A FAST-TALKING, FREE-WHEELING,
HIGH-KICKING ROMANCE . . .
AN INCOMPARABLE TRIBUTE TO
AN UNFORGETTABLE DECADE

there should have been castles

". . . a wonderful novel, a tender, warm, touching evocation of what it was like to be coming of age in the fifties . . . Herman Raucher knows all and he tells all, recreating for us in richly detailed scenes a long-ago time when idealism and illusion drifted hand in hand through a barbed-wire field of daisies. The book is at once honest, funny, unflinchingly sexual, tragic, real—and—triumphant. When his hapless, hopelessly enchanted and enchanting lovers at last find themselves and each other, you will want to stand up and cheer, as I did. I am *still* cheering, long after having turned the final page."

—EVAN HUNTER

*SUMMER OF '42
*ODE TO BILLY JOE
*A GLIMPSE OF TIGER
 WATERMELON MAN

*books published by Dell

there should have been castles

herman raucher

A DELL BOOK

Published by
Dell Publishing Co., Inc.
1 Dag Hammarskjold Plaza
New York, New York 10017

For information address Delacorte Press, New York, New
York.

Dell ® TM 681510, Dell Publishing Co., Inc.

ISBN: 0-440-18500-9

Reprinted by arrangement with Delacorte Press
Printed in Canada
First Dell printing—October 1979

For all daughters everywhere,
especially mine, Jackie and Jenny

chapter one

ben

1928–1949

I was born in 1928, an only child. All bets were on me, the longest shot since Admiral Byrd. My parents would have been better advised to get a cocker spaniel. They were about to, I'm sure, when my mother became pregnant.

By the time I was twelve I had few illusions about the world and none about myself. I was white but I was brown. Brown and medium. Brown hair, brown eyes . . . , medium height, medium build. Brown and medium, like your typical hamburger. And, I was a loner. From the day I was born I was a loner, and I could always hear my father, joking, "Ben slipped out of his mother when no one was looking. Took us three days to find him."

Crude, yes, but a fairly accurate appraisal. I always liked to stay by myself, thumbing through magazines, watching other people doing things rather than doing them myself. I liked to play with toy soldiers, to cut things out of cardboard. I preferred to be Single-O because it was the only time I never felt alone. And I loved to read. Everything from Mark Twain to Sir Walter Scott, with a little bit of Shakespeare and a book or two of Dickens.

Needless to say, some good-natured ribbing had already accompanied the first five years of my life before my father suggested that my hearing be checked, just to see if some slight impairment thereof wasn't turning me inward.

My hearing was perfect, as was my vision, as were all my reflexes and vital life signs—as was my IQ, so close to genius that they ran me through three times before recording the results in ink. After that, the jocular jibes took on a darker hue, for I found myself facing a battery of child psychologists seemingly devoted to the principle that I was either already weird or was well on my way.

My father, a strong man physically, a foreman in a shoe factory, proud of his German-English ancestry and convinced of the superiority of his genes, was merciless with my mother, who couldn't trace her origins beyond the orphanage. And often, late at night, I could hear my father grilling my mother about how come the odd progeny. My mother had no explanation beyond the obvious—therefore no defense, no hope of one, and no sleep.

Not because I wanted to, and certainly not because I felt the burning need to—but only because my mother was undergoing so fearful and endless a persecution—did I set out to establish whatever mythical virility was expected of me. I walked up to Eddie Brady who stood three inches taller and twenty pounds heavier and, without provocation, gave him five in the snout. His first reaction was to stand there incredulously, his eyes too big for his head. His next reaction was to bleed from both nostrils, a gargoyle spouting vermilion. His final reaction, as well as the last thing I remembered of the skirmish, was to unleash this outsized fist. I saw it growing but didn't move to avoid it since, as they were soon to say about Hitler—I had it coming.

No one saw the fight, what there was of it, or noticed

me peel myself from the sidewalk like an abused mustard plaster, or could vouch for the fact that I managed to walk home without the help of those legendary fourteen angels—but home I arrived, looking as though I had backed into a berserk thresher. I could hear my own breathing because my nose was in my ear, and two teeth, having barely taken residency, were lolling around inside my cheek wondering how come the rude dispossession.

My father looked up from his *Pittsburgh Courier* and stared in blessed awe at his mess of a son. "I just beat the crap out of Eddie Brady," I said, half of the consonants of that statement lost in the rubble of my mouth. My father was so thrilled he almost threw a party. And I wondered, "Is *this* all I have to do to please my father—get *killed*?"

From that point on, whenever I sensed my family's displeasure ganging up on me, I would go outside and get murdered by whomever I could motivate via the magic words, "Fuck you."

Experience soon taught me that it was wiser for me to establish my masculinity with assassins nearer my own size. Eddie Brady alone had been responsible for nearly six stitches in my cheek. Chuck Janowicz had added four more. And an additional three were happily contributed by Louie Delaney, the Mad Jew, who used me for target practice on the worst Thursday of my life. If my face was to avoid looking like that of an inept hockey goalie, I would have to start choosing opponents with greater care. Also, I would have to begin suppressing that middle-class urge to allow my opponent to hit back, tit-for-tat, because, though that was swell in a Laurel and Hardy film, it made very little sense in Carmody's Junkyard.

Consternation about me further decreased as I grew older. At fourteen I was emerging with the muscular definition of a good lightweight. And, with my father introducing me to the joys of weight-lifting and the electric thrills of isometrics, I swiftly left behind all fears that I might be of a questionable sexual proclivity. The butterfly had metamorphosed into a hair-triggered hornet which, in turn, had transformed the wary father into an idiotically happy man. Why he ever found it so marvelous to parent a potential killer was beyond my ken, and, to this day, I have not a clue as to what he expected me to become beyond a flat-nosed hooligan.

In high school I demonstrated a deep intelligence but little purpose. My grades were good but would have been better had I felt the impetus to apply myself. But I felt no such compunction and continued to maintain my reputation as High Lonesome. Reading, always reading . . . a most singular act with a most plural result, for what man was ever alone when he had Fenimore Cooper at his side and Conrad on his shelf? Because I was so good with my fists and so quick to split a lip, my singularity was tolerated and nary a derisive remark did I hear from the regular school toughs.

Though naturally athletic, I had nothing but disdain for organized sports, the only thing even mildly piquing my interest being predictably isolated—cross-country track. I tired of that the day the coach asked me to run in the rain, to which I replied "get a duck" and hung up my spikes.

I was a good boxer, perhaps the most instinctive to hit the Boys Club since Fritzi Zivic but, there, too, I had a problem. I was fine in every contest, invariably ahead on points but for only as long as my opponent could avoid bleeding. For, once the claret ran, I would immediately go into a shell and do little more than defend myself. This affliction became known to my opponents, and, between rounds, a little Mercurochrome strategically applied to my adversary's nostril or brow would, for all intents and purposes, end the bout—causing me to bicycle backwards until the final bell and the ultimate defeat.

As to the ladies, I could take 'em or leave 'em. And though I dated infrequently, I allowed my father to believe that I was cutting a swath through Pittsburgh high-school girls wide enough to slip Akron into. It pleased him to believe that I was a lady-killer as well as a man-killer.

Fascination first came in the form of Diana Schultz. It stayed three weeks and then turned into Mary Beth Mikkelson. Two weeks later it more nearly resembled Janet Dooley. A week after that it left town—

—returning in the spring via the Brobdingnagian boobs of Gloria Brundage. Though we never verbalized it, Gloria and I felt that it was a good thing to have the world believe that we were busting beds nightly. It enhanced each of our reputations . . . she as The Goddess of Love, me as The Colossus of Rhodes. The truth of it, though, was that I never laid a glove on her. She didn't want me to and I didn't care to. The upshot being that, though I never got to the plate, neither did I ever strike out.

So, at sixteen, my virginity, though thought to be on the wind, was very much intact. It didn't trouble me. I was saving myself—for who or what I didn't know, until I saw Elizabeth Satterly.

She couldn't have been more than eleven, twelve at the most. And she didn't so much walk as she did float, hovering on that tentative precipice that separated fairy-

tale from Madame Bovary. The first time I saw her I
was not yet seventeen. She bounced into view, her
feet—I do believe neither of them touching sidewalk.

She wore yellow. She always wore yellow. Everyday
I saw her she wore some variety of yellow. If it wasn't a
dress, it was a ribbon, or a kerchief, or a sweater,
gloves, a blouse. Yellow was her color, her banner, her
panache.

Black. Elizabeth Satterly's hair was black, black as
only black can be when set against yellow. And her eyes
were gray. I had never seen gray eyes before and,
though I've seen gray eyes since, never have I seen gray
of such a hue as that of Elizabeth Satterly's eyes. A little blue in 'em, a little green, a touch of pearl, a hint of
snow.

She smiled, not specifically at me, but at the world.
A Vivien Leigh smile—imp, angel, knowing, learning.
No lipstick and yet the lips were red velvet. And no
braces on the teeth for the teeth were perfection, Chic-
lets on parade.

Her breasts were embryonic but stalwart nevertheless, pressing noticeably but delicately against whatever
held them captive, giving the bend of the wasp to her
waist, the curve of the swan to her neck, the line of the
dove to her shoulder. Never had spring two such delightful precursors as Elizabeth Satterly's breasts. And I
knew even then that if the buds were to bloom no further, the roses would be no less enchanting.

Not that anyone ever knew or even suspected that I
felt that way about Elizabeth Satterly and in such terms.
Or that her legs, stepping lightly the five hundred times
we passed, triggered my heart to go at twice the speed
of light. No, I kept all of that inside me, like a mad
scientist holding fast the formula that could alter the
course of the heavens. For as surely as sunrise prodded

shadow, that's how sure I was that Elizabeth Satterly and I would one day meld—that time would diminish the distance between us. Oh, it would always be five years, but the differential would seem less each year. When I reached eighteen, she would be thirteen. When I was twenty-one, she'd be sweet sixteen. And me at twenty-four—who could ask for anything more? She would be nineteen, old enough in anyone's book. My father was *nine* years older than my mother. Not that *that* marriage was a halcyon mark of rapture. But it did prove that time closes all separations and that, if I turned out lucky, Elizabeth Satterly, gaining on me from first sight, would one day overtake me and together we'd own the moon.

So, as predicted, when I was eighteen, Elizabeth Satterly was thirteen. And when I was twenty, she was fifteen. But when I was twenty-one, Elizabeth Satterly was in Pittsburgh, whereas I was in New York City. She was behind me, a lingering radiance, still walking yellow—a daisy on Sunday, a lovely song I would always know. But what man sings "I'll See You Again" when the band's playing "Lookie, Lookie, Lookie—Here Comes Cookie"?

ginnie

1933–1948

Ginnie Maitland, me, as precocious and hateful a child as ever came to pass, was born in 1933 into a family of some artistic and professional prowess, of which I knew I was not likely to possess any. Our house, a shaky Edwardian, curlicued with 1880 pizzazz, was filled with books clenched with learning. Things hung on the walls—parchments, diplomas, awards—items that long-dead ancestors had either won or stolen, so that, long before I could even read, just looking at those framed documents told me that I was in a lot of trouble. And years before I knew who they were, I was exposed to the antique photographs of various Maitlands posing as though they knew they were really hot shit. Lawyers, politicians, engineers—they emblazoned our family tree as if laid on by eighteenth century novelists. And an uncle, Gerald T. Maitland, was then, and had been for some time, an important Republican congressman.

My father was an artist, a painter. By that I mean he had a studio and an easel and north light and was pretty much removed from reality. I don't think he ever sold anything. I'm not sure he could even give his paintings away, though I'm pretty sure he tried. He kept all of his paintings in a studio behind the house where they were all carefully catalogued and cross-indexed by title and subject. They were mostly oils, landscapes. They were pretty and I liked them but no one else did.

Certainly my mother couldn't have much cared for them since none of them was ever displayed in the house, except one portrait of her which wasn't bad. If a dollar ever came in as a result of my father's talent, I never knew it. It didn't seem to bother him. He just kept on, like a chicken laying eggs, asking no questions, making no omelets.

I wanted very much to love him. He was tall and quiet and stringy, like the birches he would always paint. And he saw to it that I always had a pony in the summer and a sled in the winter. I never once heard him raise his voice in anger or in protest or even in curiosity at the activities that kept my mother away from home for such long periods of time. He was born to wealth and never had to scratch. As such, I think he was disadvantaged. He might have amounted to something had he starved in a garret or frittered away his youth on the Left Bank. As it was, he seldom left the back country of Stamford, Connecticut, and his reputation as a talent never went beyond the twenty-three acres our house stood on. And even there the last few acres never heard of him.

He never punished either my sister or me. That may have been because he never knew we were there. We were pretty much raised by maids and nurses, polished up for holidays and sent off to various cultural, dramatic, and physical endeavors like dancing school. (Because of my scrawny and knobby legs, the family had turned me toward Terpsichore—and I was good at it. Still am, and my legs became my best feature and still are.)

Anyway, my father was always on the premises. He was around. Which was more than could be said about my mother, The Phantom of Rockrimmon Road. My mother, I guess you'd have to say, was beautiful. And she lavished great attention on her fabulous face, spending as much time on it as my father spent on his paintings. She could have signed her faces in the lower right hand corner and sold them to *Colliers* for they looked so John Singer Sargent, regal and smacking of high society.

Why they ever got married was soon enough apparent to me. My father, who was a hundred years older, indulged her. Also—she had all those paints at her disposal for all her morning self-portraits. By midafternoon her pigmented face would begin to melt, so she'd go into her boudoir for a retouch. At eight p.m. she was again the most beautiful woman in the world, still skinny but in a liquidy, high-fashion way. And she knew it. And so did we.

My sister, Mary Ann, was basically a pain in the ass. She had my mother's face only she didn't quite know what to do with it (except her mouth, which I'll get to in a minute). She was four years older than me and was nice to me only when people were looking. She spent maybe five hours a day masturbating with the handle of her riding crop. The rest of the day she spent on her horse, then in her tub, and then at her diary. I eventually got hold of her diary and it was something.

According to her diary, when Mary Ann was sixteen she was giving head to all three of her riding instructors. Up till then I had always wondered how she could spend so much time at the stables and still be such a lousy rider. From then on I no longer wondered, I marveled.

I had an incredible thing going. I found and held onto a second key to Mary Ann's diary that she must have thought she'd lost. Anyway, once a week, while Mary Ann was servicing her studs, I was home, reading about her exploits of the week before. Call it a time lag. No—call it an oral gap.

She wrote about her fellatio in great detail, describing the tools of her lovers and the taste thrills they provided. Derek Miller was "a throbbing, bananalike cartilage who hooks to the left and pulls my hair when he climaxes." Tony Borelli was "a rod of blazing steel who goes 'yip-yip' when he comes." And then there was Jud Smith who, according to Mary Ann, was "a silky avocado who can touch the back of my throat from the inside. He curses when he orgasms and tastes of maple syrup." Evidently, when Mary Ann pointed out that phenomenon to Jud, he offered to do a number on her flapjacks. I'd like to have seen that. That would have been some commercial for Aunt Jemima.

According to her journals, Mary Ann did not get laid until page four of November 15, 1946—and *that* went on until the middle of page twenty-seven. As to anyone going down on *her*, that didn't happen until June 23, 1947. But, once it did, it didn't stop until page four hundred thirty-nine of 1948 when she married Walter Harrison—which was also the day she burned her diary.

How romantic. On the morning of her wedding day, my horny sister takes her three-thousand-page pornographic diary and sets fire to it behind the house. Five hours later she has tears in her eyes as she walks down the aisle—as would *any* healthy American girl faced with the prospect of marrying Walter Harrison. For Walter was hardly the flapjack type, and if he tasted of *anything*, it could only have been Vitalis.

Any other bride would have tossed her kid sister her bridal bouquet—but not Mary Ann, she threw me her rubbed-raw riding crop. I thanked her but told her I wouldn't touch it with the proverbial ten-foot pole. She grew nervous and asked why, at which point I moved in with the *coup de grâce*, returning the extra key to her diary, telling her I wouldn't need it anymore since she had cleverly burnt that volume. Her mouth dropped open so wide she could have sucked in the Three Musketeers *and* their horses—and she was furious. Then she denied the whole thing, saying that it was just the random writings of a pubescent young girl. I'm sure some of it was but I didn't want to let her off the hook so easily so I smiled, very maturely, and asked her how husband-to-be tasted on flapjacks.

Mary Ann was nineteen when she got married. She and Walter moved to Chicago which I thought very apt since where else but the Windy City for a girl so vitally concerned with blow jobs.

What I never did tell her about was my little moment with Walter. I didn't tell her out of sheer perversity, knowing that if I *did* tell her, she would have immediately called off the wedding and I didn't want that. I *wanted* them to get married. They God damn deserved each other.

Two nights before the wedding (I don't remember where Mary Ann was, probably getting her mouth oiled) my father was in his studio and my mother was nagging the caterers, and I was alone in my room. I was in front of my mirror, wondering why the hell I was being forced to pay such a debt to society when my only crime was that my legs began under my earlobes and my skin looked like a relief map of the Dakota Badlands. At fifteen, it must be said, I was a mess. I more nearly resembled my father: tall, even-featured, watery blue eyes—not without promise. If I paid proper attention to my makeup I might just one day be pretty. My hair, blonde but getting mousy, might one day be untangleable as I was giving it the hundred lashes a night it truly deserved. I was narrow-hipped and firm-assed and my legs, thanks to dancing and gymnastics, were coming along pretty good. It was just that everything was out of synch. My legs were eighteen but my chest was twelve and a half. The rest of me was somewhere in between at irregular intervals.

Boys were interested in me but I quickly found out why. It was because of my sister's peerless reputation as a cocksucker. A boy would no sooner bring me home from a date than he'd have his tool in his hand, suggesting I give it a ten-minute tongue-lashing. One nice young man, Douglas Pennington, he didn't even wait until he took me *home*. He met me at the *door* with it, asking me if it met with my approval. I slammed the door on it and never saw him again—at least not in an upright position. As to the door, it never closed flush from that night on. I guess there's a little bit of Douglas Pennington in the old house yet.

Anyway, back to Walter Harrison, frontier accountant and my soon to be brother-in-law. There I am, stark raving nude in front of my mirror and the classy sonofabitch doesn't even knock. He just walks in and looks at me and says, "I'm looking for Mary Ann."

Brilliantly I said, "She's not here."

"Oh," he says.

Now mind you, I'm bolt naked in front of the mirror, I'm fifteen years old, my sister's betrothed (a dark, greasy type about thirty, with skin the texture of a diseased sycamore . . . all of it to be transferred to Chicago where he'll never see me again so what does he have to lose) is looking at me and I can see by the way he's standing that some evil thoughts are in his pants. Also, he's more than a little bit drunk, which is understandable for a man about to marry the bitch-goddess of all time.

Anyway, I reach for my robe—only it's in my closet, and all I come up with is a doily from my dresser, after first knocking off half a dozen bottles of my very best cheap cologne. My room immediately begins to smell like what I assumed a whorehouse smelled like because Walter got immediately excited.

"Don't cover up, Ginnie," he smiles. "You're very pretty. What the hell, we're all in the same family. You look like what Mary Ann must have looked like a couple of years ago."

"I think you'd better get out of here."

"Come on, Ginnie. A pretty kid like you? You're not going to tell me you don't play around."

"Walter, I'm only fifteen years old!"

"Yeah? When *I* was fifteen—"

"I'm having my period." What the hell, when you're in a tight spot, you *try*.

He laughed and moved toward me, trying to look harmless but looking about as harmless as Godzilla. "Ginnie—"

"Really, Walter. It's the first day and I always have a very heavy flow."

"Well," he winks, "there's other things we can do."

Christ, I think, has my sister's reputation gone *that* far? "I don't know what you're talking about." The hell, I didn't. And *if* I didn't, the sound of his zipper, opening, would have supplied me with a very audible hint.

"Listen, kid—it's a modern world we live in. And there's no harm if people like each other. I mean, we *do* like each other, don't we?"

"No, we don't. I don't like you at all."

"Yeah? Well, you like *this*, don't you?"

"No, I don't." Feigning ignorance, "What is it?"

"It's nine inches for your mouth, baby."

"No, thanks. I got two loose fillings." I was always

known for my weird sense of humor, only Walter wasn't laughing. He was just wigwagging himself toward me, like some kind of dopey farmer trying to divine water with a red-headed stick. "You better get out of here, Walter—before I call my father."

"You just don't parade around naked and not expect a man to react—you little cockteaser." He was getting nasty and impatient and larger and closer.

"Boy, I don't *believe* you. You're supposed to marry my sister!"

"Has nothing to do with it. This is you and me. Here and now. You can't tell me you're not excited, you little bitch."

"Boy, Walter—you're something." I was trying to get to the bathroom. If I could just get to the bathroom, I could lock the door and—

He was suspicious and moved to cut off my angle of retreat. "Where you going, Ginnie?"

"To the bathroom. I've also got diarrhea."

He stopped—just a split second. It was long enough for me to make my move and I dashed into the bathroom and locked the door behind me—and laughed.

"God damn you, kid! It's not funny!"

Funny or not, I was suddenly plugged in to a great truth about female self-defense. Laughter. A man comes on too strong—laugh at him. It's got to be the most destructive thing a girl can do.

He spoke, a little more calmly. "Ginnie, I'm sorry. It's just that you looked so good. You caught me off guard. I'd hate for you to tell Mary Ann."

"I won't. It's as much my fault as it is yours." I had no idea what that meant.

"And you won't tell anyone?"

"Not a soul."

"Okay. I'm going now, Ginnie."

"Stay or go, Walter. Doesn't matter to *me*." I turned on the bath.

"And—I'm sorry. I really am. I don't know what came over me. Ginnie?"

I didn't answer, just turned on the water full-out and climbed into the tub, filled with wonder at the human race, my own family in particular. But overriding all the strange comedy was my awareness that there were men out there, pointing their penises at me, and damned if they weren't reaching me, figuratively, that is. Under different circumstances I might just have favored Walter. What the hell, he wasn't all that bad. He wasn't a monster. And if he wasn't nine inches, he was at least eight inches longer than I was prepared to receive at the time.

Nor was Douglas Pennington (my first "door job") all that disgusting. It was just the situation that was disgusting. Actually, as I thought about it, Douglas's thing was kind of cute and I hated having to slam the door on it. It was like drowning a puppy. I only did it because he had been so crude. Had he asked me in a nice way, or taken me dancing, or recited a little love poem— maybe we would have been able to work something out.

What it all added up to was that maybe Mary Ann could take her loving on the hoof but *I* apparently required a little more than a twitching chunk of flesh thrust into my face without my having anything to say on the matter beyond "glub."

I lay in the warm tub and explored my goodies. I was fifteen and counting and all my equipment was in working order. It would be fun to see how long I could hold out.

chapter three

ben

1949

In a five-story walk-up in the East Eighties I read poetry to myself, not so much to learn from as to become depressed by. For what better way to endure the fruits of poverty than to read how other poets were made miserable by them. Not that I saw myself as a poet, I didn't. Not that I even saw myself as a writer. It was simply that I *identified* with poets and writers because they had the wherewithal to set their experiences down, on paper, so that others could see and learn from them and, in some way, benefit. Not that I was benefitting, I wasn't. I was barely hanging on.

It was my twenty-first birthday and I celebrated with some ninety-nine-cent wine that I had gotten for fifty cents off because no one would buy a wine that cheap unless it was really cheap—like forty-nine cents. There had been three such bottles on the liquor store shelf, so *long* on the shelf that they were seven years old by the time I got there. Never before had a man purchased three bottles of Villa Cosenza for an aggregate total of one dollar and forty-seven cents. And never before was a liquor store proprietor happier to be rid of them.

I toasted my loneliness by hoisting the first glass to the beauty of Elizabeth Satterly, she of the yellow aura and the unreal countenance. So firmly had I implanted the vision of her into my consciousness that, for the first time since coming to New York, I was aware of the fact that we had never once spoken to one another. Never once over all those years had we said as much to one another as "Good morning"—"What a pretty yellow dress"—"Will the Pirates win the pennant?" And yet I seemed to know the sound of her voice, the lyrical timbre of it—sweet and Tinkerbell, with no trace of Pittsburgh twang or west Pennsylvania slur. Amazing how the dream is novocaine to reality. But the novocaine must, in time, wear off. And twenty-one was as good a time as any.

"So, farewell Elizabeth Satterly," I said, my voice rattling through the apartment so macho poetic that I really laid into it. "Farewell thy bright walk, thy graceful carriage. Adieu the gray eyes, the honied lips, the gamine breasts never to be mine, ever to be cloaked within the bleak recesses of cruel fantasy, thy lovely voice to ring no more in my ear—because it never rang in the first place."

I never spoke that way in public, what poet ever did? Did Shakespeare, upon arising on the morrow, ever festoon himself into a sonnet? Or did he just stretch, pass wind, and shout at the girl, "What ho, bitch—fetch me a scone and move your arse"?

My rhyme matched the wine in that both were better abandoned—Elizabeth Satterly and Villa Cosenza, the former relegated to the rear of recall, the latter poured down the sink, sputtering like acid, the sound convincing me of what I had suspected from the outset, i.e., I could have gotten each of the bottles for thirteen cents, the going price of vinegar.

No matter, I thought, it marked a new beginning, a bitter taste with which to bury adolescence and Pittsburgh, two of the more forgettable items of my (up till the night before) meaningless life.

After high school I had meandered. An odd job here, an even odder one there. I had worked in a bakery, a garage, a box factory, and an A & P. In Carmody's junkyard I was paid to strip anything of value from the carcasses of dead cars. And in Patterson's Tobacco Shoppe I got hooked on good cigars.

Cigars, light of my life, Somerset Maugham had idealized them via an ode that Ivan Patterson had framed and displayed on one of the walls of his shop. It began with: "There are few things better than a good cigar" and it ended with: "For this men have sweltered long years under tropical suns and ships have scoured the Seven Seas." It so knocked me out that I committed it to memory and I still remember it, for as Maugham himself put it in that very same ode, "It is the only ambition I have achieved that has never been embittered by disillusion."

I must have stolen three thousand cigars from Ivan Patterson and they weren't cheapies. They were Havanas and Jamaicas, Upmanns, Monte Cristos, Temple Halls, and Reina Isabels. By the time I was nineteen I was smoking ten cigars a day and cut quite a figure puffing dollar Don Diegos while striding in my eight-dollar Thom McAns.

My mother took it to mean that I was earning a great deal of money. My father correctly concluded that I was heavily into pilferage. He wasn't angry, he merely suggested that I broaden my horizons by getting a job in Tiffany's. He endeared himself to me with that remark and we proceeded to get along better. And when I told him that I wanted to shake Pittsburgh, he gave me the busfare to get out of town. He was never a hugger, never a demonstrative type, but, somewhere beneath his top-grain cowhide exterior, the sonofabitch was worthy of the big shadow he cast, and I suddenly had an inkling as to how my mother could love him despite his glaring insensitivities.

They said good-bye to me as if I were going off for the weekend. That either took class, or they were glad to get rid of me. Somehow my money was on the former and, over the years, I've discovered that often the most minimum achievers possess the most maximum class.

I arrived in New York City aboard a Greyhound that should have been euthanized and carrying a valise that Willy Loman would have left forever in a subway locker. But I also had a goodly supply of cigars, one hundred of them to be exact, carefully stolen from the humidors of Ivan Patterson—and I had a battle plan to go with them. I would smoke one cigar a day, after every dinner, and by the time I had gone through the hundred, I would be well on my way to success. It was a fine plan, ranking in scope and madness with Napoleon's plan to take Moscow.

I checked into the Forty-seventh Street Y where a man could live on half a buck a day. He could also *die* at that price so the object of the game was to strive for something in between until help came from somewhere. I got a job selling greeting cards, mostly because the light was good and I could see what the poets of 1949 were writing:

> *Roses are red, violets are blue—*
> *If you're sailing to France,*
> *Don't take a canoe.*
> or
> *Happy birthday, nephew—*
> *Here's a toast to you—*
> *May all your roses be red—*
> *and all your violets blue.*

I was usually ill by noon and by quitting time I was close to retching. But it was forty-five dollars a week, which meant that, if I didn't eat or buy a shirt, I could live a life of Kafkaesque ease.

My cigars gave me a lift, each one coming as it did after a day of nothingness or nausea. I would light up and watch the smoke curl away blue, a wispy memory that put a button on my boredom and opened the door to tomorrow.

After thirty-seven cigars in a row I made a few concessions to my lack of accomplishment. I would skip a cigar here and there. So, after fifty days I had only smoked forty. And after ninety I had smoked only sixty. I had twenty-seven cigars left when Don Cook came into my life, albeit to stop me and ask, "What are you smoking—Flor De A. Allones or Ramon Cifuentes Partages?"

You could have knocked me over with a Schimmelpenninck, I was that surprised. There was a guy, not much older than myself, though considerably better dressed and screamingly more worldly, homing in on the name of the cigar I was smoking. "Take a guess," I suggested.

"It's one of the two?"

"Yes."

"Flor De A. Allones."

"Wrong. Try again."

"Flor De A. Allones."

"Right."

"You tried to trick me. Why?"

"To see if you'd stick to your guns."

"That's a sixty-cent cigar."

"True."

"Nobody who wears a mackinaw smokes a sixty-cent cigar unless he stole it."

"I don't steal mackinaws."

That exchange took place on Sixth Avenue and West Fifty-fourth Street. We stood there swapping one-liners, each of us trying to prove himself the more clever. It was a Mexican standoff so we celebrated with a cup of coffee on the understanding that *he* was paying.

We were a strange pair, me in my mackinaw and Pittsburgh posh attire—he in his Brooks Brothers triumph and Thomas Begg fedora with Tyrolean feather. Still, I had a pocketful of sixty-cent cigars, whereas he puffed a pipe packed with a penny's worth of Sir Walter Raleigh. Also, the shirt cuffs that peeked out over his wrists had a touch of the fray to them, and his immaculately knotted skinny rep tie was obviously on its last hurrah.

Don Cook was the grandest twenty-three-year-old man I had ever seen, but his grandeur was superficial and seedy. He looked like an ad for sumptuous living that had been capriciously placed in Popular Mechanics. What's more, he knew that I knew it.

He studied me as if sighting a rifle that couldn't miss. "Let me guess. You're from New Haven. No—New Brunswick."

"New Delhi. Second generation untouchable."

The smile escaped even though he tried to hold it back, and even his smile was grand, a thousand dollars' worth of orthodontia flashing out of his boney face though the upper incisors were slightly buck. "My name is Don Cook."

"I'm Ben Webber."

"I'm originally from Hartford, son of people many times divorced who dressed me in peach linen suits and wished I'd go away."

"I'm from Pittsburgh and I never had a linen suit in my life."

Don Cook spoke in public as I spoke when winging poetry aloud. He didn't do it *all* the time but *I* never did it at all. I decided that it was all bravado, a touch of W. C. Fields, a pinch of John Barrymore, a kid leading an invisible symphony orchestra, thinking he's doing *Aïda* but suspecting it's "Melancholy Baby." "I want it immediately understood, sir, that I am a thorough and irredeemable heterosexual and have no designs whatsoever on whatever body you're wearing beneath that shit-colored horse blanket."

"I'm a lesbian."

"Benjamin, I am confronted with a hapless existence and cannot pay for this coffee. I trust there won't be a scene."

"No scene, but don't have a cruller."

"I eat once a day at the Yale Club. I load up there for a dollar and can often go two days without re-eating. It is the only reason for going to Yale. Unless you can help me, I had my last meal an hour ago."

"Have a cigar." I gave him one of my Flor De A. Allones and he lit it perfectly, holding the match a half inch from the tip, drawing in the flame most aristocratically while rotating the cigar slowly so as not to induce a hot spot. And somewhere I heard Somerset Maugham say, "Well struck."

Don Cook was class from his nose to his ass. He might die in a poorhouse or under a beer truck, but whoever came to collect him would know he was picking up class. His nose had a bump in it where it changed direction slightly, but his chin was firmly chiseled and his eyes, a see-through blue, had a defiant focus to them made all the more so by the fact that they seldom blinked. Every one of his brown hairs was obediently in place, a small pompadour crowning his noble brow. And, though he was a little slight in the shoulders, there was something to his neck that said "power if needed."

"Ben," he said, "I have been trolling the streets in search of a roommate. My rent is paid through the end of the month but my larder is bare. Stock it with canned goods and Ritz crackers, give me a cigar on occasion, and I will be proud to share my bad fortune with you until the end comes. I am a superb cook, housekeeper and bulb-snatcher, a brilliant conversationalist and an incomparable dancer. I don't know what else you're looking for in a man. Think it over as you will not get another offer like this on this street this day." He flicked an ash at the world, and it's the way I have remembered him since—a Dickensian anachronism born many years after his true time.

I followed him to his apartment feeling like David Copperfield in the company of a twentieth century Steerforth. And trailing him up the five flights to his East Eighty-third Street flat, I couldn't help but notice that each of his rubber heels disappeared beneath its respective exterior ankle. A few more round trips and the heels would be no more. In short, all of Don Cook's attire was at the point of being irreparable—and yet nothing in his manner was there to indicate that his mind and spirit were in a similar disarray. The Tyrolean feather in his fedora was thumbing its nose at adversity. I was in the company of an indomitable spirit and it was brightening my life.

The apartment was a railroad type, a hallway shooting straight through, rooms ricocheting left and right. A kitchen, a bathroom, a dining alcove, a living room of a sort, bedrooms—two or three, I couldn't really tell—one of which was his and another of which had a girl in it.

As we passed the room with the girl, Don casually

indicated her presence as a tour guide might point out a local site. "That's Alice—and this is the kitchen. The refrigerator, though old, is still trustworthy though the freezer is shot and there is a certain amount of spoilage. Fish, in particular, being risky fare and—"

"Who's Alice?"

"A girl I used to know."

"I see. You don't know her anymore."

"Slightly." He looked at me, understanding that my silence had to be contended with. "Ben, Alice is a light that has gone out. She flamed for a while and then blew her filament. I loved her once but now we're just pals."

"Why is she still here?"

He expressed amazement at the question. "Benjamin, it's *her* apartment. She's *keeping* me. I think it's good of her not to ask me to leave, don't you?" He was trying to end the discussion.

"Yes."

"Then let's say no more about it." He moved on. "The sink, as you can see, drips endlessly, but if you close the kitchen door at night it's never a problem. Also, the water pressure leaves something to be desired in that, all too often, when you're in the shower, the water will go from a forceful flow to like it's a kid pissing on your head."

"Excuse me . . ."

"What *is* it?" he asked intimidatingly, annoyed at my continual interruptions and not afraid to show it by the jut of his chin.

"Alice is keeping you?"

"Yes."

"Who's going to keep *me*?"

"Alice."

"Does she know about it?"

"Did she see you walk by?"

"Yes."

"Then she knows about it."

"Mr. Cook, you will give me straight answers or I will bend your nose in the opposite direction." I could not have been more direct.

"Sit down, Pittsburgh."

"Fuck you, Hartford. I'm leaving."

"You'd let a *girl* come between us?"

"How do I know it's a girl? All I saw was a face in a blanket."

"It's a girl. Why else would it be named 'Alice'? Ben, sit down. Please?"

I sat, on a chair whose springs jumped up to meet me. "What the hell *is* this? The Fun House?"

Don was telling all. "Alice is a stewardess. You've heard of TWA? It's her apartment. She's away a lot of the time, coming and going. She likes to have somebody on the premises to kind of watch over things. A caretaker, if you will. And that's it."

"No, it's not. There's more."

"Well—she also likes to kind of have a man around. You know—to protect her against frigidity."

"Let's see if I've got this straight. I'm being brought in as what—your replacement?"

"My successor."

"What happens to *you*?"

"Life goes on."

"Alice pays the rent. I supply the Ritz crackers and the manpower—and you do what—*nothing*?"

"You're being unkind. I'm unemployed at the moment, yes, but once I get a suitable job, you will both of you be glad that you kept me on." He became buoyant, painting pictures in the air. "I will make roasts and pour Beaujolais and read to you—as you and Alice revel on percale in celebration of youth. However—" his voice came down an octave, "there *is* a catch."

"Aha!"

"You have to pass muster. Alice, of course, has no time to look and has left it to me to come up with a suitable choice. But I can't just bring *anyone* in on her. The final decision must be hers." He glanced at his watch. "All entries must be made by midnight; neatness and originality count, and Alice's decision is final."

"A straight answer. Why are you out?"

"You're a very pragmatic fellow, a very unnerving trait in this tawdry world in which we live."

"You've got ten seconds to answer—or I'm *gone*."

"I won't really miss you, but I *will* miss your cigars. So—tarry."

"I'm tarrying, but for only five more seconds."

He sighed and delivered the news. "Don't get upset, but it isn't just Alice. There's *Susan*."

"Susan?"

"And Jessica."

"Jessica?"

"They come and go. There's usually a couple nights a week when there's no one. But by the same token, there's often a couple nights when there's two. But never three. There's never been a night when there's been three. I give you my oath on that, my good fellow. I wouldn't shit you."

"Jesus Christ! What kind of girls are they?"

"They're darling."

"But—to live like that?"

"Benny, Benny, Benny—they're stewardi. They fly with death. At any given moment, on any flight—it can all end. Pfffft, like that. So, when they come home to their place, they like a little of the *good* things in life—a little fucking, a little sucking—it's understandable. If you were a stewardess, you'd understand. Good Lord, they're *paid* little enough."

"You're such a man of the world, how come you can't handle it?"

There was a small note of desperation in his voice. "I *can* handle it—to a degree. But sometimes I don't get out of bed until four in the afternoon. And often, when I do I'm tired. Too tired to go out on a job interview. And when I *can* summon up enough strength to look for a job—I look like shit." He slumped a bit. "I tell you, Ben, it's a problem. I stumbled into a young man's dream, my every sexual fantasy gratified and by experts, but it's aging the crap out of me. And I live in fear that, by the time I *do* get a decent job, I'll be either on social security or a basket case."

I had to laugh. It was the nuttiest thing I'd ever heard of. Don took heart at my laughter, interpreting it as a victory of his logic over my blind stupidity. He dropped all the dramatics and leaned in like a buddy.

"Ben, I'll level with you. The broads are a touch horny. I think it's the whole setup that turns them on. I think, in a different situation, they'd be normal or close to it—but *here*? I'll help you out wherever I can but I can no longer handle it alone. I've offered to bring in guys on a free-lance basis, but they won't buy it—that'd make them whores and me a pimp. They're very old-fashioned on the subject, kind of sweetly monogamous which I find very endearing, but I am *not* Brigham Young. Nor do I have three cocks, and, lately, the one I *do* have has been hiding. This has been pointed out to the girls on more than one occasion so that now they see the wisdom of having another buck in the wigwam, assuming, of course, that his head is on straight. Ben, they'll *love* you. You're bright and have good posture and wear sensible shoes. If we bury your mackinaw and spend a few bucks on a Wembley tie—Ben, if we pool our peckers and work as a team, together we can hack it. Alice isn't bad. A little plain, but deft. Susan? You'll *love* Susan. She comes once and falls asleep. Sometimes she's asleep *before* she comes, and you can save it for another day. And she loves to make breakfast. Fresh orange juice, Ben. None of that frozen shit. And she strains out all the seeds and the pulp. I swear, Ben, sometimes I think that, if you suck her tits long enough, Susan'll give milk."

"Sounds like a very nice, outgoing type."

"Then it's settled."

"What about Jessica?"

"No problem. She's seldom here."

"That's not what I asked."

"I know."

"What about Jessica?"

"Well—she's large."

"*How* large?"

"Well—about six feet tall."

"How *wide*?"

"Well—about as wide as your average DC-3. But Ben—she's got beautiful eyes!"

"How many propellers? So long, Don." I started out.

He stopped me. "I don't really see what you have to lose. Try it a week. Try it a *night*. You can't buy a lousy hooker in this town with just a sixty-cent cigar. We'll work out a schedule. And there's vacations. The girls have *vacations,* Ben. They fly to foreign places on vacations. Tibet, Samoa, Saturn . . . You'll have time off. You can go to the movies, smoke cigars, whittle soap. Ben, you're a good physical specimen. I'm not but you are. Right up until the moment of your heart attack, you'll have such a good time—"

"Why don't they get guys from the airlines? Why do they need you and me?"

"Company policy. The airlines frown on fraternizing. TWA especially. Alice and Susan are TWA. Jessica is Allegheny, they're not as strict but I have to be honest. Jessica *did* bring home a pilot once, but the word is out on her because—on his next flight, the guy crashed. He was a cripple on the morning he left here. I should have stopped him but I thought he'd pull himself together. The least I should've done was to call the terminal and give them an anonymous tip that one of their pilots would never get it up that day, but I didn't. I didn't want to lose him. I was—selfish."

By then I was practically rolling on the floor laughing. I didn't know how much of what Don was telling me was truth and how much was fiction. All I knew was that, inside of ten minutes, Don had gone off to walk his dog (which he didn't have), and I was standing, my pants around my ankles, in Alice's steaming room. The lighting was dim but I could see her giving me the once over. Then she sat up and ran her hand over my belly, hefting my scrotum as if she were about to roll dice, grabbing my penis as if she were about to pump water—ultimately guiding me inside her as one might lead a pony to a stall. And all the while she never said a word. Not even "coffee, tea or milk" or "Sir, your fly is open."

What neither Alice nor Don knew was that they had been dealing with a virgin. And so it was that on my first time out, I never saw the girl, never spoke to her, never kissed her. I just dropped my pants and fucked, climaxing inside her without passion, shame or skill—a triumph of friction, a poem without words, music without music—just percussion, rhythm and drums.

Still, on reflection, I have to admit that it had been

reasonably exciting, except that she kept calling me "Murray" and I could have done without that. Alice left during the night. A dawn flight to Dallas.

The next afternoon (as I was relating to you earlier) I was sitting alone in the apartment, having moved my stuff over from the Y. Toasting the memory of Elizabeth Satterly with my three bottles of Villa Cosenza, I had just poured it all down the sink and was lighting up one of my very best Jamaicas when Jessica walked in. I thought it was the Hindenburg but it had beautiful eyes, so I knew it was Jessica. That's all I remembered.

Somewhere around eight in the evening I heard Don tippy-toeing in. I felt like Maggie waiting for Jiggs, sitting there in the dark as Don tried to sneak into his room. I turned on the lamp and he froze as in a Tom and Jerry cartoon (my entire world had turned comic strip). He had a bag in his hand that smelled of hamburger. "Lose your dog?" I asked.

"Ahhhh, Ben."

"You were expecting maybe Brigham Young?"

He was looking toward the bedroom. "Jessica?"

"Either her or the whole Notre Dame line."

"No. It's Jessica. You all right?"

"The doctor says I'll be walking again in no time."

"Well, the initial outing is always the most difficult. In time you'll learn her funny little ways."

"You knew she was due back."

"Me?"

"You knew her schedule."

"Let's just say I had an inkling."

"Alice and Jessica in less than twelve hours. That oughta make me Varsity, coach."

"I knew you could do it. Now, 'fess up. It was great, wasn't it? Wasn't it a compelling experience?"

I smiled. He was right. Sitting alone, toasting Elizabeth Satterly between screwing Alice and surviving Jessica *had* been kind of lofty. "Tweren't bad."

"Only in America, eh, kid?"

"Want to give me a hint as to when Susan's due in?"

"Wednesday. You've got two days. You go back to the Y—a little whirlpool treatment, a little steam room—you'll be fine."

We laughed, had a couple cigars, and I forgot to be miffed at my unlikely new roommate. Also, I stayed on.

Don Cook had to be the most conniving, designing fellow I had ever come across in my life. Yet nothing he ever did was truly malicious. He was like a perennial college boy. Life was just a pledgeship and an alma mater and he sailed through it and over it, flying his feather and sidestepping disaster, never hurting anyone and, in his own way, always giving much more than he himself ever asked for.

Sometime later, Jessica emerged from her room dressed in an orange kimono that made her look like the entire dawn. We had the hamburgers that Don had brought back, paid for with money he had earlier lifted from my unknowing pocket but, honorable fellow that he was, he gave me his marker for the full seventy-five cents. In the years that followed I was to receive a number of Don Cook's markers. They were worthless then but later became invaluable. They're stashed away somewhere, I forget where, but I have them.

Jessica had a flight to Rochester or Binghamton and was soon dressed in her cute and mammoth stewardess outfit. She kissed both Don and I on the cheek and, saying she'd be back soon, saluted and went out. The apartment trembled slightly as she descended the stairs. Don said that it was only my imagination but I noticed him holding onto the radiator as she left. I was too much the gentleman to point that out to him.

Don relaxed when he realized, for better or for worse, that I was staying on in the tepee. And he allowed as how I was both brave and wise and that, if nothing else—if nothing good or positive ever came of it—it would still have been an interlude in my life wherein I had flown TWA and Allegheny—First Class.

We went over to Broadstreet's, where, with Don acting as advisor, I bought a sport jacket and slacks, and at Wembley's a multi-colored necktie that Don said would go with anything but a fucking mackinaw. When we got back to the apartment, Don packed my fucking mackinaw away somewhere, saying that we would always keep it handy in case Jack London ever came to call. Then we discussed financial matters.

I, of course, was solvent, my job at the Rockwell Greeting Card Store secure at least through Christmas, which was still some months away. But with Don it was another story. He was out of work, had used up his unemployment eligibility, and his father (one of them) had cut off his allowance. He owed twenty dollars to Susan and thirty-five dollars to Alice and close to a hundred to Jessica but that was alright because Jessica also took markers. The money he owed the girls, I should mention, was not for services rendered. It was hard cash, borrowed in good faith against bad luck and would all be one day paid back at eight percent per annum. The girls had as much chance of seeing their money again as England had of regaining India, but they were either very good about it or—interesting thought—Don was better in bed than he would have had me believe.

Don got a job at Bloomingdale's, as a floorwalker. It lasted one week in that it took his superiors precisely that long to discover that he wasn't walking the floor at all, he was eating the samples in the Gourmet Section, thus saving the money he would normally be called upon to spend at the Yale Club.

During that week I had an interesting experience at the apartment. I had returned from another illiterate day at the greeting card factory and found that Susan, the last of my three landladies, had arrived. I introduced myself to her and she eyed me curiously, more with amusement than with interest. Then, formalities behind us, we made love, after which she asked me if she was a better screw than Alice and Jessica. I said that she was superior in every category and every subdivision. This evoked a big laugh from Susan in that she wasn't Susan at all, she was Alice. It had been so dark in the room when we first made love that I never really saw her face. Then, she left so early that I didn't know she was gone until I came out of my trance. Fortunately, Alice was of a good nature and promised never to tease me again on the subject *provided* that I change the after-shave I was using to something a bit more inspiring than bay rum. I allowed her to choose the fragrance and she opted for something French—Guerlain, as I recall. And she placed me under strict orders to use it only with her and never with any of the other girls.

Don was soon to get a job at 20th Century-Fox, in the mailroom. He was a messenger at thirty-eight dollars a week. The meager salary didn't bother him, he was that pleased to be in show business, a field he always believed he had an affinity for. He was frankly surprised that he had gotten the job because the other young men hired were all Jewish, the result of a kind of reverse bigotry in that, in those days, the big New York-based advertising agencies were hiring, for *their* mailrooms, only Presbyterian Ivy Leaguers—no riffraff. And so, the movie companies, all of which maintained advertising and publicity staffs in New York, as if in retaliation to the ad agencies, hired *only* Jews, plus a couple Catholics, a smattering of blacks, a dash of Puerto Ricans and a random leper. Don figured that he had slipped in under the "leper" banner. "I'm their token WASP," he said. "But I'm so grateful that I will eat a bagel every day and donate a portion of my salary to the UJA."

And so Don had himself a job. He was making less than I was but his vistas were much broader. He was reading scenarios—I was reading "get well" cards. I asked him to bring home a scenario because I was curious about what a movie script looked like. He said he couldn't, it wasn't allowed. It was top secret and he could get fired. But he brought one home anyway. "All About Eve" by Joseph Mankiewicz. It was so brilliant, so simultaneously brittle and solid, that I read it a dozen times . . . after which I read it no more because I didn't have to. I had it memorized. I kept that script. Red cover, number 156. One hundred eighty pages of the best movie I ever read.

Where I worked pretty much by myself, selling retail to the card-buying public, Don was thriving behind the scenes in a world so glamorous that it almost made me cry not to be a part of it. He would tell me of the other young men he worked with, describing them so vividly that it was as though they were in the apartment with me, sharing my last cigars.

I yearned to be a part of it and asked Don what my chances were of passing for Jewish, especially since I was circumcised and was, therefore, an all-around good fellow. Don said that he could probably teach me a few Jewish mannerisms to go along with my circumcision but that my lack of a college degree would rule out all chances of my getting a job. Besides, there already was a full coterie of "Men of Tomorrow" (that was their official designation), twelve being the maximum. Nor was it likely that one of them would die and thus leave an opening.

As to my circumcision, Don felt that it could only work in my favor if I ran into W. Charles Gruber in the men's room and wanted to flash my credentials. And since W. Charles Gruber, vice-president of the whole thing, had his own private bathroom, the chances of that happening were nil and I should stop living in a dream world.

Susan eventually flew into town, putting a dent in my circumcision that lasted a week. Things eased up when Alice announced that she was leaving TWA to marry a dentist in Cincinnati. I would miss Alice because Alice was my first, even though I couldn't see who she was at the time. She gave me a farewell bang and said that I could return to bay rum if I liked. I told her that I would continue using Guerlain because Guerlain would always remind me of her so she banged me again, plus a few other things that she did so well.

Jessica still came and went like the migration of elephants, and Susan did indeed make fresh orange juice though she never gave milk. But it was Alice who I really loved and the memory of her died hard.

ginnie

1948

Mary Ann Maitland and Walter Harrison were married in a sterile ceremony in which her dearest friend, Francine Lazenby, sang "Because" though I never really heard anyone ask "Why?" Everyone was so glad to see those two get married that you'd have thought they were, both of them, pregnant.

It all went off cleanly, like a beheading, and lots of important people attended—at least they dressed that way—Uncle Gerald, the congressman, being the most important of all because he was the newly appointed Minority Chairman of the House Foreign Relations Committee and was being looked upon as a possible running-mate for Eisenhower in 1952.

Two good things immediately resulted from Mary Ann's move to Chicago. One, she was out of my life and good riddance and that went double for Old Nine-Incher. And two, I was the only child in the family and on the premises. I thought, therefore, that things would change. But nothing changed. My father kept right on painting and my mother kept on traveling. And, because I no longer had an older sister around to guide me in the paths of righteousness, I was straightaway hustled off to another private school, the lucky devils.

. It only lasted a couple of months. I caught Beverly MacNamara in bed with Louisa Demeter, which wasn't so bad in itself except that Beverly MacNamara was a student and Louisa Demeter was an instructor. An instructor in what, I'd hate to tell you. Let's just say it wasn't Home Economics.

Craftily I tried to work it to my advantage—a little innocent extortion, just to keep things alive on campus. Beverly would have to give me ten bucks a week (no big deal, her father had trillions) and Miss Demeter would have to pass me in History (my absolutely worst subject and one she taught).

It all backfired when I was suddenly hauled up before Miss Calhoun (grande dame of the whole Whittier School for Over-sexed Girls) and confronted with James Griffin (dull-witted handyman), who, it seemed, was accusing me of making indecent demands of his person. They must have paid the sonofabitch a fortune to say that because it never did set too well with his wife. But I guess, later, when he showed her the moolah, she thought better of it and maybe even spurred him on with other Whittier girls as there was no doubt a fortune to be made in such out-and-out fucking lies.

So there I was, fifteen and with a past: I had designs on a handyman, having offered to pay handily for his handiness. The man was quick to say that he had turned the money down and that nothing happened, but I was still stigmatized and shipped home like something out of *Oliver Twist*.

My father, who had been duly informed of my impending return (my mother was away, ho-hum) dropped his pallet long enough to have a little heart-to-heart with me.

I had looked forward to the talk because, though I didn't much care what the rest of the world thought of me, it was important to me that my father know the truth. So, in his den all male and outdoorsy, my bags still packed and beside me, he listened as I told him exactly what had happened, after which, with the calm of Andy Hardy's father, he spoke down at me from Mount Wisdom. "Ginnie, almost anything that a young girl does during adolescence is explainable and understandable."

"But, Daddy, I didn't *do* anything except try a little blackmail. And I only did *that* as a joke."

"Shhhhhhh, let me finish. Please. The important thing for parents to keep in mind is that a young girl's mind and body are in turmoil during adolescence. Desires crop up. 'Lust,' if that's the correct word, appears. It has to be contended with and 'conquered'—if that's the word."

Up until then I never had an inkling as to what a stuffed ass my father was. I'd never really talked to him. I had merely watched him move around, playing Master of the Manor, Squire of the Land. Could it be that, despite all the wealth passed on to him, they had allotted him no brains? "Daddy, you've got it all wrong. Really. I know they must have made it sound pretty bad, but, when you hear *my* side of it—"

But he wasn't listening to me anymore. He was listening to himself and he liked the sound of his voice and the brilliance of his paternal bullshit. "I think, Ginnie, that it's important for you to know that, no matter what you do, I'm always here for you to talk to. However, there's one rule—no lies. There must be no lies between us if I'm to be of any help to you. Do you understand that, Ginnie? Ginnie? Are you listening?"

"Yes, sir."

It was my father, pontificating as he was condemning me, and I had a quick flash of what it had to be like for my mother, always being forgiven for her transgressions when, just maybe, she hadn't been transgressing at all.

And maybe, if she was, maybe my father's need to forgive was so great that, to please him, she had to continually do things that he could forgive her *for*. Or at least *pretend* to do them. It suddenly had all the earmarks of a Gothic comedy. My beloved father was seemingly both a patronizing clod and a twelfth century bumpkin, and I could hear the idol shatter in my head. "Honesty, Ginnie, honesty is the secret of a good relationship, of *any* relationship. Honesty. If you and I can effect such a relationship then perhaps I can be helpful to you in whatever crises occur. And they *will* occur, they always do. Especially in the teen years. And I want you to know that I'll always be here, my door always open. And all I'll ever insist on is—"

"Honesty."

"Exactly. Now then, if we understand each other on that point, perhaps you'd like to tell me exactly what happened because only then can what I say have any value. Do you understand?"

"Yes, sir."

"Because if I'm asked for guidance on an untruth then any conclusion I come to or anything I say to you will have no bearing, no—validity, if that's the word."

"That's the word."

"Very well. Now tell me what happened, exactly what happened." He sat back in his big chair, all puffed up with how well he was handling what could all too easily have become a very sticky matter.

I chose the path of least resistance because I really didn't care to hang around much longer and watch my father turn into plum pudding. "Well, Daddy—about Beverly MacNamara and Miss Demeter—you ,were right. It never happened at all."

"Ahhhh." He was so pleased at having pulled the

truth from me you'd have thought the Louvre had bought one of his paintings.

"I made it all up, to cover myself."

"I understand."

"Because the truth of it is, Daddy—I mean, you *do* want me to be honest, don't you?"

"I do."

"The truth is—I offered Mr. Griffin, *James* Griffin, ten dollars if, if . . ."

"If what?"

"If he'd let me have a gander at his penis."

He didn't bat an eye. His pristine daughter, baring the depths of her debasement, and the old bloke doesn't even inhale. "And why did you do that?"

"Because ten dollars was all I had." I hoped he would laugh and see what a jerk he was being, but he didn't. He just continued on in his role of Judge Hardy, like his kid was asking for a raise in his allowance. I was so crushed I almost ran from the room. But then I became fascinated with the game of how far I could go without Daddy pissing in his pants. But he wasn't pissing and he wasn't laughing. He was just asking, like in a game of bridge, like, "Why did I play that card?" "Why did you want to see his penis, Ginnie?"

"Gee whiz, Daddy—"

"Honesty. Ginnie, we're dealing with honesty. Why did you want to see his penis?"

I straightened up like a kid doing the Pledge of Allegiance. "I wanted to see his penis because I heard, from some of the other girls, that it was enormous and attractive."

"I see. Other girls had paid Mr. Griffin to reveal his penis?"

"Half the school. I don't know how he ever got any work done."

"And did he show it to you?"

"Yes."

"I see."

"So did I."

"And how did you feel when you saw it?"

"You want me to be honest?"

"Yes."

"I felt cheated."

"Why?"

"It wasn't as big as I'd been told it was."

"Did you have something to compare it to?"

"No. I'd only been told it was huge, and I didn't think it was."

"Did you verbalize your disappointment?"

"In a way."

"How?"

"I asked for five dollars back." I was giving my father a chance to display either a sense of humor or a touch of intelligence. Failing that, I was going to give him something really fantastic to forgive me for.

"And did he give you five dollars back?"

"No. He said he had nothing smaller than a twenty."

"How did you settle it?"

"Well, gee whiz, Daddy, it's getting a little embarrassing, you know? Discussing it so clinically? I mean, wow!"

"Ginnie, how did you settle it?"

"He put his penis in my hand and I soon had ten dollars worth." I couldn't believe I'd said that, but it was my voice so it must have been me.

He took a short pause. That pleased me. At least he was beginning to wonder. Then he pulled himself mightily together and— "Then what happened?"

"Daddy!"

"What happened?"

"Well—I squeezed it—his penis. Daddy, gee whiz!"

"For how long?"

"Till he agreed to give me my ten dollars back." I waited for him to laugh. Laugh, I thought. Laugh, you imbecile!

His mouth dropped but he still hung in. "And did he give you the ten dollars back?"

"He gave me twenty."

He was fussing with some things on his desk. "I must admit, I'm at a loss as to what school to apply to. Surely they'll check with Whittier and find out everything. Ginnie, quite frankly, you've given me a great deal to think about." I turned, grabbed my bag, and got the hell out of there. When I reached the hall, I was laughing, but when I got to my room I was crying. I wanted my mother. Where was my mother?

My mother, as it turned out, was in San Francisco, some kind of clinic opening or hospital dedication. I guess she hit the main entrance with a bedpan full of champagne and they rolled the patients right in. My father had apparently gotten in touch with her because mother was home before the week was out, and all the patients had to be sick without her fabulous face to give them something to live for.

During that week my father, with my help, managed very neatly to avoid me. He was painting some kind of landscape—Iowa, I think—and had his meals brought to him in his studio. It was all terribly dramatic, the artist at work, sealing himself off from the world, holed up in Iowa while his daughter rattled around in the big house listening to Buddy Clark records and reading E. E. Cummings.

I don't know whether my father was mortified or mystified. I don't know if he realized what a dope he'd made of himself or if he didn't really see me as some kind of modern day duBarry, bedding down aristocrats and peasants alike in hopes of avoiding war with England. All I knew was that in the first trauma of my life (I'm not including Walter because that was just silly) my father chose to take the word of a schoolful of dykes over mine, and from then on it was okay with me if he *never* came out of his room. He could stay in there and paint Iowa, Wyoming, Alabama, and Greece—and then he could wallpaper the whole place with Russia; I just didn't want to see him anymore.

My mother returned and, after an hour of putting on her face, appeared at my door. Damnit, but she was beautiful. Why couldn't I look like that?

She gave me a little kiss and her perfume went delicately to my brain. I hadn't realized how young she was, many years younger than my father who I knew to be fifty-nine. She asked me to please tell her what had happened and, just to test her, to see if she didn't share the same midget intellect of my father, I told her I had been fucking since I was twelve years old—anything in pants, from Harold, our butler, to Mr. Jamison, the friendly druggist, to Walter Harrison, my recent brother-in-law.

Mother listened to it all, saying nothing. But when I included Walter in my conquests she laughed so hard that one of her earrings popped off. I guess naming Walter as one of my amours was just too hard to swallow.

Her laughter was delightful and I remember wishing that I had heard more of it in the house. She pulled herself together and asked again what happened at Whittier and I told her and she believed me and I loved her for it. And then we both relaxed and let our hair down.

She told me that she had every confidence in my

being able to handle my own life, that contrary to what my face would have me believe, I would one day be pretty and how lucky I would be not to inherit her breasts (or lack of them). She was sensational. Sitting in my room with me she was suddenly the sister I never truly had. She was bright and funny and inventive, and, since her name was Maggie would I please call her Maggie.

We gabbed—it must have been for hours—and I learned how she and my father had gotten married. It was like a Joan Crawford movie. Her father was a poor but honest plumber with the emphasis on the poor. Originally from Camden, New Jersey, she was sixteen and working in a crummy Philadelphia diner that various artists frequented when my tall and handsome father came in and ordered some terribly romantic spare ribs. She could see that he was rich and attractive and that here was her chance to get out of the hole her family had her living in. So she deliberately dropped the gooey spare ribs into my father's lap and looked so great crying that my father, evidently a boob even then, ended up consoling her over a lobster dinner at one of Philadelphia's finest seafood spots.

She posed for him in his studio but knew enough to not take her clothes off since that was what every artist's model did as soon as the chips were down (and that portrait of her was the one that hung over our living room mantel). He offered to pay her for her time but she refused, saying something like, "I just want to be in your company, to watch you work. I think you're wonderful."

He responded very well to her lying candor and physical withdrawals. He liked her innocence and was charmed by her virtue. More than anything else, he liked the fact that, in the middle of wicked, wicked Philadelphia she had managed to retain her lovely virginity.

Mother was smart for she *was* a virgin, which she quickly proved by bleeding all over the place when he finally got her onto the veranda. Poor father, so delighted that he had brought down immaculate Miranda, never minded that there was a pool of blood in his studio that looked like the French Revolution. She cried and she cried. Oh, how he had hurt her. Worse, he had stolen her jewel. She didn't want to see him again, ever—how *could* she? And would he please take her home this instant!

He called the next day but she would not speak to him. He found her later, in the diner, once again on duty as a waitress (surprise!). He sat down at her table and romantically ordered spare ribs. No fool, she again dropped them into his lap and, after two weeks of soy sauce, they were married.

From then on it was all downhill. She would have preferred it to have been otherwise but was not surprised at his dullness because dull was the color he had flashed from the beginning. She tried, really tried, hoping that he would develop into a more acceptable fellow. She was dutiful, attentive, and loving; but after five years and two daughters, she was unable to tolerate the boredom of being with him, a boredom made all the more tedious by his inability to develop as an artist. He became duller and duller, finally losing interest in her in bed. So she started moving around on her own.

She and my father had an arrangement (Ah!). They had never really sat down and worked it out, it just happened. She could come and go as she pleased as long as it was with some semblance of respectability. He was content to stay at home and paint Utah.

Maggie didn't go into any great detail about how she spent her time away from home. Just said it was "charity work." And the only reason she had told me as much as she had was that she was leaving my father and wasn't sure just when she'd see me again.

I cried because I felt that I'd just met her, and she cried, too. She would try to keep in close touch with me but that would be impossible for a while as she would be living in Europe with a man whose name she wouldn't tell me.

She hoped I'd understand. I hoped I would, too. But at the time it hurt too much for me to make any promises other than that I'd try to make the best of it until she could straighten out her life, get a divorce, and maybe send for me.

She gave me a tearful hug and swept out of my room like the tail end of a nice dream. It was all screwed up. A week before I had hated her and loved my father. Suddenly it was the other way around. And in the process I had lost them both. I had a mother and I had a father, but damned if I wasn't an orphan.

chapter five

ben

1949

On the day of my last good cigar, I quit my job at the Rockwell Greeting Card Store. I don't know why I quit. Certainly I had no other job. It just somehow seemed the thing to do and so I did it, chalking the whole pointless gesture up to splendid symbolism.

To further establish the end of an era, I went into a cigar store and bought a package of White Owls, six for a quarter. Lighting up, I most definitely felt the rumble of Somerset Maugham revolving in his grave, even though the man was still alive at the time and, as far as I knew, in the best of health.

I wandered New York, moseying through Abercrombie's main floor where everything was leather and crystal and predictably depressing. For I had decided to be depressed; I had earned it. Over the years I had learned that the best way to deal with setbacks and failures was to indulge in the depressions they inspired rather than smile and say "pip-pip" and pretend that life was a maraschino. For always, after a day or two of bottomless depression, I would become so sick of it that all the world suddenly looked good. It was the Ben Webber theory of relativity, and it worked:

$$\frac{\text{DEPRESSION} \times \text{INDULGENCE}}{\text{DAYS REQUIRED}} = \text{ENOUGH}$$

So, after three days of self-imposed gloom, I re-entered Abercrombie's and applied for a charge account, giving my last year's income as $25,000 and using as personal references Darryl F. Zanuck and Spyros Skouras, two men so high up in 20th Century-Fox that a fella had to be an eagle to get an appointment.

Not that I ever thought Abercrombie & Fitch would issue me a charge card, it was just that I wanted them to know my name, to be ready for me when my time came, and for the imperious bitch in the New Accounts window to one day have to explain to her superiors why she had failed to issue Benjamin Rex Webber, prominent eye surgeon and leading tenor at the Met, an Abercrombie & Fitch credit card. Couldn't she see, even then, that the young man was going places—like to Saks Fifth Avenue, where he similarly applied and similarly was turned down? Was she insane?

With a jauntiness to my gait I went into Thomas Begg's and bought an eleven-dollar fedora of the ilk of Don Cook's. I didn't like the feather it flew and said as much to the salesman who, anxious to please, pulled out a box of feathers that would have given a pea hen an orgasm. After a half hour of comparing color and texture, I made my selection, and not until I hit the street did I realize that I had for a feather the identical twin of Don Cook's. I wasn't surprised.

I bought a bag of hot chestnuts because it was October and chestnuts evoked images of blonde girls in camel hair coats cheering at football games. I winked at a pretty girl and stared down an even prettier one. And in the Museum of Modern Art I found myself less occupied with Brancusi than with the girls who were taking notes on his works.

It has always seemed to me that, in October, girls in the Museum of Modern Art are outrageously beguiling.

Girls in Bloomingdale's are older and more sophisticated. And girls in Bonwit's are sweet if a touch antiseptic. But girls in the Museum of Modern Art in October are descendants of F. Scott Fitzgerald, slender, fragile, waiflike, affluent things, wrapped in mufflers that go three times around their necks before bouncing against their thighs. In October, girls in the Museum of Modern Art are virginal but experienced, unembittered by cooled affairs and ever-hopeful that magic is just around the corner. And maybe the magic is *me*. Ergo—

Feeling good, I walked all the way back to the apartment, three White Owls still in my quiver. I consumed a glass of sherry and reshaped my new hat to something more nearly my mood. A tilt to the left, a crush to the crown, a flick of the feather for luck.

Our stewardesses were away. Alice was in Cincinnati being drilled nightly by her dentist-husband. Susan, the orange-squeezer, had jumped ship in Miami, holing up with a retired stockbroker whom she hoped would marry her if she read the market right. And Jessica was off on a leave of absence during which she was determined to lose weight.

With our stewardesses gone, Don and I were free to bring home anyone and anything we fancied. That we did not or could not was a testimonial to how much we missed our three First Class Fly Girls.

I was denied unemployment insurance because I had quit my job rather than rigging it so that I could be fired. But I didn't care. I still had a few bucks in the old cookie jar and if I didn't know where I was going, I at least knew where I had been, all of my decisions along the way having been made with integrity, morality, and stupidity—a combination of medically proven ingredients guaranteed to cause my death if somebody didn't stop me in time.

Most of my days were spent soaking in New York. It was heady wine and, to my credit, I was never envious of the more successful types who trod the same sidewalks as I. Most of my nights were spent with television, for I was drawn to that thing like a bee to a bud. I particularly watched the dramatic shows, all of them live and most of them written by "another promising playwright." I could be a promising playwright, too. I'd promise them *anything* if they'd let me be a playwright.

Don saw to it that my social vistas broadened. And on Friday and Saturday nights we often wound up in the Village, pretending to understand the two-beat Dixie that blew out of every joint from Phil Napoleon's to Eddie Condon's. In the mix I was allowed to travel with the guys from 20th, i.e., the boys with whom Don worked in the big brick building on West Fifty-sixth Street between Ninth and Tenth. And I liked them, every one. Big Al Epstein was a winner, had it stamped all over him. Arnie Felsen, yearning to be a playwright, took notes wherever we went, nothing escaping his goiterlike eyes. Everything had a significance to Arnie, and once I even came across him in the men's room at the 181 Club, peeing away with one hand while balancing a pencil and pad against the tile wall with the other, recording some obscure observation without missing a drop. Indomitable Arnie. Even then he was a pisser.

Bob Steinman, ex-World War II navigator, was continually homing in on provocative womenfolk and with unearthly success. With that kind of aim he should have been able to hit Berlin and end the war at least a year before the rest of the Allies finally pulled it off. One minute he'd be sitting next to me, and the next minute he'd be flying a sortie with some girl twenty yards across the room. I can't remember a night when Bob Steinman ended up alone. There had to be more action in his two-room apartment than ever took place in Europe. The best thing about him was that he never gave us any of that "I'm a combat veteran and an officer" crap. He never lorded it over us, never treated us as anything but equals. And even though he was over thirty, he never bemoaned the years he lost in the service. All he wanted to do was get laid and, I must say, it didn't seem to matter with who. If Bob shot down a dozen or so sleek Messerschmitts before our very eyes, he also knocked off a couple Piper Cubs, a handful of blimps, and an occasional turkey.

The man I felt a special affinity for was Roland Jessup. Out of an orphanage in New Jersey, Roland was a black man—but barely. By that I mean he was light enough to pass for white but simply didn't choose to go that route. It was rumored that he was homosexual but none of us knew for sure, nor did Roland ever attempt to clue us in (though we *did* know that he lived alone in a Greenwich Village apartment fixed up to look like an Arabian tent—striped drapes, purple cushions, beaded curtains, Turkish hookahs). Whatever he was, Roland was a good guy and a tireless worker—which was more than could be said for a lot of people walking the earth at that time.

One day—it was a great day—Don came home from work to tell me that the union, the Screen Publicists Guild, had bargained with management and that, as a result, two new jobs were created in the ranks of the "Men of Tomorrow" and that I was supposed to call W. Charles Gruber about one of them.

"But," I said, "I'm not a college graduate."

"You are. University of Pittsburgh. They liked that. Marshall Goldberg was an All-American there."

"But what if they ask to see my diploma?"

"They didn't ask to see mine."

"Do you mean—you never went to college?"

He shrugged, pseudo-Jewish. "Don't ask."

I called W. Charles Gruber, vice-president of the whole thing, but never got to speak with him. His secretary, though, expecting my call, told me to call Stirling Silliphant's secretary for an interview. Stirling Silliphant, soon to become a most successful writer-producer, was then in charge of 20th Century-Fox's exploitation department. I met with him that afternoon and told him that no offense but I thought I'd do better in the advertising department because of my "inherent knowledge of writing" (greeting cards). Stirling Silliphant said that Josh Meyerberg was advertising manager but that he was fully staffed and would I mind working for Dan Steier in Publicity and I said no. So I was hired and on the job the next morning.

It had all happened very quickly. I had called Gruber, met with Silliphant, was told that Meyerberg was who I should be working for, and ended up working for Steier who didn't know I was alive until I walked in and told him so.

I knew I would like being in the movie business because, from what I could see of it, it was delightfully imbecilic, no one in it ever went to college, and my being Jewish was an advantage. I haven't been Jewish since, but it was fun.

chapter six

ginnie

1949

So there I was, at The Stokely School for Girls, in Mary-
land, turning sixteen, failing at everything except jazz
dancing, and being called in for a private conversation
with Miss Marjorie Stokely her regal self. I assumed it
would be about my cavalier attitude and general all-
around beastliness. I was wrong.

Uncharacteristically, she beat around the bush for
over ten minutes, talking of life, experience, field
hockey, cabbages and kings—everything but how to rid
Malaya of crotch rot. I let her ramble on, figuring she'd
get to the point sooner or later because she was well
into her seventies and didn't have all that much time left
to indulge in a filibuster.

Marjorie Stokely's countenance was marble smooth
because she had filled in all the lines and creases with
what had to be a mixture of face powder and plastic
wood. If a high wind were to suddenly come up it
would have blown her patina to Paducah, revealing her
face for what it was—a pale prune, ravaged by drought,
in which nothing living could take root beyond two
pasty lips the width of rubber bands and maybe a dozen
beige teeth that George Washington would have turned
down. Her creped neck swiveled her head from window
to door, to ceiling, to floor but never at me. Finally, she
stopped the blathering and, looking straight into my

face, said, "Virginia, life is a fragile thing at best, and too often things we love are taken from us all too prematurely."

I figured she was about to tell me that her turtle died. I'd heard it had been sick for quite some time and was destined to be an ashtray in a fortnight. But she wasn't talking about her turtle because there it was, looking at me from its glass case, its own creped neck holding up its own shriveled head. Like mother, like turtle.

"Virginia, there's been an accident. A fire."

"Chicago again?" I asked, ever the weisenheimer.

"In Stamford."

Oh, Christ! I thought. Daddy.

"Your father." She dabbed at her eyes with an Irish linen something. Too ornate to be a handkerchief, it had to have been cut from an unused wedding dress or an unfledged shroud. "I don't really know the details, Virginia. We received a call. The fire was confined to his studio. The main house was untouched. You have to go home. I'm sorry."

She said a few other things to fill the void because I wasn't in the mood for babble. Apparently I said so little that, as I left, she seemed rather surprised. "You seem to be taking it very well, Virginia."

"Well—he wasn't my real father." I don't know why I said that. I always knew I could be counted on to say something bizarre in a delicate moment, but that one surprised even me. Maybe I was just trying to ease the hurt. Or maybe it was the way I really felt. Not that I ever doubted that it was Daddy's sperm that had catapulted me into creation. It was simply that, as I grew older, I came to realize that it takes more than a shot in the dark to be a father. I mean a real father.

As I left Stokely I knew I'd never be back. The only reason I was there was that my father had *sent* me there. With him gone, who'd give a damn where I'd go? My mother? I hadn't gotten as much as a "Happy Arbor Day" card from her since our first and last fireside chat. I wondered if anyone had told my mother that the old man had curled up his toes. How *could* they? She'd pulled off the greatest disappearance since Judge Crater. No, wherever she was, the lovely Maggie Maitland would know nothing.

So it was good-bye, Stokely, hello, Stamford, as the dumpy old train carried me back to the old homestead. I had some difficulty getting my head together. Yes, I felt mortal and vulnerable. After all, my own flesh and blood had perished. And yet, it wasn't as if some dread disease, something in the family line, had claimed Daddy, and might one day claim me. It was fire. And fire could happen to anyone. So I didn't feel all that threatened. Nor did I feel denied a great paternal crutch to lean on since Daddy had trouble enough standing on his *own* without having to steady a dizzy daughter.

Still, I did feel an overwhelming sadness. Not for me, but for him. For if he never succeeded in accomplishing anything in his life, neither did he ever hurt anybody. His was like the death of a small animal that you never know is around until you find its dead body—a hummingbird, a koala bear, a marmoset—sweet, benign bits of life, unnoticed except as echoes and shadows of their small former beings. We'd be burying an echo and a shadow in Stamford, Connecticut, in a small cemetery within a semicircle of evergreens. Who will come to the funeral of Howard Maitland? Do try to attend as hardly anyone will be there. (Betcha never knew his first name.)

My sister, Mary Ann (yecchh), and my brother-in-law, Walter (ugh), met me at the station to console me the rest of the way home. But I needed no consoling because just the sight of them made my heart dance with joy. Mary Ann, barely twenty, looked forty. And Walter, reeking of alcohol, looked ninety. Obviously their marriage had gone well (from *my* point of view), and when Walter's hand fell on my knee on the ride home, I let it stay there (eat your heart out, Mr. Nine Inches, it's as much as you'll ever get from me).

Oh well, funerals are pretty much alike, I guess. A gathering in the church, a mumbo-jumbo service, a dogmatic litany, limousines to the planting grounds—and lower away! What I hadn't counted on was my own particular reaction to it all. I was all right until the coffin was being lowered into the grave. And I would have stayed all right if I hadn't said anything. But, at the last moment, unbeknownst to me—I did speak. "Good-bye, Daddy," I said, and that did it. I almost collapsed, mammoth groans pouring out of me, huge uncontrollable spasms wracking me, and I had to be led away.

Just the sound of those words, "Good-bye, Daddy," and I dissolved. I know now that I would have done the very same thing at a stranger's funeral had the stranger's daughter said "Good-bye, Daddy." I know now that I had cried as a conditioned response to the words and not the reality, to the familiarity not the pain. And how could I ever have done otherwise? For how many movies had I seen in which Bette Davis did it? And Jennifer Jones and Olivia de Havilland and a whole host of immaculately conceived heroines who loved their parents into the grave and beyond. How many years of good, clean movie-going had primed me for that moment in which *I* would play the big cemetery scene in my own Warner Brothers melodrama?

The actual facts of Daddy's death were these: He took all of his paintings, a bottle of bourbon, a vial of pills, a gallon of gasoline—and one dry match. And he put them all together and they spelled *Mother*—in big, flaming, yellow letters. His whole studio went up in minutes, all of Daddy's paintings with it. I can only assume (or hope) that he was properly out of it when he struck the match. But we couldn't know for sure because there was no note and what they found of him was mostly ashes and dental work. It was incredible. He cremated himself and *then* we buried him. How dead can you get?

It didn't take Herculean deduction to figure out why he did it. He did it because he finally faced up to the fact that he was and had nothing—no wife, no daughters, no talent. My mother, "The Phantom Maggie," never showed up or acknowledged his passing.

The lawyers moved in immediately. Daddy's estate —house, land, stocks, bonds, etc.—came to about $800,000, give or take whatever he left to the servants, charity, lawyers and the inheritance tax. A week before the big bonfire he wrote Maggie out of the will. Even if she had shown up she'd have had a hard time contesting it as no one could honestly say she'd done anything wifely beyond desertion.

So it was $400,000 for me and $400,000 for Mary Ann (to share with the Pancake King), the only catch being that I was a minor, which meant that my share had to be held in trust with guess who as trustee. Worse, she was also my guardian. How many sixteen-year-old girls could actually say that their guardian was a cocksucker and know it to be a fact?

Within two days the real estate brokers were mincing through the house like it was kickoff time at the Oklahoma land rush. And the antique dealers with their little tongue-moistened pencil points, were tippy-toeing around, placing little tags on everything but the toilet paper. Only one art dealer came by, just to check if any

of Daddy's paintings had survived the fire, a little old
man named Mr. Peebles. Over the years he had seen all
of Daddy's paintings and saw nothing in any of them
except for the portrait of Maggie. He asked about it,
did that burn, too? When told yes he shrugged, went
"tsk-tsk" and headed for the door, with me in righteous
pursuit.

"Where the hell were you when he was *alive*?" I
shouted, surprised at how angry I was and how shrill
my voice sounded.

He looked at me while trying not to. "I'm sorry,
young lady, but your father was a minor painter."

"How would *you* know, you idiotic creep?"

"It's my business to know." He kept moving toward
the door, anxious to get out but unable to accelerate.

"Why didn't you buy something from him when he
was *alive*? Then maybe he'd still *be* alive!"

"I offered to. The portrait of your mother. He
wouldn't sell it."

"Maybe if you'd have offered more than eight dollars he *would* have!"

"I offered considerably more. Excuse me. I must be
going. I'm sorry for your trouble."

"*Everybody's* sorry around this fucking place!"

Mr. Peebles left. He was Irish, no doubt, because
only the Irish say "I'm sorry for your trouble." They
say it all the time. They say it when someone dies, when
someone sneezes, when someone's coat is stolen. They
said it to Othello, Hitler, Xerxes and Attila. "I'm sorry
for your trouble." Translated into English it means,
"It's a fucking shame your old man kicked off but what
the hell do you want *me* to do about it?" Why don't
people say what they mean? I slammed the door after
him and a vase toppled from a table and smashed. The
tag said: "#356—$148.00." Right away I owed Mary

Ann seventy-four bucks. Fuck her, I thought. I won't tell her. I'll tell her the wind did it. I'll tell her the *butler* did it.

I went to my room and cried. Not for me. Not for Daddy. Not for the starving masses in India. But just for the hell of it. And maybe, just a little, for all the painters who couldn't sell as much as a picket fence even if they cut an ear off.

I stopped crying because I became bored with it and I looked around at my chocolate box of a room that I had created for myself, on my own, no help from nobody. It wasn't that I had manifested any great talent in the decorating department that I was given the assignment. It was merely that no one really gave a damn so they left me alone with the task. I doubt if anyone ever went up there to see what I had eventually committed beyond Sara, our maid. I had done it all by myself, calling the shops, thumbing through swatchbooks, arguing prices. It had all been a great experience. Too bad the result looked like an explosion in Candyland.

I was wrong about no one coming to my room other than Sara. Someone else had been there, and recently: my father. I found the painting in my closet, pressed face against the back wall—the portrait of Maggie. And there was something on the back of it, some writing:

> Ginnie—
>   this is your mother.
>   I loved her.
>   Dad

So I cried all over again, new tears, cascades. Somehow, even in the prelude to his suicide, Daddy had determined that I, and I alone, was to have the portrait of Maggie. Somehow he knew that it was worth the not-burning, that it had a value, not necessarily in dollars but in human terms. It was the only thing he left me that wasn't catalogued in the will. Weird. All I had of my father was my mother.

I held it up to the light. God, it was good, and God, it was Maggie. That face, those eyes, the hair, all caressed onto the canvas with such perfection that I realized, in one awesome rush, that mixed in with all the oil and pigment was the one ingredient that was absent in everything else that the artist had ever done—*love*. Jesus Christ, Maggie, what did you ever do to deserve it?

There was no doubt in my mind that I'd keep the painting for myself, like a deathbed promise to my father. I'd be damned if I'd let Mary Ann know of its existence; damned if I'd argue over the possession of it or let those graspy appraisers stick a number on it or a pricetag. And as far as my showing it to Mr. Peebles, fuck him and I'm sorry for his trouble.

A fantasy swept across me. The painting was worth a fortune. Properly examined and evaluated, it would rank with the Mona Lisa. But how could I sell my mother? How? Easily. It was my father I couldn't betray. Besides, I had $400,000 even if I couldn't get my hands on it for another five years. I settled for a compromise, as follows: If I fell upon hard times before I came into my inheritance or if Mary Ann squandered my share on a vibrating phallus the size of the Alps, I would then, and only then, sell mother to the white slavers—for $250,000. That would be the very least I'd accept for her. A beauty like Maggie Maitland? Hell, what impotent old collector wouldn't be willing to pay such a small stipend to have a face like that on the wall of his study where he could get his jollies without having to tax his anatomy.

I had already decided to go out on my own, make a

run for it, hit the trail, ride the rails, when Mary Ann, the SOS Queen (Spurting Oral Spermatozoa), knocked at my door. She was allowed entrance only after I had restashed Maggie in the closet.

Mary Ann was so overflowing with filial attention I thought, for one fleeting moment, that she had become a nun when no one was looking. Wouldn't have bothered Walter; that dark-visaged stud would've probably found the idea sensational. Nothing like nailing a wife of Christ to the mattress to liven up a dull Palm Sunday.

"Ginnie, I think we should talk."

"Okay."

"After all," she continued, hands clasped in her lap as if she had lilies growing there, "we *are* sisters, and, with Daddy gone—"

"Don't you wish we'd been a little nicer to him? We all treated him like he was a *room. All* of us."

Mary Ann pressed on, no time for sentiment. "We don't know where mother is or if she's even in the country. Daddy left everything to us. It's a lot."

"Bully."

"I'll be twenty-one in a month, and, because you're a minor, I'll be your legal guardian." And then she dropped the sweet stuff. "Look at me, you little cunt. I'm not here for my health. I've been going over your record at Whittier. Blackmail and hand jobs. I don't know what I'm going to do with you."

"Who's asking you to do anything?"

"You're sixteen years old and you have no parents, Miss Jerkoff."

"I have a mother."

"You have the *memory* of a mother—that's all. As your legal guardian I'm required to see to your schooling and watch over your investments."

"And what have you come up with?"

"The Hollyridge School. It's close enough to Chicago so that you can be home with Walter and me on weekends. They specialize in maladjusted, toilet-mouthed bitches. You'll fit in well, I'm sure."

"Right. I'll tell 'em I'm your sister and they'll make me captain of the Blow Job Team." I watched her puff up like a blowfish, which I thought very much in character.

She squinted at me, as though to make certain I was still there. "I cannot tell you with what revulsion I view you."

"Me? *You're* the one who took on the Three Musketeers—and their *horses*, I assume."

"You're my only relative. God damn it, I deserve better."

"Stick around. Maybe you'll come up with hoof and mouth disease."

Right before my eyes, she turned into the wicked stepsister. "You will do everything I tell you to. You will go where I send you—and you will treat me with proper respect. And if you don't like it—you can shove it up your ass."

"A pox on you, Mary Ann. As far as I'm concerned, you can throw yourself under a car and kill yourself."

"Fuck you," she said, and hoity-toitied out.

I slammed the door after her, shouting, "I'm sorry for your trouble!"

For the next few days I harbored thoughts of running away. But all I had to my name was twenty-six dollars and maybe twenty-three cents. Jesus, I thought, is Mary Ann going to give me an allowance from now on? How could I ever survive that? I considered sneaking the portrait of Maggie over to Mr. Peebles and selling it then and there, cash on the barrelhead, whatever I could get. But that would have been like drinking my last canteen of water *before* crossing the desert. It was a problem.

I had no trouble avoiding Mary Ann and Walter. The house was big and they were both involved in the selling of things. One afternoon I went to the riding stables, doing an hour on old Snowball who was getting lame and gave me no trouble. Jud Smith was there (he of my sister's flaming diary) and he offered his condolences, asking that I extend them to Mary Ann as well. I told him thanks and that, if he'd trot over to the house, Mary Ann would suck off both him *and* his horse. He turned to stone. Best part of it was that, as he was standing there looking stupid, old Snowball drops a load of manure on his boots. I don't know, but it somehow seemed right.

Apparently, Mary Ann was as much for my running away as I was. What I mean is, I went to bed that night and, as I snuggled my hands under the pillow, what should my wondering hands come upon but a thousand dollars in unmarked bills—fives, tens, twenties and fifties. No note, just the money, in an envelope. Well, never let it be said that Ginnie Maitland couldn't be bought off. So, next morning at sunrise (it seemed fitting), I took two valises of my most practical clothes, called a cab, and took off for the Stamford station, the portrait of Maggie under my arm, wrapped in a pillow case (it was only twenty-four inches by thirty-six). It was well before the commuter rush, so I got a seat.

Old Greenwich, Riverside, Cos Cob, Greenwich— they all passed by my window, waving good-bye as I did the fifty-five-minute trip to Grand Central. That was the last stop. It was also the first stop because it was New York, and 1949, and I had busted out of San Quentin.

chapter seven

ben

1949

20th Century-Fox, in New York City, was a world within a world. It had its own boundaries, its own rules, its own heroes and its own villains. I was in a strata of that society just above porters, janitors and bootblacks, and just below office boys, doormen, and elevator operators. I was a messenger in Publicity, which meant that I had to endure a form of indentured servitude just this side of slavery.

Despite a semimuscular union, the work day was long and the take-home pay would have been more appropriately given to us in rice. The work was dull, exhausting, and often humiliating. The opportunity for advancement was slight. And though we were all of us good fellows, the competition for a place in the sun was fierce, the name of the game being get out of Publicity fast or languish there, and be forgotten.

Astride the filmic complex was Spyros Skouras, president of 20th worldwide and then some. White-maned and will-o-the-wisp, he was one of a trio of self-made brothers who, deficient in both languages, spoke neither Greek nor English well. But he was an imposing man nevertheless, seeming to be eight feet tall and to possess wings on his ankles—he covered that much ground. Messengers and lower luminaries seldom saw him but knew when he was in the building because the whole thing trembled with his presence. Also, the brass door shone a little brighter and the elevator men stood a little taller, especially around Christmas and Greek holidays when Skouras tossed out ten-dollar bills as if they were sample portions of baklava.

I guess he spent as much time in California as he did in New York, but California and all film production was headed up by the redoubtable Darryl F. Zanuck who could do fifty one-handed chinups while interviewing innumerable starlets for featured roles in upcoming films (or so the legend went). Beyond that, he was a spirited studio head with a good financial track record and that's what counted (not to us but to the stockholders).

Anyway, back in New York. The vice-president in charge of Advertising, Publicity and Exploitation was W. Charles Gruber and he was something else. Having fallen short as an independent film producer, Gruber fell back on his former experience in the marketing of films. He never made life easy for anyone and was surreptitiously referred to as "the Jewish Himmler." Under Gruber were Silliphant (Exploitation), Steier (Publicity) and Meyerberg (Advertising). But almost as soon as I got there, Steier was gone, Silliphant moved into Publicity, with Rodney Bush taking over Exploitation and Meyerberg holding fast in Advertising. There was no musical chairs like motion picture musical chairs.

So there I was in Publicity, happy to be there but already fighting to get out. Don had hipped me to the whole deal, pointing out the fate of those who hung on there too long. But we were all young, screamingly liberal, and slopping over with hope. Thus equipped, it was impossible for us to indulge in a dog-eat-dog war for some mythical advancement. Instead, we galvanized our energies into a single striking force and quietly turned it against what we all judged to be a malevolent and medieval management. We did our jobs but we clung together. It was a testimonial to the youth of our generation. Years later we'd be playing a different game.

We were caustic, critical of the scripts and films we saw, derisive of the industry as a whole, and referred to ourselves as "The Men of Last Week." And we credited ourselves with a greater awareness of what was going on in the business than that of the people we were working for.

Television at that time was beginning to flex its cables, but the studios were a long way from turning it into an ally. Instead, they fought it, denigrated it, looked upon it as a kind of "color radio." And even though the film studios were turning out the most dismal fare of all time (I defy anyone to find a more shallow film era than the early fifties), somebody still came up with the slogan MOVIES ARE BETTER THAN EVER. It became the banner for the entire industry, an "all for one and one for all" approach, whereas, five years earlier the individual studio watchword was more nearly, "If it ain't ours, fuck 'em."

What folly it was for them to insist that movies were better than ever. It was like a drowning man asking, "How do you like my backstroke?" or Icarus saying, "Catch my Victory Roll, Ace." Still they persisted, the moguls and idols, cheering us on with their brave words and gallant lunacy, charging straightaway into the Valley of Death because no one knew how to execute an about-face.

No matter. We hung the posters and stamped our envelopes and filled the media with MOVIES ARE BETTER THAN EVER, like religionists reverently believing that "Jesus Saves" (the film industry?). And in between came the financial crises, during which dissident stockholder groups merged their forces in efforts to oust the ruling powers, plus "economy firings," through which twenty people were fired so that one biggie could go on in his chosen profession of plowing 20th under with anachronisms, banalities, and inability.

The Messenger Corps suffered casualties. I will not bother to mention their names because they were too soon gone to catalogue. Roland Jessup, happily and deservedly, was transferred to Advertising where Josh Meyerberg protected him from future economic pogroms by making him an office boy.

The rest of us scroungy messengers dug in our heels, but at wages so close to bare subsistence that building pyramids in ancient Egypt began to look like a better area for advancement—and that was the catch. Management couldn't fire us, but if we quit voluntarily they didn't have to replace us. It put the five of us in a fascinating position of power. We could be uppity with management, slovenly in our dress and lope, but as long as we were union members, they had to abide us. By the same token, we could be obstreperous and rebellious with our union, rambunctious, critical and late with our dues, and no one would put us down. The members could call us "The Five Little Shits" (I heard that from the back of the meetingroom one night) but they still needed our numbers for their own insulation. Also, lest we forget, Senator McCarthy and his "Red-hunters" were in the wings, sharpening their lists; and the Guild, though free of communist taint, had recurring nightmares in which one or all five of us was reporting directly to J. Edgar Hoover.

On our nights off from work we still managed to carouse, in our fashion, which meant that Big Al went home to his wife and his efforts to make her pregnant because there was a war brewing in Korea and he desperately wanted an heir and an exemption, while Arnie Felsen went home to the Bronx where his mother was making him diabetic with Jewish cooking so heavy that to lift it from the stove was to risk a displaced disc. This left, for the carousing, Don, Bob Steinman and myself. Or, as we referred to ourselves, "King Kock and the Nuts." Bob was, as I said, a good guy. Also, he wasn't stupid. He knew that 20th would fire Skouras before they'd fire him for he was a bona fide war hero, and a Jew. And *that*, in the movie business, was like having the first four draft picks on Nympho Night in the Catskills. Not that Bob needed any help in that area, he didn't. He had such an overflow of willing women that Don and I, like jackals in the wake of a lion, had much to dine on if such was our desire.

Unfortunately for me I found there to be an unbridgeable chasm between "flesh" and "carrion"; and though Don was not too choosy whose hind quarters he'd sink his canines into, I found that I was developing tastes that were unfulfillingly epicurean. Such being the case, and for the longest time, I feasted only with my eyes, filling them with unattainable quarry, spending my evenings alone with the hunger of abstinence and the writings of Twain.

For lunch we dined at Killerman's Bakery on Tenth Avenue, choosing from any one of a dozen huge rectangular cakes at ten cents a four-inch square. A container of coffee was another dime, as was tea, though milk was fifteen cents. We sat at two little tables because Killerman's had no luncheon trade. They set up the tables to accommodate us because they knew we were Jewish and because they were German—and maybe mankind could get together again one day, over a strudel and a two cents plain.

On rare occasions we'd hit the Stage Delicatessen, just to see the waiters on parade. Bombastic, mercurial, short-tempered and hilarious, they'd argue with us, tell us what to order, spill mustard in our soup, make fun of our ties. It was all a show, of course, with the food the best kosher fare in town. And old Max Asnas, the proprietor, took great pride in knowing every customer's name. What matter that he called me "Hymie" or greeted Don as "Sol"?

On even rarer occasions we'd go to Lindy's, where you had better have a reservation and three bucks to squander. Everybody who was anybody ate at Lindy's. It was the land of Damon Runyon, his favorite haunt, where the strawberry cheesecake was immortal and men had been known to kill for the corned beef on rye.

Wherever you sat at Lindy's it was Magic Time. It was where Ed Sullivan held court and where Danny Kaye dropped down from heaven for stuffed derma. Sid Caesar, at the top of his game, showed up with his retinue of young writers, among whom were Mel Brooks and Neil Simon, only nobody much gave a damn for them at the time.

Show people, pony-tailed dancers in pink and blue makeup and rehearsal clothes, actors with scripts, agents with deals—they all hit Lindy's. The place was alive with theatre, movies and TV, and it whetted my desire to be a bigger part of it than, as Arnie so poetically put it, "a schlepper and a schlemiel."

Things began to happen just at about the time I thought they never would. Unbeknownst to me, Roland Jessup had put in a good word for me with Josh Meyerberg. More than that, Roland had encouraged me to take home some scenarios of upcoming 20th Century-Fox films. He told me to read them and rough out some advertising lines that he would then show to Meyerberg.

I had no way of knowing whether my work was good or bad. I had never really tried to write anything until then except phony excuses that would get me out of high school assignments (and those I forged my mother's name to). So I read some scripts, came up with some copy lines and accompanying layouts, and gave them to Roland each morning as I went past the Advertising department on my way to Publicity. For three weeks I did that, feeling as though I was making ransom drops to kidnappers who had already killed my child. Then I received a phone call from Josh Meyerberg's secretary. Could I find the time to stop by his office? Yes. How was three o'clock? I'll be there.

Willa Nichols, Josh Meyerberg's secretary, looked down her perfect nose at me for five seconds. Had it been her old nose it would have taken a half hour. "Yes?" she said finally. She was about thirty and lumpy, and it occurred to me that, as long as she was having her nose redone, she should have had her body smashed and made over also. Even if she came out as William Bendix it would have been an improvement. She was superior without cause, a quality I've never been able to tolerate in women, cats, and quiche Lorraine. "Whom do you wish to see?"

"President Truman, but I'll settle for Josh Meyerberg."

"Is he expecting you?" She only asked questions. Many people do that. Even their declarative statements go uphill and have question marks hung on the ends of them.

"Yes. He's expecting me."

"And you are—?"

"Spotty Ginsburg."

She was confused at the inconsistency between name and note pad and ran her finger up and down the page in her appointment book as if she were goosing a moving bug. "Do I have your name here?"

"I don't know. Do you?"

"Ginsburg?"

"Yes. Spotty."

"Spotty?"

"As in Spofford."

"Spofford Ginsburg?"

"I also use the name Webber."

"*Ben* Webber?"

"Yes. Maybe *that's* it."

She seemed cross with me and her voice dropped. And even though it was a question, it was also an invitation for me to stop the shit. "Are you Ben Webber?"

"My God, yes! Are you Josh Meyerberg's secretary?"

"Am I?"

"Then will you please tell President Truman that I'm here and do not wish to be kept waiting?"

"President Truman?"

"Jesus Christ!" I slumped into a chair. She inhaled as she stood, so strongly that both nostrils pinched together as if someone had clamped a clothespin over them. She disappeared into the office beyond—and returned as Josh Meyerberg.

"Ben?" He shot the word at me as one might say "duck!"

I stood up quickly. "Yes, sir."

"Come on in." He turned and went in and I followed. As I went in, Willa Nichols went out. By the tilt of her perfect nose I knew that I had lost a friend. Either that or her nose was still setting and she couldn't put it down.

"Sit down." Meyerberg was to the point. No time to waste. He walked fast, talked fast, and, judging from the Alka-Seltzer on his desk, ate fast. But he also was pleasant, a handsome, black-haired man of thirty-eight or so who worked with loosened tie and rolled-up shirt-sleeves. He had my advertising suggestions on his desk, a pile of them. I had no idea I had turned in so many. "Who told you you could write advertising?"

"Nobody."

"He was right. Most of these are awful, but so are most of the ads *we* turn out."

"I'm sorry." I didn't know what the hell else to say.

"Therefore, you could slot in here very easily. However, a couple of these are almost *good*. Which can only mean that you're liable to upset our whole operation if you're not careful."

"I'll try to be careful."

"This stuff you did on 'Fireball'—" He read my copy aloud. The picture would star Mickey Rooney and was about the Roller Derby. " 'Rooney runs riot on the Roller Raceway'—that's so bad, it's good."

"Thank you."

"This line of dialogue you have him saying— 'Nobody's throwing rose petals on the road to success'—does he say that in the film?"

"No."

"Then why do you have him saying it in the *ad*?"

"Because that's his attitude in the film."

"There *is* no film. Not yet. Just the script."

"Well, that's his attitude in the *script*."

"There's still time. Do you think we ought to call Darryl and tell him to put the line in the script?"

"No."

"Why?"

"Because it's not dialogue. I mean, as dialogue it would be lousy."

"Why?"

"Because the character he plays would never say it."

"Then why would you have him say it in an *ad*?"

"Because, in the ad, *we're* saying it and it's all right if *we* say it but it's lousy if *he* says it." I was enjoying the exchange and every fiber of me told me that *he* was enjoying it, too. He was taking my measure and I felt up to it.

"Roland Jessup is a good copywriter."

"I'm sure he is."

"A lousy office boy but a good copywriter. That's why he's being moved up. What I need now is a good office boy."

"Yes, sir."

"But *not* one who'll develop into a lousy copywriter."

"No, sir."

"I'd rather have another lousy office boy who'll develop into a good copywriter, rather than the other way around. What do you think?"

"I think I can be a lousy office boy."

He pressed the button on his intercom. "Willa, see if Charlie's in his office."

W. Charles Gruber was in the steam room so I waited until 5:30 to see him. Where Josh Meyerberg's office was Spartan and open, Gruber's was all cushy and tucked away, guarded by a secretary somewhat more attractive than Willa Nicholas—Patricia Jarvas, a skinny redhead, about nineteen or twenty, whose face was dotted with greenish freckles and whose nose was so snub that it was hardly there at all. She had a nose that Willa Nichols would have killed for and, the more I looked at her, the more I liked her. Skinny she was, and pale and ill-at-ease and annoyed, but there was something there. Beneath that flat chest something was lurking, something sensual and untapped, a mother lode just waiting for some prospector's pick-axe.

"Whatcha lookin' at?" she asked, in an accent so indelicately Brooklyn that I thought perhaps she was kidding.

"Pardon?"

"You're starin' at me. I can't help it. I gotta sit here. Do I stare at *you*?"

"No."

"So cut it out, all right?"

"Yeah. I'm sorry."

"He'll be back soon. You gotta be patient."

"Yeah. I know."

"And I can do without being ogled, will ya?" She picked up whatever magazine she had been reading, answered a few phone calls and continued to be uncomfortable in my presence. I couldn't help but wonder why Gruber would have a secretary like Pat Jarvas. Either she was very good at her job or he was banging her. But why would anyone like W. Charles Gruber want to bang anyone like Pat Jarvas? Maybe he wasn't banging her. Maybe someone simply left her on his doorstep with a note to please take care of her and hide her if the dog catcher comes. And yet, by God, there *was* something about the girl that was downright sensual. Must've been her elbows.

W. Charles Gruber swept so quickly past that I didn't even see him. But I smelled him. He was wearing Guerlain, the same cologne that Alice had me wearing. Could it be Alice and W. Charles Gruber? Never. I believed in coincidence but not in the supernatural. "Bring your pad." He was obviously talking to his secretary, which was just as well as I had no pad. She took her pad and went in, closing the door as quietly as death.

I waited. Another half hour. Looking at the autographed photos on the wall. Linda Darnell. Susan Hayward. Betty Grable. All of them dedicated "to Charlie" with love, or devotion, or everlasting affection. The phone rang a couple times but was answered inside. I waited some more. He was making me wait. It was exactly what I had expected and I immediately grew comfortable with the situation, like an actor familiar with a script the very first time he picks it up. And it struck me that everyone I had met since coming to 20th acted as though he or she were in a movie. I attached no significance to it because, after all, any large company and its people were but a microcosm of the rest of the world and Pat Jarvas was standing there, looking at me as if I were crazy. "Hey?" she said.

"Huh?"

"I said you could go in."

"Oh. Thanks."

"And watch out. He's in a lousy mood."

"So am I." That made her wonder. I had her respect. What I'd ever do with it was up for grabs. I went into Gruber's office, feeling as though I should be doing it in a tumbril. But I wasn't scared. If anything, I felt just the opposite. He was just one more bully I was picking a fight with in Carmody's junkyard. And goddamnit, after waiting so long to see the sonofabitch, I'd be fucked if I'd back off or knuckle under.

W. Charles Gruber was round. Round body, round head, round hair (what there was of it). And he had squinty eyes that made him look like a dimpled dumpling. So this was the scourge of 20th Century-Fox, I thought. This was the ogre who made men quake. I have many recollections of that man but the strongest, most all-prevailing one is that there was no way for anyone to have liked him at first sight.

"What is it?" he asked as though he'd rather not, as though he had a million things to do but was seeing me because, as King, he had to set aside thirty seconds a day to hear the problems of the peons.

"Mr. Meyerberg asked me to see you."

"I know." He leaned back in his chair, his belly going up so high that it just about obscured his chin. "You want to be transferred to Advertising."

"Yes, sir." He didn't invite me to sit down. He just had me standing there—some kind of perverted psychological ploy calculated to break me down.

"So why do *I* have to see you?"

"I don't know."

And so he told me. "I have to see you because I am responsible for all personnel in this office. No one transfers, or is fired, or goes to the crapper without seeing me first."

I nodded my comprehension of his powers. Then I sat down and crossed my legs and got comfortable because fuck it.

"I didn't ask you to sit down."

So I stood up.

"Sit down."

So I sat down. And I had the weird feeling that the sonofabitch liked my style. It wouldn't have mattered to me if I was wrong because *I* liked my style.

"I can quash your transfer, you realize that."

"Yes, sir."

"Usually we keep messengers in Publicity until they either quit or die. Why should you be transferred? Why not somebody else?"

"Beats me."

"Josh says you've written some copy, that some of it is good, and that he's moving his office boy up to apprentice copywriter, and that he wants *you* to take over with the ink wells and the pencils and the paper baskets and all that shit."

"Yes, sir."

"He can't have you unless I approve it. Why should I approve it?"

"Because you respect Josh and he thinks I can do it."

"What do you *really* think?"

"I think you're a tub of shit."

He leaned forward, his smile vanishing, and he took a few seconds to try to wither me with his fierce squint. When that failed, he said the obligatory words. "You're fired. Get out."

"Fuck you. You can't fire me."

"Why can't I fire you?"

"Because you have no reason to."

"You just called me a tub of shit."

"You *are* a tub of shit. But nobody'd believe that a guy up for advancement would say that to your face."

"So what?"

"So the Guild will pull a strike. They all know it's going to come to that anyway one day. They'd be happy to go out fighting."

"The SPG is full of communists."

"So is Russia, but they can't fire me either."

"How come you're so brave? You got a lot of money?"

"Yeah. I own a hotel on Boardwalk." I was going full tilt. I had shot off my mouth and had survived. Better than that, I was gaining ground, making points in whatever moronic game we were playing.

"Where'd you go to school?"

"I didn't."

"It says here University of Pittsburgh."

"I deny it."

"Says you played football."

"I did. Under the name Marshall Goldberg."

"You Jewish?"

"You?"

He laughed so hard that his chair went all the way back, causing his head to bong against the wall. It didn't bother him, he just kept on laughing, his feet seeming to pop out from under him, kicking at the ceiling like a mindless slut trying to rid herself of her panties.

I will never know why I was so brave or if it was bravery at all and not some other madness. Certainly it wasn't smart. But I learned something about myself that day. I had a thermostat, a setting, call it a "bullshit setting." I could tolerate anything this side of the bullshit line, but go beyond it and my balls would clang and I'd come out swinging. I think I got it from my father. He had it but it never served him well. Anyway, I got the job.

Though hardly a job for royalty, it was at least four castes above the pariahs who labored in Publicity. I was encouraged to write copy, not that any of it would be used. It was like being a pitcher warming up in the bullpen, ready in case I was called in but knowing that if I was called in the game was already lost.

There were three real copywriters. There was Roland, newly raised to forty-five dollars a week. There was Mickey Green, a thin lunatic of a man with only a fragile connection with reality. And there was Dora Leindorf, a small lady whose husband was a junior partner in some seventeen-name law firm, a fact that Dora used as an excuse to never attend union meetings though no one ever truly saw the connection. Dora paid her union dues, wrote tidy copy, was always a lady, but remained premeditatedly apart from the rest of us, coming and going like a sanitized society girl, even though all three writers and the new office boy worked in a green glass-walled fishbowl where you couldn't pick your nose without someone saying, "Ha! Caught ya!"

Dora Leindorf never picked her nose. She blew it. Loud honks that drowned out nearby churchbells. They would come with a suddenness, like the sharp trumpeting of moose, causing us to leap from our chairs because the sky was falling. And we'd look up to see her, tossing Kleenex like a drunken semaphorer. Then it would subside, having registered a 5.2 on the Mount McKinley seismograph, and the people would return to their homes, grateful at having survived what could only have been the anger of Zeus.

Roland, even though our desks were adjacent, was as aloof and as foreign as always, bringing in his lunch, speaking to strange people on the phone about strange show business deals, but performing his job admirably, all the while maintaining a brand of isolationism that was easily the equal of Dora's. The pair of them, like cogged wheels, touched only in the performance of their duties, the rest of their 359 degrees being spent in the turning away from each other. Roland chain-smoked and Dora blew her nose. They were a great comedy team—"The Hales"—"In" and "Ex."

It was Mickey Green who took me under his wing, skinny as it was. Mickey, thirty-four years of thin, with purplish lips and a complexion the color and consistency of a dried-out pen-wiper, was, by his own admission, the greatest movie copywriter of all time. He had been doing it for years and knew all the tricks, like putting the paper into the typewriter at an angle so that the copy ran rakishly off the page. He knew how to use three dots, exclamation points, underlining, and caps, and how to write variations of the traditional movie puffery, such as:

Always to be remembered—
The never-to-be-forgotten story of . . .

A MOTION PICTURE AS BIG AND AS SPRAWLING
AS ALL OUTDOORS . . .

Together Again for the First Time . . .

NOW—from 20th Century-Fox—
the Studio that Gave You . . .

Mickey also wrote great "SEE" ads, such as:

SEE The Palace of the 1,000 Sorrows!

SEE The World Beneath the Twelve-Mile Reef!

SEE Two Great Stars Together Again
for the First Time
in a Never-to-be-forgotten
Motion Picture as Big and as Sprawling
as All Outdoors.

Mickey could do it all and he did. When no one could decide whether "Cinema" and "Scope" should be one word or two, it was Mickey who split the difference and astounded the world with "CinemaScope." And it was Mickey who got the West Coast office to pose an unknown actress looking seductively over her shoulder at the camera while walking away. The actress was Marilyn Monroe.

I strongly believe that Mickey Green knew more about movie advertising than anyone I've ever met, but he was so out of focus on everything else that he always translated as some kind of mystical quirk barely able to function more than ten feet away from his desk. He had a wife, a son, a new car that he never drove because he had never taken driving lessons, a wristwatch on each wrist because one was fast and the other slow and so, to get the proper time, he took an average. He had socks that never matched ("I've got another pair at home just like 'em"), suits five sizes too large ("I like 'em snug"), hair that he couldn't manage ("I've had three combs shot out from under me"), and an ethnocentric view on politics ("I'm voting for Alf Landon or Davy Crockett—whichever is best for the Jews").

There was a certain insanity to it all in those days. Things were changing in the industry, yet we were like the palace guards, loyal to the czar but not knowing why. Fresh breezes were blowing that we could have filled our lungs with, but, fascinated with what the movie business once was, we took our places on the parapets alongside the very people who would have tossed us to the Red-hunters if it meant saving their own asses.

Spyros Skouras secured the motion picture rights to *The Greatest Story Ever Told* and, gathering his advertising and publicity people into 20th's bronze-crusted screening room (designed in 1930 by Mrs. William Fox on a day when she should have been committed), he told us how hard we would have to work on "ziss beautifully motioned pixture." Peppering his speech with archaic English words and phrases, he went on to paint the eventual glory of it all. "Pixture, if you will, how audiences will be mesmerized at the panorama of Christ and his desiplus at the Final Luncheon . . ."

That one almost put us under our seats. This *next* one *did*. "Gentlemens and laddies, I offer you an oath. Ziss motioned pixture will be bigger than *The Twelve Commandments!*"

That's the way it was. The old moguls, sensing the end of their dynasties, were flailing against their fate, flogging their underlings to tote one more barge, lift one more bale. The courts were giving them a hard time, too, for no longer would they be allowed to both produce the films and own the theatres. There had to be a divorce in that they had been in clear defiance of the Sherman Anti-Trust Act and had been since the beginning.

Rumors flew. Zanuck was out. Zanuck *and* Skouras were out. 20th was bust. 20th was being purchased by the United Cigar Corporation ("Everything's going up in smoke"—Big Al Epstein). And, at the height of it all, in the middle of all that marvelous uncertainty, with people looking for other jobs in other businesses in other towns—I was drafted.

I had gone for my physical some six weeks earlier, not of my own volition but at the insistence of the land I lived in. And it was there determined that though I was hardly perfect, I was well enough to serve. I was a little deaf in one ear and a little blind in one eye (those fights in Pittsburgh) and had two floating cartilages in my knees, a lumbar situation in my back, and some separated ribs through which my heart could easily pop out if I ran fast and stopped short, *but,* they were still going to take me because I was such a sporty guy.

They stamped my papers "Limited Service" and told me to go home and not worry because, unless the Chinese came down into Korea from across the Yalu River, the US could handle it and without military conscription.

Wrong. The Chinese came down and if the US could handle it, they couldn't *quite* handle it without *me.* I was punchy. Too young for World War II which I had dearly wanted to get into, there I was, among the first to be called for something that wasn't even considered a "war." It was called a "police action" ("So why don't they send cops?"—Arnie Felsen).

The day before I left they threw a farewell luncheon for me at the Howard Johnson's on West Fifty-seventh Street. Everyone came except Gruber who was in the steam room, and Skouras, who was in Europe, and Zanuck, who was on safari. Josh Meyerberg was there and made a nice speech, after which everyone applauded, and gave me a nice watch. It was a beautiful thing but hardly worth going to war to receive. I made a speech, too, a silly one because I was uncomfortable. I thanked my coach and my blockers and my offensive line and, believe it or not, Patricia Jarvas cried and had to be helped from the room. When she came back she received more applause than I had.

After it was over they all pumped my hand and wished me well. Dora Leindorf blew her nose, three quick blasts, denoting emotion rather than chilblains (I had learned to differentiate and interpret her basic nose calls). Roland just shrugged and walked away, feeling guilty because, as a devout homosexual, the Army had no use for him. Mickey Green, who had served in the Pacific in World War II as a cadaver, 3rd class, bet me ten bucks that on my return he'd be able to drink five bottles of cheap champagne in a half hour. I accepted the bet and Mickey slunk away, his shoulders very small in his too big jacket. Big Al and Arnie asked me to drop them a line when I had a chance and I said I would. Don said he'd see me later at the apartment because all that breast-beating was breaking his collarbone.

It was Bob Steinman who grabbed my arm and steered me off to an Eighth Avenue bar. He was very supportive, telling me that I would have no problems and that, with any luck, it would all be over soon. Also, according to Bob, being Limited Service was a bona fide guarantee that I'd never come close to combat.

He also told me that he had been wounded and shot down over Germany, waking up in a hospital where for two days he was afraid to look down and see if he still had his legs. After he had recuperated he was transferred to a prison camp, where he remained until the end of the War. The worst thing about the prison was that American bombers came over nightly and, unable to distinguish one target from another, they just pasted everything. Whenever the American POW's heard the warning sirens they had to duck for cover under anything available—out of windows, under tables, into holes—and they suffered twenty-five percent casualties as a result of American bombings.

It wasn't a cheerful story and I wondered why the hell Bob was telling it to me. Still, I was grateful at being let in on a story that he had apparently told very few people. We had a few drinks and Bob picked up and tab and smiled that very winning smile at me. "Ben, you're gonna have it all. You're gonna be fine." He dropped me off at the apartment and cabbed on to his, where, no doubt, some girl was waiting.

When I got up the stairs, Don was there. "How you doing, kid?"

"Fine."

"Bob get you to tie one on?"

"A little, yeah."

"You don't want to report for duty with a hangover."

"Why not?"

"They're liable to make you an officer."

"You mean I'm not? See what happens when you don't check the small print?"

"How come you never asked my draft status? You know I took a physical, too."

"I wasn't interested."

"I'm 4-F."

"Nobody's 4-F. You must be dead."

"Rheumatic heart."

"As long as it's not your cock."

"No such thing as rheumatic cock."

"I'm glad to hear it."

"Had it since I was a kid. Rheumatic heart. I'm ashamed of it. I mean, it's something I don't even want my doctor to know. I'd rather the world think I have hemorrhoids."

"I'll tell Hedda Hopper."

"Anyway, I wanted you to know. Not that I'm disappointed at not being drafted. It's just that I'd prefer that my affliction be somewhat more glamorous, like a football injury, or a sabre wound, or third degree burns suffered while pulling six kids out of an orphanage fire. Also, I don't know how I'm going to pay the fucking rent with you gone."

"Take in a new roommate."

"Yeah. But not right away. I'm hoping you'll desert. Maybe you'll desert."

"Maybe I won't even go."

"Speaking of roommates. There's somebody in your room."

"Really?"

"Yeah. It's a surprise. At least it surprised the hell out of *me*."

"Not Roland."

"No. He was busy."

"Who?"

"Someone who evidently has a strong feeling for you, who wants to do something for your manhood."

"Mr. Geppetto?"

"Benjamin—go to your room."

Patricia Jarvas was in my room. She wasn't drunk. She wasn't crying. She was just talking. "I'm sorry. I mean, I'm not *really* sorry. I mean, if you mind or you're offended I'll go, but—I took this moment, because of the situation, because it's dramatic and who knows if you'll ever come back." Her Brooklyn voice was very high. Then it lowered and came out with a smile. "I've had a couple drinks, ya know."

"Don talk you into coming up here?"

"Oh, no. It was my own idea. My very own. *I* approached *him*. Told him that—oh, Jesus—told him that I had this strong feeling for you and that, if you weren't busy tonight, neither was I."

I was getting used to the dim light. She was sitting up in my bed and she was naked, holding the sheet up to her chin as if being surprised by a private eye in a motel. She was there. She looked good. And she was ready.

I started to take my clothes off, unable to say anything particularly pertinent and not caring to.

"You've got a good built," she said.

"Thank you."

"Very masculine."

"Yes."

"I'm glad you're not angry. You see—everytime I'd see you, in the hall, at meetings, at screenings—I din't know how to express my feelings. I tried reaching you through telepathy."

"Yeah, well, I never get my messages."

"Anyway, I think—in this day and age—I think that a girl can tell a fella what's on her mind and—that's what I'm doing, Ben. I'm afraid I'll never see you again so—you know what I mean?"

"Oh, yes." I slipped into the bed alongside her, kind of lazily kissing her neck, running my hand up her flanks to her washboard ribs, behind which her heart was pounding like a nonstop tennis ball.

"Ben—" She snaked her arms around me, then her

legs, more strongly than I would have imagined her capable of. "You gotta fuck me, Ben, or—" She was reaching for my penis which, clever girl, she knew exactly where to find. "You gotta do it, Ben."

"All right."

"Yeah—*Oh*!" She was pulling me by the root of it, urging me on but causing me some pain and disenchantment.

"Easy. Easy, kid. It's hooked on, you know."

"Oh, Jesus—" She was on top of me, spinning around, getting in place, handling me as if she owned me, as if getting the pipe ready because the drill had struck oil. "Ben! . . ."

"Yes?"

"Ben! Oooooh!"

She was having a difficult time getting me in and, because it occurred to me, I thought I'd ask. "Listen— Pat?"

"Wha? Oooooh!"

"Are you a virgin?"

"No. Oooooh! I'm married. Ahhhhhh!"

Fortunately I had just made my entrance when she gave me that little bit of information, otherwise I'd never have made it. "Married?"

"Divorced. Shut up! Fuck!"

"Well, I—"

"Just fuck! Will ya just fuck? Oooooh! Aaaaah!"

At her suggestion, we fucked. We fucked for quite a while. Until I climaxed and the skinny girl went limp, rolling off me as though lassoed from somewhere across the room.

Moments later, moving like a collapsed lung, she wiped the perspiration from her body with the sheet. "Listen, I gotta go, okay? I mean, I'd like to stay here, but I can't. Unnerstand?"

"I'm afraid not."

"God, you are so *cute!*"

"Thank you."

"I mean, your prick fits me like I'm a glove."

"I'd rather it fit you like you were a catcher's mitt."

She laughed. "*God,* you're cute!" She was smoothing
the sheet. "Little wet spot here. *You* did it so *you* clean
it up. Listen, I gotta go. My car is waitin'."

"Your car? You have a chauffeur?"

She laughed. "Yeah. Kinda. Maybe we can do this
again, when you come home on a furlough or somethin'. On the sly, huh?"

"On the sly? Why on the sly?"

"Oh, shit. I din't tell ya, did I?"

"No, you din't."

"I belong to Charlie. Charlie? You know, Gruber?"

"Ahhhh, Charlie."

"Yeah. He sent me over as kind of a goin' away present. In his limousine yet. Everything but a gift wrap."
She was just about dressed and bent down and across
me to lay a kiss on my dead snake. "Mmmmmm.
Maybe next time we'll go French, huh?"

"Oo-la-la."

"French is what I give Charlie. I take lousy dictation
but I give great head." She gave me a few seconds of
coming attractions and then pulled away.

"Whoops," I said.

"Ben, I'd really like to stay longer but Charlie said
no longer than eight. Where the fuck *were* you? I been
waitin' here a couple hours."

"Had I known—Listen, do you really have to run
off?"

"Oh, I gotta go. But *one* day—when you get back—I
mean, I could tell you such stories you could write a

book." She worked her hand up and down my very confused shaft. "Keep up the good work, huh? huh?"

"Yeah."

She got up and headed out. "Don't get yourself killed, Ben. Just think of me, waitin' for you."

"Okay."

She raised her imaginary glass in a toast. "To the perfect fuck."

"Amen."

"I think that's Hemingway."

"It ain't Louisa May Alcott."

She left. In the other room I could hear her saying good-bye to Don and then go down the stairs. After which, Don came into my room and surveyed me, all laid out, as on a crucifix.

"Jesus Christ," he said.

"You got it."

"Was good?"

"Was *very* good."

He sat down on the edge of the bed and pondered. "I never thought that about her."

"Neither did I."

"Think Charlie knows?"

"I doubt it. Even if he did, the old fart probably couldn't handle it."

"Makes a guy wonder about secretaries."

"Yeah."

The next morning at four A.M. my alarm rattled my brains and I lost my place in a dream in which skinny girls the world over were lining up at my bedside, ready to work wonders. I got up gropingly but aware. Don was asleep and I didn't want to waken him, especially as we had said good-bye the night before. Had I known how long it would be before I'd ever see him again, I might have tossed down a few more beers with him before sacking in. I packed a small bag, toilet articles and such, and I left ye olde pad, the wild smell of Patricia Jarvas still clinging to both my body and soul.

Two things occurred to me as I went down the stairs. One, for some reason in W. Charles Gruber I had a friend. And, two, for the first time since meeting him, I had not shared a confidence with Don Cook.

Was I trading up or trading down? Was I being corruptible or pragmatic? Was I a prince or a prick? In that dichotomous state did I deliver my bones to the Army of the United States, where persons other than myself would help me render that judgment.

ginnie

1949

It wasn't much of an apartment, but I really didn't want it to be. Up till then I had never lived in anything even approaching squalor and somehow I felt that, if I was to develop into anything at all, I had first better experience some of the drearier things that life had to offer. Also, the absolutely last thing I wanted to do was shoot up all my money on frilly duds and fancy digs. For though admittedly a bit of a flip at the time, I did have enough marbles to know that a sixteen-year-old girl in the big city becomes immediate shark bait if for too long she shops drunkenly at Bergdorf's while living lavishly at the Ritz. Also, to abuse the point further, the prospect of my calling home for more money was so low on my list of "things to do in an emergency" that it came just after suicide and just before going to bed with Walter the Repulsive.

So, squalid it was, my little pad. And meagre it was, my menu. But between the rent and the groceries, I knew I could make it on something like twenty-five dollars a week. That meant that my thousand dollars getaway money (less train fare to New York City and cab fare to Greenwich Village) would last me for almost a year, even if I never got a job. And if, after a year, I couldn't make it in New York, I'd willingly face up to the fact that I wasn't worth it and I'd turn myself in to my "guardian" and sit around some other girls school, masturbating and matriculating, until my 400 grand came due, after which I'd turn alcoholic, buy a ballet company, marry Vincent Price, write my memoirs, and die of the dropsy in an Old Folks Home in Darien. So, as you can see, I was not without a plan.

Nobody asked any questions on my first day in New York, so I volunteered no information that might be used against me. I looked older than sixteen, my luggage was presentable, and I had a painting under my arm, which meant that I had either painted it or purchased it (or stolen it)—so the landlord took the first month's rent in cash, for which he gave me three things: a receipt, a key, and a dirty look.

Like I said, it wasn't bad—except comparatively. By that I mean it wasn't the back country of Stamford, but neither was it the puke bucket of Peking. It was all in the way one chose to look at it, and I chose to look at it positively. It was one room with a bathroom and a kitchenette, but it was mine, all mine. The refrigerator worked, the john flushed, the radiator hissed, the bed held, the door locked—Old McMaitland had a flat, ee-eye, ee-eye, oh.

I cried for an hour. Didn't know it was coming. Never do. I didn't even know *why* I was crying. But there I was, one minute smiling with triumph, my paisleyed bags brightening my new kingdom on the Hudson. And the next minute I'm bawling like a kid whose toy poodle got galomphed by an elephant.

I chalked it up to rampant puberty and unpacked. The next thing I did was run out and get a radio because I couldn't live without Guy Mitchell, Frankie Laine and Patti Page. Then I went out again and got some cleaning things—soaps and sponges, disinfectants and detergents—and I went to work.

The apartment was furnished—technically. There was a broom teethed on by the Werewolf of London, and a mop that Monstro the Whale had spit up. And some pots, pans and dishes that the Red Cross bought from South Africa *after* the Boer War. But there were no sheets or towels, no dust rags, no toilet tissue, and dishes so greasy I couldn't get a grip on them—so I went out again, throwing caution to the wind and thirty-five dollars to Woolworth's, and when I came back I had it all—the whole shootin' match. From Pepsodent to Drano, my pad was complete, functional, sanitary, staffed, and stocked. I hung up Maggie's portrait so that it collected the light from my one window, and I was home.

It was a big building, maybe three stories and ten tenants. And mine wasn't the only basement apartment. There was another, lived in by a black lady named Mona, who, at all hours of the day and night, had men and women lining up outside her door. I, of course, thought the worst, but was wrong. What she was doing was cooking chickens. In those wee hours, she would cook chickens for people. Musicians, mostly. And hookers, I'm sure. But for a buck and a half, Mona would give them a completely cooked chicken. And any time of the day or night, there was a line outside Mona's door like a hit movie was playing.

There was something depressing about the Village. It seemed to have had it, except its denizens didn't quite know it. They'd scuff around in sandals and dirty clothes, quaffing capuccino at coffee houses and coexisting with Oriental lesbians and sequined faggots as though that's all they had to do by way of paying dues. Oh, some had talent, I suppose. Some could paint and sculpt and knit—but *all* of them? Hardly. And why couldn't they see it? I could see it and I was barely an apprentice nincompoop.

It took me awhile to realize that many of them did see it only they blocked it out, huddling together in the Village because they simply couldn't, or, rather, wouldn't, take a shot at the outside world—choosing instead to bestow on the Village the aura of Paris after World War I. Well, it wasn't Paris. It wasn't even Poughkeepsie. It was just a big, fat hiding place for veterans and runaways, and neophyte hookers and unrevered poets. It was just a big garbage pail that people were jumping into and rattling around in and putting the lid on from the inside.

Yes, I would enjoy Greenwich Village, for what it offered: abandon and rebellion and dereliction. But I would also keep it at arm's length because it was, at the same time, dulling and meandering and toxic.

On the first rainy day I bleached my hair. Not just blonde, baby, but Harlow blonde, raging blonde, so platinum it was white. I was afire with it. Ablaze. My blood was blonde, my tendons, my toes. The change, though sudden, was natural enough in that my skin was fair and, in the summers, gorgeous with maybe twenty-three freckles. And my eyes, blue-blue, were reborn beneath the vividness of it all, finally seeming as though they truly belonged in that formerly vacant face.

My body, too, once an alien thing, had come together in New York and, in leotards or tight jeans, with my yellow hair in a pert ponytail pointing straight down to my best feature (my ass), there wasn't a citizen on MacDougal Street who didn't take me for a ballerina and want me for a quickie.

Fitting action to fiction, I signed up for a modern dance course. Madame Getrude on Jane Street. I did that at night, working during the day in a leather shop that specialized in belts, taking the job because I got tired of sitting in my apartment watching my plants not grow. How I loved working in that shop, for it smelled of boots and saddles and reminded me of home and of my sister's three riding instructors, those stallionesque men of her diary's delight, those well-proportioned lads in bulging jodhpurs and constant heat. Just stepping into that shop and handling those belts and I would go moist in the crotch. You might say that, working in leather got me into a lather. More on that later.

I had no friends but wasn't trying for any. There was something crashingly marvelous about being among all those people, all that life, and not talking to anyone. And I didn't want to ruin that wonderful isolation with chit-chat and balderdash. Also, putting a clamp on my mouth seemed to sharpen my eyes, turning me into a kind of Christopher Isherwood lens that took snapshots, a million a minute, that I could then reduce to microfilm and file away in that part of my brain entitled: *New York City—1949. In which our heroine sets up house in wicked Greenwich Village, bleaches her hair, and tries to discover her true identity.*

I lived like that, in the leather shop by day, alone with my reading at night, like something out of O. Henry, the big difference being that I had over $900 in the cookie jar, whereas O. Henry never had that much in his life.

I decided to broaden my vistas. Helping me in that decision was my comprehension of the financial facts of my life—I had a balance-of-trade deficit. I was spending more than my leather-shop salary was earning. I was dipping into my savings, and, if I was to reverse that trend without subsisting solely on brown bread and V-8, I would very soon have to knock over a gas station, or turn hooker, or both.

I discussed the matter with my employer, Patsy D'Amico, suggesting to her that I might work on some kind of commission, say, ten percent on everything I sold over my thirty-seven-dollar-a-week salary. The poor girl then showed me her books, tearfully explaining how she was losing money by keeping me on at anything over twenty-five dollars a week. I pretended to see her point, offering to take a twelve-dollar cut so that they wouldn't foreclose on her two-bit tannery. Then, after she dried her grateful eyes, I told her to go fuck herself, only I didn't hang around to see if she did.

No job, no unemployment insurance (because of my age and the fact that I had never applied), little Ginnie Maitland looked for new work; and, though the Village had many possibilities, she began to feel that she'd no longer like to labor as a salaried menial but as an entrepreneur with her own business. (Shit, somewhere down the line, *someone* on my father's side had done it or else how come all the money?)

I read the Classified section of *The New York Times,* looking for "business opportunities." A lot of people had ideas or growing concerns, but needed capital, and I had over $900. Yes, I was willing to invest it, provided that whatever I put it into had a good chance of success, not that I was any judge.

I thought I had it in a clothing store that featured only suede. I loved their name—Easily Suede—and I went down to chat with the owners. But if that stuff was suede then I was queen of Yugoslavia, so I got out of there almost before I went in, the smell of hairy tarpaper rebounding in my nose as I walked further down the street to where destiny truly awaited me. For what should I stumble upon but a brand new store front, shiny and seductive, all glass and chrome with its name in confident caps:

Kosher-Japanese
Cuisine
S A Y O N A R A

permitees   Sy   &   Ira
Fein   Tanaka

I went in even though the sign on the door screamed
in Day-Glo pink that the Grand Opening was still two
days off. It was all clean and Formica, little booths in
red vinyl, candles in squat fish-net glasses, adjustable
chandeliers hanging on single strands that one could
raise or lower with the snap of a wrist. And on the
walls: on one side, framed travel posters of Japan; on
the other side, likewise framed posters of Israel (which,
at the time, wasn't two years old so all that the posters
displayed were camels against a Star of David).

There were two men sitting deathlike in a corner
booth, like new additions to be picked up by Madame
Tussaud on her next buying trip to Greenwich Village.
One was about fifty and Caucasian. The other about
thirty and Oriental.

The Caucasian looked up at me. He was quaint,
Humpty-Dumpty in a sleeves-rolled-up C.C.N.Y. sweat-
shirt, that revealed enormous forearms, like Popeye's. He
had a round, flushed face and a full crop of rust-colored
hair that began at the very top of his head, giving him
the look of a bald man who had gotten his head caught
in a rusty porthole.

"Sign says two days," he said. "Come back in two
days and we'll still be here, in this booth—dead." And
he waved his hand as if to dispense with me magically.
He was Sy—Sy for Seymour, I guess—Sy Fein, and he
was always able to see the darker side of life.

The other man, the Oriental, was Iri. Iri Tanaka. He

was smaller than Sy in every dimension and every direction. He tried to smile at me because that's what Orientals do if you just stare at them and say nothing. "What the man is trying to say," said Iri, "is would you mind leaving us alone?"

"What's the matter?" I asked, a little aggressively because I sensed a business opportunity and knew that it had to be pursued. "This is a very nice place."

"Make us an offer," said Sy, immediately beginning to laugh, slapping Iri on the arm and quipping, "gallows humor, eh? Eh?"

"Yeah, hysterical." Iri got up and went into the kitchen, muttering Japanese, tossing a napkin ahead of him and kicking it further along.

Sy stood and said "Oy." He said "oy" every time he changed his position. It was like a sound his body made. The Tin Man creaked, Sy Fein oyed. Beyond that, they were similar in that each of them wanted a brain. "I'd have my head examined if I could afford it. But when a man puts his entire life's savings into a new and stupid venture, he's got nothing left to shoot on a psychiatrist. That's the long and the short of it. Period and goodbye."

"I guess I don't understand," I said, but I was beginning to.

"Okay, Blondie, I'll tell you." He wanted to talk out his misery and I was elected. "You see this place? Beautiful, right?"

"Right."

"A beautiful American story. A Jew-boy and a Jap. Kosher-Japanese food. Not easy. Not even legal, I suspect. But if he don't tell Hirohito, I won't tell Ben-Gurion. So, here we are—a nice place, yes?"

"Yes."

"No!" And his arms flew apart, as if they would fly

off. Then he tugged at one of the chandeliers, bringing it down to mouth level and speaking into it as if it were a microphone and he were introducing two leading heavyweight contenders. "Ladies and gentlemen. We are in hock to our eyeballs!" Then he looked at me curiously. "Why am I talking to *you*? Who are *you*?" And he tugged at the chandelier and it shot up to its previous height.

"Well, I—"

He pointed toward the kitchen in which Iri had disappeared. "I would have sold *him* but he has no value as he was made in Japan." He walked around, touching tables as if they were marble and chairs as if they were thrones. "I'll make a long story short only because *I* find it boring. Every dollar we both have, every yen, is in this place. We have the finest of everything. Stoves, refrigerators, pots and pans of such a chrome you could wear it on your Chrysler. A sprinkler system could have put out Chicago. Auxiliary generator you could light up Venezuela. And clean? Even the cock-a-roaches are clean. I make them shower every day with Dial. You're waiting to hear the catch, right?"

"Right."

"So here comes the catch. Ready?"

"Ready."

"The catch to the whole thing is *this*—" He yanked down another chandelier and yelled into it. "Thank you, Mister Sonofabitch Union! After all our expenses *you* make us put up a bond for our waiters and dishwashers—two weeks! Two weeks advance for seven momzas who won't do anything except get their beautiful hands dirty!" He snapped the chandelier and up it went as he pointed again to the kitchen. "The cooking *he* does. The buying, worrying, and glad-handing *I* do." He tried to calm down. "So, all right, we say, to get it going, to get it off swinging on a star—*we* will work for nothing. Zip! Me and the Jap—no pay, no love, no nuthin'."

"Excuse me, but I never heard of Kosher-Japanese cuisine."

"The reason you never heard of Kosher-Japanese cuisine is that there *is* no such thing. It's all in the mind. A dream. A vision that comes to me in the night and says 'Sy, for openers half of New York is Jewish. Next, with the war over for years, having a Jap cook on the premises can be very chic. So, Sy, make a partnership.' "

"I still don't follow."

"You don't follow for two reasons. One, you're not a businessman. And two, with a ponytail and a tochis like that, everyone follows *you,* so what are you worried about?" He looked at me searchingly. "How old are you?"

"Twenty-five."

"Thank you. I needed a good laugh." He continued with his catharsis. "So my friend in there, who has been working as a cook in the home of a wealthy manufacturer of Jewish clothing, and has managed to pick up a few pointers on kosher cooking—you following yet?"

"I think so."

"Nifty. So he sees me and I see he and we work out a scheme because in me you are looking at an old pro from the restaurant business." He shouted into another quickly yanked-down chandelier. "I have failed in five previous restaurants and have a right to sing the blues except *six* is my lucky number and, by Jesus, this time I am gonna *make* it!" He almost threw that chandelier back up into the ceiling, after which he faced me. "Still with me, Blondie?"

"Yes."

"Splendid. So we have this idea, me and Iri, in which I call him Ira instead of Iri because what's in a name anyway? And we come up with 'Sayonara' which in Japanese means 'So long, buddy. See you later when your legs are straighter.' A play on words, yes, but a nicely turned phrase nevertheless. And we raise $7500 and we get a license to sell the pee that passes for Japanese beer and we're in business, right?"

"Right."

"Wrong. Seventy-five hundred dollars goes immediately down the toilet because fully staffed and ready to throw out the first ball guess what?"

"What?"

"You ready?"

"Ready."

"We have not money to buy *food*! What with having to pay deposits for the Electric Company and the Water Works, and having to mortgage Baltic Avenue to post a bond with the fucking union—pardon my fucking—I can't buy a fortune cookie! I can't even buy a hot washcloth a fella shouldn't have to use his sleeve after a plate of pastrami-teriyaki. Still following?"

"Yes."

"Glorious. So as we speak, my partner is in the kitchen with Dinah, hopefully committing hara-kiri and naming me as beneficiary. And I am in here, talking to a cutie-shiksa while, inside, my gall bladder is attacking. If you have a pencil, I'll write a note. 'Pardon me for killing myself and please take care of my cat.' "

"How much do you need?"

"A three-cent stamp, the letter should reach my wife without being returned for insufficient funds."

"How much do you need for your *food*?"

"You have investment capital?"

"Maybe."

"You have—pardon the expression—money?"

"A little."

"And how much is a little, pray tell."

"Five hundred dollars." I figured I'd better hold onto the other four hundred dollars in case it turned out that Sy's lucky number *wasn't* six.

"You have five hundred dollars?"

"Yes."

He walked toward the kitchen. "Go home. You're a mirage." He turned and walked back. "Blondie, cutie-pie Blondie, you have five hundred George Washingtons?"

"Yes."

"Which you would invest in a cockamamie Kosher-Japanese restaurant?"

"I might."

"What are you—a crazy Vanderbilt?"

"No, I—"

"—that you would invest five hundred samoleans for a share of the profits the formula of which we'll work out later?"

"Possibly."

"And the moolah is not in Deutschmarks?"

"No."

"Iri!" He called. "If you haven't already killed yourself, come out of the kitchen! If you *have*—don't bother, I'll go it alone!"

And so I was in the restaurant business, turning $500 in cash over to Sy Fein who yelled at me for not getting a cashier's check because how could I know that he and Iri were on the up-and-up, was I out of my *mind*?

As insane as it may sound, the restaurant worked, becoming a fixture and a meeting place where Christopher Street crossed West Fourth. Crazy Sy Fein, given my five hundred dollars with which to buy food, made the thing work. Iri handled the kitchen, Sy clanged the cash register, and I waited tables but only for as long as it took daylight to come shining in. And when I quit, it took two girls to take my place. Hah!

On Sunday mornings we'd split up the take. Mine wasn't much but then, how could it be? They had put up $7500. I had only put up five hundred dollars. Still, it was a Dow-Jones miracle. My money was earning money—more each week. The reputation of Sayonara spread, blanketing the Village and moving uptown like Donovan's Brain, causing people to trickle in from faraway places—Flatbush, Staten Island, East New York, Nassau. Jackets, ties and reservations were required, especially on Friday and Saturday nights. Iri took on another chef, Lenny Abelson, whose specialty was "lotkes tempura" (potato pancakes in soy sauce). Sy added a maitre d' out front, Oshiru Matsuoka, an expert on cheap wine as, yes, we got a true liquor license and made a phony wine cellar out of a spare john.

What it meant for me was emancipation. I didn't have to work. After getting my five hundred dollars back, my share of the daily take, after expenses, was coming to almost thirty dollars a week, more than enough for me to live on. Sy arranged for me to put my remaining money into a "legitimate bank" with Sy as trustee, because of my age. He was shocked at my age but promised to keep it a secret from the white educationalists. At that time it wasn't all that unusual for minors and runaways to be floating all over the Village. The trick was to stay out of trouble. Keep your nose clean and the police would turn a deaf ear and a blind eye. Needless to say, I maintained the cleanest nose in town.

What did I do with all my time? I breathed. I sucked it all in. As a kid I didn't speak a word until I

was five. And there I was again, so anxious to sop it all
up that I was willing not to speak—to anyone about
anything. I floated up to the UN, skinnying in, telling
officials that my uncle was my father: "I'm Congressman Maitland's daughter." (He was with the UN at the
time but I never contacted him lest I be hustled off to
Chicago.) Once inside the UN I would listen to the
translation machines, turning the dials on the chairs,
putting on the earphones and tuning in to any one of six
languages. I learned Russian, a little. And Chinese, a
little less. But they were more fun than French or Spanish. Also, if they were indeed coming to get us (the
Russians and Chinese), then I sure as hell wanted to
know what they were talking about when they registered
at the White House.

Fritz Kreisler. I adored Fritz Kreisler. The cognos-
centi dug Jascha Heifetz but I loved Fritz Kreisler. He
made the violin sing. Heifetz could make it stand on its
ear and do tricks but Kreisler was liquid gravity and
musical poetry. When Fritz Kreisler played Carnegie
Hall I went to every concert. I hung around outside and
followed him down the street. I would sit in the lobby of
his hotel, waiting to get a look at him. I got to know the
ushers at Carnegie Hall and they'd let me back-stage to
watch the rehearsals. I was a Kreisler freak and he must
have thought he had two shadows.

At the Forty-sixth Street Theatre I went to see *Guys
and Dolls* over and over. It was an incredible show because neither the cast nor the audience was ever allowed to relax. Two, three, four nights a week I'd go.
And each performance I'd watch something else. I'd
watch the dancers because I thought I could do that. I'd
watch Sam Levene and Vivian Blaine and Isabel Bigley
and Stubby Kaye—how they moved, their anticipation,
their timing. I watched the conductor pointing in the

pit, making different instruments do their individual thing. I watched an oboist for an entire performance. Then the drummer, then the French horn. I gathered it all up, harvested it, threshed it, stored it—the techniques and emotionality of musical theatre. I would know it from a thousand different angles—a million. No one beyond myself would ever know *Guys and Dolls* as well for no one beyond Damon Runyon and Frank Loesser and Abe Burrows and George S. Kaufman and Jo Swerling could ever muster the time, endure the rigors, and apply the love to really distill what made the magic, how the music, why the laughter, whence the exhilaration.

And when I finished swallowing *Guys and Dolls,* I likewise dined on *South Pacific,* after which I consumed *Wish You Were Here.* I glutted myself on Broadway musicals, moving from afficionado to addict. I was hooked on them and on New York because New York didn't just permit it to happen, it insisted on it.

I began to bathe myself in New York. The air of it and the light of it. I would take it and rub it all over my skin as if it were Revlon and bottled. A few weeks before—six, maybe—I had kept New York at arm's distance, distrusting it, condemning it. But now I was a part of it. I could see it and feel it, running up alleys and spilling onto sidewalks. At four in the morning I could open my single, ground-level window and look up and out at how the world was doing. Yes, there were derelicts and druggies and crazies, some of them pissing in the street—but, Christ, it was going on, life was going on. So what if the old sot was pissing directly on my window, banking it off my wall and shocking the shit out of my one geranium, I was in the middle of a solar explosion, a musical extravaganza gonna play

Broadway, you bet your ass. Box seat, Maggie, wherever the hell you are.

Boys. Yes, there were boys. In all shapes and sizes.
Weird ones, nice ones, cute ones, gay ones—emphasis
on the latter—like Glenville. I guess Glenville was
about thirty. He had bleached hair and plucked eyebrows and see-through shirts, and he followed me
around with his tortoise-shell comb. Whenever he'd see
me, he'd zip out his comb and start combing my hair.
He'd see me from across a street or out of a doorway
and come skipping after me, like a cat or a dog that
knew me. And he'd comb my hair all the way to where-
ever it was I was going. Sometimes I wouldn't even talk
to him just to see if it would stop him. Other times I'd
make as though he wasn't even there, gliding along like
a disinterested fish. It never bothered Glenville. He still
came after me. Then one day Glenville just upped and
disappeared; I never knew what became of him.

Aldo, the dope addict. Kept his hair slick, like Cab
Calloway, and his eyes wide like Jerry Colonna. He was
in his early twenties and had to know that I was a lot
younger than legal. He was always singing, always flashing teeth so white that, whenever he smiled, his mouth
looked like it was rolling dice. Aldo never touched me
and I had no idea he ever wanted to until, one night, he
said to me, "You're driving me crazy, so I can't see you
anymore." And he disappeared.

It had taken Aldo two months to be driven crazy.
Had I known it was going on I might have tried to enjoy it. I mean, hell, that was pretty torrid stuff he was
dishing out. As to why he was called a dope addict, I
had no idea. I never saw him do a thing that was the
slightest bit strange except, as I said, on the last night I
saw him. I should tell you that he was crying when he
left. Smiling, rolling his white dice teeth, but crying. I

don't know whatever became of Aldo. I'm not sure he knows either. But he was the first boy to ever say he loved me and that ought to count for something.

Maxwell Bodenheim bought me coffee. He was at that time the waning poet-laureate of the Village even though he lived in Brooklyn with his bedraggled Medusa of a wife. He was craggy, boney, emaciated, had popping eyes, long slidy hair with things in it (some of them alive), and a hatchet nose that also could have served as an ice-breaker. He would have been perfect casting for Raskolnikov. And he always had with him his ragged leatherette portfolio of aimless rhymes, word things he would read aloud and with feeling to anyone who chanced by his bench in Washington Square Park. He was like a spider, sitting in his web, waiting for some unsuspecting victim, then—*wham*—a poem came at you from out of nowhere, numbing you, fixing you where you stood. And, if you remained stationary, or if you even slowed, there'd be another poem and another, shot into the back of your neck—*whump*—until you were dulled to death and spun into a pupa that he would dine on for the rest of the afternoon, after which he would buy you coffee that *you* had to pay for.

He was shaggy, smelled bad, was ninety percent nuts; and the dog-eared poetry that gushed from his folder was, to state it mercifully, incomprehensible. And yet, maybe because I was young and searching for some evidence that there once was an Atlantis, I listened to the fossil, pretending that the relic was a god and that the ravings were clues to the universe.

Maxwell Bodenheim read some thirty to forty poems to me over some ten cups of coffee, and people began to notice me if only because I was sitting with him. I liked that. Maybe I didn't understand his poetry, but after a while I began to understand *him*. He was trying not to die. They were burying him, smacking him topside with their shovels, but he was still dodging the blows when I met him. One foot in the grave, the other in his mouth, the poor, brave, cast-aside poet was trying not to die— an admirable goal and one that sustained him, I'm sure, right up until they found him, murdered in a basement, beneath a cellar, under Brooklyn. Who would murder Maxwell Bodenheim? Any information leading to the apprehension and conviction of that individual would be a little fucking late, don't you think?

Another incident of passing interest was the night there came a knock on my door, somewhere around midnight. Prepared to tell whoever it was that Mona the Chicken Lady was just one door down the hall, I opened my door, only to find that there was no one there—at least not at eye-level. But, allowing my gaze to drop, I was soon confronted with the bare ass of a man. It was looking up at me like something from a Breughel, winking. And just below it, peeking up and out from between two hairy thighs, was the upside-down head of the ass's owner. "Hello," said the head pleasantly, its hands holding its trousers and its underwear at about its knees.

"Hello," I said, struggling for poise while wondering how I'd gone through the looking glass without ever knowing it.

The inverted head, quick to see that it had parked at the wrong address, said, "Oh, excuse me." After which its owner righted himself, pulled up his clothing, and turned and smiled at me like Marlon Brando because, bless all elves and woodfolk, that's who the hell it was.

Never having seen a star before, I said, "But, aren't you—?"

"No," he said, clicking his belt into its buckle and swaggering down the hallway. "I'm Fred MacMurray."

So much for my meeting up with Marlon MacMurray, an important event in itself but all the more important in that it triggered something rather disquieting in my head. The man's behavior was typical of a kind I had never experienced until coming to the Village but was experiencing more and more every day; i.e., people were going to great lengths to not say "hello, can you help me?" It was very "in." Very "cool." Saying hello from under your ass was evidently a very funny and hip thing to do. I guess I could have shut the door and forgotten the whole thing except that Marlon Brando was my genius, my Stanley Kowalski. And if he could reduce himself to an asshole aimed up at whoever answered a door, what was going to become of me?

I took the question back inside with me and it raised other questions, like what motivates people? Why the strange, aberrant kidding around? Saying to a person "Jesus, you're a sonofabitch"—is that supposed to mean "I love you"? Because it doesn't. It means, "Jesus, you're a sonofabitch." Will I get to a point where *I* do it—and like it? When will love reveal itself to me and what do I do about it? *Aha*—love. That was the word all the time, wasn't it? Finally pushing through.

Never having tasted of love I began to think that, since it could easily be around any corner or in any pair of pants, I'd better get ready for it. I'm talking physical love, okay? The other kind? I had seen enough of that to know to pretty much leave it alone. I was beginning to ponder the issue rather clinically. For on more than one occasion had I awakened in the middle of the night unable to get back to sleep without first introducing my finger to the task of "eight hours peace through sexual release." It didn't upset me. I had masturbated before, but that was merely to see if my body really worked, if I could really press the button and get a charge. But now

my body was saying to me "Hey, big shot, you're sixteen and you're ready. It's going to happen soon, so
why not, before you get raped in an alley, pick a fella of
your own choosing and get the deed done?"

That was one way of looking at it. Another way was
to 'fess up that the idea of sex, with or without emotional involvement, scared the bejeezus out of me because I had yet to find one person, beyond poets and
liars, who was ever made anything but miserable by the
inserting of a penis into a vagina—or, in the case of
Mary Ann, a mouth, or an ear, or wherever she was
taking it at the time.

Okay, then, I said to myself, calling a spade a spade,
sex is scary but can no longer be ignored by burying it
in the removable crotchpiece of nylon pantyhose. And
since it takes two to tango—are there any volunteers?

There being no one in my room at the time, no dashing volunteer stepped forward, and I knew it would be
up to me to make the selection. I also knew, if it was to
work, that it would have to be a man who had nothing
to gain and nothing to lose by making love to me. I
made my selection: Alan Braden, thirtyish and groovy
in an unhandsome yet attractive way. I called him on
the phone, not to tell him the good news (how head-on
could one be?) but to ask him if he'd be at Madame
Getrude's dance class that afternoon. For Alan, like
many actors, took dance class so that his body might be
as supple as his mind, so that, on stage, he could trust
his body and move it and ask of it things it might never
be called upon to do offstage.

At any rate, yes, he would be at Madame Getrude's
for three-o'clock class and, yes, he'd love to meet with
me afterwards for a Coke and a walk and a seminar on
theatre. On other occasions, Alan and I had behaved
like Hansel and Gretel, holding hands and running

through Times Square, knocking on doors and yelling "Flood!," subwaying to Coney Island for hot dogs at Nathan's, and generally encouraging each other to be eight years old. Having first met at Madame Getrude's, we had known each other for about a month and we liked each other. I was pretty sure he was married, unhappily, and that he had a couple of kids but all the better, I thought, a man of experience.

I should tell you that I never missed dance class. Not once. And on days when Madame Getrude's was closed, I'd take class with Mae O'Donnell, or Frank Wagner, or Pladova, or with the immortal Luigi, perhaps the greatest of them all. He had studied with Jack Cole and taught jazz dancing in a studio that always had live music, piano and drums, *something*. Ask any New York dancer. Luigi was "it."

I loved dancing. I could do it quickly. I could pick it up immediately, faster even than those who were at it longer and more easily than those who were more accomplished. I could dance without thinking, it never gave me a headache, and it forever provided me with substitute orgasms. Because, if you danced well and full out, you didn't need sex (at least that's what they told me).

Anyway, Alan Braden and I regularly took class at Madame Getrude's, which was fast becoming the most "in" studio in town. Madame Getrude, a little Jewish sparrow of a thing with vision so bad that she'd often miss her own studio by two blocks, never insisted on being paid. Evidently she was of a moneyed background and was not using her studio to derive income. That in itself guaranteed attendance in her class to run from "full" to "Look out, we're capsizing." But recently she was into "Island Dancing"—Caribbean dancing, a style first introduced by Catherine Dunham in the forties. It was being dusted off and reintroduced at Madame Getrude's by a former Dunham dancer, Annice Chatterton, a black giantess, six feet of slink, and utterly brilliant. As you might imagine, beyond the usual crowd there were then a lot of black dancers coming to class, not all of them professional but, wow, all of them born to those Afro-Haitian, bongo-birdcall rhythms.

We all plugged into the music of Martinique and Jamaica, and we watched, fascinated, as a barefoot Annice, costumed in ruffles and rivulets of white skirt, crowned with a wild turban and dripping with glass beads, stepped around as though she owned the whole Caribbean. The music came out of the phonograph hot and voodoo and absolutely shameless in its sensuality. Each of us was asked to try it and Alan was a hoot, looking as though he were trying to put out a lit cigarette with bare feet. The blacks did it best, of course, but that didn't bother me. For when my turn came I jumped up and did it like I had six hips and three belly buttons. I didn't know if I was good but man, I was into it, on top of it. I was living it. And that's all I remember—beyond receiving a lot of applause. That kind of dancing is so raw, so steaming with natural power and jungle grace that, to this day, whenever I hear that music, I'm not to be held responsible if I bite a chicken's head off and dive into a live volcano.

Alan and I had our hamburgers (I paid for my own, always did). And then we went back to my place to listen to Fritz Kreisler records and put my plan of seduction to work. I was nervous but resolute, unsure just how I would do it but convinced that it would be done.

It didn't take all that long. Alan was ready, spurred on by my Caribbean performance earlier that afternoon. "Jesus, you were something, Ginnie."

"I was?"

"You mean you didn't know?"

"Well, I enjoyed it, but I don't know if I was any good."

"You were good." He was sitting next to me on the floor, our arms touching as our backs leaned against the sofa.

"Can I get you something?" I asked, suddenly willing to jump up and run down to the corner pizzeria—in Dubuque, Iowa.

He held my arm. "No. Sit still. You did enough jumping around this afternoon." He looked around the room, seemingly uncomfortable. "Is that the only music you have? Fiddle music?"

"It's Fritz Kreisler."

"I'm getting a little tired of it."

"Well, what would you like to hear?"

"Do you have any of that Caribbean stuff?"

"No, but I can run uptown and—"

"What the hell you doing?" He was holding my wrist, keeping me from getting up. "Why'd you want to see me tonight? You're acting all fucked up. What's wrong?"

"Well . . . nothing."

He got up. "First thing we do is give Mr. Kreisler a rest." He removed the record. "Next thing we do is cut down on your electricity bill." He switched off a few lights and then turned to where I was sitting—and trembling. "What's wrong? You're shivering."

"I think it's my old malaria cropping up. Got it at Guadalcanal."

He laughed. "You're afraid of me."

"Afraid? A-ha-ha-ha."

"You are."

"Not."

"Are."

"Not."

Ever so gently, he took me by the shoulders and placed me on my back, on the floor, my head at a painful angle against the leg of the sofa. His face hovered over me, seeming all magnified, and his voice, though a whisper, came at me as if through a bull horn. "Listen, Ginnie. You listening?"

"Yes. Sir." I was afraid. I had prodded the sleeping tiger and, sonofabitch, the cage had come open and the beast was coming out all erect—and I don't mean on his hind legs.

He rolled on top of me, his hands doing predictable and clumsy things. "Ginnie, you know how I feel about you."

"No, I don't. Tell me."

"What?"

"Tell me how you feel about me. But first—hey—can I move my head a little? It's gonna break off."

I moved and he kissed me, with deadly aim. Right on the mouth. He was talking and kissing, simultaneously. "Ginnie . . . Ginnie, I . . . Ginnie? I . . . Ginnie . . ."

"Yes? What? Alan? Hmmm?"

He pulled back and tensed up. "What the hell's wrong with you?"

"I'm trying to tell you. My head's in a funny position."

"Then move it! Move your fucking head!"

"Yes. Thank you. I'm moving it. *There*."

He tried to recoup. "You comfortable now?"

"Me?"

And he flared. "Who else is in the room?"

"Well, you never know."

He turned cold. "I'm not gonna wrestle with you, kid. I'm not gonna play games or let you be coy."

"Coy? Me? A-ha-ha-ha-ha."

"You know how I feel about you."

"Well—"

"So it's time to stop the shit."

"What time *is* it?"

"I'm not even gonna honor that question with an answer."

He was unbuckling his belt and making so much noise that I had to say "Shhhhh."

"What?"

"Nothing."

"Listen, I wanna be tender. I really do, but you're acting very freaky. Are we going to do this or aren't we?"

"I don't know." And I didn't.

"To me that means yes."

"Yeah? To me it means 'I don't know.' " I was up on the backs of my forearms, like a sunbather looking at her toes.

He pushed me down again, climbed aboard, and was wiggling all over me. "Ginnie, I hate to do it this way . . ."

"Alan—I'm scared. I mean, I am goddamned terrified."

"I know. I know. I'll be tender." He was working on my clothes.

"Alan—I'm only sixteen."

"I wouldn't care if you were nine."

"You're tearing my sweater!"

"*Fuck* your sweater!"

"Alan—there's something I have to tell you."

"Tell me later. Jesus."

"I've never done this before."

"I know."

"You do?"

"Yeah."

"And it doesn't matter?"

"It did. About ten minutes ago. Now it doesn't." His hands were dancing under my sweater. He kept trying to stay on top while I kept trying to roll him off. All I could think of was Miss Marjorie Stokely's turtle trying to stay on its slippery rock. His left hand went under my sweater, a diversionary action to keep me busy there. His right hand was grabbing at my belt.

"Alan *please*!"

"So you're a virgin! So fuck it!" He was all breathy and determined and out of control.

"Alan, I—" My hand reached down in the fight for possession of my belt buckle and came upon his penis.

"Oh, Ginnie—"

"Oh, pardon me." And I let the thing go. But it quickly found its way back into my hand, obviously possessing some kind of homing instinct. I tried to shake it out of my hand but his hand was on top of mine, clamping it. "Alan, I don't think you understand . . ."

"I understand, I understand! Jesus Christ, Ginnie!"

"You have to let me explain . . ."

"No! I have to fuck you! That's what I have to do! So, for Christ's sake, stop the phony resistance!"

"Yes, I'm sure, but—Alan? I *can't* fuck."

That stopped him. "What?"

"I'm trying to explain." Even as I was talking, I wondered just what I was going to say, what weird fiction I was going to come up with that would save the day, the moment, and my virginity.

He kept his penis in my hand, that silly bit of cartilage jumping all over the place like a landed ten-pound trout. But I wasn't moving a knuckle. He would have had more action had he stuck his dopey dick into a bathtub faucet. "What the hell you talking about?" he asked.

And it all came out, amazing even me. "It's not a pretty story, Alan."

"I'm sure."

"I was born in China. My father was a missionary. When the war was over we had to literally walk out of China. All of us. My father, my mother, my sister and me. I wasn't twelve years old. Alan, they raped me."

"What?"

"The Chinese, the Japanese, wherever we went, just walking, east, east to the ocean." I was marvelous. Tears came to my eyes and I tried very hard to have a few of them land on his penis, an act which brought me dangerously close to the enemy but which was worth the risk. "Alan, I've *never* been a virgin. My father had to sew me up. Six, seven, eight times—maybe ten. I'm all scar tissue, Alan. I have a very little opening. I can't take insertion." And I turned away, half waiting for the applause.

He was consoling. "You poor kid."

"No, it's okay. I've come to terms with it. There are things—exercises I do to limber myself up, but I'm not ready yet. I have no elasticity down there. My first Tampax? I practically had to hammer it in."

"Oh, Ginnie . . ." He was hugging me, rocking me. And I consoled, hugged and rocked him back.

"It's all right," I said. "I've come to terms with it. In a year or two—maybe less—I'll be able to—accept a man."

"You poor baby. What about your mother?"

"What about her?"

"Did they rape her, too?"

"Oh, no. She was too old. They weren't interested in her, just—the young stuff."

"Your sister?"

"My sister? Oh—that's another story."

"What?"

"Well—she loved it." Nothing like getting a zinger in on Mary Ann Marvelous. "She was fifteen and loved it. Fucked her way right out of China. If it weren't for Mary Ann taking the pressure off me, I don't know, we might still be there. In a cage in some kind of Chinese brothel."

"Jesus what a story." He rolled off me and lay on his back alongside me, his penis going with him because, well, it didn't extend all that far. "No wonder you dance like you do. It's all sublimation. You perform sex in your dancing."

"Yes, Alan. As shameless as it may sound, yes. I dance the way I'd like to fuck—*if* I could fuck." I was having such a good time with my melodrama. I moved to kiss him. "It's something to look forward to, though, no?"

He sighed. "Yeah. I guess so."

I realized he was hurting and I was sorry. I hadn't thought about him at all, and I liked him. "I should have told you. I shouldn't have let you go this far."

"Forget it."

"I think—if you want to—you should take care of yourself." I, myself, wondered what I meant by that.

"I will. When I get home. Only it'll take a year to get there, as I'll be doing it on my hands and knees."

"Do you hurt?"

"No. I *always* wear my schlong in braids."

"Can you take care of yourself—here?" If he did, I'd leave the room, of course, being a lady.

"With you?"

"Well, I—"

"Your mouth?"

"No, that's not exactly what I had in mind."

He got ugly. "Something wrong with your mouth, too? What'd they do? Rip your mouth open and force root canal work on you?"

I reached for his penis, instinctively. Grabbing a man's penis is like rubbing the stomach of a dog. It pacifies and temporarily defuses. Immediately disarmed by the act, Alan stopped bitching. "Alan, I don't want you to go home angry and tense." I sounded like a commerical for Anacin.

"Aaaaah, shit."

He lay there, all rigid, as if whatever I was doing to his penis would shortly happen to the rest of him. Inside of five seconds he was taking on the dimensions of a telephone pole. "Does this make you feel better?"

"Ginnie, that's for kids. I can do that myself."

"Okay."

"But do it anyway."

"Yes, Alan." I distinctly remember feeling no excitement at all. Holding his sex in my hand was about as thrilling as holding a Russian salami, neither of which did I ever have any intention of eating. But I liked Alan and I owed him that much. What the hell, what was the big deal? If that's what he wanted—

"Oh, Ginnie."

"Yes, dear. Just relax." Ginnie, the expert.

"Ginnie, I love you. Ginnie—"

"I know. I know." The hell he loved me. He just loved my hand. It was like the old adage: "The hand that holds the penis, rules the world." And I held it. Like a rudder. If I twisted left, his right leg went up. If I pushed it forward, his head rolled to the side. And if I pulled down on it, his whole body trembled as if he were breaking through the sound barrier. I was Smilin' Jack at the joystick. With the right amount of pressure I

could have sent him into a fatal power dive, a terrifying
tailspin. Only my grasp of things, plus a working knowledge of aerodynamics, was all that stood between Alan
Braden and another kill for the Red Baroness.

"Ginnie—"

"Shhhhh."

"Ginnie—?"

"Shhhh."

"*Ginnie????*"

"Alan, what *is* it!"

What it was was that he exploded all over my sweater
and my jeans and my nice carpet. It must have made
him feel terribly foolish because he immediately stood
up, zipped up, and walked out, saying, "Pretty fucking
humiliating, Ginnie. Thanks a lot."

Well, you could have fooled *me*. I was under the distinct impression that he had been enjoying it. As I
cleaned up the mess I began to realize that sex and me
were not going to be all that compatible. The idea of it
was grand and I loved it, but the putting of it into practice was something else. I liked Alan, about as much as
I had ever liked any boy or man, but I simply didn't
want to make love with him. I could hold him in my
hand. I could relieve him. I could give him his little-boy
hand job. But it was all ice cold and premeditated. I
was not transported to Olympian heights by it. I was not
sent skipping to my diary to giddily record my first
jerk-off. I was simply aware that I had behaved stupidly
and clumsily with a man I rather liked and, in the process, had set back US-Sino relations about three hundred
years.

Meantime, I quietly turned seventeen and, back at
Madame Getrude's, Annice Chatterton is slowly but
surely (and very expertly) developing a group of dynamite boy and girl dancers, of whom I am one (and the

only white one). I mean, there I am, all blonde and
blue-eyed and screaming of Scandinavia, prancing
around in the middle of a tribe of blue-black Negroes
and Negresses who move with the rhythms that flowed
out with them when the water broke in their various
mothers' wombs. How long would it be before Annice
would up and say, "Hey, Vanilla, yo' is discharged from
the shebang."

Well, the hell. I didn't care. I just didn't. I was simply
determined to keep on showing up, sweating with the
rest of them, doing interpretively what came to them
anthropologically. Besides, damn it, not only did I enjoy
it, I was good at it. If I was going to be hustled off the
floor it would have to be as the result of pure, head-on
bigotry, and they'd know it. And if they didn't, I'd goddamn tell 'em.

One Sunday, one of the boys (not a professional dancer; matter of fact, he never danced at all, just hung
around and took notes) took me aside and asked if I'd
have a Coke with him. His name was Roland Jessup
and it didn't take me long to realize that he wasn't just
another silly dancer. Rather, he was bright, well-
spoken, mature, and worked in the advertising department of 20th Century-Fox somewhere uptown—so far
uptown it could just as well have been Canada.

Roland told me what I had already begun to suspect.
Annice Chatterton was gathering a troupe of dancers
for a review that would open in some posh uptown club.
Catherine Dunham had done it in *Cafe Society,* and
now it was time for someone to do it again.

Roland went on to say that, though he worked full
time at his job, he often dabbled in private ventures and
was very much involved in the organization and coordi-
nating of the Annice Chatterton Dancers. The selection
of the dancers was up to Annice, of course, but the ne-

gotiating and contracting—all the logistical work—was solely his responsibility.

Well, to get right to it, Annice wanted me in the troupe but wasn't too sure but that the black kids might resent the hell out of me. Also, would the paying public find it destructively gratuitous? Wouldn't she be better advised to settle for a lesser dancer and keep the whole show black?

Apparently, Annice was ready to go the all-black route but Roland wasn't certain it was the right move. After all, wasn't the idea to get the best dancers and not the best black dancers? Annice had given Roland her proxy. If Roland wanted to sound me out on the subject, and if I found the idea to my liking, fine. But it would then be Roland's job to acquaint me with the possible side effects of joining the group.

"Like what?" I asked.

"Like having a dozen black girls not talk to you."

"They don't talk to me now."

"Like having them make you miserable by letting you know that, if you woke up dead, they might just jump for joy."

"I don't care what people do after I'm dead."

"You have to give it serious thought." His voice was deep, a Paul Robeson voice but with a flip on it, always accentuating words, emphasizing them as if he were an effeminate school teacher.

"Okay. I thought about it. I want to do it."

"I'm not asking for a decision this very moment, Virginia."

"I know. But you *got* it."

"You must understand. If the group does well at The Blue Angel, we may want to tour it. You'll be living with black girls."

"I don't do windows or any heavy work."

He laughed so hard his cigarette-holder fell out of the space between his teeth. "You are a fantastic dancer, but you're going to look like an oddity, as though we put you in to shake things up. For you to survive, you're going to have to be ten times the dancer the other kids are. Otherwise, the critics and the audiences are going to crucify you. You're going to have to be better than Jackie Robinson."

"I can't move to my left."

He smiled. "How old are you?"

"Oh, shit."

"We'll have to get you a union card. AGVA. If you're a *minor*, one of your parents'll have to go with you."

"What if I have no parents?"

"Your guardian."

"Forget it."

"We'll work *something* out. Pay is sixty dollars a week."

"I'll take it."

"—for which you will work so hard—"

"It's okay."

"You'll rehearse all day. Two shows every night."

"Okay."

"And if the show goes on the road, darling, you'll be living with black people."

"That's *their* problem."

"Once you leave New York, I can't help you."

"Who's *asking* you to."

He sat back, puffing his strange-smelling cigarette. "Well, Joan of Arc was sixteen."

"Was she black?"

"At the end, baby, she was charred."

I got my union card but don't ask me how. Roland and a black girl went with me and told the man at the desk that I was black, and the man just didn't want to fight it. I had my card, I had my contract. And I had a share of a very successful restaurant. Things were good. Alan called a couple of times but was so belligerent I just had to hang up on him.

I was working very hard. The fun and games were over. Annice drove my ass off in rehearsals but I didn't resent it. She simply wanted to make it impossible for any of the other girls to say I was hired because I was white. I was hanging in—losing weight but hanging in. Even after rehearsals I would go back to my apartment and work out all over again. I even went down the street doing my snaky routine, once stopping a helluva lot of traffic coming out of a Safeway store on Stuyvesant Street.

I was really on top of things when it happened. I was fast asleep. Out cold in my apartment. So beat from the physicality of dancing that I was into something more nearly approaching a coma. I never heard a thing. Not the sirens, not the screaming, nothing. But I smelled it—the chickens, burning.

The smell came under my door and I knew immediately what was happening. I opened the door and the flames almost knocked me over. I'd never get out that way. I didn't panic. Panic was not my style. There was still my window, my one window, but could I squeeze through it?

I pulled a chair over and stood on it. Though the window was about one foot by two feet, it just didn't swing open enough for me to wiggle through. Six inches—that's all. I pulled the window closed and then smashed it with a lamp. Then I knocked off all the ragged glass edges that remained. If I hadn't done that, going through the window's frame would have been like going through the mouth of a shark.

The flames were licking under my door, even through the keyhole, the smoke curling across the floor like a ground fog aimed at my ankles. There wasn't too much I could take with me and not all that much time in which to make my selection. So I took things that seemed to have the most value—my workout clothes and Maggie's portrait.

Hands helped pull me through my ex-window. Police, firemen, water, lights—it was like opening in Vegas. And there I stood, in all the noise and all the color, wet from the fire hoses, my legs shivering below my baby doll nightie, holding onto my leotards with one hand and my mommy with the other. I knew I looked forlorn, so I cried.

Good-bye, apartment. Good-bye, li'l haven, first sweet place of my own. And fuck you and your chickens, Mona. I hope you fry in Mazola.

ben

1950

Let's say it right off, clearing the air of all possible misconceptions: the Army and I, as a team, as a marriage and an act, closed after a long run during which all the critics agreed that the US would have been better advised to surrender than to attempt to mold Ben Webber into any kind of fighting machine, unless, of course, the purpose of such an attempt was the complete and total demolition of the United States itself, as an army, a nation, and an ideal.

It just didn't work, gang, what else can I tell you? From the beginning it didn't work. From the bus ride to Fort Devens, Massachusetts, during which two men vomited and the air-conditioning failed through the lunch stop at Springfield, where three men, sworn in that very morning, made for the woods with six MP's in pursuit, it didn't work.

Flashback. Young Benjamin Webber, on a bright and brisk morning at five A.M., takes the oath of allegiance, in which he promises to defend his country, is fingerprinted, pushed onto a bus with forty other similarly delighted lads, and is sent—through puke and desertion—to the Fort Devens Reception Center. It is eight degrees above zero and snowing. Five of the new recruits are crying, and young Benjamin has to wonder, "Are we being executed? What is this place? Where is the band playing Sousa? Where the smiling girls with the doughnuts and coffee? Where the grateful civilian populace clamoring its affection, covering us with kisses, offering us its women, its wine?"

Fraud. Fraud, deceit, misdemeanor, felony, coercion, and bullshit. There are no women, no doughnuts, no music, no wine. There is nothing but eight degrees, snow, and a fat southern sergeant shouting at us in something approximating English, but more nearly sounding like Pig Fart.

I was issued my clothing and assigned to my outfit, the 42nd Quartermaster Group, Headquarters Company. Basically, it was a Pennsylvania National Guard outfit that had been mobilized when no one was looking, clearing out the gyms, garages, sawmills and churches of all eligible men. The colonel in charge had a dry-cleaning business. The lieutenant colonel, second in command, was a bank teller. And none of the noncoms was over nineteen years of age. All of them were Pennsylvania Dutch, which meant that they washed regularly, said "fuck thee," and were in for a big surprise.

Mixed in with the National Guardsmen (NG's), were a sprinkling of Regular Army men (RA's), all of them noncoms, and a handful of World War II Reservists (RES) who, stupidly, to hang onto their rank, joined the Reserves at the end of the war in 1945. Basically, the Reservists were good guys, in their thirties, but contemptuous of a situation that had them in their second war within five years.

Please understand the array: forty-five National Guardsmen, fifteen Regular Army men, six Reservists, to which are added thirty-five draftees (US's). It was an impossible amalgam. The NG's were painfully young, and if they had ever been laid, it would have had to have been with horses. The RA's were old drunks who saw the Army as their home. The Reservists, Army-wise and pissed off, would rather America lose the war than serve another week. And the US's were, for the most part, street smart, crafty, and not to be broken easily to the bit.

Of the NG's, only Captain Francis Grace was for real. Despite the double feminine name, he had been a Marine officer in the Pacific theatre of operations and, following World War II, though properly mustered out, had somehow felt compelled to sign on with the Guard. When the Guard was activated, Captain Grace found himself attached to a unit in which he was the only officer with any combat experience. He could not have liked being billeted with those egg-pluckers.

The two colonels, I suppose, were all right, but they were distant. Colonel Cranston, as I said, had this dry-cleaning business and was very big on inspections. The band would play "Cruising Down The River," he'd stand up in his jeep, salute, and then drive off. How he'd be in a war was anybody's guess. *Clean* would be a good word; *pressed* would be a better one.

Lieutenant Colonel Beakins, our bank teller, always looked as though he was about to ask, "How would you like it, sir? All in fives?" As to the rest of the NG officers and men, they ran from "tolerable" to "middling" to "God help us," though Master Sergeant Luther Holdoffer was easily the most inexcusably stupid human being whose canteen I ever had the pleasure of peeing in.

The RA's and Reservists I'll deal with as events unfold, but I *would* like to sketch out two of the US's who, to this day, have my admiration, respect and affection. Raggedly individualistic, they could not knuckle under to authority any more than I could. As a result they helped make my Army life bearable and, on occasion, pleasurable.

Johnny Munez was half Spanish, half Italian, and all swarthy. He was from Brooklyn, drove an eighteen-wheel trailer truck as a civilian, stood five-foot-seven and was built like the stump of a Sequoia. Resourceful, intelligent, troubled by his lack of education, Johnny had determined that the real enemy was the National Guard. And together we waged a guerrilla war against the Guardsmen of such an intensity that, only now, years after the events took place, do I dare make the facts known.

My other good friend was a laughing man with sparse hair so blond as to seem either white or nonexistent. Painfully Polish, lantern-jawed and blue-eyed, why Tony Wesso laughed was forever beyond me because, of all the draftees, he had the most to lose by doing a stint in the Army. He had been the leading left-handed pitcher for the (now defunct) Jersey City Giants, but it was all behind him. He had been wrenched off the mound, put in a new uniform, and told to stay loose. Instinctively happy, Tony laughed because everything seemed truly funny to him. He never complained. He was so coordinated that nothing in our basic training ever truly tested his skills. But there was an impish side of him, a Halloween side, that of a born prankster.

Tony Wesso, Johnny Munez, Ben Webber—plus a few other carefully selected US's—posed a greater problem to the security of the United States than did a dozen Communist Chinas.

Being attached to a quartermaster company can be, and usually is, a very cushy situation. But being attached to the headquarters company of a quartermaster outfit is beyond all of a drafted man's wildest dreams. Easy jobs. Frequent passes. Clothing that fit. It had all the earmarks of an eighteen-month vacation at the expense of our rich uncle.

The fly in that ointment, we soon found out, was that all the rank, all the good jobs, were already spoken for and held down by the NG's. That meant two things: no chance for advancement, and all the shit details were ours automatically. It was as though I was back in the mailroom of 20th Century-Fox.

Our basic training was a laugh riot. Most of us draftees were Limited Service, which was why we were assigned to the quartermaster in the first place. I mean, my body was a breakaway body, not unlike the suits that the old burlesque comics used to wear (pull a sleeve and the whole thing flies off). I could pull a hamstring, strain a back muscle, pop a knee, just from moving from a canter to a trot. My body could not be relied on in a stress situation. And all of it was made worse by the fact that my fists were clenched in frustration thirty-six hours a day.

Johnny Munez's limited service was due to his being blind in one eye. Which eye, not even he knew. And Tony's was due, believe it or not, to chronic athlete's foot that he had allowed to fester for years because it felt so good when he scratched. However, some of the draftees were 1-A in that they had good bodies, weak minds, and were ideal candidates to have their heroic asses shot off.

Faced with this utter waste of time, what else could Johnny, Tony, and I do but behave like bad little kids? Where could they transfer us to? All the so-called shit brigades were totally staffed by Negroes (the Army was segregated and blacks were seldom called upon to do anything that didn't come under the heading of slavery).

So here's what we did. We created a designation

called Draftee of the Week. It was Tony's idea and he
kept the chart, hidden, of course. The idea behind it
was simple enough. A dozen of only the most trusted
draftees would meet every Thursday prior to whatever
passed for the dinner meal, and we would vote in, as
Draftee of the Week, the one US who had done the
most to noticeably aggravate the shit out of the NG's. If
that draftee was not a member of the inner circle of
twelve, he would be told of his award and would be
offered full membership.

And what was the award for being Draftee of the
Week? Simple. For the week following his award,
the Draftee of the Week rated a full salute from all the
other draftees in the program. That may not seem like
much to you, but, it you had been there to see the faces
of the officers and noncoms and NG's and RA's and
Reservists, to watch them watch me walk down the
company street in my dirtiest fatigues and have all the
draftees snap to and salute me as if I were MacArthur,
some of them doing it three and four times within a
five-minute span—well, you would have realized the
importance of such a program to our morale.

Now, you may ask, how does one *earn* Draftee of the
Week? Well, in my case, here are just two of my accomp-
lishments (directly from the commendations as written
up by Private Marty Ransom, former star reporter of
the *Staten Island Herald* and later to become a successful advertising executive).

1) On the day of a short twenty-mile hike, the men
   of the 42nd Group being required to complete
   that hike without being issued canteens of water,
   Master Sergeant Luther Holdoffer was seen pouring hot tea into a canteen that he then flaunted
   on his cartridge belt. Private Benjamin Webber,

assuming great personal risk, somehow managed to exchange the tea for urine. Sgt. Holdoffer, true to form, was unable to detect the difference. Due to Private Webber's courage and resourcefulness, the hike was enjoyed by one and all, especially as Sergeant Holdoffer vomited all night.

2) Before reveille on the morning of March 2, 1951, Private Benjamin Webber, US, noticing that the Cadre Room door had been left ajar, slipped unnoticed therein and deposited into each of Master Sergeant Luther Holdoffer's highly-lustred boots, a generous helping of ripe shit. He was assisted in this action and in the procurement of the excrement by Privates Stovall and Morelli who had eaten Mexican chili the night before while feeling somewhat adventurous. At the sound of reveille, Sgt. Holdoffer, as is his wont, leapt into both boots and shortly got the message. For your creativity and courage, Private Webber, the men of the 42nd salute you. Never has better use been made of Mexican cooking.

Much of my malice, as you may have picked up on, was directed at Master Sergeant Luther Holdoffer. This was no accident. Holdoffer personified everything wrong with the National Guard. He was thick in the coco, humorless, mean, and had the intelligence of a plant. He had green teeth and a reeking mouth. He had red dandruff, the body odor of a beached crab, scratched his crotch incessantly, had the blind strength of a pair of oxen, and was the quintessence of random sadism. But more upsetting than anything else, he had master sergeant's stripes. He was topkick, sergeant of sergeants, cock of the walk, king of the hill, prick of pricks. He had authority. As such he could not be questioned and he could not be stopped. Nor could he be anticipated because he was never able to frame more than three thoughts in a row. In short, he was a sadistic Goliath who loved rubbing our noses on the rocks. On two separate occasions he had goaded a draftee into challenging him to a fight in an official ring, with an impartial referee. Both those draftees emerged so busted up that one of them took five weeks to recover, and the other, hung up with untraceable internal injuries that the army couldn't treat, was given an honorable discharge with a twenty-five percent "service-induced disability."

Bringing the cruel ogre to task for his crimes against humanity became my one consuming military aim. North Korea, China, Russia—they were too far away to mean anything to me. Holdoffer was visible, present, active. He was the consummate villain, the universal tormenter—and my one reason for being. I would have his hide.

And he would have mine, for somehow it had gotten through to him that I was the bee in his asshole (not surprising, as anyone of a dozen NG's could have told him that). And one night he cornered me coming out of the PX, on one of his "drunk nights." Nobody knew why, but Holdoffer always got drunk on Tuesdays, Thursdays and Saturdays. When he was that drunk he never scared me. His sodden condition was such an equalizer that I'd be able to hold my own with him or, failing that, outdistance him. It was dark and his death-breath reached me before his words did. "Webber, you motherfucker . . ."

"Ah, Sergeant Holdoffer. I recognized your cologne."

"You fuckin' motherfucker."

"That's redundant."

"I know it's you, you fuckin' kike."

"Actually, I'm a fuckin' Presbyterian." I kept walking.

"If I say you're a kike, you're a kike."

"Yazzah. Listen, Sarge, I'm off duty. Anything you want to say to me is going to have to wait till tomorrow." I tried to walk around him but he blocked my way.

"Fuckin' Hollywood smartass. Yeah, I looked at your file. You come from 20th Century-Kike in Holly-kike, Kike-a-fornia."

I managed to walk around him. "Whatever you say, Sarge." And I walked away.

But he was walking alongside me, a foot taller, and bumping me as if he were pushing me off the road. "You shit in my boots, dincha?"

"You kidding? I wouldn't go *near* your boots."

"And you pissed in my canteen."

"That was tea. I don't pee tea, see?"

"You mothers are doin' somethin' with all that salutin'. Don't think I don't see."

I saw Johnny and Tony. They were right behind us, coming out of the PX, so I stopped and faced Holdoffer, figuring that they'd catch up. "Listen, imbecile, you lay a paw on me and you'll be up on charges so fast your skin'll clear up."

He saw Johnny and Tony, too, and he included them in his remarks as they came up to flank me. "The three of you fuckin' kikes, I'm gonna make you eat shit. You're gonna cook it, cut it, and eat it."

Tony smiled at Johnny. "You mean that stuff they're servin' *ain't* shit?"

And Johnny smiled at Tony. "I didn't know you were a kike, Wesso. When did that happen?"

"Beats me. I don't remember being barmitzvahed." He

felt around on the top of his head. "Jesus, I lost my beanie."

I looked again at Tony and realized that, though he wasn't as tall or as heavy as Holdoffer, he might easily be just as strong or stronger. Certainly he was in better shape, a better athlete. Also, he was a few years older, and the difference between nineteen and twenty-three could also be the difference between a boy and a man.

Holdoffer was not intimidated. "Wesso, you're a motherfuckin' Polack. And anytime you wanna step in the ring with me—"

Tony busted in with a smile. "Sarge, before you and I part company in this army, I'm gonna throw a forkball, two hundred miles an hour, right up your ass."

"Try it, Polack," said Holdoffer. "In the ring."

"I wouldn't last one minute in the ring with you, apeshit. The smell would knock me out."

"Fuckin' shit-eatin' kikes." Holdoffer slunk off, his various smells going with him, circling around him like fruit flies.

A few mornings later, Captain Grace called me in. He directed me to be at ease, closing the door and asking me to sit down as though we were chums. He began to talk, informally, lighting up a cigarette and clomping his feet up on his desk. "Explain something to me, Webber."

"Yes, sir. I'll try."

"Why are you so angry? You're not the only man being asked to serve. Everybody's unhappy, as they should be. But you—you're angry."

"I'm not angry, sir."

Captain Grace was not one for zig-zagging. He had the face of a Hollywood marine, lean, lined and leathery. He reminded me of Sammy Baugh who used to quarterback the Washington Redskins—not handsome, but riveting. And when he threw the ball at you, you either caught it or it went right through you. "Straight answers, Webber. I have no time for side trips."

"Yes, sir. Well, sir, maybe 'angry' isn't the right word."

"Then, please, tell me the right word."

"I think 'frustrated.' "

He was holding my MOS file. "Yes. You had a good job. Okay, you'll have it again. It'll be there when you get back because that's the law."

"Yes, sir. If you say so, sir."

"Webber, I'll tell you something. I don't like being attached to this outfit any more than you do, okay? They offend me. They concern me and they bug me. But there's nothing I can do about it except to keep applying for transfer, through proper channels. Meantime, I do not sit around and bitch, and stir up trouble. I do my job."

"I'm not stirring—"

"Bullshit. You've got this whole company divided like *Mutiny on the Bounty*. It's tough enough keeping four such dissident groups together. I've got two colonels in an ivory tower and a lieutenant in a perpetual fog, and I have to run this bastard of an outfit on a day-to-day basis. I could use some help." He took a long draw on his cigarette. "I'd like you to stop baiting Holdoffer."

"Yes, sir."

Because if you don't, you're going to get the pointy end of a very long stick. Why do you do it?"

"Well, sir—"

"Straight answers."

"He's a sadist, sir."

"Think so?"

"Yes, sir. He's a sadist and a bigot and, very likely, a moron."

"He's a master sergeant."

"Same thing."

He tried not to smile, then he leaned forward. "He's also Colonel Cranston's nephew."

"Oh, Christ."

"The whole unit, Webber, they're all from the same towns. Every one of them is related in one way or another."

"Colonel Cranston's nephew?"

"Yes. What I'm trying to tell you, Webber, is that if you work on that moron long enough—he *is* a moron—he'll go to Uncle and *you'll* go down the latrine."

"Yes, sir."

"So I want you to back off. If he maltreats you or any of the men, the Army will take care of him."

"How, sir? If he's the Colonel's nephew, how?"

"I don't know how, but it will. Also, in case you're unaware of it, you can apply for transfer, too. With your background, maybe Special Services'll be interested in you."

"Yes, sir."

"Only I have to tell you, other men have requested transfers but Colonel Cranston always turns them down."

"Why?"

"Evidently he thinks it reflects on him."

"Then I can't get out of the 42nd, can I?"

"You can. You can apply for Officer Candidate School. If you're accepted it's not considered a transfer. It's considered self-improvement and is encouraged by the Army. Consequently, no group commander, or anyone, can stop it.

"I'm Limited Service."

"The Chinese have shot up a lot of our second looies. The physical requirements are no longer so stringent."

"You mean they'll take anyone who shows up."

"Anyone who can walk in, stand up and spell his name, yes. But it will add three years to your tour of duty."

"What second looie in Korea is going to live three years?"

He smiled. "It's a dilemma."

"Yeah. Sir."

"Think it over. Meanwhile, let me reiterate. Stay out of Holdoffer's way or you're aiming yourself at more trouble than your quick mind is going to be able to handle. *And*, starting tomorrow I'm on Holdoffer's side. You do understand?"

"Yes, sir." I saluted. He saluted. And I left.

I explained the situation to Johnny and Tony—that we had to lay off Holdoffer. They had a strange reaction. They felt that without Holdoffer to vent their dissatisfaction on, something marvelous would be going out of their lives. They were concerned, however, with my possibly signing up for OCS. I immediately put their fears to rest. "Gentlemen, I'd rather do two years with Turd-Head Holdoffer than three with Charlie Chan." They applauded my comment and we then went off to become semidrunk.

From time to time I received letters from Don. They were newsy and fun, my one link with the outside world. And when they came I'd find a private place in which to read them, a place where I would not suffer any interruption, where Manhattan would miraculously show up and embrace me—if only for a few minutes.

Dear Glorious War Hero and Demi-God,

I report to you on a variety of items, all of which I trust you will find interesting or else why the fuck am I wasting my time? 20th Century-Fox still thrives, still turning out garbage but still paying salaries. I see very little of Arnie and less of Big Al who hurries home to screw his wife each night because they'll soon be drafting married men who are not fathers. Poor Laura, went from virgin to harem girl in record time.

As to Bob Steinman, he still seems more interested in screwing than in climbing the ladder of success. He just kind of loafs through the day and fucks through the night and doesn't care about the next day any more than he cared about last week.

Oh, new messenger in Publicity. Some kind of monster. 5'6", he must weigh half a ton, and his arms come down to his ankles. His name is Sam Gaynor and his father was evidently some kind of 1920's crooner who the world loved until he got so fat that his voice couldn't squeeze out. Sam never lets us forget who his father is which is fine because it lets us forget who Sam is. He never stops talking, talks only of himself and how much talent he has and how everybody at 20th is a fool. He intends to be a director but, at the moment, has his eye on your job in the ad department. But Mickey and Dora and Roland told Meyerberg that they'd quit if "Mighty Mouth" was brought in as your temporary replacement, so the status is quo. The guy is 4-F—"diarrhea of the mouth." Speaking of Roland—you know how I've been having trouble paying the rent on this barn and how I've been looking for a roommate to help share the tariff.

Well, old Roland comes in one day with a great-looking girl and says that she needs an apartment because she just got burnt out of hers and needs one uptown because that's where she'll be working. Her name is Ginnie Maitland and she's a dancer with legs that won't quit. Blue eyes, blonde, but insists that she's a Negro. I find her to be slightly strange but, what the hell, she came right up with the rent money.

Patricia Jarvas asked to be remembered to you and would like you to drop her a line. Also— would you call her the first time you're on furlough as she—and I quote—"has a warm spot in her bed for you."

Love from the Home Front,
Don

Captain Grace got his transfer. I was pleased for him, we all were. He deserved better than the 42nd and had somehow convinced Colonel Cranston that his transfer be approved. It never occurred to us that Colonel Cranston might be downright pleased to get rid of an officer whose very presence subverted his own image. Also, it moved Lieutenant Rankin up a notch, displacing Captain Grace with a man who in civilian life worked at Colonel Cranston's dry-cleaning company. Talk about blind loyalty, in Rankin Colonel Cranston had practically his own sheepdog; and in too soon a time we all got to appreciate how good and fair and intelligent a company commander we had had in Captain Grace.

Lieutenant Rankin was about twenty-eight. He was kind of odd physically in that he was a beanpole with a paunch—skinny except around the middle. He had a receding crew cut, a weak chin like Andy Gump's, and he wore G.I. eyeglasses (round, metal frames). His hands were most definitely female, and when he walked it was as though he were walking a tightrope, his eyes aimed at the ground as if he believed that, with one false step, he might just fall off the earth. He smoked a pipe filled with chocolate cake that was forever going out, giving us the feeling that he was not an experienced pipesmoker, that his pipe was just some kind of prop he was using to project an image of tweedy masculinity, mostly, I suspect, to reassure himself.

And so it came to pass that, on an incredibly cold day, Lieutenant Rankin decided to establish, once and for all, both his authority and his masculinity, for he seemed to sense that we doubted both. He ordered a twelve-mile hike to an overnight bivouac, for everyone except a dozen NG's who would remain behind and run the command post and water the colonel's plants. By the way, neither of our colonels accompanied us.

It was hard to believe. We hadn't been in the Army three months and were off on a maneuver that seasoned veterans were seldom asked to undergo. The NG's, bright-eyed, bushy-tailed and dense, took to the whole idea as if it were a hike to a hoedown. They were in good shape, and, even though they hadn't done it in the depths of winter, they had hiked full-pack any number of times before their unit was eventually activated.

But the draftees—the majority of us—were Limited Service and technically not required to endure such nonsense. And the Reservists, all of whom had combat experience, felt it an affront to be included in such a whimsical exercise. As for our RA's, all of whom were in some state of drunkenness twenty-four hours of every day, they were in such God-awful physical condition that it was highly doubtful any of them could go half the distance without dropping out as if it were the Bataan Death March.

And, it was snowing. Christ, was it ever snowing, as if the gods had decided to assist Rankin in the testing of our mettle. Clearly I could see that we would either make it or freeze, or drown, or rust.

We started out immediately following a stomach-turning breakfast. Full packs: rifles, entrenching tools, blankets, K rations, canteens. Why we were taking canteens was beyond us; the water inside them would freeze within a mile. Plus, we didn't need water. If we wanted it all we had to do was scoop up a helmetful of snow. Before leaving the barracks, Tony, Johnny, and I emptied the water from our canteens, refilling them with something purported to be bourbon. Barely palatable, it was so highly alcoholic that it was guaranteed not to freeze. As to the other men, they were on their own. Some had bourbon and some didn't. Some had rye, rum, whiskey, beer, and cider. All had something, it was just a question of degree (or proof).

We stepped out, our arctic boots mushing oafishly through the Mixmaster snow, and I never saw Holdoffer so fulfilled. The cold, the snow, the ice beneath the snow—nothing slowed him. He seemed to skim over the surface like a low-flying bird. He was the point man and set a pace so doggedly hurried that, almost at regular intervals, he could be seen a hundred yards ahead, screaming at us like a galley foreman, waving at us to catch up as surely as John Wayne had waved in any number of better-written movies.

Lieutenant Rankin, hardy soul, walked the first two miles with us. After that he never appeared except during breaks, seeming to materialize out of nowhere, looking fresh and smelling like cake. He didn't fool us, the sonofabitch, because we could hear it—the jeep—always about a quarter of a mile behind us. What he'd do was drop back off the pace, wait for his jeep, and then ride to a point just short of where we'd be taking our break. Then he'd walk through our ranks as though coming up to accept his Academy Award for special effects, pretending that he had walked all the way just as we had. And yet he had to know that we were onto him. Strange man, Rankin. As long as no one told the emperor that he had no clothes on, then he was not naked.

Ultimately we stumbled into the bivouac area, a few metal markers starkly indicating that we had reached our destination. Holdoffer moved among us, shouting at us to set up our pup tents. It had to be ten below zero. Six inches of new snow had fallen since we had started, and, once we pushed that aside, it was close to impossible to sink a tent stake into the rigid earth below. Some of us managed to do it, after which we helped those who couldn't. Even then we couldn't get the stakes in firmly enough to keep the tents from wobbling like wash on a line. It was getting dark and a wind was building, the snow ripping in circular patterns as though spun off a cotton-candy machine.

Holdoffer kept moving in and out, so strong, so transported by the role he was playing that he was almost admirable. He had a flashlight that he swung like an incense burner, and he shouted at us that we were on our own until morning. We could eat our K rations whenever we wished, and we could crap wherever we chose, as long as we made our drops at least 100 yards beyond the perimeter of the bivouac area. All of us decided against exercising our bowels for fear of freezing our jewelry off. Better to die full of shit, like a soldier, than to live on as a eunuch.

Johnny, Tony, and I set up our tents so that they butted up against one another. Another thing that Johnny had us do was to break some twigs off the many firs and pines that grew all about the area. These we spread directly upon the ground to give us an extra layer of insulation. It wasn't in the manual but we did it anyway, and, once it got dark, we told the others to do likewise, which most of them did.

When it got real dark, when the night and the snow and the wind triumvirated to completely mask our struggles, we uncapped our canteens, got comfortably high, and fell asleep. During the night I heard Holdoffer. Either he was very close or upwind because his voice had an alarming presence. I could almost touch it. Johnny and Tony heard it, too, for none of us was so stupid as to have allowed himself to get blotto drunk in so unfriendly a setting. We had consumed just enough bourbon to keep our pilot lights lit. The rest of the fuel we were saving because we knew not what the morrow would bring.

Anyway, I heard Holdoffer and he was chewing out Sergeant Deyo (RA), who was protesting in his distinctive, high-pitched, hermaphroditic voice. He was doing more than protesting. He was begging. "Don't. Listen, I need it. I got poor circulation. Listen, Sarge—Luther—" Only Luther wasn't buying. It didn't take long for me to get the picture. Before setting out on the march, Deyo had apparently filled his canteen with liquor, as had we. His mistake was in drinking too much and getting properly pissed in his pup tent, singing and laughing and drawing attention to himself. Holdoffer, alerted, had come by and was appropriating Deyo's canteen.

"Fucking old fag, what makes you think you got privileges nobody else is got?"

"Luther, please—"

"And don't go fuckin' callin' me Luther, either. It's Sergeant, got it?"

"Luther, *Sergeant—I'm* a sergeant, too. Oh, Jesus.

I've been in the army over twenty years. I'm old enough to be your father."

"You ain't anybody's father, you drunken jockstrap, shit-eating homo. Don't think I don't know you and that queen, Kuyper, aren't sucking cocks and swapping assholes."

"Sarge, please! Don't take it! I swear, I may have taken a little too much, but—"

"You get back in your fuckin' hole, Deyo! Go on! Back into your hole! Back, you mother! Take Kuyper with you, but don't let me catch you, you—"

That's all we heard of it. Holdoffer, crazy mad and probably foaming at the chops, then stomped emphatically about the area, up and down and between the ranks of tents. We could hear the crunching of his boots and the tone of his voice. He was like a revenuer looking for moonshine in the Tennessee hills, reaching at random into unsuspecting pup tents, sniffing men's breath, pulling out any canteen that smelled the slightest bit alcoholic, and all the while screaming over the wind, "You mothers! You fuckin' pencil pricks! Any of you with booze, I'm gonna bust your sausage! If you got it, get rid of it! Throw it out! Don't let me catch you with it or I'll have your noses up your own asses!"

Tony, Johnny, and I knew that he was looking for us. As stupid as he was, he knew that if some of the troops had liquor, it was *guaranteed* that Munez, Wesso and Webber had liquor. He was on an all-out seek-out-and-destroy mission. All that saved us from discovery was that our tent, unlike the others, did not protrude conically out of the snow. Ours was flat and, with an hour or two of snow on it, could look only like a harmless mound. Holdoffer never found us, and, when we began to realize that he wouldn't, we giggled anew and toasted each other and drank to all the enemies of the United

States of America, from bad King George to Mao Tse-tung, our allies all.

In the morning, Sergeant Walker J. Deyo was dead, frozen to death during the night. The snow had stopped. The sun was coming up, a wan peach blur. And the wind had blown itself out, scooting over the snow like an unseen spectre. At no time could anywhere on earth have been as still as it was where we were. Soldiers were standing around, leaning on trees or swinging their arms and marking time against the cold, their breath spiraling up like tepee smoke. And Sergeant Deyo was lying on a blanket, on his back, his beer belly a foot higher than his nose.

I don't know who started it, possibly Johnny, but soon all of us, draftees, Guardsmen, RA's and Reservists, were slowly banging our mess kits with our forks. Like imprisoned convicts hitting their tin cups against the iron bars that held them, we rhythmically voiced our protest. It wasn't loud, it wasn't angry—it was constant, slow as in the beat of an Indian's tom-tom, once every three seconds, so dirgelike that it was far more chilling than the arctic air that Massachusetts was laying on us.

Holdoffer was not the slightest bit remorseful as he explained the situation to Lieutenant Rankin. "The old homo had booze. He was drunk. He kicked off his fuckin' blanket and froze to death. It's a fuckin' good lesson for everyone else, sir."

But Rankin wasn't worried about giving lessons. He was worried about his ass. He knew from the soft din we were raising that we condemned the action and would not lightly allow the ghost of Sergeant Deyo to go out as a vapor on the morning. He looked into our faces and then looked away, totally in command of himself yet absolutely terror-stricken. He was the officer in charge. As such he was responsible even if he could pin the responsibility on Holdoffer. It would still be his ass. He looked at us again, or tried to, again feeling our wordless judgment, again unable to face us for more than a gnat's flicker.

Tony, Johnny and I hadn't moved. We stood over Deyo, looking down at his bulk. He had hardly been an ideal soldier. Like many RA's, he had chosen the Army rather than face civilian life. Now he was dead. Yet all that separated him from us was a canteen of booze that he had been denied.

Holdoffer was standing behind us. "Okay, Andrews Sisters, now that you've viewed the stiff, let's see you break down his tent and gather his gear, as he don't much look like he can do it by himself." He laughed, his foul breath seeming to squirt at us all.

Tony turned to him, speaking through gritted teeth, "You miserable shit."

"Watch that stuff, Wesso," said Holdoffer, unconsciously taking a backward step.

"Why couldn't you let him have his goddamn booze?"

"I don't owe you any fuckin' explanation, Polack. It was against regulations. Matter of fact, I'd like to see *your* canteen."

"It's on my belt. Take it from me." Tony had his feet planted and was ready to kill Holdoffer if this man moved as much as a fingernail to take the canteen.

Holdoffer considered the challenge for a moment and then smiled. "Polack, I'm gonna let you take the first punch. You know the penalty for striking a noncommissioned officer?"

"In your case—the Medal of Honor."

"Then do it, Polack." Holdoffer hung his chin out toward Tony. It was a most tempting target. "Come on,

Polack. Hit the fuckin' sergeant." Holdoffer was speaking loudly enough to get everyone's attention. He wanted witnesses and he had them. "Come on, you Polish scumbag—kiss me."

Johnny and I moved simultaneously, almost as one man, both of us knowing that Tony was about to take Holdoffer up on his kind offer. I had one arm and Johnny had the other, and together we wrested Tony away, but it was like hanging onto a crazed bull and we could have used five more men, and some rope.

Holdoffer laughed. "That's right, fuckheads! Back off! Back off, you Polish fart-smellers!"

Tony was barely in our grip and two other men had to jump in to help us restrain him. He was screaming at Holdoffer, the veins popping so prominently on his head that they looked ready to burst. "I'm gonna kill you, Holdoffer! You Nazi! I'm gonna kill you! Wait for it! Know it's coming!"

"Yeah, yeah, yeah," Holdoffer laughed as he walked away, not quite willing to take his eyes off Tony. "I'll wait. Anytime you're ready." Then he turned his embarrassed wrath on the others, screaming at them, shoving them, swatting at the air as they stepped aside to let him pass.

Tony relaxed in our grasp, we could feel the strength going out of him. "It's okay. I'm okay."

"You sure?" I asked.

"Yeah. I'm fine. Thanks."

We let him go and he walked off. He was okay. We looked at Deyo again. We had hardly known the man, never really ever spoke to him. Yet there he was, the first dead man that either Johnny or I had ever seen. I knew I'd remember that puffy, red-nosed face for as long as I would live. "What do we do with him?"

"Nothing," said Johnny. "He'll keep."

We were all heading back to the post when the ambulances came out to meet us. We had covered only four miles but, apparently, somebody had enough brains to realize that the HQ Company of the 42nd Group was out there, in killing weather and without radio contact. Colonel Cranston took the credit but later we heard that it was a captain from the 317th Field Artillery Battalion who had given Cranston the idea.

Lieutenant Rankin was transferred out of the outfit almost as soon as we got back to the post. That wasn't Cranston's idea either. That was the post IG's who, upon learning of the incident, saw to it that Rankin was in the next train west, attached to an infantry division as an officer replacement. Rumor was that he was killed within two weeks of having arrived in Korea. But that was only a rumor.

I wrote to Don of Deyo's death—just a quick note without all the grisly details. It helped me to know that Don knew.

Four men had serious frostbite. One of them, Corporal Lightman (NG) lost an earlobe to the surgeon's knife. Sergeant Deyo was buried on the post with full honors. We all attended the lavish ceremony and had the feeling they were burying MacArthur. He was awarded the Purple Heart posthumously. It went nicely with his purple cock and purple nose and purple lips. His boyfriend, Sergeant Kuyper, didn't cry. He just saluted like a toy soldier.

Holdoffer still prevailed, like an evil spirit in the second act of a morality play. Tony calmed down but, when asked, still quietly claimed that he would kill Holdoffer; he was simply looking for a way to do it without incriminating himself. There was no doubt in my mind that Tony Wesso would one day do it.

Johnny Munez went his stoic way, never connecting with anything, just allowing the days to come and go, almost reveling in them because his life as a civilian had been so predictable and uneventful—anything was an improvement.

As for me, I was merely strung out. Frustrated. I sensed the waste of time and energy. I began to pick out my own overtones in everything I was saying. Cynicism and sarcasm were my watchwords, peppering my speech, overloading my attitude. If the US kept winning wars it could only mean that our enemies were stumble-bums. And if I was to get killed in the name of the U S of A, then my ghost would find the ghost of George Washington and kick its ass back to Valley Forge.

I wanted to be W. Charles Gruber, with a limousine and a girl I could send to my friends. I wanted to be Zanuck and Skouras, kings of all creation. I wanted to be Stirling Silliphant and Josh Meyerberg and Tyrone Power and Victor Mature. I wanted to be out of the fucking Army and back at 20th Century-Fox, protecting my job against the new man in town. I missed Alice and Susan and Jessica and Patricia Jarvas and all the nameless girls at the Museum of Modern Art. I wanted to go home. To New York and Don Cook. To Pittsburgh and Elizabeth Satterly in her yellow dress. To Carmody's Junkyard, Patterson's Tobacco Shoppe. To my mother and father whom I never deserved in the first place.

Meantime I was drinking a lot of beer at night and rolling in drunk where Johnny and Tony, both of them made of better stuff than me, calmed me down and got me off to sleep and up the next day and back to my appointed tasks of guarding a door, cutting a pipe, reading a manual, answering a phone, suppressing a scream.

Letter from Don Cook:

Dear Ben,

Bad news. Terrible news. Bob Steinman. He was with this girl, in his apartment, screwing her I guess—at least that's what the police figure from the story she didn't tell all of. There was a big fire on the street and every fire truck and prowl car arrived at once—sirens all over the place. Bob must have thought he was under fire or something because, as the girl told it, he yelled "Cover!" and dove through the window. Six floors. He died on impact. Crazy story, strange guy. But we all liked him. Funeral was yesterday and it was a big military thing at this temple on the West Side. Lots of brass, very impressive. They gave his mother a flag. Anyway, I thought you should know. I'll write again soon, hopefully with better news.

Best—
Don

I read the letter three times and then screamed. If Tony hadn't been able to subdue me I'd be running still; off the post, out of the Army, back toward whatever sanity might still remain. Tony tackled me and wrestled me back to the barracks, incoherent, I'm told, for almost an hour. *Coherent* would have been a better word, for it was then that I began to fear that Deyo's death was but a preamble to Bob's, and Bob's but prologue to mine.

chapter ten

ginnie

1950

Standing out there on MacDougal Street, barefoot in the middle of the goddamn night, holding my portrait of Maggie while watching my dandy-keen basement apartment wither into embers, I really didn't have a solid thought in my head as to what I was going to do or where I was going to go or how I was not going to freeze to death in my dopey shorty nightie.

A policeman pulled me aside, a little roughly I thought, and asked if I lived in that building. "No," I said, "I always walk around half naked, selling paintings." He then turned to a fellow officer and said, "She's in shock. Take care of her." But I was gone before the law could make a move at me.

It was absurd, of course. The streets were cold, and I cut myself nine million times but I just kept on walking. To where, I had no idea. All I knew was that it was all over back there on MacDougal Street and that there was no sense in hanging around and letting my name or picture get in the papers because I was still underage and didn't want to blow my cover.

I hadn't really developed any friendships in the Village other than with Sy and Iri, both of whom lived north somewhere. So there I was, no one to go to or drop in on or even telephone.

Then I remembered that Roland Jessup lived right

around the corner from me, on Sullivan Street, and I walked there. Because of the wandering route I had taken, it took me close to an hour. After an hour walking barefoot on New York City streets, I was lucky to have arrived there with all my toes and ankles.

No bell, so I clanged the brass knocker (a lion's tongue), and Roland appeared like a genie summoned. He was wearing a violet velour robe with crimson rolled collar and golden slippers that curled up at their Turkish tips. I looked at him through the tears that had come to my five-year-old eyes. "My feet are all cut and I feel awful."

"Love your costume," he said, trying to take the edge off my discombobulation. When he closed the door, I could see that I had stepped into *Scheherazade*. Billowing curtains and drapes like the sails of faeried clipper ships, and dripping beads and cloudy cushions and different colors climbing different walls at different angles and a ceiling-to-floor portrait of a knock-out black lady in silver sequins and shining feathers—Roland could see my dumbfoundedness. "Just a few things I picked up during my voyages with Sinbad."

"Who's the chocolate sundae?"

"Josephine Baker. Who's your pink lady?"

He was referring, of course, to my portrait of Maggie which I was still clutching. "My mother."

"Couldn't get a wallet-size?"

"It *is* wallet-size." He laughed and I set the painting face-against-the-wall, as if to not let my mother see where her daughter hung out at three-thirty in the A.M.

Roland gestured for me to flop on one of his pillows. "I think the mauve will go well with your chiton."

I sat in and disappeared in the mushy thing. When I came up for air it was because my feet were being tickled. Roland was examining the soles of my feet. "Is it bad?" I asked.

"Yes. Filthy. The bottoms of your feet are blacker than mine."

We laughed and chatted and I filled him in on the events of my morning in Manhattan. He daubed Mercurochrome on my feet and asked that I walk only on the red squares of his red and purple carpet.

Roland made some tea and we talked the sun right into the window. He had an idea where I might find a place to stay, and he made me feel very safe, safer than I could remember either of my parents ever making me feel. We fell asleep amid all the pillows, with me hugging him as if he were Winnie the Pooh and him hugging me as if I were the black man's burden. It was the first and last time I ever embraced a man without feeling either threatened or shat on.

A few hours later, the sun really at work on the day, he let me wear his cape-coat and a pair of his too-big sandals. In that attire I went to my bank, managed to identify myself, and withdrew enough bucks to get some jeans, sneakers, a dumb jacket, with some money for extras. I waited in Roland's apartment for his phone call, as instructed. It came at eleven thirty A.M. At six thirty that night I was in Don Cook's endless apartment. Roland had found me a place to stay.

I liked Don Cook. He was all uptown and well dressed and spoke like someone auditioning for the part of Don Cook. He expressed only slight amazement at my arriving with only the clothes on my back, plus Maggie's portrait. But when I explained about the fire, he quipped, "All I ask is that your cow not knock over my GE three-way lamp."

The apartment was nutsville, a railroad-type thing

with different rooms like in a hotel. There were three bedrooms. One was his. One was mine. And one was Ben's.

"Who's Ben?"

"My roommate. He's in the Army."

"Ah."

"Hasn't been back since the day he left. Roland says you're a dancer."

"Yes."

"Nice legs."

"Yes. Roland does have nice legs."

"Had any dinner?"

"Nope."

"I'll split a tunafish and grilled cheese with you. I think it's ripe now."

"No, thanks. I have to get some clothes and go to work and have no time for Continental cuisine."

"You're in a show."

"Yes. The Annice Chatterton Dancers."

"They're black."

"Yes."

"And what are *you*? An albino?"

"Black. Don't let the blonde hair fool you."

"And the blue eyes?"

"A flaw in my ancestry."

"How old are you?"

"Eleven."

"You mean I should stay away from you."

"Well, Roland said there'd be no problem."

"Have no qualms, Nell. If you're eleven, there'll be no problem."

We laughed and split a flat Coke, our territories outlined, our mutual respect clearly established. He would make no demands of me other than my share of the rent and expenses. I told him he'd probably have to do all the shopping as I'd be working nights and sleeping days. He saw no problems.

I hung Maggie's portrait in my new room and hustled down to Capezio's, still open, picked up some additional workout clothes, and then went back downtown to The Blue Angel, just in time for an eight thirty P.M. rehearsal. Roland was there and I thanked him for hooking me up with Don. Roland, embarrassed at being thanked, could only shrug.

Annice worked our asses off. The little stage didn't afford us much room to go all out. To make up for it we had to shorten our stride. As Annice put it, we didn't have the Caribbean to step around in, so we might as well get used to it. Besides, there were a dozen of us—eight girls and four boys. But worse than anything else was Annice's announcement that we'd have to cut the group to fit the stage. She was sorry but it was the only way. She hoped that once the act got on the road we'd go back to the original dozen; so, following the next day's rehearsal, she'd announce the cuts. And that was it, except that we were to be there by one P.M.

Roland bought me an ice-cream soda and we discussed the problem. I just couldn't see how Annice could cut a black girl and keep me. Roland wasn't sure, though he did say that Annice was perfectly capable of making an unbiased decision. If I was a good dancer, I had no worries.

I walked the twenty-eight blocks to my new home, trying to figure out just what it was I was supposed to be doing with my life beyond wandering, dancing, and trying out new places to sleep. I stumbled in somewhere around eleven-thirty, closer to death than to exhaustion. The five flights of stairs didn't help. Don was still up, going over some papers and things. And the big lug was in his bathrobe. Uh-oh, I thought, here it comes.

He smiled at me, like a husband. "Hi."

"Not tonight, darling. I've got a headache."

He laughed, got up and went to the kitchen, and came back with a cold glass of something. "Iced tea. I thought coffee'd keep you awake."

"Oh, can I ever use that. Thanks." I took the tea and collapsed into a chair. "I think I need a shower."

"Don't worry about it. I never shower until I get fourteen anonymous letters from people in the neighborhood."

"What're you working on so late?"

"Just going over some correspondence. Ben writes a letter for every one I write him, and I owe him. Here's a picture he sent. He's the one—"

"No. Don't tell me. Let me guess."

"Sure."

I studied the photo. It was very small. There were about a dozen soldiers, all standing around in a bunch and mugging for the camera. Not all of them were mugging. Some seemed serious. But only one of them was Ben. Don't ask me how I knew—but I knew. I knew exactly which one was Ben; the one in the top row, on the extreme right, in the group but not quite, trying to look like one of the boys but not fooling me for a minute. Oh, the sadness to his even-featured face. Oh, the anger behind the eyes, the pucker to the mouth that said, "Take my picture but don't mess with me." "This one," I said. I had my finger on the face and turned the photo to Don.

"Sonofabitch. How'd you do that?"

"I don't know."

"Yeah, that's Ben. Even when he's happy he's angry. What the hell he's doing in the Army is beyond me. If there's more than three people in a room he tenses up. And there he is, in with a hundred thousand idiots, all in green, all with short haircuts, all with their individualities destroyed."

"His isn't."

Don studied the photo again. "I guess not."

"How'd you meet?"

"On the street. He was dressed in rags but was smoking a sixty-cent cigar, like an exiled monarch. Proud . . . so fucking proud. Nothing going for him on the surface, but, Christ, what insides he had."

"So you became roommates."

"Yes. Because, as I suspected, the raggedy king had a few drachmas and, with the rent coming due, I suggested a merger of our two nations. He would contribute to my depleted treasury, in return for which he would receive a naval base in the bathroom, a bedroom in which to rehabilitate, and landing rights in the other bedroom."

"Landing rights?"

"Yes." He didn't seem anxious to explain. "There were other roommates, fly-by-nights. But it's too long a story. Besides,"—he stood up and yawned—"I've had it and I'm going to sleep. Would you like to sleep with me, Ginnie?"

"Thank you, but no."

"Very well. I will ask you again, you know. It's the hospitable thing to do. But I will never force myself upon you because, judging from your legs, I might get hurt. Good night, Ginnie. I'll stock the kitchen tomorrow."

"Do you need some money? I have some."

"No. I get paid tomorrow. We'll settle up then."

"Okay. Good night."

"Good night."

Don went off to his room and I sat there alone, just me and my iced tea, which I put aside, and the photograph of Ben, which I held onto. I was so tired, so very, very tired. I really wanted to get up and take that shower, but I knew I'd never make it. The best I could do, I figured, would be to summon up enough strength to reach over and turn off the lamp. I tried, but my hand fell short, landing instead on the pile of letters that Don had left on the table. Ben's table. I was in Ben's room. I had lost my way and was in Ben's room. Crazy.

Ever the eavesdropper, ever the diary-peeper, wicked Ginnie Maitland pulled the letters over to where she lay, suddenly alive with curiosity. I had never read a man's letters before. I would have preferred them to be love letters to some nameless female, swearing eternal devotion and filled with explicit sexual details straight from the *Kama Sutra, Fanny Hill,* and de Sade. But, under the circumstances, I was willing to settle for letters from Ben to Don, especially since Ben might just be reporting on the marvelously dirty things he was doing on his time off from the Army. I sat up and read them, in order, one at a time.

Dear Don,

I am in the Army. As such I am surrounded on all sides by an excruciating lack of intelligence. I am an island in a sea of ignorance and the waves are knocking on my shore. I pray that it is only due to the fact that I arrived here at high tide and that the waters will eventually recede and leave my senses undampened.

Two men puked on the bus, which had no windows and faulty air-conditioning. At Springfield, three others bolted for freedom but were captured and flogged and keelhauled (by a bus?). At camp it was snowing and freezing. (It is not at all like summer camp. I do *not* like my counselors, and the boy in the bed to my right was jerking off all last night while sobbing that he missed his mommy. Some mommy. Luckily he hooked further to the right, so I avoided pregnancy.) All today I have been outfitted with the very kind of clothing that my mother used to throw out. The food is inedible but plentiful, so I take a lot and don't eat it. In one day I have lost 45 pounds. (Are you sure Mahatma Gandhi started this way?)

I have no friends and no hope of escape. If I send you the Queen's ring, please use it to gain access to this fucking place and get my ass out of here. I love my country but, apparently, not enough.

> Yours truly,
> Private Shit-Head Webber
> (that's what the sarge calls me)

P.S.—burn this, or eat it. Or both.

Dear Don,

I received your letter and carry it around with me next to my heart because it's very important that I know that the weather in New York is clear, with temperatures in the 30's and with no snow anticipated. You are the worst fucking letter-writer since the Count of Monte Cristo . . . and I charge you, sir, to come up with something more creative or not to write at all.

Nothing new here except that Jackie Jerk-Off has been given an honorable discharge for his discharge. Once the news got out that Jackie got out, everybody began stabbing his own individual rabbit ceaselessly. No one sleeps, the noise is unbearable, and the walls are so insulated with dried sperm that the barracks sergeant has been able to turn down our thermostat five full degrees.

It is 4 degrees above zero in Fort Devens, Massachusetts. The sky is clear and a warm front is moving in from Alabama. And if you don't write me a real letter soon, I will join the meat-beaters and end up with a forearm like Popeye and a full disability.

Yours truly,
Uncle Wethbee

P.S.—no rain in the forecast for Wednesday and Thursday, and the stars at night are big and bright, Deep in the Heart of Texas, you prick.

Dear Don,

Sorry to hear that you're not all that thrilled with the way things are going at 20th for you. I agree that, by now, you should be out of the Messenger Corps and onto bigger things, but I don't yet think it's time for panic. Certainly I don't think there's anything to be gained by going in to Gruber and suggesting that he shove the entire operation up his ass. For one thing, it is not gentlemanly. And, for another, if Gruber truly shoved up his ass everything that people suggested he shove up—well— what room would there be for your suggestion? Hang in. Give it a little time. Maybe something will break in radio-TV publicity now that management is waking up to the fact that television can be used to sell films and not fight them.

The National Guardsmen are idiots. We played them touch football and won 42-6. We gave them the six because they were threatening us with post-game shit details. If we play them again we'll try very hard to lose but don't look for miracles.

Also—there is a sergeant, a Frankenstein type name of Luther Holdoffer who is indescribably imbecilic and bestial and makes life worth living as he is a target for all our wrath. He's right out of central casting, the consummate finky sergeant. Last night we put a little surprise in his boots and it was like a dream come true.

We have instituted a program called "Draftee of the Week." It's too complicated to go into here. Suffice it to say, it's very dangerous, marvelous, ridiculous, and necessary.

> Write soon, and don't quit.
> Regards to anyone who still
> remembers me,
>
> Benedict Arnold

Dear Don,

Thank you for your letter. I'm sorry but I can't advise you from this far away. If you really can't stand it anymore then, yes, you have to quit. I just wish you had something else to go to. Also, I don't know how the hell you'll swing the rent. If we were married I could send you my allotment, but "going steady" doesn't count with the Army so maybe you'd better send back my fraternity pin. I have some bucks in the post bank which I'll send you as a money order, first chance. No, it's not charity. It's just in case I get the firing squad for killing Holdoffer. I'd want you to have that money to erect a monument to me for service to my country.

Meantime, keep looking for a roommate, someone who can help you get up the rent money. I know there's no one else who could ever replace me in your heart . . . but a buck's a buck, so don't be a schmuck.

Write, you fool,
Ben.

Dear Don,

Two things I think you must now do: 1) Tell Gruber to shove it up his ass. And 2) get yourself a roommate before you lose the apartment for nonpayment of rent. Above all, don't lose the apartment. We'll never get another like it. Ask around for a roommate. Put up posters in the office. Somebody has to know somebody.

Again I have been named Draftee of the Week and it makes me very proud. Johnny, Tony and I are very thick; it's almost fun. No furloughs yet but we do manage to get a Sunday off every now and then and we bus into Boston, go to the USO . . . and get bored to death.

I wish I were in love. Where is she? I need her. Someone to write to. Someone whose picture I can carry around in my helmet liner like in *Guadalcanal Diary*. I am in great need in that area. Write me a letter as if you were a girl. On second thought forget it. Just send me some 8 x 10 glossies of Debra Paget, Helen Westcott and Mitzi Gaynor . . . and sign them all in a different hand.

Missing in action—
Ben

That was the last letter and for some reason it moved me to tears. Ginnie "the Gush" Maitland was crying again. I placed the letters back on the table and dragged my sagging remains back to my own room. Or was it Ben's room? I didn't know where I was anymore—and I walked between the two rooms until I figured for sure that I had the right one. Then I fell upon my bed like a brick. Only it wasn't my bed because it wasn't my room. Goddamnit, it was Ben's room, the light from the hallway coming in at a different angle, outlining a different table, a different bureau. It had a different feel, too, and a different smell. And it was a different time, a somewhere else. A nice place, a safe place. I cuddled into the pillow and snuggled the blankets around me, a mouse holing up for the night. And I knew, even as I dropped a thousand feet straight down into the deepest of sleeps, I knew I'd be kept on by Annice. Ben Webber would be my luck.

I awoke. Almost noon. Shit. It took a year for me to figure out where I was and another year to figure out who. I walked into the shower like a zombie, and out like a mummy. I looked at the time. Twelve-forty P.M. Rehearsal was at one. I had twenty minutes.

I didn't quite make it, arriving at one-ten, the rehearsal in full swing. Nobody looked at me or made any move that might indicate I was there at all. To prove that I was either there or not, I got out onto the floor between Weesa and Vanessa and squeezed my body into the number already in progress.

The piano and drums were going, really going—pow, bam, zocka-zocka-*chung*! It was like live-sacrifice time. And all twelve of us dancers were jumping and leaping as if auditioning for the last Ed Sullivan show of all time. I gave it everything I had, toe-stepping and hip-churning, pushing my pelvis in directions that only an out-of-its-mind compass could track, grinding my ass north and south, swiveling my tits and shoulders east and west, shaking one knee toward Haiti, knocking the other at Minneapolis.

"Ginnie, if you're quite finished—" That was Her Eminence, Annice.

"Well—" I huffed, still dancing, unable to stop, Jumbo going downhill. "I was ten minutes late, so—"

"Please sit down," she said, and so I applied the brakes and, wet and embarrassed, found a chair in which to be mortified. Everyone else was already seated, either laughing or trying not to. How long had they been watching me go on and on like a crippled toy? Oh, well, I thought, if nothing else my Caribbean carioca had cut the tension wide open; and whichever of us were getting the ax, at least we all would have had a good laugh.

Annice was great, what a lady. "Okay, chillun. Here's the way it is. I can't cut any of the boys because all I've got is four to begin with. As to the girls, eight is just too many. I've got to cut it down to no more than six. I knew last night who I was going to cut, but I just wanted to make sure. *And,* it has nothing to do with performance, because you're all so great it's impossible to choose—except on size. I'm cutting the two shortest girls. Cramped together on stage the shortest girls just seem to lose their lines. They seem squat when what I must have is elongation. You know who you are— Diane and Betsy—*BUT,* I want you both as extras, in case something goes wrong; in case someone gets hurt or sick. *ALSO,* you'll both be on full salary, so what's everybody bitching about?"

There was spontaneous applause, followed by hugging and crying, all of us so slick that we slid off each

other like eels. There would be two more days of rehearsal before we opened. And Annice was right to
have made the cuts. With more room to move around
we were each of us ten times as good. It was a tight-knit
group. Black dancers didn't work all that much and I
knew the kids needed the loot. Anyway, we all went
crosstown to Confucius' for a midafternoon Chinese
bacchanal, all except Annice, who always stayed aloof
from the troops and also had to rehearse her own numbers. After stuffing myself with a ton of Moo Goo Guy
Kibbee, I waddled up to the apartment to tell Ben the
good news. Excuse me—*Don.*

Two men were with him and he introduced them to
me. Big Al Epstein was a mountain of a man with a
smile on it; Arnie Felsen was a little feller with eyes
the size of Rolls-Royce headlights. They all worked at
20th and none of them seemed too happy about it.

Anyway, as the conversation didn't really concern
me, I excused myself and plopped into a hot tub where,
an hour later, the Chinese food surfaced in my throat
and I thought I was drowning in the Yangtze. The walls
were so thin that I couldn't help but overhear what the
boys were talking about. That, plus my being a congenital and skilled eavesdropper, made my bath both restful
and informative.

Don's point was that they were getting nowhere and
had better face it. Also, the new man, Sam Gaynor, uni-
versally disliked, was making a strong pitch for Ben's
job. With the exception of someone named Bob Steinman, there was no one at 20th (beyond the three of
them) worth passing the time of day with.

The conversation went on and on and the next thing
I knew there was a knocking at the bathroom door.
"Ginnie? Hey, you all right?"

I had fallen asleep in the tub and Don was worried. "Huh? Oh, yeah. I'm fine. Must've fallen asleep."

"In the tub?"

"Don't be silly. On the john."

I dried off and came out, in my robe, of course. Big Al and Arnie had left, leaving Don alone with a bottle of Scotch that he was doing a good job on. He was obviously unhappy and I didn't think it vital that I tell him how well things were breaking for me.

We talked and we talked, and he filled me in on all the people at 20th, and the politics. He was teetering, I could see it. Ready to crack. All that marvelous veneer, all that poise and assurance, it was as though it were peeling off as the night wore on, chipping away, flaking off—and it was hard to keep him on the subject. In the process, I learned more about Ben, about his job at the greeting-card shop, about how great a copywriter he was, how he was such a natural and a sure bet.

Cleverly I tried to find out about Ben's love life, who he went with, the kind of girls he liked. I was very close to overdoing it when the phone call came. Bob Steinman was dead. Suicide or accident—they couldn't tell at the moment. The funeral would be the next day, Jewish people not being big on letting the dead hang around too long.

Don didn't say another word that night. He just sat in his chair and I sat alongside him, filling the air with all the gratuitous wisdom a seventeen-year-old runaway could muster. Finally, I got him to go to sleep, helping him into his room, easing him onto his bed and taking off his shoes. He was talking dopey. "You'll like Bob Steinman. He's a genuine war hero." That scared me, so I never really went to sleep, just kind of dozed in his room while he lay on his bed, in the dark, all night. His eyes never closed.

When it started to get light I took a look in the kitchen to see if Don had really done some shopping. He had lots of junk food, exactly the kind of garbage *I* would buy if turned loose in the A & P. But there were eggs and coffee and juice, so I had breakfast already going when Don came out of his room.

He was all dressed up in a blue suit, white shirt, and maroon tie. "Wouldn't have a hat on you, would you, kid?"

"Sorry."

"Well—they'll give me one at the temple."

We ate quietly, most of the chatter supplied by myself. I was tired and not very good at it. Then Don became talkative, frighteningly so, his eyes all red, magnified by the tears he refused to release.

"Bob was my last friend. I can't count on Al and Arnie. They go their own way. I don't have many friends. Never did. Scare 'em away with my large mouth. Virginia, child, you are gazing upon a jigsaw piece to the wrong puzzle. I do not fit in."

"I think you're wrong."

"Will you come with me?"

"To the funeral?"

"Got anything better to do?"

"I'll have to get some clothes."

"You've got a few hours. Come with me. Everyone'll be there. Maybe you'll be discovered."

"Yeah. By the truant officer."

We went to the funeral. It wasn't much fun. Part of it was in English and part in Hebrew, but none of it made any sense. I mean, putting a man in a box and parading him around and invoking God and telling God that He knows best. As usual, I cried, as did everybody else. An American flag was on the coffin, and a lot of

Army people had come. And when it was over, they folded the flag up very ceremoniously and gave it to a tiny woman who I guessed was Bob's mother. She accepted it very graciously, as though knowing that if she watered it every day, her son might grow out of it. I didn't know what she'd really do with it though. What do you do with a flag that's given to you when your son dies? Do you hoist it on the Fourth of July? Do you hang it in the window on his birthday? Do you flop it across the piano as a decoration? Or do you put it away in your attic? What if you have no attic? How about a drawer? Yes, you put it in a drawer. That's what you'd do with your son if they'd let you keep him. You'd put him in the drawer. "Hello, nice to see you. Want to see my son? Oh, Morris?—which drawer do we keep Bobbie in?"

We didn't go to the cemetery which evidently was so far out on Long Island that we'd have needed passports to get there. Big Al led me out of the temple. Arnie Felsen led Don. Jews seem to know what to do at funerals. I felt very lonely, very vacant. Somebody I almost knew was dead. And somebody I wanted desperately to know was almost there. It was all very mixed up. They put Don and me into a cab and sent us home, like we were deaf-mutes in Afghanistan.

Don was laughing. So I asked, "What's so funny?"

"Arnie got his notice to report. He got it this morning."

"Is that funny?"

"No. It's hilarious. We put Bob away and send Arnie to take his place. What else could happen to fill out this grotesque day?"

What else could happen was in the mailbox when we got back. A letter from Ben.

Dear Don—

We buried Sergeant Walker Deyo today. On the post. Full military honors. He wasn't much, not really. A fat little man who drank so much that he pissed 100 proof. He joined us on a little bivouac in the cold and he froze to death by morning. It was Luther Holdoffer who was responsible, but it's the Army that creates the Luther Holdoffers. Tony will kill Holdoffer. It's just a matter of time. Everyone knows it. And if he doesn't then Johnny and I will. And if we don't, then God will. Like I say, Sgt. Deyo wasn't much. But yesterday he was alive, and today he isn't . . . and as Arthur Miller wrote, "Attention must be paid."

My best to you all. And please give a special hello to Bob for me. The knowledge that the Armed Forces can turn out men like him allows me to accept the facts of this very cold day without running AWOL to the moon.

> Oh, to be in Vienna again—
> Ben

Don read the letter to me aloud. And when he put it down, he said to me, "Ginnie, my child, the world is on its last legs. It cannot stand up another year." He said it without hysteria, as a simple statement of fact. I didn't contest it because I suspected it might be correct. It was awful. I couldn't help Don. I couldn't help Ben. I could barely help myself.

The next day, first thing in the morning, Don quit his job at 20th. Just as I had returned from a shopping spree and was coming up the stairs, he told me.

"Well," I asked, " do you have another job?"

"Nothing."

"Is that smart?"

"No. But it's necessary. I'm never going back. It's a master stroke."

True to his word, Don never went back.

We opened at The Blue Angel. Smasheroo! Two shows a night and every show sold out. We had a full seven-piece orchestra and lights that swirled oranges and yellows so hot that the front tables got sunburned. Yes, there were real people out there, some of them rude, yes, but, for the most part, they were appreciative. And applause. We had applause. I had never heard it before—and what a glow it gave me. Only a few of the kids had ever danced professionally, and, when we came off following our first number, we were so stratospheric that to the casual observer we had to look like junkies. In any case, I was hooked. I mean, I just loved it. Pow-bam, zocka-wocka-*chung*!

Reviews? They were great. Almost all of them mentioning "the tall blonde girl in the all-black group." I was interviewed a couple of times but stuck to my story, maintaining that I was a Negress and proud of it. The reporters didn't know what to do with that one so they just quoted me and let it go at that. Roland was very helpful in that area, heading off the ratty columnists and steering me only at the good guys.

We were all having a fine time. We worked hard, yes, but you work hard in a turkey, too, only without the praise and the money and the applause. My first professional job and I was a hit. The *Variety* review praised Annice, of course, because she was nothing short of brilliant. I mean, she took the floor tall, loose-limbed, a brown python so slinky-sexy that every man in the audience had his tongue out so far that it looked like his necktie. But there was also this nice paragraph about me:

> . . . special mention must be made of the one, it would seem, Caucasian in the group. Her name is Ginnie Maitland, and, though she claims to be from the inner regions of the Dominican Republic, she more nearly looks as though she hails from the outer reaches of Sweden. Long-legged, blond and blue-eyed, she dances so convincingly Negro that, five minutes into the lush choreographic jungles of Haiti, her story of being the albino daughter of a black coffee-worker father and a black cotton-picking mother seems almost plausible. In any event, her presence as one of the Annice Chatterton Dancers is no mere concession to publicity— the girl is good, very good. Check that—the girl is *marvelous*.

We ran for six weeks and could have run forever except that the bookings were piling in from out of town where the clubs were bigger and the money better. And so we all got ready to go on tour—Chicago with Danny Thomas, Cincinnati with Polly Bergen, St. Louis with Martin and Lewis, Pittsburgh, Denver, Los Angeles, San Francisco—supporting the biggest names in the business. And, in some cases, *we* would be the headliners. We, the Annice Chatterton Dancers, and me, Ginnie the Jungle Girl.

My life opened like a pat straight flush. And money was burning holes in my leotards. I bought fantastic clothes at the three B's (Bloomingdale's, Bergdorf's, and Bonwit's) and people actually knew me when I traipsed down Fifth Avenue like it was my own private street and what were *they* doing on it? I was not yet eighteen but looked older. Men were sending me flowers but Roland kept me away from them, saying that they only wanted me for the thrill of bagging a black girl.

I liked Don. Very much. I respected his mind, he was so clever. But I was also drawn to him by the sadness that was gathering around him. He was looking for work but was coming up empty. I couldn't blame him for turning down those so-called great opportunities. They weren't great at all. They were dead ends; over-the cliff hopes of landing in a pot of honey. Why couldn't the world see what he had to offer?

He would be up when I got home and, as tired as he was, was always pleasant in our predawn chats. He always had something waiting—coffee, tea, hot chocolate, cookies, crackers and cheese—something, anything. It was all wrong, of course, and we both knew it; but it was our own little platonic world and we enjoyed it to its fullest, especially since we both knew that it was all winding down, coming to some kind of natural end.

I didn't sleep in Ben's room anymore but I still allowed that fantasy to fester because I really wanted a lover and Ben was perfect because he couldn't say no. I would talk to his picture, sleep with it under my pillow, and pray that he would come out of the Army in one piece and soon. It was a little sick, I must admit, and dreadfully juvenile, but so was I. And his letters, more mature than in the beginning, contributed to my belief that he was really with me, in the apartment, in my room, in my bed. And many's the time I'd fall asleep, hugging the hell out of my pillow, sleeping lengthwise alongside it, pushing it down to my belly, wrapping my legs around it. Sick, sick, sick, but nobody knew but me and God; and one thing about God—he could keep his mouth shut.

Letter from Ben:

Dear Don:

I have no words of wisdom for you. You're right, you just have to sweat it out. Yes, the travel business sounds good so, yes, you should pursue it. But even then, don't be too hasty. Don't go jumping right in.

Winter is showing signs of leaving town, for which I'm grateful. It's been a bad time for us all. Holdoffer still swaggers but he's calmed down a little. Methinks we make him nervous (me, Johnny & Tony), so he tries to steer clear of us. Tony still swears he'll kill him and we all have a fine time devising various perfect crimes.

Met a fine female in Boston, serving coffee at the USO. Very pretty, very charming, very well-educated. Society, I think, but it's all been surface talk so far. I keep finding myself drawn to her, so I go there whenever I can get off the post.

New York is still too far to go and come back from in just one day and, as the new company commander, Lt. Collings, is a stickler for there being no car accidents because of guys speeding back to camp to make Monday morning roll call, we simply aren't allowed to go further than a fifty-mile radius. Still, some guys do it, and—if I get desperate, I may just pop in on you.

With winter doing a slow fade, spring is kind of whispering into the picture. It's strange how spring and autumn are so alike and yet such inversions. You can wake up on a day in either April or October—the air, the temperature, it can all be indentical and yet you know there's a difference. Spring, I think, is a promise whereas autumn is a threat. One says life and the other points to death. I'm glad it's April and not October and I hope that, any day now, you'll be glad, too.

My best to your Ginnie and tell her that I thank her for taking such good care of you and our place.

Let me know the minute something happens,
Ben

My reaction to that letter was twofold. First, come home, Ben! Come to New York! Break the fifty-mile radius line and do it soon, please, before I leave town! And second, Ben, you bastard! How can you be playing with a girl in Boston when you know how very much I love you here in New York?

Sy Fein called and asked if he could come to see me. I took it to be a bad sign. Up till then my checks from the restaurant had been coming in pretty regularly—thirty dollars, forty, thirty-five, thirty-seven. Each week, the extra money I'd put in my new bank. Don was out on an interview somewhere, so when Sy arrived I was alone in the apartment. I hadn't seen him in months. After the fire and my move uptown, we conducted our business on the phone and through the mail. And when he stepped into the apartment, oying from the climb, I suddenly realized how much I'd missed him, so I gave him a hug to end all hugs, saying, "Oy, my Jewish mama!"

"Hello, Blondie." He stepped back, holding my hands in his big paws while looking at me. "It is you, no?"

"Yes! You dope!"

"I couldn't be sure. From all I've been reading I expected maybe a colored girl."

"I *am* colored."

"Thank you. And I'm Cardinal Spellman." He looked around at the apartment. "Nice place. Big. You live here by yourself?"

"You *are* my Jewish mother."

"Just asking. Of course, what do I know from modern living? Maybe you sleep in one room on Monday, Wednesday, and Friday and in this other room on Tuesday, Thursday, and Saturday. And look at this—a Sunday room. Some business. Tsk-tsk-tsk."

"Sy, I don't live here alone."

"A boy or girl? Don't tell me."

"A boy."

"I told you not to tell me."

"His name is Don."

"*Uncle* Don, he's not."

"He's very nice. It's very platonic. We're sharing expenses."

"Why tell me? It's none of my business."

"Sy, it's okay. I swear. I promise."

He smiled. "Good. Mind if I sit?" He sat. "That's some flight of stairs. A man has to be a human fly."

"It's so good to see you again."

"It won't be so good the next words you hear."

"What's wrong?"

"First, let's talk about *you*. I hear great things. You're a star, yes?"

"Well—"

"Now, let's get down to business. The restaurant is dying."

"Why? What happened?"

"Who knows? People stop coming. The quality of the food was never better but suddenly we're out of vogue. Also, a ridiculous restaurant opens two doors down. Absolutely ridiculous. You ready to hear about it?"

"Ready."

"Take a guess at what it's called."

"Schrafft's."

"Close. It's called The Outside Inn. And right next to it, three doors down, take a guess at what its partner is called."

"Well—"

"You guessed it. The Inside Out. I give it three weeks. Meantime, to stay alive for those three weeks, Sayonara needs more money—to stand the gaff, as Iri says, whatever *that* means. You go in business with a Jap and you have to be prepared for strange things to happen to your native tongue."

"How much do you need?"

"Another five hundred dollars, but I can't accept it."

"What?"

"I can't let you do it. Forget I asked."

"But you did ask."

"Make believe I didn't. I'm going. Good-bye and good luck."

"Sy, I can give you the money."

"You must be out of your mind."

"I've *always* been out of my mind. I'll write you a check."

"I can't accept it."

"But you came all the way *up* here."

He smiled. "To bid an official good-bye to my blondie partner. Also, to give you your last check from the last profits, which was two weeks ago if a day."

"Oh, Sy—"

"Don't 'oh, Sy' me. It's no big thing. Here. Three dollars and forty-six cents. Invest it wisely. I hear Coca-Cola is a good thing."

"But you're going to let the restaurant close?"

"I already let it. Last week." He waved at last week

as if pushing it out the window. "But it's not all that bleak. Iri and I got some of our money out of it. Iri's going back into service, in the kitchens of Mrs. Samuel Pincus, in Scarsdale, where he'll lay low and make a comeback next time there's a Pearl Harbor. As for me, guess what? I'm going for number seven, my new lucky number. A candy store on Third Avenue and East Thirty-second Street. A prime location for bankruptcy. If you're ever in the neighborhood and you need a Raisinet or a Goober, come in and I'll overcharge you only slightly. Until then, Blondie—Alf Weeder's son."

He was at the door, smiling, his huge arms stretching toward me, beckoning for a hug. I ran over and hid there.

He patted my back, as if to burp me. "You're some Blondie. Ready to give me another five hundred dollars at the drop of a needle. If I was thirty years younger— you wouldn't even be born yet." He broke away and went down the stairs. "Keep in touch. And don't forget, Third Avenue and Thirty-second Street. Guess what it's called?"

"What?"

"Sy's Candy Store. Has a good ring to it, yes?"

"Yes."

"Good-bye, Blondie. Let's have lunch." And he was gone, oying his way down the five flights of stairs, the top of his red head descending like a Jewish setting sun.

So—I was out of the restaurant business. I felt bad, not for myself because I was swinging, but for Sy. He was so damned unstoppable. I knew they'd never beat him down. If I could have crossed Sy Fein with Don Cook, what a hybrid I'd have had—a brilliant, tireless, verbal, gutsy character that could quote Spenser while spicing it, in meter, with dramatically interspersed *oy*'s.

I tooted over to The Blue Angel where we'd be closing after that night's two shows. Annice wanted us all to meet following the last show, at which time she'd give us our itinerary, our tickets, and tell us how we'd be living on the road.

The nine o'clock show was great. But the midnight show was like we had never been before. I mean, the beads flew, the skirts unfurled, and the drums rattled the pots and pans out in the kitchen. Like a jungle telegraph. We were soaring. Annice was inhabited, stepping around in her black glory, and the rest of us got right up in the trees with her. I counted twelve curtain calls before the stage manager decided that enough was enough and left the curtain drawn.

Still in costume, still steaming like race horses, we assembled backstage where Annice applauded us and we applauded her and each other—and then we all collapsed on the floor, laughing and crying and not knowing what the hell we were doing.

Annice made a lovely speech, very courtly, in her precise English just tinged with Jamaican sing-song. It was all filled with gratitude and hope, running over with visions of how far we'd be going, how much of America would see us and love us. Roland gave us our tickets and instructions as to where we were to meet the next day—what time, what train—all that. Then we cheered like Notre Dame and broke up like we'd never see each other again but would always remember our beloved alma mater.

I looked at my ticket and my typewritten instructions and at the little note I almost missed because it was stuffed so far back into the envelope. It was from Annice; would I please come to her dressing room?

Where all the kids shared one barnlike room backstage, Annice, as befit her station, had her own dressing room. I went there fearfully, wondering if the plans hadn't changed, if maybe I had indulged my "black" image so much that Annice felt I was stealing her thunder. I knocked on the door so softly that not even I could hear.

"It's open," Annice called. I went in and sat down. Annice was in her shower. Her dressing room was very Afro-Cuban. Wood sculptures, ebony, and weird and exotic draperies. It was almost as nice as Roland's. "Ginnie?"

"Yes."

"Relax. I'll be right out. Sit down."

I tried to relax in that one big chair, stuck out in the middle of the room all by itself, as if for the third degree. What an odd place to put a chair.

In a few minutes she stepped out of the shower, a coffee-colored princess, six feet of statuesque majesty, moving lightly, in sections, one pushing the other, like a snake—dreamlike, almost in slow motion. Wow. Nude, she glided over to her red robe, hung on a big brass hat rack. I had never seen her naked before. None of us had. She wrapped herself in the robe, drew it closed, and made a loose knot in the belt to hold it. "Well, Ginnie, what do you think?"

"What do I think?" I was punchy. Her perfume was everywhere, something like Jungle Gardenia.

"About our show. Our future. The fun times ahead."

"Oh. Well—I think it's sensational."

"We've got to economize on the road a little bit so we'll be doubling up, all of us." She poured some rum into two small glasses and handed one to me. "You'll be with me. I hope you won't mind." She stood there, sipping her rum.

"Mind? I'm flattered." I took a sip of rum and it flew to my toes. I looked down to see if they hadn't lit up like Christmas bulbs.

"I'm flattered, too. You're a very lovely girl. Skin."

"Pardon?"

"Skin is what it's all about. The texture of skin. You have beautiful skin, Ginnie."

"Yeah, well, keeps my bones from falling out."

She laughed, but I was beginning to get a very bad message, one I hadn't expected and didn't want. She moved about like a lioness, so graceful that I had to continually look to see if her feet were truly touching the floor. Even her hair was special, short but rich-looking, silky. I had never been aware of her hair before because she had always been wearing a turban.

She circled the entire room, as if she were stalking me, two times, three, coming closer each time until, finally, she was standing directly in front of me. She reached down with those long fingers and held my face so that it looked up into hers. And she smiled down at me. "Ginnie?"

"Yes?"

"What do you know about me?"

"Well, I know you're a great dancer and—"

"I mean, what have you heard?"

"Heard?"

"Yes."

"Nothing."

"Really?" She was untying her robe and drawing it back like a curtain, and I was suddenly looking at that exquisitely sculpted stomach—flat, muscular, yet classically female. Mocha and marvelous. "Give me your hand, Ginnie."

Only I wasn't interested. "Listen—"

"Give me you hand."

I wriggled free and stood up, knocking the chair over. "Excuse me, but I think you've got the wrong girl."

"Do you?" She was still smiling, undismayed.

"Yeah. You see, I don't know about these things and—"

"There's nothing to know."

"Well, I think there's a couple books I should read, and I think I ought to go home and brush up on my Sappho."

"You're frightened."

"Well—I'm a little off guard."

"Is it because I'm black?"

"No. It's because I'm yellow."

She laughed. "Oh, Ginnie, you are a marvelous thing, truly." And she started to glide toward me again.

"Thank you, very much, but—I've got this dentist's appointment and it's in a half hour and—"

"You'll make it."

"—it's in Phoenix. Arizona?"

"Ginnie, we all have our little perversions, you know."

"Oh, I know."

"Mine is skin."

"Mine is being on time for dentists' appointments."

Her smile was vanishing. "I'm not about to chase you around the room, Ginnie."

"I'm very sorry, Annice. I wish—but, I just—it's not for me."

"I gather."

"So, er, though I'm terribly flattered and all—that you like my skin—you ought to see it in the summer, when it's peeling. Looks awful, like a skinned rat."

"I understand." She knew that the romance was over.

"Also—I'm having my period, and—when I was a kid, in China—"

"You may go now, Ginnie."

"I'm really very sorry, Annice."

"And please don't come back."

"I guess not."

I got out of there and heard the door slam behind me. Then I bumped into Roland, which wasn't exactly accidental because he was waiting for me. And I knew that he knew. I walked passed him and on into the big dressing room. It was empty.

I sat down before the mirror and began removing that awful stage makeup that had, by then, turned into rainbow-smeared oatmeal. In the mirror I could see Roland come in. He stood behind me and we played the whole scene through the mirror, very dramatic.

"I was hoping it could be avoided."

"Thanks for warning me, old buddy."

"Darling, if I told you ahead of time, you'd never have been able to dance."

"No, but I'd have been able to run."

"I was hoping that Annice would not give vent."

"Give what?"

"Vent."

"What's that, another Jewish word? Why don't you people speak English?"

"She gave vent, didn't she?"

"Yeah. She gave a whole lot of vent. She gave, and I vent. So it all worked out."

"Virginia, you did the right thing. You live with Annice, on the road? With that 'skin'? She'd have you doing things that haven't been invented yet."

"It's just so damned unfair. I never would have turned black if it also meant I've have to be a dyke. Oh, well . . . I think stars should quit when they're at the top."

I went back to the apartment, deep in philosophical thought. In less than eight hours I was out of the restaurant business and out of show business. Don was awake, waiting for me, and in a good frame of mind—not because anything particularly wonderful had happened to him that day, but only because he was aware of what a wet blanket he had become. I told him about what had happened and that I quit and that my restaurant had folded and that I didn't want to live anymore and that the two of us were the losers of the world and that we should sign a suicide pact and climb to the top of the Mark Hopkins in San Francisco and plunge into the Hudson, leaving no notes, just bubbles.

I was tired, punchy. Don helped me undress and led me to the shower, which I cried all through. He pulled me out before I could turn into a prune and wrapped me in a big towel. He led me to my room, helped me into my bed, pulled the covers up to my nose, gave me a daddy kiss, and said he loved me. I said I loved him, too, only I called him Ben.

Poor Don, how that must have hurt. Poor Sy Fein whose lucky number was 577 only didn't know it. Poor Bob Steinman, just a neatly folded flag in the front parlor bureau. Poor Sergeant Deyo, deader than last week's news. Poor Little Rich Girl crying herself to sleep.

ben

1951

The deaths of Bob Steinman and Sergeant Deyo, coming so close together at a time when my own hold on reality was none too secure, had turned me self-destructively inward. I did my jobs, I did what I had to do to earn my keep in the Army, but I maintained very little contact with anyone other than Johnny and Tony. I was kept additionally off keel by the continuing news that Don was having as much trouble hanging on in the outside world as I was having hanging on in the Army.

Facts became elusive, untrustworthy. If someone said it was Thursday, I had to think about it for a day or two before I could accept it. If someone said "Good morning," I'd find myself thinking, "What did he mean by that?" Tony, a good Catholic, suggested that I have a chat with the chaplain. Johnny, a bad Catholic, said I'd be better off talking to Charlie McCarthy.

My temper had an exceedingly short wick and I knew it. I had been an ornery loner my entire life and there, in the middle of more pointless humanity than I had ever before had to elbow around in, I was a vial of nitro with the jostle tolerance of a mile-high souffle.

All that saved me from spontaneous combustion were those weekday nights and Sunday afternoons when I was able to get off the post. On most of those I went into Boston without Tony and Johnny. They were good about it, never felt hurt or acted miffed. My definition of a friend, from that point on, has always been someone who, out of love or loyalty, blindly elects to understand behavior in another human being that is incomprehensible, indefensible and maddening. They helped me, those two. Even alone, walking the Boston Common along any one of a dozen radii, I could feel Tony and Johnny alongside me. When my war with the Army was over, I would strike a medal for each of them—the Ben Webber Decoration for Unflinching Friendship Under Fire—the last recipient of which was Don Cook.

I didn't really know Boston except as a place to catch a bus to from Shirley, Massachusetts, having earlier switched over from an Army bus at Ayer, the whole trip so wretchedly long that it left precious little time to do anything other than stagger into the USO and sit in a corner and wonder why I had gone there in the first place.

There were ladies (not many) at the USO piddling about, serving coffee and conversation in equally tepid doses. During World War II, I had heard, the USO really jumped. But WWII was over, and all the drama and romance surrounding it had eased into the history books with it. This "Korean thing" lacked the glamour of its predecessor. It didn't have the dynamism and propulsion to inspire that its departed sibling had generated. And those of us poor khaki-clad slobs who inhabited it seemed more victimized than heroic. One had to look no further than the hostesses on the job. No heiresses or Beacon Hill Brahmins or high-cheekboned tennis-playing Celtic princesses had we, just itinerant housewives, high-school kids, petrifying matrons, and a couple of pratish alcoholics—with one exception.

I never got her name my first two times there because I was never really alone with her, there being other eagle-eyed servicemen able to separate the pearls from the oysters. Also, where the other hostesses wore name badges that screamed their identities, *she* chose to go nameless, a decision I respected in that it paralleled my own feelings about the Army; "In a garden where all that grow are weeds, flaunt not your name but rather go nameless—in hopes that someone, anyone, may see you as a flower."

Anyway, either because she had been unaware of it and someone had reminded her that she wasn't wearing her badge or because it was a rule that some USO official insisted be followed, when she smiled at me on that drizzly Sunday she was wearing a badge, and the name on the badge was Mrs. Barringer.

I don't know how old she was. To this day I am an inept judge of a woman's chronology. To me Deanna Durbin in her heyday looked a chubby fifty-five, while Ingrid Bergman, if she lives to be 109, will always be twenty-three in my heart. What did bother me was her marital status. Pretty presumptuous of me, I'm sure you'll agree, to think that the "Mrs." on her badge was all that would preclude her falling in love with me. But that was my initial reaction and my face must have shown it.

"Are you all right?" she asked, her face cocked quizzically sideways so that only one green eye showed.

"So that's your name. Mrs. Barringer."

"Yes. What's yours?"

"Ben Webber."

"Some coffee, Ben?"

"No. I'd just like to stand here and look at you."

"Then you'd better have some coffee." And she drew a cup from an urn that, in a prior life, had been a deep-sea diver's helmet. "Here you go."

"We've talked a few times before, you know."

"I know. You're stationed at Fort Devens."

"Most of us here are."

"True," she said, nodding at the *A* patch on my arm. "First Army."

"Yes. And I hope it's the last."

"You're always by yourself. You see? I do remember."

"Thank you. Sometimes I feel invisible."

"You're hardly invisible."

"What does that mean?"

She drew back. "It means we're talking in a manner that is not all that proper, considering who and where we are."

"Well, I know who I am, but who are you?"

Her smile was tinged with admiration. "All that charm—and you're only a private?"

"In civilian life I'm a general."

Two bumpkins came by and wanted coffee, so we were interrupted for a few moments. I took note of her figure when she turned away from me—so trim in flower-print blouse and navy-blue skirt. And how well she moved, likening the giving of doughnuts into the knighting of knaves. "I'm off in fifteen minutes." She had turned back to me and was smiling.

"Where can I meet you?" I knew I was being outrageous but I didn't care. It was like a game that both of us knew we were playing, the young soldier and the beautiful lady. Hardly an original script but tried and true, and she wasn't exactly discouraging me.

"There's a side entrance," she said. "Do you know it?"

"I've seen it, yes."

"I'll meet you there, but—I do have to go home."

"Fifteen minutes."

"Fifteen minutes." And again she turned away, three

sailors garnering her attention. So casually did she look away and not look back that it occurred to me that she would never show up, because she'd never remember, because I was simply not worth the remembering.

Still, it was about as exciting a thing as had happened to me since last I saw dreamy Elizabeth Satterly glide past me in Pittsburgh. I went around to the side entrance. It opened on a street that hosted very little traffic. In fifteen minutes she appeared, out of the side door. As she did, an endless black barge of a limousine sidled up, stopped, and a liveried chauffeur popped out on cue, holding the door open for her.

She took my arm without breaking stride. "Come on, Ben, I'll drop you at the bus depot," and I was sitting beside her in the moving limousine. She smiled coquettishly. "Like my flivver?"

"Yeah. It's cute."

A glass separated the front and rear sections and she spoke to the chauffeur through an intercom. "Fletcher, can we drop Private Webber at the bus depot?"

"Yes, Mrs. Barringer."

"But I don't *want* to go home," I said, feigning a lower-lip sulk. "I want to go with you."

"Mr. Barringer might not appreciate that."

"Isn't he playing golf or something?"

"He doesn't play golf or something."

"My bus isn't for three hours."

"That's the last bus. There's four before that."

"Tell Fletcher to take us to Kansas City."

"You're a very precocious young man."

"In that case, tell him to make it Chicago."

She said nothing, just slipped her arm through mine and pulled herself very close to me. It was an undeniable gesture of instant affection, unedited, candid, and clearly indicative of things to come. Then she bounced back to the way she was, as if to apologize for having taken such a liberty.

"You can do that again, if you like," I said.

"Some other time."

"When?"

"Some other time, I don't know." She moved further away, withdrawing her arm from mine. "I'm sorry. I shouldn't have done that. It's not to be misinterpreted." She spoke into the intercom again. "Can we go faster, Fletcher. Private Webber mustn't miss his bus."

Fletcher, evidently having once driven at Indianapolis, sliced in and out of what traffic there was as if the passenger section was on fire and he wanted to stay ahead of the flames.

"You're trying to get rid of me," I said. "That's no way to treat a serviceman."

She was contrite. "Can we stop all the sparring, please?"

To which I could think of no retort. We drove on, silently, inexorably toward the depot. She had so disarmed me that I began to fear that I was out of my league. A few phrases I might have said did come to mind, but vanished before they ever reached my lips.

With her eyes on Fletcher's rear-view mirror, she spoke to me without noticing me. "If I tell you where to reach me, if I give you a telephone number—can you remember it without writing it down here?"

"Yes."

And looking out her window she said, "It's a private number in Wellesley Hills. 534-9766. Do you have it?"

"534-9766."

"If I'm not there, tell them you're the Greenway Florist and ask when you can call back."

"All right."

Fletcher was guiding us into the bus depot. "If you don't call," she said, "it's all right."

"If I don't call—I'm dead."

Fletcher's voice on the intercom: "We're at the depot, Mrs. Barringer."

"Thank you, Fletcher." She turned and smiled at me and drilled me like a secret agent. "Tell me the number again."

"534-9766."

"Well, then," she said, her smile broadening, "here we are."

The car stopped and Fletcher was holding the door open for me. I smiled at her and played out the game. "Thank you for the lift, Mrs. Barringer. I'd have missed the bus for sure."

"My pleasure, Private Webber."

I watched the limousine pull away. It looked like the Queen Mary. Then I walked over to the bus which wouldn't be leaving for forty minutes. I got on anyway. Moving from the limousine to the bus was like going from caviar to farina, and I had to convince myself that the whole thing had actually happened. I wrote her number down on two separate bits of paper, one of which I put into my shirt pocket—which I then buttoned—and the other of which I put into one of my back trouser pockets. I buttoned that one, too. Unless I lost my shirt and my ass, I would always have that Wellesley Hills number.

The thought of Mrs. Barringer sustained me. It came with a rush in the morning and it sat on my shoulders through all the collecting hours of the day. It lay beside me at night on my painfully narrow cot—the flowers on the blouse dropping off one by one until the pair of us lay naked, clasped together in a bower of blossoms,

Johnny once waking me with a rude shove to say, "It's okay to hump your mattress, Benny-boy, but the fucking bed squeaks. So how's about you go to the latrine and beat your pudding and let the rest of us monks sleep?"

There were letters from Pittsburgh, from my parents with whom all was going well, letters I answered immediately rather than allow to gather because I knew that, should I ever fall behind, I'd never catch up—and my parents deserved better than that. Funnily enough, I kept in closer contact with them in the Army than I ever had in New York, because they were more concerned and I was more dutiful.

Luther Holdoffer, still an infernal figure, strutted less annoyingly that week because I knew that, come Sunday, I'd call that number in Wellesley Hills and speak with that fine lady and arrange a rendezvous and, in so doing, cause the foul sergeant to disperse like a fart on a breeze. And the earth, parched where he had stepped, would spring green in a miraculous reaffirmation of life and love. And it struck me that the time the army sliced from a draftee's life could be made amazingly tolerable, providing that that man had some dream to retreat to— a face, a smile, an implied promise, a self-deception, even an outright lie. All that was required was a living creature with an honest-to-God identity to attach it to. A badge on a lapel would do, "Mrs. Barringer" immediately coming to mind.

On Thursday of that week I received a letter from Ginnie Maitland:

Dear Ben,

You don't know me but I know you because I've peeked at your letters to Don and, I must say, you do use naughty words. I think you know I'm

living in your apartment and that I contribute to
the rent which is why I'm writing.

Don has been very low because nothing is happening for him and this morning, when I got up, I
found that he was gone. He left this note which I
think you should read before you read the rest of
my letter.

I turned to Don's letter which Ginnie had clipped to
hers.

Dear Dancing Lady,

I am off to Los Angeles, but don't ask me why.
I woke up at 3 A.M. and it seemed a good idea at
the time. I've used up New York and I have to
face it. I can't get a job here even as a derelict, so
why not give L.A. a shot?

I know I'm hanging you with the rent money
but maybe, if you write to Ben, he can knock over
a PX and send you some loot.

Please apologize to Ben and yourself for me, but
I'm suffocating here so I'm heading West. I will
send you post cards, and, hopefully, some sheckles
to keep the bank from foreclosing, but until I do,
please do whatever you can to keep the pad. The
Landlord comes by the first of each month and
asks no questions if you pay him in cash. Hail and
farewell—

Love—Don

I resumed reading Ginnie's letter.

So you see, Don is gone, which is bad enough.
But I'm not working (a long story). I do have

some money but have been living off it for a couple weeks while trying out for some shows. Nothing seems to be open and when it is, they always go for the girls with musical comedy experience.

Anyway, I'm writing to alert you in case my money runs out. Meantime, don't send any money till I tell you to as, who knows, I may get a job and the whole crisis will blow over. My name is on the little mailbox downstairs so I do get mail—only nobody writes because I don't know anybody who *can* write, except you. Will you be my pen-pal?

Respectfully yours,
Ginnie Maitland

I folded both letters away, placing them into my footlocker. Things were changing in the world I'd left behind. A triple play was occurring in the old apartment—Jessica to Don to Ginnie—and, unless the ump was blind I was out at home. I could only hope that Ginnie would find a way. Meantime, my immature sense of honor dictated that I send the girl some money—a money order for $150 plus an encouraging letter: "Yes, I will be your pen-pal if you will stay on and make me pockets. Love from Never-Never Land—Peter Pan."

Sunday came and I bussed my way to Boston. Immediately upon disembarking, I dialed the enchanted number—534-9766. A woman answered, a maid. Mrs. Barringer was away and would not return until the middle of the week, would I care to leave a message? Yes. Tell her that the Greenway Florist called and that they will call again, some other time.

What an idiot! What a callow simpleton to not have phoned *before* leaving the post. What incalculable illogic to have come all the way to Boston on the teenage assumption that my love lay waiting where the lilies grew.

On the outside chance that she might be at the USO I went over there to see. No such luck. Finding it impossible to drink giraffe-shit coffee or play Ping-Pong or suffer any exchange of dialogue with the autowaxed ladies on duty, I went back to the depot and caught the next bus, another disheartening triple play—Boston to Shirley to Ayer. I wasn't exactly "out at home," it was more like "left at the post."

The barracks were empty. Only a fool would hang around on Sunday, and I was looking at him—in the mirror over the sink where I was splashing water onto his stupid face. The next time I looked, there were *two* fool's faces—mine and Holdoffer's.

"Hello, Hollywood," he said, flashing those brown-glazed teeth with the little sweaters on them. His breath hit me full in the face, prompting me to wash it all over again, two sinks to the right. He followed me. "Nothing to do on a Sunday?"

"I've already done it. I slipped a bomb up your ass when you weren't looking. Please don't be near me at five-fifteen."

He laughed, landing his big hand on my shoulder. "Hollywood, you got style. I think we should be friends."

"Let's discuss it at five sixteen." I shucked his hand off and walked out of the latrine and back into the barracks. He followed me like a witch's familiar.

He smiled and sat on Johnny's bed. "Hollywood, we're gonna be awardin' PFC stripes soon—couple weeks maybe. My recommendations are gonna count. Wooncha like to be a PFC?"

"Yeah. In the Russian army. Will you leave me alone, Holdoffer? And while you're at it, take a shower.

You smell like a bag of year-old jockstraps. And brush your teeth, too. Teeth are not supposed to have moss growing on them."

He refused to be riled. "You got the makins of a good soldier, Webber. We'll be goin' overseas soon. You can be a corporal by the time we ship out. More pay. No shit details."

I put the magazine down and looked at him. "Okay. What do I have to do for it?"

"Be my spy."

"Okay. Consider me your spy. Just call me X-9." I picked up my magazine again. "I'll expect my promotion by next week."

"Wesso's out to get me. He's crazy and he makes me nervous. What I mean is—" He was picking his nose with his thumb. "—I could use a little advance notice on anythin' he's plannin' that has to do with me, okay? I'll keep it fuckin' confidential. I mean, you're no use to me if I tell people where I'm gettin' my information from."

"Too risky."

"Think so?"

"Yeah. If I was to spy on Wesso, you'd have to make me, at the least, a captain. Unless—"

"What?"

"—unless you sweeten the deal with a little cash."

"Forget it."

"Then it's no deal."

He thought about it. "How much cash?"

"Ten bucks for every piece of information I give you."

"I dunno."

"Then let's just drop the whole thing."

"No. Let's *do* it."

"Ten bucks in advance. As evidence of your good faith."

"Five."

"Seven fifty."

"Five, Webber. Take it or stuff it."

"What if I can't get any information?"

"Then you don't get paid."

"I don't know."

"Whaddya think, I'm stupid, Webber? Come on." He could see that as I thought it over my position was weakening. "Yes or no, Hollywood. I ain't got all day."

I played it all the way. "And you'll put in a good word for me? About the promotion?"

"That's what I said I'd do."

"Well—okay," I said. "It's a deal."

Some people are stupid but they know it and can deal with it. They are the *smart* stupid people. The *stupid* stupid people are those who are so stupid that they think they're *smart*. Holdoffer not only fell into that category, he owned it.

I told Johnny and Tony about it, of course, and we rolled on the floor laughing. And each time I'd pass Holdoffer, he'd whisper to me, "Anything?" and I'd nod no and he'd walk away, shrugging, as if to chastise me with "No info, no money."

Finally, to demonstrate that I really was digging for information, I told him of one of Tony's discarded plans. "Luther, stay out of the Day Room tonight. Wesso and two others are gonna jump you, throw a blanket over you, and drop you in the grease pit." Holdoffer smiled, peeled off a five-dollar bill, and nodded his comprehension of the insidious plot. To establish the veracity of my information, I made sure that Holdoffer saw Tony, Johnny, and Morgan return to the barracks that night carrying a blanket and some rope. Holdoffer winked at me, as if to say, "Keep up the good work."

The weekend struck and I phoned 534-9766 from the post. Again the maid and again the same story—Mrs. Barringer was away. And again I left the message that the Greenway Florist had called. I didn't go into Boston that day. I went into Leominster, about eleven miles off the post. Nothing specific in mind. I just wanted to get away and be by myself. I wandered around rather aimlessly because the whole town was Sunday-closed. Then, after having sat for three hours, ducking pigeons, I returned to the post, bothered by the disquieting hypothesis that the lovely Mrs. Barringer had only been playing games and never had any intention of honoring her tacit promise of wild and unbridled sex. Still, she had given me the correct phone number. If her purpose had only been to knock the starch out of me, why wouldn't she have given me some phony number? Why risk my saying the wrong thing to whoever might answer when I called? It was all a touch unsettling and I could have done nicely without the guessing games.

Letter from Ginnie Maitland:

Dear Ben,

Thank you for the $150. I put it in the cookie jar which I bought with three dollars of it. So there's only $147 in the cookie jar plus a couple quarters which I really must save for the Laundromat. Anyway, the pressure's off. After working as a waitress in a pizza palace, I got a job! "Guys & Dolls"! My favorite show! I can't believe it! I was one of four girls selected! I start in two days. Wish me luck because I AM SCARED! Also, I get to say some lines! How's *that*? I'm a star!

No word from Don yet but I have to tell you about something because maybe you can shed a little light on it.

I came home from the market and there was a girl in the apartment. I asked her what she was doing there and she asked me the same thing. I told her I lived there and she said she did, too, and she showed me her key. Her name is Jessica and she seems to know all about you and Don and also says the lease is in her name and in the name of two other girls named Susan and Alice and that it was in a drawer—and there it was.

Would you explain it to me, please? She is an airline stewardess only I think it would take a bomber to get her off the ground. Also—she brought this man with her, a Captain Stykes, who flies for another airline but who is sleeping with Jessica. I put them in Don's room and told her you were in the army and she sent you her regards and disappeared for the night.

Question is, do I charge her for part of the rent? Do I charge Captain Stykes? Shouldn't they pay for food and electricity and linen and such? Should I change the lock on the door? And what do I do about Captain O'Neill who is sleeping in your room and coming on very strong with me? What kind of place are you running here and can I get in trouble because I'm underage?

Please call as it is quicker than a letter and you can reverse the charges because we're splitting the phone bill anyway.

> Confusedly yours,
> Ginnie Maitland

I called Ginnie late that night.

"Ginnie? It's Ben."

"Ben?"

"Yes. I got your letter."

"Ben? Is it really you?"

"Yes."

"It feels so weird."

"It's me."

"I mean, I feel like I know you. And here I am, thinking about what to do, and the phone rings, and there you are."

"Here I am."

"Wow."

"Congratulations on *Guys and Dolls*."

"Thank you, but what do I do about Jessica?"

"Nothing. She's your guest."

"Well—she's all right. It's just that she acts like she owns the place."

"She does."

"Yeah. I knew you were going to say that."

"Is this Captain O'Neill giving you trouble?"

"He's gone."

"Ahhh."

"Captain Hennon took his place. *He's* giving me trouble."

"Can you handle it?"

"I think so. Yes. I just wanted—verification. From you. That this is the way it is."

"That's the way it is."

"Am I ever going to meet you? Do you ever get a furlough? I mean, I think I miss you. Does that make any sense?"

"Some."

"I mean, it's like I know you very well."

"Really?"

"How you doing with your girlfriend in the USO?"

"Pardon?"

"I've read all your letters. I told you."

"Oh. Well, she's away."

"And Holdoffer? He still giving you a hard time?"

"I can deal with him."

"Well, I don't know what else to say except—I'm glad you called and cleared things up. It was very nice speaking to you. Give my regards to Johnny and Tony."

"Yes. I will."

"Will you call again? It's nicer than letters and you can make it collect."

"Well—I'll try. First chance."

"Bye, Ben. Take care of yourself, okay?"

"I will. Bye, Ginnie."

And we hung up. It was the strangest conversation. We'd never met yet she knew all about me. It was—provocative. There she was, living in my apartment, socializing with my friends, concerned with my welfare, and I didn't even know what she looked like. All I knew was that she was a dancer with long legs and was good enough to be in a Broadway show. Period.

A few days later—sonofabitch, there it was on the bulletin board. I had made PFC. Whether or not Holdoffer had anything to do with it did not stop him from pulling me aside and taking full credit, reminding me in the process how one hand had effectively washed the other, to which I suggested that with both hands he effectively wash *himself* lest some nearsighted gravedigger with a highly developed sense of smell come by and, thinking him dead, bury him in a trice. Holdoffer found that very funny and laughed, his breath enveloping me like a sheet of hyena spoor.

Tony and Johnny congratulated me, saluting me all

the while, and, were it not for the fact that five other draftees had received similar promotions, I'm sure that I'd have been drummed out of the Draftee of the Week program. As it was, if the NG's had wanted to destroy our subversive movement, they could not have come up with a better way to do it than to give us promotions. Somehow, with that extra stripe on our sleeves we were less prone to be capricious. Anyway, though it still survived, the Draftee of the Week program had received a telling if not fatal blow by the promotion of six of its most vindictive members to the dizzy rank of PFC.

Flushed with glory and wanting to tell someone, I phoned Ginnie to tell her the news. The kid was half-asleep and kept congratulating me on having made lieutenant. I hung up, feeling at odds with destiny.

I then called the magic number in Wellesley Hills, what the hell. Again the maid and again my spirits flagged. But wait! What was that? Mrs. Barringer was *in*? Oh, unbelieving heart, to have had so little faith! I waited, trying to think of what I might say to her. Telling her that I had made PFC suddenly had all the chic of telling my old Aunt Frieda that I'd learned to ride a bike. Telling her how much she was on my mind could only be followed by my asking her to come with me to the pep rally. Telling her that her breasts were like pomegranates and that her—

"Hello?"

"Mrs. Barringer?"

"Yes."

"Greenway Florist."

"Who?"

"Greenway Florist. *You* know."

"Perhaps you'd better refresh me."

"Ben Webber. You told me to call."

"Oh—Ben! Of course! How *are* you?"

"Fine. You've been away."

"Yes. Down to the Islands. It was lovely."

"That's nice."

"What's on your mind, Ben?"

"What's on my mind?"

"Yes."

"*You're* on my mind. I've called a couple times."

"Yes. I'm sorry."

"I left messages. Like you told me."

"Yes."

"I'd like to see you."

"Yes—well. I'd like to see you, too."

"I'm off Sunday. Should I come in to the USO?"

"No."

"No?"

"Meet me at the Ritz-Carlton. Do you know where it is?"

"I'll find it."

"I have a room there. Room 503."

"503."

"503. When can you be there?"

"In the morning. Eleven thirty—twelve."

"All right. Don't ask for me at the desk. Just wait for me in the lobby. Only—don't notice me. Give me five minutes to get to my room, then come up. I'm sorry, but—"

"I understand."

"Room 503, Sunday. All right?"

"Yes."

"Ben?"

"Yes?"

"I want you . . . Sunday. Good-bye."

"Good-bye—

—darling." I said the "darling" after I'd hung up. I wanted to say it over the phone but didn't want to appear too forward. What a day! I had made PFC and I was going to make Mrs. Barringer! What a parley! Like leading the league in stolen bases as well as in home runs. How could I miss being selected Rookie of the Year?

It was Tuesday. If Wednesday came, could Sunday be far behind? Could anything stop Sunday? No, nothing short of dyspepsia. I knew I had to stay healthy, lots of sleep, proper diet. Be careful crossing streets, cut out sweets (ooo-ooo). Keep my nose clean, stay on the good side of Holdoffer. Pass inspection. Check the duty roster—was I on KP that weekend? I looked. I wasn't. Sunday, eleven thirty, the Ritz-Carlton, Room 503. The whole fucking globe could blow up on Monday, it wouldn't matter as long as I had my Sunday with Mrs. Barringer.

Tuesday made its way into history with nothing untoward blemishing its page. I hit the sack early that night, disdaining Tony's and Johnny's suggestion of a couple beers and another Doris Day film at Post Theatre Four. They were curious but didn't press me as to why the sudden introversion, for they were beginning to understand that I could never be understood. I did not sleep an hour Tuesday night but it was a sweet insomnia, Mrs. Barringer populating my head, heart, and other vital organs.

Wednesday was monumentally uneventful, couldn't have been better. A few rain drops but better the rain in midweek than on the weekend. Thursday the rains came, tall black clouds collapsing on us. So great a deluge did occur on Thursday that it could not possibly rain again for a month of Sundays. Twenty hours of it had turned the company streets into impassable swamps. Even the indomitable jeep could not progress a yard without first giving up a foot. I loved it, the smell of freshly drenched earth so damply clean. Thursday was inspirational and I wallowed in it, slogged through it like a mudcaked moron, kicking at it like Tom Sawyer, coveting it like John Silver his treasure.

Friday? Friday was not a good day. Friday my luck ran out. Friday the mud turned to shit and the stars to bile.

Some fool of a general (time has mercifully obliterated his name from my memory), having nothing particularly important to do, took Friday to discover that the men of the 42nd Group HQ Company had never gone through the infiltration course. Delighted with the news because it had been such a dull day until then, the general rang up Colonel Cranston and pointed out the oversight. Colonel Cranston, an heroic boot-licker, was quick to state that he had been waiting for just such a rigorous day on which to schedule that most vital maneuver and that he would get on it immediately, which he did after first assuring the general that he had been typing up the order when the general called.

With a bare fifteen minutes' notice, we were all of us called away from our pertinent jobs (me from watering Lieutenant Colonel Beakins' potted miniature pine tree). I mean *all* of us—NG's, RA's, US's and Reservists, the latter group bitching all the way to the area in which the foul deed would take place. And I mean bitching, because they had done it in combat years earlier and there they were again, in the twilight of their service careers, having to walk, full packs, three miles off the post because the 6×6 transport vehicles selected for the task had sunk into the mud halfway up their wheels upon venturing out of the motor pool.

So it was shanks' mare through the gook, the slop coming up and spilling over the edges of our boots no matter how well we bloused and rubber-banded our fatigue cuffs. Five steps out of the company area and we could just as well have been barefoot. The only difference between the mud inside our boots and the mud outside our boots was that the mud inside was warmer—and was laced up.

The sun was incongruously shining, heightening the insanity of what we were doing by playing a spotlight on our fretfulness. From our waists up the mud had dried and caked like cow dung, allowing us all the freedom of movement of a plaster of paris cast. From our waists down the mud ran and oozed like unset pudding. We slid, slipped, fell, cursed and continued—and got there feeling no sense of achievement in the arrival.

The only vehicle to make it to the infiltration course was the ambulance. Without the "meat wagon" there could be no exercise. It was regulations. It parked off to the side, staffed by three men—a bald captain and two bored medics.

None of our officers came that day because they suddenly had thousands of things to do; therefore, it was Sergeant Luther Holdoffer himself who had gotten us to the course. A lesser man could not have done it. A better man would never have attempted it. Only a Holdoffer would have enjoyed it, haranguing us, cursing us, moving up and down the line like a demon, dominating us with his will, destroying us with our own accomplishment.

It was so degrading, so invalidating to be squishing around in all that primordial slime that we were past complaining. Standing about in lumpy groups of three and four, it was as though we were about to be executed, right there, and it all seemed fitting, for, like fools, we deserved to die, if only as payment for the folly of having followed.

Before us was the infiltration course. It was about

forty yards wide and a hundred yards long, like a football field. Only no Bronko Nagurski could have made it
across. There was barbed wire everywhere, haphazardly
strung out, no pattern to its many directions, no thought
to its configurations, just barbed wire, a menacing crisscrossing of steel designed to passively rip flesh if at-
tacked head on.

And there were rocks. And holes. And dips and gul-
leys—all of it filled with a glutinous mud. The ungodly
field looked as though the battle of Verdun had been
fought in it five times, as though the French and the
Germans had hacked away at each other in it, jumping
from trench to tree stump, following the command of
some fool of an officer with a whistle and a pistol. I felt
as though I had stepped back into 1917 and that it
would never be 1918.

Facing it all, as if set up smack on the middle of the
nearest goal line, was a thirty-calibre machine gun, its
ability to traverse the field clearly restricted by the rectangular wooden brace through which it protruded. The
machine gun could move laterally rather freely. It could
spray most of the field from side to side, but two vertical stanchions, one left and one right, prevented it from
moving further sideways and thus firing off the course.
The machine gun could not move vertically at all. Two
horizontal guardrails, one above the barrel and one below, both running parallel with the imaginary goal line,
allowed the machine gun not an inch of vertical play.
The bullets would pepper over the course at the precise
level of the machine gun's barrel, thirty-six inches
above the ground. Anything below thirty-six inches
would not be hit; anything above it would have its ass
blown off.

The machine-gunner was an experienced man (judging from the hash marks on his sleeve) who wore cor-

poral's stripes and a troubled skin. He sat behind the weapon, looking so much a part of it that, had he been painted black, one would have been unable to see where gun ended and man began. He was not in battle garb but rather was incongruously decked out in his dress khakis, obviously having been called as suddenly away from his office work as we had been. And he seemed more interested in not muddying his uniform than in readying his weapon for its scheduled task.

The range officer, a captain, also seemed a bit teed off at having to be there that day. He, too, was in his Sunday finest and it disturbed me that he was so shamelessly lackadaisical about what he was there to do for on his ability to instruct us depended all of our lives. Never had an officer such undivided attention. Never were troops more restive.

Sergeant Luther Holdoffer, who himself had never gone through the infiltration course, called for our attention. "Okay, you men, look at me. This here is the range officer, Cap'n Mackie. He will explain everything to you so give him your attention so's he can explain. Cap'n Mackie . . ."

A couple idiots in the rear applauded. It did nothing to contribute to Captain Mackie's happiness. A stolid man, graven and paunchy, he placed his hands on his hips and addressed us in a dialect so "suthin" that it came at us as if out of a cotton gin. "Maybe yawl won't think it so funneh bah the tahm this day is out."

"Settle down," quacked Holdoffer. "This is for your own good so give him your attention, you muthahs. Sorry, Cap'n."

Mackie droned on, talking dully and by the book, as if reading last year's minutes. We had to strain to hear what he said and it went, give or take the English language, something like this:

"This heah manoovah will have two beats. Fust, yawl do the course without any fah. It will be a drah run to innerduce you to the turine an' the obstacles thereon. Second, yawl do it again *without* it's bein' a drah run. Yawl do it under fah, under combat conditions. The ideah bein' ta do it raht the fust tahm so that the second time yawl do it even rahter."

He turned his back to us, facing the course, so that his voice became totally garbled. "This heah is the machine gun witches loaded with bullis, among witcher traysa bullis witch'll come out wunnin evra fahv rowns. Yawl see 'em inna ayer buvyo haids. Keep yo butts down an' yawl be air rot. Astoe the barbra wyer—one man lyzon his back an' hols the barbra wyer wahl thuthah man slits through the space, an so on an so fawth. A haht of thutta-sex inches, blow witch yo oh rot, but above witch, man, yawl stan up too hah an you ass gonna flah toe Bawstun town an' beyon. Carra yo weppin, keepin it clara mud. Get mud in you weppin an' yo gonna have to do it again. Axes to the fah enna this course is gain via slit trench awf to the raht. Yawl will go ten men atta tahm, lannin' up inna slit trench dreckly oppsit wheyah ah am now lookin'. Spread out proxly three-fo yahds tween each man. When yawl heah the whistle, yawl come ovah the top of the slit trench an' head back heah. Raht in frunna this gun izza nothah slit trench. Yawl reach it an' yawl okay. Yawl jess ploppin an' crawl out. Thenna nex groupa ten men move out."

Caesar having thus addressed the Roman Forum, Captain Mackie strode gingerly over to the mud where his jeep and driver were parked. He climbed in, wiped the mud from his trouser cuffs, gave Holdoffer some kind of high sign, and then sat in the back seat of the jeep as if he wasn't there.

"Okay," Holdoffer shouted, "you heard what the

man said. Single file into the trench on the right and move down to the far end. Move it. Move it."

We obeyed like barge slaves on the Nile, walking knee-deep in the slop-marsh, through the side trench toward the back trench.

"It's hot shit. That's what we're walkin' in," grieved Tony who was in front of me. "We're clamming in hot shit." And he shouted to the others. "Don't eat the clams, men."

Johnny was for laying back and he restrained me. "Go last."

"You're crazy," I said. "The last ones to go will be over their heads in this shit. It'll all be loosened up. We'll drown."

"No," said Johnny, also pulling Tony back. "In the dry run, I wanna see which wires are the easiest to get under, which ones guys get stuck on. And on the second run, I wanna see where the charges go off."

"What charges?" I asked.

"They're spotted all around," said Johnny. "Stuck in the middle of rocks, strung around with barbed wire. You can't touch 'em and they can't hurt you. But if they go off when you're near 'em, they're gonna knock your teeth loose and you won't hear for a week."

"Where are they?" I asked. "I don't see them."

"They're supposed to be marked with whitewash but there's no whitewash out there today," said Johnny.

I cautioned him. "Johnny, if you're standing and looking when they blow—"

"No. The tracers'll show which direction the machine gun is moving in. When they're goin' over the far side, I can pop up and take a look. Listen, dummy, do as I say."

One thing about Johnny, if he said he knew something, then he knew it and wasn't to be questioned by mortals. Tony and I dropped back with him. We'd be the last to go, which was fine with the others because they, like me, figured it was best to go first.

The first ten men made the left turn into the back trench and took up their positions as instructed. Johnny then leaned against the wall of the trench we were in and poked his head up to reconnoiter. A whistle blew and the first ten men went up and over. I wanted to see, too, so I poked my head up alongside Johnny's, and Tony stuck his head up alongside mine.

"Fuckin' rifles are fulla mud," said Tony, trying to wipe his rifle barrel clean.

"They're *all* full of mud," said Johnny. "Forget 'em."

"We'll have to do it *again*," said Tony.

"Everybody'll have to do it again. Don't worry about your rifle, just your ass. And shut up. Just watch."

We watched the first ten men suffer their way over the course, some of them with their tails so high that, if the machine gun had been blasting at the time, the very least that would have been shot off would have been their canteens. We could hear them grunting and talking to each other, instructing each other where to go, who was to hold the wire, did anybody see an extra rifle? Some of the idiots were even giggling.

"When we go," said Johnny, "no talking. Just gestures and hand signals."

"Why?" asked Tony before I could.

"Because on the second run the gun'll be going and you won't be able to hear *anything*. Look at where Pollar is. That's where the wire is easiest. Look at that, even fat Morgan got under that one." Johnny kept up a running commentary, pointing out things that would be useful when our turn came. The only noise that interrupted us was the noise of the guys bitchin' in the mud, calling to each other, and, of course, Holdoffer at the far end, bellowing out his own expert observations.

"Stovall, Morelli, Kirkpatrick—your asses are up! Get 'em down! Ransom, you moron—hold the wire for the next guy! Move it! Move it! That shit hardens, you'll *never* get out!"

"Best place for us is the far side, about ten yards in. The ground is lower. We can get under the wire easier." That was Johnny.

Holdoffer was going strong. "Who is that? That you, Fusco? You ain't that old! Move it! Newland, Aronson, Lightman—that ain't no beauty bath! Stop *layin'* in it! Get *out* of it! Move it! Move it!"

"Okay," said Johnny. "I got a fix on it. Just let's stay together, the three of us. It's better than two."

The first group of mudders completed the course. It took them about four minutes. They plopped into the front trench beneath the stoical machine gun, some of them head first, their legs waving so high in the air that, had they been under fire, their legs would have been shot off at the knees.

"Don't do it that way," said Johnny. "When you get to the front trench, *roll* into it—sideways. Drop into it. Don't dive."

I peeked up to see what was going on back at Captain Mackie's jeep. Nothing was going on. The man had his hat off and his face to the sky. He was sunbathing. At the ambulance, the bald captain and his two henchmen were having a difficult time not laughing. I began to feel as though I were in the Roman Colosseum. The citizens were enjoying the spectacle but the Christians weren't too thrilled.

Holdoffer blew his whistle and the next group of ten went over the top. By then the course was considerably more muddy and, in no time, faces became as obliterated as uniforms. Everyone looked like wounded alligators, slithying in the tothe. Even Holdoffer couldn't make them out, and when he chewed them out he couldn't do it by name. It was just "You there! Get your fuckin' head down! That man on the left— congratulations! You just loss your ass! Move, you niggers! Move, you fuckin' black samboes!"

Johnny had a few more observations, which Tony and I listened to very carefully, as did a few other men in our vicinity. There wasn't much laughter anymore. The comedy had waned. The realization that we could get killed had finally gotten through to us. The second group made it in five or six minutes. Basically, they made the same mistakes that the first group had made, it was the mud that added to their time. Too bad there was no officer to point out their errors.

The whistle blew and the next group flew over the top and damned near drowned in the glop, which was more liquid than earth, going more readily down the windpipe.

Our group's turn came. We slid ourselves over the top and looked over the lip-high muck. "Don't shout, you'll make waves," gurgled Tony, quoting the punch line of a very old joke. We could barely discern the barbed wire. Pulled at, torn at, coated with mud, it so perfectly blended with the brown-drown that we couldn't really see a strand of it until we were practically stuck on it. But Johnny had marked our course well in his head. He went first, then me, then Tony. And we were good. We were flat and we were fast, working as a team, slipping between the wire, sliding over the mud, communicating with each other without a word. We reached the front trench and rolled in. I had put no clock on it but it was fast, well ahead of the rest of our group. Even Holdoffer was impressed as he watched the three of us pull ourselves out like seasoned retrievers.

"Who's that?" Holdoffer said. "Ah, the Polack, the spic, and the kike." (He winked at me as if to say, "I'm calling you kike so as not to blow your cover.") "Pretty good. Pretty good." He shouted to the rest of the group that was still mudding in, "You assholes—you let these three scumbags beat you to the goal line! What the fuck is the world coming to?"

We got to our feet and scraped the mud off ourselves as though our hands were windshield wipers. I noticed Johnny looking at something and Tony and I looked, too. One of the stanchions supporting the machine gun brace had settled slightly into the viscous earth— enough so that, if the machine gun were to be firing to the left (the side *we* would be on), the bullets would travel at a slightly lower elevation than the prescribed thirty-six inches. By the same token, if firing to the right, the ground clearance would be slightly more than thirty-six inches. If the stanchion were to settle into the mud no further, the differential would be no more than an inch on either side. But it could be an important inch. Johnny nudged me and said "Signals off. We go to the high side." Tony and I nodded.

The dry run completed (it was hardly dry), Captain Mackie deigned to come down from his perch. He tippy-toed as though through tulips so as not to get un- necessarily soiled, picking his way over to us assembled mudcakes and addressing us anew.

"That was fahn. But ah do not believe theyah is one clean raffle among yo, so ah guess yawl jess gonna have ta do it again."

And we did. All over again. Another "dry" run. Not that any of us cared a fuck by then. It was just that the sun was beginning to set and the bog was beginning to chill, and if men could get arthritis and lumbago from just one such exposure, we'd be bent into pretzels by moonrise.

When we picked ourselves out of the mud following our second dry run, Johnny, Tony, and I took notice of the machine gun stanchion. It did not seem to have settled any further.

"Seems to be okay," I said to Johnny.

"Wait'll the fucking gun is being fired," said Johnny.

"Shouldn't we point it out to them?"

"I suppose so."

"You want *me* to do it?"

"Holdoffer's your friend, not mine."

"Okay."

Captain Mackie, in his jeep throughout the second dry run just as he had been through the first, was again tippy-toeing toward us as I drew Holdoffer aside. "Listen, Luther," I said, "that machine gun is gonna hook to the left when fired. Maybe you ought to point it out to Mackie."

"You're imagining it, Hollywood."

"Look at the stanchion. It's already sunk an inch."

"You chicken, Hollywood?"

"No, I'm not chicken, death-breath, I'm just observant." The slob was pissing me off with his superior stupidity, and, cold and miserable as I was, I simply blew my cool. The old hair-trigger Webber temper.

Holdoffer looked at me, wincing in annoyance. "What'd you say Webber?"

"I said you were a shit-faced fuck-up and, to support that statement, you'll get my letter in the morning."

He shoved me. "Get your ass back with the others, kike." And he shoved me again.

"What's this?" asked Captain Mackie, by then standing alongside us.

Holdoffer wasted no time. "This man don't want to do it anymore, Captain. He's a little yellow Jew and—"

"Now, now, Sergeant," said Mackie, suddenly the voice of tolerance. "No need for rayshill sluhs." And then he looked at me and he was not so tolerant. "Yawl do it, soljah—else yawl do two and a half yairs on the rock pahl, ah do bleeve."

"The machine gun stanchion's sinking in the mud, Captain—"

Holdoffer broke in. "It isn't, sir. He tried that on me. I measured it and it is not sinking. He just plain don't wanna do it."

Again Mackie was tolerant, but barely. "Ah know yawl scared, boy. But the day is turnin' dark an' we got no tahm foe cowardice. Now, the sergeant says he checked the gun an' that it is fahn, an' so that is fahn with *me*, so—"

"Sir," I said, hanging in like Larry Leech, "if you will examine it yourself, I'm sure you'll—"

And Mackie blew. "Ah am not gonna examine *nothin', boy*! Yawl can get in lahn with the othahs, or yawl can drop out and face a courts martial, and not the chief Rabba of Droozlim's gonna save yo bacon!" He had to smile at his own wittiness.

The case for my pressing the issue further was fading quickly, especially with Johnny a few feet away from me, clearly indicating by face and gesture that I should drop the issue and get on with the rest of my life.

"Yes, sir," I said to Captain Mackie. "But if it does slip, I will bring the matter to the attention of the post inspector general and—"

"Back in line, kike!" said Holdoffer, shoving me so hard into Johnny that the both of us almost toppled. Tony caught us and kept us from belly-wopping in the mud.

"Stupid bastards," I muttered.

Tony was straightening me out. "Come on, Ben. You ain't gonna win that one."

"The fucking stupidity—it's like a disease!" I was so angry I was shaking, my hands clenching and unclenching as if they wanted to hit someone. They were not totally under my control.

Captain Mackie moved ahead in the day's events. "Vurra well, men. Yawl have had the 'vantage of two drah runs. An' now it is tahm yawl did it with lahv ammo. No big trick, jess do what yawl did the fust two tahms, rememberin' t'keep flat onna groun' at all tahms as that machine gun is gonna whip awf anythin' flahin' too hah in the skah. Ah should point out that they is a coupla charges gonna go awf at very-us innivals, but—if yawl jess pay attention to what yawl is doin' it shoont cause yo' enna hodship whotsoevah. Carra on, Sergeant."

And Mackie began to tippy-toe back to his jeep. But the evening was taking on a chill and the jeep was uncovered, and so he glanced over at the ambulance and, noting that the two medics and the bald captain were warmly ensconced inside that vehicle, he executed a tippy-toe turn and joined that privileged trio inside the ambulance, where it was warm and dry. In so doing, Captain Mackie disappeared from our view and his post.

We all filed into the side trench, third time. And again Tony, Johnny, and I lay back at Johnny's insistence, watching the others trudge to the head of the line.

"Shouldn't we go first and get it the hell over with?" asked Tony.

Johnny nodded in the negative. "Fucking gun's liable to sink with the first round that's fired."

"But, if it doesn't," I said, "it just might do it on the *last* round."

"Could be," said Johnny. "I don't know. Could happen any time or not at all. Luck of the fucking draw."

"Shouldn't we tell everyone to stay over to the left?" asked Tony.

"God damn it, Tony! It's every stupid slob for himself!" It was the first time I had ever known Johnny to get angry and it got me a bit nervous, like watching the Rock of Gibraltar twitch. "We can't have *everyone* on one side!" Johnny went on. "We'd be crawlin' all over each other!" He softened, faking a smile. "Listen, relax. It may never happen. Just stay to this side and let's get through the fuckin' thing as fast as we can. That way—"

The whistle blew and the men in the first group went up and over, not as an integrated group of soldiers, but as rabble, as ten straggly bugs with the perception of a blur. And all hell broke out. The first thing we heard was the machine gun, blatching like a jackhammer into a microphone, splitting the air and shaking trees. Then we saw the promised tracer bullets, coming as phosphorescent fingers that pointed over the course at ten-yard intervals, purpling by so low that they almost seemed to be at ground level. The tracers sprayed over the course like a well-regulated garden sprinkler, fanning left to right and back again, the gunner obviously knowing his trade, the stanchion obviously holding. With the tracers swinging and flying over the far side of the course, we stuck our heads up like groundhogs to see what we could see.

The men were so low in the mud, pressing themselves so passionately to China, that there was no way any of them was going to get hit. Also, I had the suspicion that our machine-gunner had somehow elevated his weapon because the tracers very soon seemed to be going over the course in a noticeably ascending line, disappearing over the far end at something like five feet above ground level. It pleased me to know that somebody back there had some sense and that our buddies, unaware that they had nothing to fear unless they jumped up and sang "Apple Blossom Time," were all the same performing the maneuver admirably. The tracers came swinging around and back toward us, so we ducked.

Some charges blew, not as loudly as they might have had they not been so buried in the ooze, but loud enough; and, when the tracers speared over the far side of the course, we again popped our heads up to see how our boys were dealing with it all.

They were dealing with it well, going about their muddy business, crawling through the paste, spreading the wires for one another, aiding and abetting one another and, for one quick moment I could see why America did well in her wars. It was because the average buck private, the lowest man on the totem pole, be it by instinct or conditioning, even when commanded by twerps and nerds, was able to take care of himself in untidy situations. And I found myself cheering them on so loudly that between the machine gun and the cheering I was unable to hear the grating bellow of Holdoffer's voice.

The first group made it without incident, somehow knowing not to dive into the safety trench but to roll into it, instinct triumphing over panic, marvelous. The machine gun relented and we watched the gunner feed another ammo belt into its side. The charges ceased, too. I only remember four of them going off, five at the most.

"Six," said Johnny and I figured he knew.

The whistle blew and the next ten men went over the top. Again the machine gun ratcheted. The tracers flew, three charges blew, everybody cheered—and everybody got through. It was a game and the good guys were winning.

It continued on until there were but two groups left. Tony, Johnny, and I were among the last ten men who would go. We moved into the back trench, taking the places of the men who had gone up and over when the whistle had sounded. The tracers were still zipping over the course, still passing over our heads by that very comfortable five feet. It was so clear that no one was going to be hurt that we stood straight up and peered over the rim of the trench like box-seat customers. It was a mistake.

Just as Johnny said, "Stay over to the left," because Tony and I were too far to the right, the machine gun stanchion sank into the mud as though driven by a sledge hammer. I could see the tracers suddenly cutting at too low an angle, and Tony's head flew away, his helmet clanging like a shooting gallery gong.

I couldn't believe it. He was still standing next to me, still holding his muddy rifle, but he had no head and blood was gushing out of the tubes in his neck. It bubbled and fountained down his field jacket, over the caked mud, down his trousers, mixing with the slime below—all that precious blood. I grabbed his neck with both hands, trying to cover it, to stop the blood from leaving, but it kept coming, gushing out from between my fingers, spurting, pulsating, shoved out by an angry heart. I was crazy, shouting at the headless body, "Cut it out, Tony! It's not funny! Cut it out!"

Johnny was pulling me away. I looked into his face and it was frozen. I screamed, pulling Tony's body to mine, hugging it, trying to make it well, rocking it as if it were my baby.

The firing had stopped. I looked around at the men standing in the trench with me, at their faces. They all looked hollow-eyed dead, spotted about like skulls in a cannibal's hut. Some turned away and groaned, and slipped. Some vomited.

I looked at Johnny—Johnny Munez—so chillingly calm. "Ben, let go." His voice was so controlled that it quelled my hysteria. And I relaxed my hold on Tony and Johnny took him from me, gently, allowing Tony to settle into a sitting position—a headless soldier taking a break. At ease, soldier. Rest.

Then the sounds began to filter in. Crying. Moans. And not all of it was coming from our trench. Some of it was coming from over the top. Johnny was steadying me. "You're all right, Ben. You are. Ben?"

"I'm all right."

"You know what happened?"

"The stanchion gave."

"Right." He peered over the top and I did likewise. The men to the left were crawling in every direction, some toward the finish line, some toward the side trench, some back at us. The men to the right, four of them, had been hit. Only one of them was moving. Lying on his back he was raising his hand in the air, his index finger pointing up as if hailing a cab. I couldn't see who he was.

Down at the far end, nightmarishly, Holdoffer was raging, yelling at the machine gunner. "Shoot shoot shoot! Who told you to stop! Shoot shoot shoot!"

But the gunner had no intention of loosing another round. He just sat at his gun, attempting to secure it so that it could not do that again.

Holdoffer was screaming into the gunner's face, all that foul breath, "They gotta *learn*! It's *part* of it! Commence firing, Corporal! Commence firing! Corporal!"

There was movement back at the ambulance. The

medics were in motion, readying equipment they never thought they'd have to use. They were fussing with a stretcher, dropping it twice into the mud, face down. The bald captain was sloshing clumsily toward the wounded, slipping, getting up, swinging his arms scythe-like to gain leverage over the mud. He had forgotten his helmet and his head looked like a white ass.

Only Captain Mackie was motionless, evidently unwilling to dirty his uniform. He just stood there, surveying the scene from the ambulance, as if watching a dull polo match.

Johnny was looking at me, his eyes searing into mine, his voice terrifyingly controlled. "That's the enemy, Ben. You hear me, Ben?" There was blood in his eyes. Real blood. His eyes were bleeding. Something had popped in his head, some vein, some something had given way and the whites of his eyes were red. "And now, Ben—now we go after them." And casually he climbed, up and over, and I went with him, walking toward Holdoffer, toward where that man was screaming at the gunner who simply wasn't buying, who was, instead calmly taking down his equipment as though the whistle had blown for lunch.

No one else walked with us, just Johnny and me, and it was unreal. It was also familiar—newsreel footage: "Doughboys advance at Chateau Thierry." "GI's Move up at Remagen Bridge."

The bald captain and his two flunkies were out on the course, their white bandages fluttering like surrealistic banners, turning muddy in moments. I didn't look to see which of the men had been hit. It didn't matter. NG, RA, US, Reservist—it just didn't matter. Any face that I would be able to recognize would be the face of a friend. Johnny was right. The enemy was up ahead.

We kept walking, not bothering to slip under the

barbed wire, just stepping over it, our rifles in front of us in the prescribed position as if our bayonets were fixed, as if our mud-clogged rifles could be fired.

Holdoffer saw us coming, and if he wasn't crazy before, he was crazy then. With the ammo box he clobbered the corporal, lifting it high and bringing it down upon that man's head so hard that he simply folded up and lay still. Holdoffer picked up the machine gun, which was already detached from its tripod, and, cradling it in his arms as lightly as if it were balsa wood, he stepped out toward Johnny and me, jumping across the trench in front of him as easily as if he were a panther. He advanced on us at the same pace that we were advancing on him.

It was not happening. How could it be? How could we be replaying every battle movie I'd ever seen? What the hell were Johnny and I doing walking into the muzzle of a machine gun? It was all so far beyond my ability to think about that I just kept moving forward without thinking. Munez and Webber had rifles without bullets. Holdoffer had a thirty-calibre machine gun. Where the hell was Randolph Scott?

We were no more than thirty yards apart when Holdoffer's finger curled around the machine gun's trigger. I could see it do it. I could see it squeeze. But I couldn't hear the gun fire because there was no ammo belt hooked in.

That didn't bother Holdoffer. It didn't bother him and it did not dissuade him. He just kept walking toward us, through the mud, past the medics who didn't look up, past the bald captain who couldn't do anything for the first man so he sloshed through the gook to the second. Holdoffer was grinning and squeezing the trigger and making like a machine gun—"Eh-eh-eh-eh-eh-eh-eh-eh!"—spraying the area with bullets that came

only from his mind. He never broke stride, never slack-
ened his pace. Something had snapped in his head. And
something had snapped in ours. We were going to kill
him. We were going to bash his head in with our rifle
butts. We hadn't discussed it, Johnny and I, but that's
what we both knew we were going to do. We were going
to end the existence of Sergeant Luther Holdoffer and
we wouldn't be hurting for witnesses because they were
all around us, quiet as death and as watchful as vul-
tures. I wanted someone to stop us. A word would have
done it, a sound, a small tick of rationality. A laugh, a
burst of profanity, a song—Bing Crosby, Kate Smith,
somebody from home. But there was nothing. Nothing
from anybody because everybody wanted us to do it.
The drama would play to a conclusion, nobody to be
seated during the last five minutes of the show.

The two factions were no more than fifteen yards
apart and closing when a figure came running up at
Holdoffer from behind. Holdoffer never saw the man
who bridged the separation swiftly, in defiance of all the
awkward footing, but he felt the blade, plunged so hard
into his kidney that he dropped immediately to his
knees. It was Sergeant Kuyper, Deyo's lover, and he
had performed the vindictive deed with the longest
blade he could find in his trusty Swiss Army knife.

Holdoffer looked up at Kuyper and recognized him,
which was what Kuyper wanted. Then he sagged into
the mud, plopping over onto his side, lying there, alive
but barely, the knife sticking in his kidney, its red handle and white cross the only clean metal on the course
that day.

Kuyper looked at us blankly, then turned and walked
back to the others, as though he had suddenly remembered to go back and turn off his car lights. Johnny and
I reached Holdoffer and looked down into that twisting

face. We wanted him to see us, too. He did. And his lips moved in some inaudible curse, his teeth so brown that, played against the brown of the mud, it appeared as though he had no teeth at all. Then his head turned sideways so that the slime he was lying in began to trickle into his mouth, gravity and suction doing what man could not, shutting the mouth of the obscene animal, stifling its bestial noise.

By then the medics had established that the first three men were dead and moved on to the fourth, the one with the index finger in the air. He was alive and so they worked on him, glad to be able to save somebody that day because their pride was at stake. The man would live but, in the time it took to save him, Holdoffer quietly died. Not of his wound but by drowning. And we stood there and watched, Johnny and I, as his head rolled over like a capsizing ship and the last bubbles pushed up through the mud.

Five men had died on that worst Friday of my life: Private Dickie Stovall, US; Private First Class Junior Lightman, NG; Corporal Alan Kirkpatrick, NG; Private Anthony Wesso, US; and Master Sergeant Luther Holdoffer, NG. Private Paul Morgan, US, was wounded but survived. Corporal William Simmons, RA (the machine gunner) received a concussion but survived. Who was guilty? Where did the responsibility lie?

Sergeant Frank Kuyper, RA, was charged with homicide. He was arrested and jailed. Captain Albert Mackie, Range Officer, was confined to quarters pending further investigation. But Colonel Herbert Cranston of the 42nd Group, and his next in command, Lieutenant Colonel Terence Beakins, and Lieutenant Wyatt Collings, Company Commander—none of whom had showed up that day—lay low. Very low indeed.

The dead were shipped every which way: Dickie Stovall to Brooklyn, New York; Junior Lightman, Alan Kirkpatrick, and Luther Holdoffer to small places in Pennsylvania, all near Lancaster; and Anthony Wesso to Norwalk, Connecticut, where they buried what was left of him, throwing his baseball glove into the coffin to see if he could pitch his way out of it.

None were buried on the post. The situation was too hot and the Army wanted the bodies dispersed, scattered to the winds, divided and conquered and forgotten.

The Inspector General of Fort Devens, Lieutenant General Kenneth McArdle, hero of Anzio, Salerno and Monte Casino, spent all that remained of Friday and all that there was of Saturday gathering his facts and formulating his conclusions. High on his list of men to be talked to were Private John Munez and PFC Benjamin Webber.

Johnny went in first and came out ten minutes later with nothing for me but a blank look. I walked in as he walked out.

General McArdle was a large man, well over six feet tall and 250 pounds wide. He was in his forties, a West Point graduate, a career soldier, and a very troubled human being. I saluted and he gestured for me to sit down. "We'll drop the formalities as this goes considerably beyond military pomp and circumstance. If you want to smoke, smoke. If you want to take your shoes off, do it. If you want to pass wind, pass it. But, for Christ's sake, Webber, help me with this situation."

"Yes, sir." I sat down and faced the general. There was much I wanted to tell him and I'd be damned if I was going to edit myself.

"Munez gave me nothing. I don't know what he thinks he's proving, keeping it all inside."

"He's like that, sir."

"Corporal Simmons, the machine gunner, I spoke with him only briefly because of his condition. He said that the gun slipped and that he stopped firing as soon as it did. He said that Sergeant Holdoffer directed him to continue his fire but that he refused. He said that Sergeant Holdoffer was deranged. Everything that Simmons said is corroborated by the handful of men I've so far managed to speak with. Is that your interpretation, too?"

"Yes, sir."

"Can you tell me more?"

"Yes, sir. Holdoffer was a prick and a sadist."

McArdle let it go, didn't even raise an eyebrow. "I can't speak with Sergeant Kuyper until counsel is arranged for him. As you know, he's charged with homicide."

"He should be given a medal."

"Why did he kill Holdoffer?"

"Ask Holdoffer."

"I want you to be informal—not insulting."

"Then ask Kuyper."

"I intend to. But right now I'm asking *you*."

"He had his reasons. Someone was going to kill Holdoffer sooner or later. Johnny and I were on our way to do it. Kuyper got there first."

"You're lucky."

"No, sir. It would have been a privilege."

"Kuyper's in deep trouble. He's the one man whose fate is sealed. I'm trying to find out who else is guilty."

"The following people are guilty: Colonel Cranston, Lieutenant Colonel Beakins, Lieutenant Collings, Captain Mackie, Sergeant Holdoffer—dig him up and shoot him. *You're* guilty. The *Army's* guilty. And *I'm* guilty."

"Let's take 'em one at a time, shall we?"

"Yes, sir."

"Why is Colonel Cranston guilty?"

"Because he sent us out without an officer."

"Lieutenant Collings was supposed to have been there."

"He wasn't. It was Cranston's responsibility to see to it that he was. Cranston is Holdoffer's uncle and—"

McArdle broke in. He didn't want to tangle with that one. "Why is Lieutenant Colonel Beakins guilty?"

"Because he's an ass and has no business commanding men."

"And Captain Mackie?"

"Because he doesn't like to get his pants dirty, can't speak English, and wouldn't listen when I told him that the left stanchion of the machine gun brace was sinking in the mud."

"Was it?"

"Yes. I told Holdoffer and I told Mackie."

"And they did nothing about it?"

"Nothing."

"Who else knew about the stanchion?"

"Johnny Munez, myself, and Tony Wesso."

"Nobody else knew?"

"Nobody."

"Mackie will deny it."

"I know."

"Okay. Next you said—Holdoffer. We can skip him."

"Why?"

"Well, for one thing, he's dead."

"Hitler's dead. Should we skip him?"

He sighed. "Let's not get into political science."

"Holdoffer got himself a hero's funeral. His name's going on a plaque alongside the names of a lot of men who deserve better company."

"Webber, there is nothing to be gained by—"

"Then why didn't we allow them to put up a plaque for Hitler?"

"I understand your feelings. I may even agree with them, but I want to get on with *this* investigation, not Hitler's, okay?"

"Yes, sir."

"You say *I'm* guilty."

"Yes, sir."

"Why?"

"Because of the way you're handling this."

"Care to enlarge on that?"

"Yes, sir. You're concerned with procedures and legalities and technicalities. You're not concerned with morality. You're seeing things through 'Army-colored glasses.' Five men are dead and you're not trying to figure out why, you're trying to figure out who. Hell, you can figure out who everytime it happens. But if you'd try to figure out why—just once—it might never happen again."

"You also said you were guilty. Why are you guilty?"

"Because I accepted it."

"Accepted what?"

"Everything. I accepted being drafted. I accepted the indignities of having to take orders from people who couldn't properly order around chickens. I accepted the existence of sadists and jugheads in positions of authority. I accepted the nepotism that allowed a man like Holdoffer to get a master sergeant's stripes. I accepted treatment in the Army that outside the Army I wouldn't put up with for five seconds."

"Like what?"

"Like a man freezing to death for no reason."

"Sergeant Deyo?"

"Sergeant Deyo and whoever else has frozen to death up here and gotten himself buried and had a bugle blown over him—after which everybody went out for a beer."

"All right, Webber, tell me, if it were up to you where would you fix the blame? How would you proceed? What would you do if you were me?"

"I'd blow my brains out."

"That's something that has never occurred to me."

"Take off your glasses and it'll occur to you."

Under the circumstances, he was more tolerant of me than I had a right to expect. "You're a very bright young man. You speak very well. You make a lot of sense."

"Yes, sir."

"From now on it is not necessary that you interrupt me when I'm talking. I just want you to listen. I don't want to hear your voice until I ask you a specific question. Understood?"

I nodded my understanding.

"You're a very singular man. Being singular is great. It's a great trait—in the *outside* world. But, in the Army it's catastrophic. If every man in the Army was like you, we'd have no country—because, in a war, we'd have no Army, no men willing to take orders—*blindly,* if need be. All we'd have would be a lot of individualists, who in situations of stress would take off in a million different directions because their 'consciences' would dictate that they do so. We'd be like China used to be: millions upon millions of people, going their own way, contributing nothing to the nation, accomplishing nothing for themselves. Believe me, now that the day has come that the Chinese take orders from a central authority, China is a force to be reckoned with. Do you agree?"

"I don't know, sir. That's political science."

"Go easy on the sarcasm, fella. I'm beginning not to appreciate it."

"Yes, sir. Sorry, sir."

"Any more than I appreciate your 'Draftee of the Week' program."

"I didn't originate that, sir."

"No, but you perfected it."

"Yes, sir."

"If I were to call every draftee on this post into this office, one at a time, if I were to tell each of them, in private, that if he wanted to he could go home and never have to come back, how many of them do you think would take me up on it?"

"All of them."

"Exactly. Now then, if I were to have them assemble, all of them, on the parade grounds, shoulder-to-shoulder, in uniform, with division flags flying and the band playing, and I were to make them the same offer, over a loudspeaker, how many do you think would take me up on it?"

"I don't know, sir."

"None. Believe me, Webber. None would do it. They'd either feel ashamed that they'd look like cowards or be afraid that it was a trick . . . but they just wouldn't do it. They'd just hold their ranks, no one daring to be the first man to bug out. And *that* is what the Army is all about. We *want* to destroy your individuality. We *must* shave your heads, and dress you in olive drab, and rub your noses in shit collectively because it's the only way in which we can *maintain* an army. You call it dehumanizing, we call it mobilizing. We're at war—it's a sticky war, undeclared, no one really cares for it. We wouldn't have a chance in it if we couldn't take a million free thinking individualists and turn them into an unquestioning mass of willing servility. Yes, we'll make mistakes. Yes, we'll put the wrong men in charge from time to time. Yes, that will happen. But over the long haul we'll hammer out an Army in which the best men will be recognized, and through which our country will be properly represented in battle. Is any of this getting through to you, Webber?"

"Yes, sir. The philosophy is. I understand why you're doing it. I just don't happen to care for it."

"I know."

"I'm sorry."

He picked up a folder from his desk. I recognized it. It was my folder again. My 201 file. "You know what this is, don't you?"

"Yes, sir."

"It's pretty up-to-date. A lot of unflattering things—and yet, you recently made PFC. How'd that happen?"

"I duped Holdoffer."

He didn't want to play with that one, so he continued to make whatever point he was making. "There's a letter in here. It's written by Captain Grace, your former company commander. May I read it to you?"

"Yes, sir."

McArdle read the letter:

Private Benjamin Webber is a very intelligent young man with undeniable leadership potential. Unfortunately, that potential will never be realized in the Army—not for lack of opportunity, but for limitations in the man's makeup. He cannot really be trusted to *give* an order because he cannot properly *accept* one. He would have been fine serving with George Armstrong Custer but in today's Army, never. He is intuitive and candid, but often to his own detriment. I attach this memo to his 201 file because he and I had been discussing the prospect of his going to Officer Candidate School. I feel that, as much as I like the young man, if

asked I would disapprove of his officer candidacy.
He is too much the individual and not enough the
team man. As an officer, in my opinion, he would
be a disaster.

"And it's signed, Francis Grace, Captain, US Army."
McArdle put the letter back into my file. "Do you
agree with his evaluation of you?"

"Totally."

"Think you'd make a lousy officer?"

"The worst."

"Worse than you are an enlisted man?"

"Ten times worse."

He wasn't smiling. He was no longer the casual in-
quisitor. He was the cryptic judgment-passer. "Webber,
the infiltration course incident will be settled with or
without your assistance or approval. Responsibilities
will be fixed and punishments will be set. Even before
you came in here I had a small buzz on how it all happened and what would have to be done to see that it
never happens again." He laid into that last phrase, for
my benefit.

"Yes, sir."

"I didn't think you'd be terribly helpful because that
doesn't seem to be your style. Nor did I think you had
any idea as to how much you might have contributed to
this tragedy. And I was right. You don't."

"No, sir. I don't."

"There's no place for you in the Army, Webber.
You're a square peg and all we've got are round holes.
Wherever we put you, you'll make trouble. And the
worst part is that you won't even know you're doing it.
Colonel Cranston informed me of how you continually
baited Holdoffer. Lieutenant Colonel Beakins knew all

about your Draftee of the Week program. Pissing in a canteen, Webber? Shitting in a boot?"

"I pissed but I didn't shit, sir."

"Shut up."

"Yes, sir."

"They may not be your idea of good commanding officers but they did know what was going on in their HQ company. And they did have you slated for a change in MOS number—944-Rifleman, going to the Far East Command as a replacement. Want to see it?"

"No, sir. I believe it."

"I'd have approved it, too, except, after studying your record, it seemed to me that you were a good bet to be leading a battlefield revolt within ten minutes of reaching Korea."

"Yes, sir, but I don't think—"

"Shut up." And he continued, angry but under rein, the fury of his words made all the more telling by the modulation of his voice. "If you had gotten to Holdoffer before Kuyper did, our worries would have been over. It would be your ass and not Kuyper's. But no, no such luck. Kuyper's in the stockade and you're standing here and—just so's you know how I feel about the pair of you—I think Kuyper's a dozen times the soldier you are. So what if he's a faggot. I wouldn't care if he fucked *trees*. He's a damned good man, as witness the fact that when the moment came *he* was the one who killed Holdoffer, not *you*. You never would have done it."

"I think you're wrong, sir."

"Shut up."

"Yes, sir."

He went swiftly to what he had been, up till then, only dancing around. "There's a thing we have in the Army now, we didn't have it in World War II. It's called Convenience of the Government. You familiar with it?"

"No, sir."

"It's very simple. It's an honorable discharge in which the Army, in effect, apologizes for having drafted you. In which the Army states that though you're not making it in the Army, there is no reason to believe that you cannot make it in civilian life. A lot of men function beautifully as civilians but fail as soldiers and have to be mustered out: malingerers, congenital AWOL's, thieves, fools, cowards, malcontents. In World War II they were given 'Section Eight' discharges, which implied that they were mentally unfit. In too many cases that was too sweeping and unfair a designation, and those men suffered when they returned to civilian life because 'Section Eight' was stamped all over the papers that prospective employers asked to see. Well, we don't do that anymore. Now we have 'Convenience of the Government' and it slots neatly between 'Section Eight' and 'Honorable Discharge.' And Webber, at the convenience of the government you're going home. It's not a decision I've come to lightly. If it were up to me personally, I'd ship your balls to China. But the Army tells me I can't do that; that as an officer I have a responsibility to all my men, even to you; and that if I see you as unable to function as a soldier, yet do honestly believe that you can function as a civilian, I *have* to send you home—for your sake and for the sake of other soldiers whose lives you could easily jeopardize in an emergency situation." He pushed a paper across his desk at me. "Read it. All you have to do is waive all claim on any Army-incurred disability that you may have—and then wave bye-bye. Wouldn't you like that, Webber?"

"I don't know, sir."

His smile was riddled with contempt. "Hey, fella, I'm saying you can go home. Don't you want to go home? Or do you think you'll be embarrassed to tell your buddies that you and you alone out of the entire company are the only guy the Army can't use? Well, you needn't feel too ashamed. You'll be in good company. Bedwetters, night-criers, masturbation artists, fainters, sneezers, hiccoughers, one testicle, two cocks, three assholes—there's a whole bunch of things a man will do and say to get out of the Army. We don't fight it anymore. Our feeling is that if a man will go to such extremes—if he is willing to wallow in such excrement and cause such conflict—we don't *want* to keep him. He's no good to us. There's just no time to make him over, no time at all. All we want in the Army are two kinds of men: those who give orders and those who take them. Anybody not in one of those categories gets to go home, and with our apologies. All the freaks, degenerates, fakers, Philadelphia lawyers, agitators, fellow-travelers, college debaters, Draftees of the Week—we apologize to 'em and kick 'em out. You're Limited Service, kid, knees, back, ears. Just tell your buddies they all went bad at once and that the Army put you in a bag, declared you dead, and sent you home."

"I don't think I can do that, sir."

"Sign it, Webber. Because, if you don't, we'll toss you into the psycho ward a couple days, just for observation—and *then* when you go home, it'll *be* as a Section Eight."

"Yes, sir, but—"

"You behaved exactly as I knew you would, Webber. Exactly as your record indicated you would. The best thing I can do now to shore up the morale of the 42nd HQ Company and get it functioning, is to clear up this infiltration-course business by getting rid of those men responsible—directly, indirectly, obtusely or intellectually. And you're *one* of them. We can't use you, son. Sign the paper, accept our apologies, and get the fuck out of here."

He had his back to me as I looked over the form. It was difficult to read—all that small print plus all the confusion in my own mind, for there it was, my ticket home. But it was all happening too fast and McArdle knew it. And without turning to look at me he said, "Take it with you. Read it over. And don't salute when you go, I won't return it."

I discussed the matter with Johnny who thought I was nuts to not sign it before the Army changed its mind. I wasn't sure. By signing it I'd be admitting to myself that everything that McArdle had said about me was true, and I didn't want to believe that. Johnny, of course, ever the realist, said that the trick was to not believe and to sign it anyway. That way, I could eat my cake, still have it, and have enough left over to shove up the Army's ass. The logic was irresistible. Still, I couldn't bring myself to sign the form, somehow feeling that I would be less of a man from the point of signing *on*.

We were all allowed out that night, McArdle giving the whole HQ Company Saturday night and Sunday off. He was right to do it because it broke the tension and dispersed the group, dividing us into duets, trios and quartets, each going somewhere else. And no one was left hanging around the barracks to feel sad, angry, futile—or to go bananas.

Johnny and I headed for Leominster and Tiny's Bar where we hoisted a half dozen beers to the memory of that stylish left-hander, Tony Wesso. We cried on each other's shoulder, reminisced, joked, and puked. And rolled into Camp at an hour so ungodly that no clock would give us the right time. Just before falling into a sleep that more nearly resembled a trance, I signed the Convenience of the Government form, congratulated myself on my pragmatism, cursed myself for my lack of character, and accepted myself for what I was: an incomplete, befuddled, befouled young man whose buddy was in a fresh grave but whose cock was twitching like a metronome at the thought of the next day with Mrs. Barringer.

I sat in the lobby of the Ritz-Carlton, watching people skim by who were so far removed from where I was at the time, who were so deep into the pleasantries of civilian life, that it actually jolted me to hear them speaking English. For English had become for me, by then, a rude language in which every third word was a profanity, and to realize that people could truly make themselves understood without a "fuck" or a "shit" to get them over the rough spots was, frankly, an astonishing rediscovery.

At eleven forty she entered the lobby—nonchalantly beautiful as she looked quickly over the room to see if I was there. Afraid that she might not be able to pick me out (there were other soldiers sitting about), I raised my hand. She continued on to the elevator and I couldn't tell whether or not she had seen me. It was of no consequence for I already had my orders.

I waited five minutes and then went to the elevator. I got off at the fifth floor and walked to room 503. I knocked, softly. Too softly. No answer. I knocked again. Louder. Nothing. I tried the door. It was open and I went in, my heart banging pans in my head.

The room was fairly dark, the drapes all drawn, no lights on. Still, I could see well enough to note that it was more than just a room, it was a suite. She appeared in the doorway to the bedroom, looking like a fantasy, wearing something silk and flimsy, no slippers, her toes painted, polished and flexing, digging into all that lavish Ritz-Carlton pile.

I started to speak but she put her fingers to her lips as if to indicate no talking. Then she moved toward me, taking my hand like a kid in a park, leading me into the bedroom. Then she turned and faced me and she smiled, as though knowing some great secret that she was about to share with me, and slowly she reached up and loosened my tie. It came off and she was unbuttoning my shirt. The shirt came off, and the T-shirt. And soon I was standing in the middle of that most elegant room stripped to the waist, astonished, a monkey's uncle smile on my Little Tommy Tucker face.

Delicately she touched my arms, running her hands over them, then over my shoulders, my chest, my stomach, all the while looking into my eyes and saying not a word, her mouth just slightly open, her breathing contemplative and feline, her perfume swarming. She was so urgently present, everything about her so screaming with promise, that I reached out to touch her. And she brushed my hand away. I was not to touch her. Again her finger flew to her lips. I understood.

She slid easily to her knees in front of me, her face and hair slipping passed my belt, her hands also, butterflying over my fly, never really making contact yet tracing my periphery like a blind person forming an image.

She was untying my shoelaces and I raised each foot, one at a time, so that she could remove my shoes and my socks. I was retrogressing, getting younger every minute. I was twelve, on my way to ten. Still on her knees she looked up at me and again I couldn't help but reach down to cup that unbelievable face. Again she shook me off, a touch more angrily than before. I was ten, going on nine.

Her hands found my belt buckle, her actions then like those of a safecracker, expertly unbuttoning my pants as though knowing the combination well in advance. My trousers dropped obediently and, cleverly, I knew to step out of them. Some change fell out of my pockets but I knew not to mention it. I was seven.

She got to her feet and walked behind me, staying there, her hands snaking around me so that I could see them and watch them as they probed, feeling for the waistband of my undershorts, her thumbs curling inside, slowly peeling at my shorts, rolling them down. They dropped to my ankles and I stepped out of them, kicking them out of the way. They flew to a lamp and hung there. I was down to dog tags and wristwatch and, to show her that I knew my way around, I removed them. I was six.

And I was naked. And she was behind me where I couldn't see her. She had touched me all over, everywhere—but had yet to touch my penis, that silly appendage so confused by it all that it pressed hard against my stomach like a bazooka aimed at my nose. Her hands again played on my arms, my sides, and her lips, making no kisses, whispered across my shoulders and over the back of my neck. Then—small bites and hot breath, and hands no longer playing but feeling, kneading, stroking.

I was completely immobilized, standing with my back to her like wet clay being shaped, like a department store dummy being stripped. Her left hand went outrageously between my legs, from behind, finding my scrotum and surrounding it with fingers. In that, too, she was expert, squeezing me just short of screaming, though I do believe I said "Eek." Her right hand, coming from the side in a flanking action, found my penis, and those fingers were *not* so gentle, grabbing and hanging on as if to strangle. I could not move and dared not move. I was witless, not a thought as to what to say or do. I could not see her, only her hands, one caressing, the other clamping. Ten fingers working me over—left hand a kitten, right hand a vise. Dichotomous dickery. I was three.

Then both hands let go and she appeared again before me, standing. But her eyes were not for my eyes, they were for my penis. So I looked at it, too, to see why the wide-eyed fascination. And there it was, where I had left it, but swollen beyond pornography. It was a rock, red-blue with dumbfoundedness, still looking up at me, its one eye moist with a few tears of pre-ejaculation.

She leaned over, touching it with nothing but tongue, and the little drops went lizardly into her mouth. If she were to touch it again—with anything, her elbow, the heel of her foot—I'd have released like Hoover Dam. But she was too knowledgeable to allow that to happen.

Taking me by the hand, she led me to the bed, lay me on my back and once again manipulated my genitals with her hands so that my penis seemed nine times as large as I had ever envisioned it becoming. And it no longer belonged to me. It belonged to her. *I* belonged to her for I was, by then, nothing more than a pulsing phallus with a soldier boy attached. Never had I, or have I since, been so thoroughly in the possession of a woman. Nor did we ever speak. Everything was done wordlessly. Two mutes fucking in oil. Two giraffes, with cotton in our ears, banging away in a soundproofed room. Every move we made was of her creation and at her direction. Whatever it was that the lady had done to me with her hands, it had rendered me incapable of ejaculating. She had so retarded my orgasm that my toes and fingers twitched in bewildered palsy. I was stupendously erect and, though continually at the brink of ejaculation, I was unable to pull the pin of the grenade.

Meanwhile, stunned at how I could hover in such a pained state and still enjoy it, I watched her slip out of her robe, the confident champion about to take on the cocky challenger. The bell rang and I was immediately down, and she was toying with me, using me as if I were a circus animal—a trained bear, a rabbit on a string, a lion lunging through a flaming hoop, each time from a different direction.

I entered her from above, from behind, from beneath, from beyond, from the next room, from the chandelier, from Altoona. I entered her from positions I had never before dreamed anatomically possible. And each insertion and its accompanying plunges touched off a climax in her so total in its violence that things spun amazingly into reverse, making me feel as though she were trying to catapult me *out*, trying to slam me against the far wall. But something held me in and kept me there. It wasn't her legs because, though often wrapped around me, they were usually flapping like canvas in a gale. What it was was me, thrusting determinedly through her contracting rings and revolving bearings, fighting to remain in her because, damn it, that's where I wanted to be.

All of this took place without a word, causing me to wonder if I hadn't lost my hearing, if all my adolescent masturbations hadn't brought about deafness rather than the promised blindness—and if blindness wasn't next.

My lady wanted oral sex and oral sex she got, pulling my head down and into her so that I wore her like a mask. Never terribly experienced in that department, I learned fast, her body telling me, wordlessly, when I was doing nobly and when I was losing ground. I would have stayed down there forever, willingly, happily. I would have gladly died down there, buried in the frills and folds of her, bathed and boiled in the essence of her, but she saw no reason to carry the sport so far. And somewhere—who knows when—she disengaged herself from me and, rolling voluptuously onto her side, lay on her pillow like an oil-painted nude over a Yukon bar, wearing nothing but an impish smile and a "come fuck me" look.

She stroked my face with a lazy tenderness that belied her former passion. And she spoke. Hurrah, I was not deaf! I was merely beat. "Poor baby. I wore you out."

"Not at all. I'm fine."

She laughed. "Ah—a gentleman. You were very good. Do you know that?"

"Oh, I thought I was all right."

Again she laughed. "Never had it like that before, did you?"

"Oh—"

"Where you're nothing but a tool." She was playing with my penis. It was so hard that I thought for a moment that she had somehow had it bronzed when I wasn't looking. "Poor thing—all the way from Fort Devens, and the lady didn't let you come. Poor little Peter, how nice he was to me."

"I just hope the damned thing goes down. Be pretty embarrassing on the bus."

"Men are invariably so selfish, that's why I turn the tables. Ladies first. I take care of *me*, after which—" Her face was on my stomach, her hair passing over my nakedness like a silken scarf, "—I take care of the sweet soldier." And she began to do things to me with her mouth, her lips, her tongue, talking to me as she did. "This is what I love the most. I love—a man in my mouth. If you knew, Dear Ben. Mmmmmm. I love it more than peanut butter. You'll be fine soon. Relax. I feel you—getting ready. Don't hold back. When it comes, go with it. Give it to me."

Obeying her instructions, I fired myself straightaway into her head. I just reared up, gathered my buttocks, and let go, the stalwart lady never backing off, never losing hold, never tiring, never disappointing. And when it was over, when the infernal cannon had fired, re-coiled, and cooled, she held the poor remnant in one hand, while patting it with the other, like ladies pat kittens. "Good boy."

"Better than peanut butter?"

"Better than cream sherry. Did you know that—men taste different. Some taste bitter, some taste sweet."

"Which am I?"

"Sweet. Oh, sweet." And she started on me again, licking me like a lolly.

"Listen, if it's all the same with you—"

She laughed, almost choking on me. "Yes. I know. You're tired. But your friend, here, he has other ideas."

"Don't listen to him. He's just showing off."

"No. He's coming back. Look at the size of him." Once again my penis filled her hand and she stretched it out so that I could see, and held it like a prize trout that she'd caught on a one-pound line.

I marveled at it. "Look at that."

"The next one's for you."

"The next what?"

"The next fuck, darling. Whatever you want. I'll do whatever you say."

"Yeah? Well—"

"Ben, you're ready. What is your pleasure?"

"Well—?"

"Don't miss this opportunity, soldier. The lady is all cunt. Spread-eagled and smoking. Let's get rid of that good conduct medal and give me that splendid cock."

My record had been, until then, seven orgasms within a two-hour period, my partner in that accomplishment being the dutiful Alice. But records are made to be broken, as are beds if one is too ardent. And if the woman involved is not split asunder, and if the man on duty can rise to each occasion, and if all the moving parts are working together and obedient inertia joins the fray, and if the cops don't bust in, there are no limits as to how many orgasms can be achieved by a young man of purpose. By my count the new record was ten.

I have no idea how long we were at it or why I was still alive. My body had turned to sponge, my magic penis telescoping so far back into its sheath that only its corona remained, as a lookout. The lady was working over me like a battlefield nurse—Molly Pitcher with a wash cloth—washing my boneless body, talking me back to life. "Ben? Are you awake?"

"No. I'm dead. But don't stop."

"You were rather remarkable, you know." She was toweling me dry and sprinkling me with talcum.

"Best you ever had?"

"No. Tarzan was better. But *he* swung from a vine. There. How's that? You're all ready to be diapered."

"What to hear something ridiculous?"

"I *always* want to hear something ridiculous."

"I only know your last name. What's your first name?"

"Maggie."

"Maggie Barringer. Nice name."

"It's not Barringer."

"No?"

"No. I just live with him. Oh, Ben—let's be honest about everything, shall we? It's so tiring to pretend. Can we be honest and not get hung up in the bullshit of the times?"

"I think it's worth a try."

"I'm not married to Kevin Barringer. I just live with him. He's rich, generous, charming—likes to fuck, when he can. And he allows me to be what I am."

"And what's that?"

"I don't know. A wastrel, I guess. A hoyden. A nymph. A nymphomaniac, maybe—only nymphomaniacs, I'm told, can't orgasm. And I can."

"Yes. I'll vouch for that."

She was lying next to me, talking, and I knew that the sex was over, at least for that day. "Anyway, I live with Kevin, in this palace, and sometimes I travel with him when he wants to show me off. He's in the oil business, cartels and things. He's forever going away. We're both back from Europe for maybe a month."

"Does he know that you—?"

"Fuck around? I think he does. As long as I don't make a big display of it, it's all right. He likes that I give some time to the USO. So do I. I've been lucky there twice."

"Who else?"

"A young sailor. Fucked like he'd been at sea for five years. He shipped out—and you shipped *in*."

"And Kevin doesn't suspect?"

"Maybe. But he doesn't badger me. He doesn't know I have this suite. Actually I think he *does* know but is glad I get some loving on the side because he's getting to be sixtyish. I wear him out. Whenever I've got eyes for someone else, I give Kevin a fucking that'll last him a month."

"Sounds sporting."

"I have suites in New York, Paris, and London, too. And, Ben, I have two daughters. One's a teenager. The other's twenty-two and married."

"That's hard to believe."

"I abandoned them. Just walked out. It's indefensible, of course, but necessary to my sanity. I'm just not maternal. Fertile but not maternal—the curse of the Incas."

"Do you know where they are?"

"One's in Chicago. At least she was the last time I looked. She's married. The other's in a girls school somewhere. My husband's in Stamford, Connecticut. He paints. After years of trying to play mother while fucking frantically on the side, I just picked up and left. I'm telling you all this so's you'll know everything about me, and it's all bad. I'm afraid I have no redeeming features except in bed, which I'm told is colossal. I move around—from man to man. I suppose it'll catch up to me one day. I guess it's catching up now. When it does, maybe I'll go home. They're very forgiving. I'll wear lace, settle down, blow an occasional milkman and grow old gracefully. For all I know I'm already a grandmother. Would you mind fucking a grandmother?"

"I hear Marlene Dietrich's a grandmother."

"Will you come back next Sunday and do me again?"

"I'll have to check my appointment pad, but I think I can squeeze you in."

"You might get scared. I mean, after thinking it over you might not like the idea of being an old lady's plaything."

"No. Never. It's just that I don't know how long I'm going to be around. I'm being discharged. It's all very honorable. The Army just doesn't think I'm good for anything."

"If they'd listen to me, they'd make you a fucking general."

"Yeah, well, don't tell 'em. I'm as sick of them as they are of me."

"A rebel. I love that. I'll miss you. We were just getting to know each other." She sprinkled more talcum on me. "Good-bye, old buddy, it was just one of those things."

"I may be around for a while, though. They don't let you out right away. They like to pull your wings off."

"Where is home?"

"New York City."

"I can meet you there. I've a suite at the St. Regis."

"Great."

"What do you do? Do you have a job?"

"I'm a movie mogul. I write advertising for 20th Century-Fox."

"You're kidding?"

"No."

"I know a lot of people there. Skouras, Winnerman. Clark. I don't bed down with them, I just see them in my travels."

"I work for W. Charles Gruber. Know him?"

"Yes. Watch out for him."

"What do you mean?"

"I mean watch out for him. He's gay."

"Gruber? Come on."

"Has he fixed you up with a girl, yet?"

"Why should he?"

"Because, now that I look at you, you're *exactly* the kind of young stud he'd just love."

"You know him?"

"Oh, well—yes—I know him. I mean, dear Ben, I do get around. I just don't want to play 'fuck and tell,' okay? I've told you too much already."

"Just tell me why Gruber'd fix me up with a girl."

"Because that's his game. He fixes you up, makes you happy, gets to be your friend—and the next thing you know he's up your ass."

"Jesus, the things you can learn in Boston."

"I have to go now. Kevin's having some people over. I think they're digging for oil behind our house. You can stay here if you like. Order up something from room service. Whatever you like. They'll put it on my bill."

"What time is it?"

"About five."

"Maybe I'll have a beer before I go back."

"Be my guest. And I'll see you next Sunday, okay? Same time, same station."

"How about earlier?"

"That's my boy."

I watched Maggie get dressed. She was magnificent. Everything about her was just right. So natural. No hang-ups. Crazy as a loon if you'd ask some psychiatrist but perfect for me at the time. Before leaving she kissed me on the cheek, like an aunt. And then I was alone in my suite at the Ritz-Carlton.

I ordered from room service. A beer. Lobster thermoidor. French pastry. And a pot of coffee. I signed Maggie's name and included a big tip for the waiter because he asked no questions. And I wondered if he hadn't had a shot at Maggie, too. Could it be that I was jealous? I'd have to watch that kind of thing.

I went back to the post and sacked out. The very next morning I submitted my "Convenience of the Government" form. Two days later I was transferred to a medical holding detachment. General McArdle wasn't wasting any time.

chapter twelve

ginnie

1951

With Don gone I came very close to craziness. I had broken with Annice and her group, Sayonara had folded, I had no prospects, and Don had skipped to LA—all of it leaving me with a few hundred bucks and a barn of an apartment, whose rent I would have to swing all on my own.

I spoke with Roland about it and he suggested that I inform Ben of the situation, that, if Ben couldn't help out with the rent, I give up the apartment and look for something smaller, and that, until I found a place that made sense, I could stay with him.

I didn't want to move back to the Village. It seemed like a step backwards. Also, I didn't want to lose Ben, a desire you'll have to admit was pretty flaky in that I had yet to meet him and, for all I knew, never would.

Anyway, being very big on "first things first," I wrote to Ben and informed him of my circumstances. He sent back a hundred and fifty dollars and signed his letter "Peter Pan." I loved him so much for that that I knew I could never let him lose his apartment.

So, while auditioning for a whole flock of musicals and never being picked, I went in for waiting tables again, at a restaurant on Lincoln Square called Chips. They hadn't built Lincoln Center yet but everyone was talking about laying aside that land, which was at the

time kind of slummy. It was right around the corner
from ABC and was about the only restaurant taking
root in that area that wasn't just a convenient bar for
fall-down drunks. At least with ABC around, a lot of
people and performers were coming around because,
not only was Chips the only game in town, it also served
pretty good Italian food.

But it bored me a lot and depressed me even more to
be waiting tables as my mother once had done, and to
make the smell of marinara go away I would work on
accents. I would pretend to be French on one night and
English the next and see how many people I could fool.

As to the pay—that was the worst part. The pay
was good, so good that I didn't dare quit. Chips was a
small place, most of its business done after eleven P.M.,
and no one really cared to work such late and long
hours but me. It didn't matter to me what time it was.
To this day I seldom know what time it is.

But life was passing me by. It wasn't what I wanted
to do. It wasn't the way I saw myself. Also, because it
was dark and late and boozey my ass was getting a lot
of pinches it could have done very nicely without. My
butt was beginning to bloom with blue polka dots, not a
nice sight to see upon stepping out of one's shower.

Well, it all ended on a rainy morning at about two
A.M., when one of the customers, hypnotized by my
short skirt, slipped his hand between my legs so fast that
I never saw it happen. I only felt it. I thought it was a
bat trying to get into me, and, goddamnit, if I was going
to lose my virginity, it wasn't going to be to a
Parmesan-reeking vampire I hardly knew at all. On my
tray at that time, by mere happenstance, was a
mushroom-and-onion pizza, large, heavy on the mozza-
rella, and gluey with tomatoes. With barely the flick of
my wrist, it upped and flew away, almost hitting the low

ceiling before flipping over and coming in for a landing on the head of the bat's owner. The sonofabitch looked as though he'd been swimming underwater and had come up directly beneath a pizza that had been innocently floating by. In seconds he was wearing it like a Dali-esque watch, only I wondered why no one was laughing but me. Well, the reason no one was laughing was that the gentleman under the pizza was chief of detectives for the twenty-third precinct, upon whom much good will depended since it was he who saw to it that the drunks were picked up as soon as they touched Chips' front door and that the two hookers who nightly occupied the corner table were allowed to do their business there, especially as the house got a cut.

Not that that would have made any difference to me, a bat in the crotch being a bat in the crotch regardless of who its keeper might be. I had reacted purely on reflex. If it had been Mayor Wagner under my skirt, he'd have gotten the flying pizza just as quick as Detective O'Hare. Governor Harriman would have gotten it, too, as would have President Truman, though I like to believe that, had it been Clark Gable, I might have been more patient—like a half hour.

At any rate, a small discussion ensued, the gist of which was that I was clumsy, ill-tempered, and fired. It was "Good-bye, Mister Chips," and it was raining as I trudged across Central Park to my apartment, out of work, out of luck, out of the frying pan, into the crapper.

I ate a can of sardines and considered my options. I could go to work as a receptionist, maybe at ABC, because I was cute and knew some of the people there who often ate at Chips. Or, I could apply for a job as an experimental corpse at Roosevelt Hospital, which, if nothing else, would be more fulfilling than being a receptionist at ABC. Or, I could panhandle because I was cute and there weren't too many cute panhandlers. Or, I could cry myself to sleep because I was good at it and could do it immediately and still keep all my options open for the next day. I did the last because that's what I always did.

When I awoke I reached over for my copy of *Variety*. I always read *Variety* because the obituaries cheered me up. They were not only heartfelt and creative, but they also meant that people in show biz had died and that jobs were open as a result, such as a tightrope walker, usher at the Roxy, and a trained dog. There was also a small blurb stating that open auditions were being held for dancers for chorus jobs in *Guys and Dolls*. I didn't waste a second cup of coffee.

There were more girl dancers at the Forty-sixth Street Theatre than marinara spots on Chips' walls. And most of the girls were pretty if not outright beautiful. I mean, show me a man who doesn't respond to a long-legged girl in black leotards and I'll show you the man who headed up the auditions that day.

I didn't get his name, I only knew that he was bored, rude, and gay. There was a piano player and a drummer and a work light, and that was all. The girls went onstage in groups of six after first watching our bored, rude, gay choreographer (he was *not* Michael Kidd) do a quick rendition of "A Bushel And A Peck"—so quick that it was over almost before we had our leotards hitched up. There was simply no way in which a dancer could come in cold and do what he did without looking like a gimpy marionette on tangled strings. But I knew *Guys and Dolls* inside out. I had seen it maybe forty times. I could do the choreography of "A Bushel And A Peck" blindfolded. And I damned near did.

And as I did, I became aware that the other girls

were just melting away, walking off the stage, vaulting back into the orchestra, and plopping into their seats (just as when I had danced like mad for Annice, to avoid the cut). And when I had finished, they all applauded sarcastically.

The faggy choreographer looked up at me. "Ever do this show somewhere before? In stock maybe?"

"Nope."

"You know it so well."

"I've seen the show."

"How many times?"

"Two or three." I heard the girls laughing. "Maybe four."

"Pray, tell us your name."

"Ginnie Maitland."

"Ever dance professionally?"

"Yes. The Annice Chatterton Dancers."

"That's a Negro group."

"Yes, I'm—I danced with them."

"Oh, yes. You're the white girl."

"Still am." I thought that was funny. Nobody else did.

"Who's your agent, Goldilocks?"

"Don't have one."

"No matter. You'll work for scale?"

"Yes, sir."

"Okay. Be in Tuesday afternoon. Twelve thirty. The rest of you, thank you very much. Just fill out the cards and leave 'em with Clancy. We'll be in touch. Next six, please. Hurry-hurry."

I had it! I had the job! *Guys and Dolls*! All that hanging around had paid off! Frightening! If I'd hang around Alfred Lunt I could be Lynn Fontanne! I was so elated, so knocked out, I immediately called Roland at his office and it was so good to hear his booming laugh. Then, before going back to the apartment, I went to the A & P to stock up for my eating orgy. Four bundles of junk food—I had to get a cab to get home, and make two trips up the five flights of stairs. And when I finally opened the door and went in, a girl was there. An immense girl in a stewardess outfit who smiled and said her name was Jessica.

I smiled and said I was Ginnie and would she please get the hell out, and that went for the man with her who was either a pilot or a doorman.

To make it brief, she knew Don and Ben and claimed to own the lease along with two other girls, and she didn't appear to be making it up. I put her and Captain Stykes (his name) into Don's room and would have explained about the refrigerator and the sink and the shower, except she knew all about them.

Another pilot, Captain O'Neill, was on the couch, having crash-landed there while I was out auditioning. He was either from another airline or another hotel, though he might have been a postman or a drum major. I helped him into Ben's room because he was too drunk to make it on his own. It was all getting a bit tight and, swearing to travel only on trains and busses from then on, I wrote to Ben for advice on how to deal with the situation.

The next day Jessica rolled out of her room but only to get something to eat. As to Captain Stykes, I guess he was eating Jessica because I didn't see him again for two days. Actually, there was so much of Jessica to eat that it's a wonder he wasn't in there till Lent.

I went over to the theatre to get fitted for costumes and to Capezio's to get some ballet shoes and sneakers. When I got back to the apartment, Jessica and Captain Stykes were in a holding pattern in Don's bedroom but Captain O'Neill had taken off, his place in Ben's room taken over by Captain Hennon, of Barnum and Bailey Airlines, or so it seemed because he came at me like a tiger.

For the next few days there was a lot of heavy air traffic in the apartment. Ben called, saying he'd gotten my letter. He confirmed Jessica's story and asked if I could handle it all. I assured him that I could and we chatted. And when I hung up I felt better about things and slept very well. In the morning, Captain Hennon was gone. I was alone. Thank God.

I continued to work my way into the show as one of the Hot Box Girls, and was scheduled to go on in a couple days, rehearsing my one line, which I wanted desperately to say right, with feeling and professionalism.

Anyway, I'm back in the apartment, alone, working on my one line, giving it all the nuances I can come up with, working so late into the night that I don't fall asleep until maybe dawn. And then, deep asleep, I hear the phone ringing and I grope to pick it up and it's Ben, only I'm so out of it I don't know what the hell he's talking about. Something about a first-class promotion which I figured upped him to lieutenant or something, only I didn't want to grill him on how a man could go from a private to an officer just like that. So I just congratulated him, hung up, fell back to sleep, and when I got up I wasn't even sure I'd spoken with him.

Some days later, convinced that Ben *had* called, and feeling sublimely confident that all doors were swinging open for me and that, no matter which one I chose, it was guaranteed to lead me to fame, fortune, and bliss, I walked over to Saks Fifth Avenue to take a gander at what 1951 had to offer—money being no object, but thirty dollars being my limit as who knew what disaster the next day might serve up.

I found a nifty blouse, $23.95, blue with white polka dots, the opposite color scheme of my ass when I was working at Chips, which is why I probably bought it. Back at the apartment the phone was ringing. Fort Devens, Massachusetts, PFC, Ben Webber on the line. Nothing important, just that he was getting out of the Army and was coming home.

My sweet Ben. He was coming home. My dear, beautiful, coming-home Ben was coming home.

I changed the lock on the door. What the hell, though I didn't legally own the lease, I did have squatter's rights; and with Ben due in soon, I wanted very much to discourage people from barging in on us highly unannounced. If they phoned ahead, fine—I'd try to accommodate them. But they couldn't just come by and flop in like I was Traveler's Aid. Those days were over.

After rehearsing my way into *Guys and Dolls*, it was time for me to go on. My first Broadway show and, understandably, I was scared titless. All the other replacements had been in Broadway shows before so they were relaxed. Also, because the show had been running for a while, there was no pressure on anyone to do or die for dear old Runyon. Vivian Blaine and Sam Levene and Isabel Bigley were gone but, happily for us, the audiences were enjoying the show almost before they sat down, practically applauding their *Playbills*, and when the overture played, they sang along, knowing the lyrics perhaps better than the composer.

But not me. During the overture I was in the john, throwing up. There I was, in this sexy costume, wearing a merry widow bra that started above my hips and ended below my boobs. It was all boned in so that, if I were to raise my arms too suddenly my tits would fly off to the second balcony. As it was, even if they didn't fly off, they were pushed up so high that I looked like a double-chinned squirrel with the mumps. I mean, I was ready to pop.

Anyway, I'm about to write a suicide note when this other dancer, Florrie, who had befriended me because she had five cats and what was one more, comes by and hauls me out of the john, consoles me, and tells me that it happens to everyone and that I shouldn't let it get me, that the curtain was going up and that if I was not out there I'd fuck up the whole show, so I'd better get my high tits onstage even if they fly off to Havana.

"But Florrie, I don't know my line!"

"It'll come to you."

"If I blow my line, the whole show'll stop!"

"Your line isn't for twenty minutes. Your tits are due *now*. Come *on*!"

And out I went. And I was fine. I mean, everything I'd heard about being scared backstage and how the only cure is to go on, and how, with going on, all fear evaporates, it was all true.

So—Adelaide and her Hot Box Girls do their number and we all leave the stage so that Adelaide can be alone with Nathan Detroit, her boyfriend. And then it's time for my line and I'm ready. I come back onstage because I'm supposed to be looking for my earring, and I'm supposed to say to Nathan, "I'm all dated up with Society Max and he goes and breaks it on account of your dopey crap game." It's an important line because it furthers the plot in that it tips off Adelaide that Nathan is running the crap game again after having promised Adelaide that he wouldn't. Without that line the audience would not understand why Adelaide was getting mad at Nathan—and—because it was the third scene, it would confuse the thrust of the rest of the show, okay?

Okay, so there I am. Adelaide is alone with Nathan,

and out I come, prancing, leggy and loony and confident, and I say to Nathan, "I'm all dated up with Society Max and he goes and breaks it on account of your crappy dope game!"

Now you must understand that I have done two weeks of tediously being on people's asses over that line and have no idea that I've done a spoonerism on it, saying "crappy dope game" instead of "dopey crap game." I mean, to *me*, it sounded right, only I know that *something's* wrong because Nathan collapses into a wet raspberry and I see the spittle coming out of his mouth, firing over the footlights like a hydrant.

Then Adelaide goes up, also spouting spit, and then the audience goes, and I don't understand anything because Nathan and Adelaide aren't doing what they're supposed to be doing. And so I freeze and figure, "Oh, shit—my boobs have popped!" And I'm afraid to look down and see, only the audience is hysterical and the stage manager is falling on the floor and Florrie is trying to keep from peeing, so I look and I see that my boobs are still there, still tucked under my chin like grapefruits on the rise. So then I think, what if I'm split? I mean, I'm in fishnet stockings, no panties, my boobs are still in place—what is going on that I can't see? It has to be that I'm split and that my entire bottom is hanging out like it's in Macy's window. And now I have to go over with my ass aimed at the audience and bend down and pick up this earring.

Well, I figure, Ethel Merman would do it. Mary Martin would do it. The show must go on. So I go over, and I find the earring, and I say, "Oh, here it is." And it's a colossal stretch because I'm not supposed to bend my knees. And the audience is plotzing so now I'm sure I'm split and that everything from front to rear is showing.

Well, I say to myself, what's done cannot be undone. If the world has seen my crotch, so be it, all girls have crotches and I'll stack mine against anybody's so why all the hoo-ha? So I do my walk-off like nothing has happened and I get applause like Lynn Fontanne, nude, never got.

Back onstage, Adelaide retrieves the day by saying, "What she meant to say was dopey *crap* game—not crappy *dope* game," which gets another five minutes of applause and which also tells me what I've done.

Delighted that I hadn't flashed my vagina, I was all the same crushed that I had blown my one line. But, if onstage my boo-boo received applause, offstage it received an ovation. The cast, the crew, even our silly-dilly choreographer came over to lay hands of congratulations on me. What had I done? Two things. I had livened up the show, saving it from falling into a pattern of dull sameness that every long-running show risks, and I had shown pluck—not my vagina and not my ass, but pluck. I had gone on with the show. When all about me had lost their heads, I had held onto mine, holding it high in the process.

So I was awarded the Gypsy Robe, a tradition that had started a few years earlier in *Gentlemen Prefer Blondes* when one of the girl dancers, upon leaving the show, gave her dressing robe to one of her successors. The robe was passed from show to show, from gypsy to gypsy (*gypsy* being the affectionate term for a dancer), and I had it, a once pretty thing that started out as white satin with a white mirabou fur shawl collar but had had things added onto it that had to do with each show it turned up in: a banana peel from *Top Banana*, some beads from *The King And I*, a ribbon from *Most Happy Fella*. It was a bit tacky by the time I got it but it was the thought that counted, and someone had thought to bestow the Gypsy Robe on me.

I was a star—of sorts. A fucking star. My language, bad to begin with, was fast becoming worse than a longshoreman's, but so was Tallulah Bankhead's so what the fuck else was new?

Word of my triumph spread quickly and I was encouraged to keep my inverted line in the show. It livened things up and added to my growing legend as the dumbest fucking girl in town. Only I wasn't fucking anyone. I was saving myself for Ben. Yes, admirers came around. And, yes, I went with some of them to dinner. But the game stopped at the front door to my apartment because no one was allowed in. Only Ben.

ben

1951

I was moved into the Medical Holding Detachment barracks which meant that I was billeted with psychos,
weirdos, and finks. All the madmen and misfits of the
Army, waiting to get out, were herded and restrained in
the same corral.

Oddballs abounded, most of whom I met during my
one night in the psycho ward, it being standard proce-
dure that anyone leaving the Army with anything other
than a perfect honorable discharge be made to go that
route. It seemed little enough price to pay for the gaining of one's freedom, so not even those of us who considered ourselves normal objected to that one night in
paradise.

The windows of the psycho ward were on the outside
of the cages, and wisely so, in that more than one sicko
had attempted to hurl himself through a window, only
to bounce back in ricochet surprise. Three of the men
had stayed all night on the mesh screen, like roosting
birds or pondering apes. They never moved—except
their bowels—so one was well-advised to give them all
vertical leeway.

We were allowed no sharp objects, our only eating
utensil being a flat wooden spoon. Needless to say, we
ate mush. And any of us wishing to shave could do so
only under the supervision of two muscular aides. As to

the blades we were provided with, they were so dull that it wasn't a shave at all, it was a rub.

No belts or shoelaces either, and pyjama drawstrings were removed with the diligence of a urologist guiding a jagged kidney-stone out of a spiralled penis. It would have been difficult enough to garner any sleep in the psycho ward, but it was made all the more futile because of O'Connell, the Mad Bunny, so named because he went from man to man, throughout the night, asking if he could take the Easter eggs out from beneath our beds. I told him that he could have all the eggs he could find, and he was so pleased at my generosity that he promised me a chocolate egg by morning. I had the good sense to not ask how he'd get it chocolated. Still, the next morning, when he brought me that imaginary chocolate egg, I ate it graciously, shell and all, because he said it was the best part.

Also that morning, Major Howard Hochman, the psychiatrist in charge, came by to see how I had passed the night. I suggested to him that if he left me there one more night, he needn't return ever. He smiled, checked me out of the ward, and I went with him to his office for consultation.

Major Hochman was a bright man, fifty and balding but magnificently clear-eyed. Having served in the Army during World War II, he had gotten called back into service to treat the nutsies of the Korean conflict. He had had to leave a healthy practice in New York City to do so but didn't seem too upset by it, being one of those scientific men who was forever learning, forever squeezing something worthwhile out of every adversity. I liked him because he had no time for bullshit. He was not interested in impressing me. He only wanted to help me. And he started right in.

We discussed my case with my 201 file open on his

desk. There it was again, my Jauvert, forever hounding its Jean Valjean—and the good doctor's evaluation of me was not calculated to contribute to my peace of mind. He said that I was angry—where or how it started was no longer pertinent—that, though unaware of it, I had approached all of my problems with an unconscious desire to disrupt rather than overcome, and that I hosted a whole slew of antagonisms which, if left unattended, might eventually bring about my doom.

The profile was neither flattering nor satisfying and, like Scrooge, I vowed to make myself over before it was too late. I would do it for Tony and for Deyo, two men whose deaths I had helped bring about, if in no other way but by my continual baiting of Holdoffer. I had contributed to Holdoffer's death, too, prick that he was, and to the deaths of Dickie Stovall and Junior Lightman and Alan Kirkpatrick. By virtue of all my subsurface anger, I had touched off an entire chain of subversions, all of which I had been able to sidestep but for which others had to pay. Captain Grace had spotted me. And General McArdle had my number. And Major Hochman had nailed me to the cross. Still, I'd be getting out of the Army soon, and how I used the time remaining to atone for my deeds and salvage what remained of my conscience was suddenly a matter of utmost importance. I didn't have much time left. A week, ten days—who knew? And I wanted to use that time well. So I called Maggie and she was in. And I tore up that unflattering photo I had developed of myself because I'd be damned if I'd let it show up in my high-school yearbook.

I strode through the Ritz-Carlton lobby like Patton. And it was good. I had the entire day off, all twenty-four hours of it, and Maggie the Marvelous was around the bend with new clevernesses to institute and old ones to reprise.

As I got on the elevator a woman got off. I'd say she was about thirty and kind of cheap-looking. Lemon hair, pitted skin, broad-shouldered and flat-waisted. At first I thought it was a man. She smiled at me. "Ben?"

"Yes?"

"Some other time." And she was gone.

I went up to room 503 and Maggie answered the door. "Did you see Betty?"

"Yeah. I think so. Who's Betty?"

She smiled. "Someone I didn't think you were quite ready for yet."

"I may not be ready for her ever. I thought she was a man."

"She thinks so, too. Come on in. Relax." Maggie was in a robe, looking good but obviously a bit tired from her workout with Betty. "Well, now you know the depths of my degradation." She lit up a cigarette. "You will admit that Betty is about as low as a girl can go for a lover."

"I don't know. She seemed kind of an all-around good fellow."

"Take your clothes off. You'd think, with the money at my disposal and the circles I move in—you'd think I'd come up with a lesbian with chic, not a dyke with muscles."

"Oh? She a dyke?"

Maggie laughed. She laughed a lot and often too quickly, and sometimes when there really wasn't any reason to laugh. "Well, I tell you, whenever I feel that I'm not all that bad, I call Betty and she comes over and brings the truth with her."

"I don't think you're so bad."

"When it comes to me, you shouldn't think *anything*.

You should just get it while it's hot. It's part of your
growing up. There's women and there's woman. Big fish
eat little fish. Eat or be eaten. Come over here."

Naked, I walked over to her and she put me into her
mouth as if I were an ice cream pop she had forgotten
she was eating. "How's that?"

"You're doing fine."

She slipped out of her robe. "Come with me please,
sir." She walked into the bedroom and I followed. The
bed was rumpled, echoes of Betty. It didn't stop us. We
rumpled it some more. She was incredible. I was like a
toy. She took me right out of it, out of wherever I had
come from and whatever was on my mind. Finished, I
felt completely new. Not even tired. "Dear Ben, it's all
happening to you so quickly, isn't it? When shall we do
it again?"

"How's five minutes?"

She laughed. "You know what I mean."

"I don't know. My orders could come through almost
any time."

"And you'll be going home."

"I guess so."

"Well, if you're still around, give me a call during the
week. Only I don't know either. Kevin and I may be
going to London. Think you can stretch your cock that
far?"

"Sure. But how do I get back?"

She laughed and then grew sober. "I'm suddenly very
sad. This may be the last time we ever see each other."

"Should we write to each other?"

"Christ, no! No letters! If you're still around, call.
But no letters, okay?"

"Okay."

I got dressed and she didn't. She just walked me to
the door. "I don't mean to rush you but I do have to get

back. Some maharajah from somewhere is coming for dinner."

"You going to eat him?"

"I don't think so. I don't like Indian food. Too much curry."

We were at the door and she opened it, standing naked in the doorway. It didn't bother her. Actually, I think she'd have liked it if somebody came by. "Well, Maggie—"

"No long good-byes." She was smiling but there were tears in her eyes. "Good-bye, Ben." And she moved her face to mine and our lips met in the sweetest of kisses. And I remember thinking at the time that, despite all the randy sex we'd had together, that was the first time that she ever truly reached me—and the only time that I ever truly felt anything for her.

Back at Fort Devens my orders had come through. I was out. Me and the Army were through. Kaput, fini and good riddance. I would miss Johnny; I would miss Maggie. But the rest of it? So long and I won't look back.

Major Hochman gave me another bit of information. It pertained to the infiltration course investigation. General McArdle had concluded his findings, which had to be submitted to the judge advocate for approval, of course, but which still represented a final ruling in that the judge advocate had undoubtedly been a party to its conclusions.

Sergeant Frank Kuyper was to be brought up on a charge of homicide. Considering his record and the weird circumstances, it was not likely that he'd get the firing squad. Still, twenty years to life seemed the best he could hope for.

Captain Albert Mackie, the range officer, was cited

for dereliction of duty, reduced to the rank of first lieutenant, and confined to quarters pending even further investigation. He would probably be encouraged to resign from the Army, no questions asked, and he'd be an asshole if he didn't snap at the offer.

Colonel Herbert Cranston of the 42nd Group was transferred to Fort Riley, Kansas, and placed in charge of a laundry company where his battlefield skills in that field could be made proper use of and where his stupidity as a commanding officer would never be called upon again.

Lieutenant Colonel Terence Beakins remained on as second-in-command of the 42nd Group but only for as long as the new first-in-command chose to keep him on in that post—which was not likely to be long. Lieutenant Colonel Beakins would then stand a fine chance of disappearing within the folds of some fuck-up bridgade where his talents as a fool could be properly utilized.

Lieutenant Wyatt Collings, our company commander who forgot to show up, was busted to sergeant and sent directly to Korea, where we all had every confidence that he would be killed, probably by an American.

Corporal William Simmons, machine gunner, was exonerated from all blame as he was judged to have been only doing his duty, four men having been killed as a result of his zeal, so maybe he'd do it again one day and make Sergeant.

Johnny Munez and Ben Webber got drunk one last time together. They did it at PX 5 and they did it well, both of them carving their initials on a wall so deeply that they would last there a millennium. The next day I was on a Trailways bus, barreling toward New York City. I had written ahead to Josh Meyerberg to tell him of my impending release from service and that I was looking forward to getting my old job back. I just thought I'd let him know in advance so as to disarm that apparent snake, Sam Gaynor.

A disquieting note. On the bus I found a Boston newspaper, and in it was a report of a train crash near Pittsburgh. Naturally, I read the story to see if anyone I knew had been on that ill-fated train. There had. Elizabeth Jane Satterly, aged eighteen; killed. Farewell Elizabeth Satterly, yellow your color, black your hair, grey eyes of such a hue as never had I seen before. And I wondered, had she been leaving Pittsburgh finally on her way to New York to find me?

As to my new roommate, Ginnie, I had told her that I'd be coming home soon but had deliberately not chosen to tell her *when*. I wanted to surprise her.

chapter fourteen

ginnie

1951

Guys and Dolls went on and on and on until even I was getting bored with it. Yes, it was my first Broadway show, and yes, it was all very exciting, but it was also hard work and getting harder, bordering on drudgery, with hours better suited to goblins and Karloffs than to humans. Finishing up at eleven thirty each night, we'd then go out for dinner, a small army of pancaked chorus girls and screaming faggots all determined to be young and gay noisying up the streets, staying frantically out until three or four, and stumbling into bed only after the sun had come up over the blanket.

Well, that was okay for a while, but when you threw in two matinees with the regular six performances a week the whole thing was suddenly not so delightful. The dressing room stunk and was cold. The girls were always bitching and the boys were even bitchier. My body ached. I was smoking and drinking too much, not getting enough sleep. The pay—$115 a week—was lousy, and the caste system, at parties, was intolerable. We were only replacements. We were the four hundredth *Guys and Dolls*. Even kids in a flop show that had opened and died were more highly thought of than we were. They were "openers." We were "tail-enders," and the snobbery stuck in our throats like old toe shoes. So, after a tour of duty in *Guys and Dolls*—the greatest

278 herman raucher

show I'd ever seen, my all-time favorite, the one show I'd have killed to get into—when Florrie came to me with this crazy idea, I gave it a good listen.

"Ginnie," she said, "I think it'll work." My friend Florrie was a thin kid, originally from Brooklyn, whose father parked cars and whose mother worked for the phone company. They lived together in a basement apartment with five cats and three hundred water bugs coming up through the floor each night that were so big that they looked like mice—which is why the cats. Florrie had enormous blue eyes and beautifully capped teeth (which is why I knew she'd be a star). And her legs— well, she had the most unbelievable insteps in town, a straight line from her knee to her toe tips. And she had a baby way that made her seem like Little Miss Innocence, even though her language was so filthy that, coming out of an ordinary-looking girl, it would have earned a crack in the mouth. But coming out of Florrie all it got was ignored because people just believed they'd imagined it. Still, when she got to cursing in that wee widdle voice I often had the feeling that the paint was curling off the walls. "Richie is a helluva fuckin' dancer and, if we formed a trio—two girls and a boy—we could bust out of the fuckin' chorus and do club dates and maybe some television and live like human beings."

"Why does Richie want me?" I asked. "He can go with Annie or Ethel or Shellie."

"Wanna know the truth?"

"Yes."

"They all turned him down."

"Swell."

"But that's because they're assholes."

"Maybe they know something we don't."

"They don't. They're all pushing thirty—from the wrong side. And they're tired and looking for husbands,

only they're never gonna find them in the chorus line. I
tell you, Ginnie, you're eighteen and I'm twenty-one
and we can dance the tits off all of 'em. Richie'll accept
your inexperience because he knows you can learn. As
to the others, all they'll learn from now on is how to
grow older. And, sweetie-puss, ain't nothin' less saleable
than an old chorine. So, whaddya say?"

"I don't know."

"You don't know? It's a chance you may never get
again!"

"I understand."

"Why don't you know?"

"Well, I may get married."

"What?"

"It's not definite, but—"

"Who? Not the dentist! Jesus Christ, not Murray the
stammerer-er-er-er!"

"No."

"The guy from the garment center?"

"No."

"Phillie the fairy?"

"No."

"*Who?*"

"I can't talk about it yet. Things still have to be
worked out. He's getting out of the Army soon and—"

"The Army? He's in the Army? What is he, a *gun*?"

"He's a very unusual and special person."

"You're describing a three-legged elf."

"Cut it out, Florrie. He's very nice and—I love him."

"Shit, you get married now and knocked up, and it's
the end. End of the fucking line."

"Maybe."

"Listen, Ginnie, shack up with the guy, but keep the
door open. What is it? Ah, he's married, right?"

"Florrie, I really can't talk about it."

"What am I going to *do* with you? Richie Pickering's time has come. He's got the talent, the drive—we can be dancing at Bill Miller's Riviera in no time. Monty can get us on *The Joey Magnuson Show*. He's already spoken to Noah Sobel about it. We'll be The Pickering Trio. Shit, you got a fella stashed away somewhere, swell! But it doesn't mean you have to let your career go down the toilet. You *know* Richie's good."

"Yes."

"You know he's not just jerking off."

"Yes."

"Then at least talk to him."

"Okay."

I talked with Richie Pickering. He was a sensational dancer and everyone knew it. About thirty, he'd had featured dance roles in *Brigadoon* and *Finian's Rainbow,* and though I suspected he might be gay, his dancing never showed it. His dancing was masculine, very butch. And the rumor was that he'd done a lot of choreography in other shows only never got credit for it. He didn't try to high-pressure me. He wanted me because I was fair and Florrie was dark and we complemented each other. He'd pay us during rehearsals, and, if I liked, we could begin rehearsals without my having to quit *Guys and Dolls*. It would mean about twenty minutes sleep a night, but if it didn't work out I'd still be with *Guys and Dolls* and would've lost nothing but a little sleep.

I couldn't find anything wrong with what he said so I agreed to give it a try. We rehearsed a couple hours every day, two separate routines: a wild jazz number to "Sing, Sing, Sing," and a sophisticated kind of Caribbean interpretation of "Sweet Georgia Brown." And if there was a music I was good at, it was Carra-bee-an, bay-bee.

As usual, I picked up very fast. Lucas Harrison arranged our music, gratis. We could pay him later, if and when. Charles Strouse played rehearsal piano for us while his partner, Lee Adams, leaned on the water cooler and told us how great we were. (A few years later they would clobber Broadway with *Bye-Bye, Birdie.*) Everybody was very supportive and the act was pulling together. It was *très chic*—mostly jazz dancing, modern, but with enough ballet peppered in to give it a wildly distinctive style.

After two weeks, some agents from William Morris ambled by to catch the act. One guy was named Lenny and the other was named Bernie, or vice versa. If you're in show business long enough, you learn that all agents are named Lenny and Bernie and call you "kid" and tell you that "you've got the goods"—and, to prove it, they set up auditions for important people who have nothing better to do with their time and want to feel that they're really being swell so they come. For us they set up an audition with Noah Sobel, producer of *The Joey Magnuson Show,* a weekly Saturday night TV show starring (you guessed it) Joey Magnuson. It always got such high ratings that the other networks seldom put on anything against it but puppet shows, wrestling and test patterns.

We gave it a go, showing up wordlessly terrified in a rehearsal hall just opposite the City Center because that's where Sobel had his headquarters and that's where he was at the time because that's where he was *all* the time.

Joey Magnuson wasn't there, which came as a relief because we'd heard that he was a perfectionist and we were far from perfect. But Noah Sobel was there and he was the man we'd have to convince. Also present, eating hero sandwiches because it was lunch hour, were all the writers, among whom was Florrie's boyfriend, Monty Rivers. They were all mad and funny and helpful, making it so easy for us to be good that, when we finished up our two separate four-minute routines, sweaty as we were, we went around hugging everyone as if we'd been hired, like boxers trying to convince the judges that the decision was in the bag. We hugged Charles at the piano and Lee at the water cooler. We even hugged Lenny and Bernie, soiling their white-on-white shirts.

We didn't hug Noah Sobel because that would have been a little much. Once we got started, I never looked at him, and only when we'd finished did I dare look to see if he was there. He was, as silent and unmoving as he was when we first came in, as though he hadn't seen anything and was waiting for us to begin. It threw me and I felt my stomach go queasy. Could it be that we hadn't auditioned yet?

Then Monty, laying aside a hero sandwich he said had died a coward's death, hopped onto his chair, whistling and applauding and yelling things like "Velez and Yolande look out!" and "All the good Jewish dancers are not dead!" Then, sticking a big cigar in his mouth, he sidled over to Noah Sobel and said, loud, so that everyone would hear, "Noah, boychik, these kids are going to the tippy-top. Akron, Duluth, Ecuador. There'll be no stopping them. If you don't sign them, Ziegfeld will, because, as you know, no one has a better eye for young talent than Sid Ziegfeld. Don't be a schmuck, Noah. Don't lose 'em like you lost Hitler. Hitler was a great tap-dancer. If you'd of signed him like I suggested, millions of lives would have been saved. But no, you told him he had no talent and that he should grow a mustache and comb his hair funny and—whacko—he declares war. Noah, if you don't want to be responsible for

World War III, sign 'em. Sign the Richie Hitler Trio. And if you do, for comic relief, I'll throw in Herm, Fats Göring and the Panzers."

Noah Sobel allowed a smile to push up his ears and he stood up and left the room, motioning for Lenny and Bernie to follow him. They did, as if they were carrying his train. We felt that something good was going to happen.

And it did. We were given a spot on *The Joey Magnuson Show*. Of course, the fact that Florrie was going with Monty didn't hurt. Monty had assured her that, if Richie could put a really good act together, he, Monty, would guarantee that Noah Sobel would buy it *because* (The Gospel according to Monty) Monty was blackmailing Noah at the time, being the sole possessor of information and photographs (and catchy tunes) that linked Noah Sobel with the Raisinets smuggling trade in the Catskills and with that infamous eccentric dancer of the French Revolution, George "Taps" Richelieu, who also went by the name Lanny Ross. Madness unchained—that's the way it was with Monty Rivers. Still is.

We rehearsed and rehearsed and the act got better and better, and Lenny and Bernie wanted us to sign with William and Morris but Richie didn't want to sign with anyone just yet, which pissed off all four of those gentlemen. It troubled me a little because Lenny and Bernie had gone to all that trouble and had every right to assume that we'd sign with them, but I didn't know Richie well enough to question his decision. The Morris office did, however, get the commission on that booking, and, afraid to alienate Richie in case the trio really took off, they chose instead to hang around with offers to help out—no charge—wherever they could. Richie had a good thing going.

Monty lent us some money to have composites made up, photographs and flattering biographies which he himself had written. I was very impressed with what I read about myself:

GINNIE MAITLAND—long, lean and lovely, is a graduate of the Orsen Sather Ballet Company of Seattle. A native of the Big Tree Country, the lissome beauty came east only at the insistence of the respected choreographer, Annice Chatterton. Once in New York, the blonde beauty captured the eye of the prominent producer, Noah Sobel, and has fascinated such choreographers as George Ballanchine and Richie Pickering, the latter prevailing upon the blue-eyed ballerina to leave her featured role in *Guys and Dolls* and join him as one-third of his new and provocative Pickering Trio. After a group of dance concerts with the trio, Ginnie may opt to go to the Soviet Union, at the invitation of that government, to work with the Bolshoi in hopes of demonstrating to Russian audiences her distinctive American style.

Just above all the lies was a dramatic photo of me on point, looking as though I had just completed a twenty-nine-foot leap and landed on the big toenail of my right foot, holding that position while the Boston Symphony played the entire overture to *Swan Lake*. The truth is, I have never been able to stay on point for longer than a blink, and the photo was actually of Maria Tallchief but with my head and ponytail pasted on. Still, it was all so terribly impressive that I actually found myself looking forward to my trip to Russia and to the adoration of its dance-knowledgeable public.

Florrie's biography was no less unbelievable, except

that she was French, a half-sister of Zizi Jeanmaire, and a heroine of the French Underground who danced for Charles de Gaulle during the most despairing moments of the German Occupation. No matter, we were going to be on *The Joey Magnuson Show* and if that wasn't exactly caviar, neither was it borscht.

We were rehearsing like mad because now it was for real. And when we had it down so pat that we could do it in our sleep, we moved over to the studio at NBC where we would soon be rehearsing with a full orchestra. Everything was "live" then. No film, no tape. You went on and you did it. You got one crack at it and, if you fell on your ass, the whole world saw it. But, being a featured act backed by a huge orchestra was worth the risk. Besides, all of Russia would be seeing me soon and I needed the experience.

Florrie and I gave proper notice to the *Guys and Dolls* management, who, on hearing the news, yawned. They replaced us with two other nameless girls who would be around for the closing party and could cry and feel a part of some great theatrical tradition.

Richie Pickering made a pass at me but I think it was only to establish his position as boss, the result of his somehow equating heterosexuality with authority. It was a feeble attempt, sadly half-hearted, in which he whispered in my ear that he'd like to make it with me. Diplomatically I remarked that I liked him very much but that I was about to be married and what would the neighbors think.

He let the matter drop—only to come on stronger two days later. I didn't know what to think. How do you say no to a man who seems to be saying "fuck me or you're fired"? It hadn't come to that as yet but it was getting there. So I asked Florrie her opinion.

"He's straight," she said, chewing her nails nervously.

"That's what I was afraid of," I said, chewing mine.

"But it's bad business. If you ball him and he gets tired of you, you're out. But if you don't ball him he'll get pissed off because he'll think that you think he's a fag. And you're out just the same as if you did ball him. So—" she was thinking it through, "if it was me, I'd just as soon be hung for a chicken as for a turkey."

"What?"

"I'd ball him."

"But—"

"No. Wait a minute. Check that. There's a middle ground. Tell him you're a dyke and that your girlfriend'll beat the shit out of you, and, while you're at it, tell him I'm your girlfriend because he's been coming on with me, too, and I can do without Monty coming over and cutting Bobby's balls off with a machete."

"What do I do?"

"Tell him you've got the clap."

"Think it'll stop him?"

"Well, let's just say it'll put a crimp in him."

"Gee, I don't know."

"Tell him you have syphilis. If that doesn't stop him, nothing will and you might as well ball him. I don't know what else to tell you, kid. He seems to have his hard-on set on balling one of us and it ain't gonna be me. So, I guess it's every man for himself."

"Why couldn't he be a faggot like everyone else?"

Florrie shrugged. "You can't have everything."

"Why don't I tell him that as a child I was raped by Chinese guerrillas and that, as a result, I can't fuck *anyone*?"

"That'd stop Monty."

"It would?"

"Yeah. He'd die laughing."

"What do I do?"

"Grow a cock."

"Yes. A good idea. Thank you."

"You're welcome."

We weren't scheduled for *The Joey Magnuson Show* for a couple weeks. Noah Sobel, about as smart as they come, knew it was our first time and he didn't want to rush us into it. We kept rehearsing, getting better and better, cutting fifteen seconds from our first number and twenty-three from our second. I don't mean in steps, I mean in time. We were whizzing through some very tricky routines, which made them look better, smoother. I thought all that speed was risky because it increased our chances of goofing. But Richie disagreed, feeling that the faster we went the less we'd think with our heads and the more we'd think with our bodies. He wanted our dancing to be as involuntary as our breathing. He wanted us to go out there and do it by reflex because that's what *all* the great dancers did.

I came home from rehearsal after first stocking up at the A & P, and when I had finished climbing my five flights of stairs, I saw this soldier sitting against my door. He looked up at me and I looked down at him and all my bundles just slipped through my arms as if greased—eggs, milk, juice, splat, glop. "Jesus Christ!" I said.

"No. Ben. Ginnie?"

"Jesus Christ!"

"Really? You don't look like any of your pictures." He got to his feet.

And I ran into his arms. "Oh, Ben!" And came all apart. "Oh, Ben—I don't believe it! I don't! Is it really you?"

"I'm pretty sure. Wait—I'll check my dogtags."

But I wasn't of a mind to take my arms away from his neck. I just hugged him and hugged him, nothing in my head but hugs. Nothing in my arms but Ben. Of course, I cried.

He was very consoling. "Don't cry. I'll buy you more groceries."

"You're home. Jesus Christ, you're home."

"Yeah. Sorry the resurrection took so long. It was my first time and—"

"You're home. Oh, Ben, I thought you'd never get here."

"I had a few doubts myself."

I stepped back to look at him and he was beautiful. Even through my tears I could see how beautiful he was. Taller than me by at least five inches (thank God) and strong and straight and Ben. I pulled myself together before he'd think me a perfect nut and run. "You waiting long?" I asked, digging through my mammoth rehearsal bag for my key while wiping my nose on my sleeve.

"An hour. Somebody changed the lock."

"You're kidding."

"No. My old key doesn't fit."

"I've got a new one for you inside. I made two." I found my key, opened the door, and we went in.

"Anyone home?" he called, then turned to me and smiled. "From your letter and phone calls I expected to find a few bodies strewn about."

"That's why I changed the lock. You still in the Army?"

"Nope. Out."

"You're still in uniform."

"None of my civilian clothes fit."

"Gee, that's a shame. You have such nice things. When you said you were coming home I had all your clothes cleaned. Jackets, slacks, shirts, socks. You favor blue. You seem to have a lot of blue clothes."

"Not my underwear."

"Couple of your BVD's are plaid."

"How many?"

"Three. Three are plaid. Four striped. Two torn. And the rest white."

"How many white?"

"Nine."

"How many—pairs of socks?"

"Twelve. All blue." I saluted.

"Shoes?"

"Four pair. Plus some sneakers, slippers, and something that looked like a pair of loafers which I had resoled." I saluted all through that speech.

"I got it!" he exclaimed, snapping his fingers. "You're a customs official!"

"Come on, I'll show you *your* room."

"How many rooms do I have? Quick! Quick!"

"Oh, shut up."

I showed him his room and he liked the way I had kept it. "Gee," he said, "just the way it was the day I died." He dropped his duffel bag on his bed and it bounced. He took off his Ike jacket and he looked beautiful in brown. Brown was not a bad color for Ben. No color was a bad color for Ben.

"Want to see *my* room?" I asked, like a kid wanting to show her latest toy.

"You mean—? There's a nursery?"

I showed him my room and he was very complimentary. I had thought to take Maggie's portrait off the wall and had shoved it into the closet. I just didn't think he'd be impressed with a girl who kept a portrait of her mother over her bed—especially when we got to making love.

"You've really fixed it up nicely. The whole place looks a lot better than when just Don and I lived here."

"*Just* Don and you?" I asked facetiously.

"And Alice and Susan and Jessica, several of whom I believe you've met."

"Yes."

"Where *is* Don? Have you heard from him?"

"No. Have you?"

"No." And he looked concerned.

"I hope he's okay. He was pretty low. Nothing was breaking for him."

"He must've been feeling lousy to just up and leave the whole city."

"What happens now? I mean to *you*?"

"Well, today's Tuesday. I go back to work after the weekend."

"The 20th?"

"Yep."

"Five days."

"What?"

"You have five whole days before you report for duty."

"I guess so."

"Any plans?"

"Nope. I just wanted to get home. Beyond that, nothing else was on my mind."

"I'm solvent again."

"*Guys and Dolls?*"

"Better. I'll tell you over dinner. Unless, I mean, have you made any plans for dinner?"

"I thought I'd eat."

"Can I take you to dinner?"

"You mean pay?"

"Well, I think I've got more money than you."

"I'm sure you do. Let's go to Le Pavillon."

"I was thinking more along the lines of Horn & Hardart."

"I need a shower."

"I need a bath."

"Flip you who goes first."

"You go first. I take too long."

He took a shower and I saw him when he came out of the bathroom, a towel wrapped about his waist, its folds moving with him as he walked, his body tight, a conspiracy of 300 smooth muscles playing about his navel—so classic, so marble-carved, so badly did I want him it was a wonder I didn't just open my big mouth and say so—"Hey, Ben, give it here. Give us a try, big boy, ten cents a whatever."

Instead I took a bath, lying in the tub, my entire life playing against the far tile, a bad movie on a cracked screen. Mommy, Daddy, Mary Ann, Walter, their faces hoisted up out of ancient archives, slapped against the bath mists and allowed to caper before my eyes like some kind of hung jury—I knew why they were there. They were there to tickle my conscience, to prick it—so to speak—because that's what was on my mind and on my agenda, to be pricked, verb form of the masculine anatomy. To be laid, finally and irrevocably; fucked by the prick of one's own choice; the long-awaited moment a confrontation to rattle the rafters and test the bedsprings. Come one, come all—wrestling on Mount Olympus, bringing together, at long last, two popular crowd-pleasers: Ben Webber, the Fort Devens Kid, pitted against that up-and-coming virgin of the Connecticut back country, Ginnie Maitland, current holder of New York's diamond-studded chastity belt. Fifteen rounds or to a conclusion, with nobody losing but conformity, hypocrisy and the Stokely School for Girls.

Time to get ready, to meet the challenge. The girl is in shape, best legs in town, flattest tummy, pertest ass. A little perfume here, a little oil there. A little robe—

the Gypsy Robe—a little sashay out of the bathroom
and into his bedroom. What? He isn't there? Then on to
the living room where—ah, there he is. Unaware of me.
So I'll pose in the doorway, like so. One arm on the
door frame, one hand on my hip, and one knee forward,
protruding from under the robe. Provocative. Irresistible. He senses. He turns. And wide-eyed he says,

"What the hell is that?"

"What?"

"What the hell are you wearing? What is it?"

"Oh—*this* old thing. It's the Gypsy Robe. I forgot to
give it to someone else."

"It's got bananas on it—"

"Yes, well, *that's*—"

"And feathers!"

"Yes. It's one of a kind. No other robe like it."

"You're not going to wear that to dinner, are you?"

"Don't be silly. I only put it on to hand you a laugh."

"Well, you got your laugh. Now, let's get dressed and
go to dinner. I'm starved."

So much for romance.

We had dinner at a little French restaurant on West
Forty-ninth Street. Le Champlain. Lots of atmosphere
and passable food at $5.95 a setting, wine included. I
wore to dinner a very high sweater, turtlenecked to my
chin, a baggy jacket that Abbott and Costello used to
fight in, and a dirndl skirt that would have made Deli-
lah look like Edna May Oliver. I was overreacting, of
course, a touch foolish at having been turned down with
a laugh and a "what the hell is *that*?" I had gone crazily
in a desperately opposite direction, dressing down to
such a degree that the nearest thing to a female that I
could possibly have been mistaken for would have been
a frumpy nun going to a masquerade party as an awn-
ing.

I had the dreadful feeling that Ben had yet to take a good look at me. I mean, when I met him I was in tights, the outlines of the greatest body in the Western Hemisphere just a grab away. When I had stepped out of the bathroom (we'll forget the robe, shall we?), my hair was piled on my head and doused in enough perfume to bring down a rhino. And there, at the restaurant, wearing practically widows' weeds, I had yet to hear a comment on any of my many disguises. It was disheartening, to say the least, so I overate.

"That's quite an appetite," he said.

"So what? I'm paying."

"That's no reason to eat like a brontosaurus."

"I'll eat like whoever I please. I happen to be very hungry."

"You can't still be hungry."

"I am. Order me some more escargots. And get some more bread. You ain't seen nothing yet."

He refused to order anything else for me to eat, which was just as well since he had gotten the point that I was unhappy. Still, it was hard for me to be all that angry with him because he had to have been very tired from his trip and couldn't possibly know that he was breaking bread with a nymphomaniacal virgin.

Conversation soon took a turn for the better as I told him of the Pickering Trio and of my upcoming television appearance (I left out Russia, which is what the UN should have done). He told me about the infiltration course incident and about the deaths of Tony and Holdoffer and the others, and I was afraid it was the wrong time to ask about the society lady he had met up with at the USO.

We walked a million miles back to the apartment and he held my hand which was nice except that it had no significance other than to keep me from falling into a pot hole or a sewer or something.

We climbed the stairs and it got silly.

"Well," he said, turning to me at the door, "thank you for a lovely evening." And he opened the door with *his* key.

"You're welcome."

"And for the nice dinner. It was really delicious and I hope we'll be seeing each other again and—" He gave me a quick kiss on the cheek. "Good night." And he stepped in and pulled the door closed, leaving me standing like a lump in the hallway.

"Hey!" I said, knocking on the door.

He opened it a little. "Yes?"

"What're you doing?" I was hopelessly off balance.

"Well, I'd ask you in but it's only our first date and—"

"I live here, too, remember?"

He thought for a moment, very concerned. "You don't have another place to stay?"

"No."

"Hmmmmmm, that *is* awkward."

"What?"

"I guess you'd better come in."

"I guess I will," I said, going in, wondering whatever had become of my legendary sense of humor.

"You can sleep on the couch, if you like."

"I have my own *room*, remember?"

"That's right, you do. Well, then—by all means—go to your room."

"What?"

"I'm going to sleep. It's been a long day."

"So who's stopping you? You want to go to sleep, go to sleep!"

"I don't see why you're so angry."

"Who's angry!"

"You are."

"I'm not angry! I'm *pissed-off*!"

"Why?"

"Because—" My sense of humor was returning, but I still played it miffed. "—when a person takes another person to a very nice dinner, that person expects a little more than just a little good night peck on the cheek!"

"What did you have in mind?"

"How about a little fuck?"

And he laughed so hard he actually fell to the floor. And I laughed so hard I fell down next to him. And there we were, the pair of us, lying on the floor, holding on to each other, laughing in the dark like drunken loons. And in that position, in the dark, on the floor, laughing till it hurt, I lost my precious, invaluable, irreplaceable virginity. It was not at all as I had imagined it would be—breathless and promising and sighing. It wasn't at all like that. It was just a fucking laugh.

ben

1952

It had been one helluva long time since I'd been in New York, almost a year and a half. I would miss Don's mad presence but still, in that bus that was grumbling into the Thirty-fourth Street terminal, I felt as "coming home" as Caesar. No brass band, no welcoming committee of mayor and alderman, none of that, but the smells came up and said hello, all of them oppressively familiar, slamming up my nose as if shoved by a huge, wet palm. Cracker Jacks and popcorn and frankfurters, gasoline, urine, beer, dog shit, vomit—a congealed Mulligan stew of foul odors curling hazily dank out of aromatic subway holes. The Manhattan skyline is for tourists and foreigners. But it's not what says home to New Yorkers. Smells are what say home. Smells first, the other stuff later. That's the way it works. Duffel bag on my shoulder, I headed uptown, walking slowly through the last simper of a freaky January rain.

At about Fifty-second Street I'd had enough of starry-eyed hiking with a fifty-pound duffel bag on my shoulder so I took a cab the rest of the way. It made me feel very affluent and I overtipped Marvin Wittenberg, who smiled and said, "You're an officer and a gentleman."

"Wrong. I'm a civilian and a schmuck."

"Ain't we all." And he drove off, richer for having known me.

The five flights were not easy, not with the baggage I was carrying. But I made it, only to find that ye olde key no longer fit ye trusty lock. I rang the bell—no answer. So I sat down in the hallway, my back against the door, and I thought about a lot of things for I don't know how long.

About Don, of course. Poor guy, I couldn't blame him for going for a change of climate. Still, all that wit and intelligence, he'd make something happen. Somewhere and somehow all the pieces would come together and something good would happen. I just wished that he'd kept in touch. That he hadn't I took to be a bad sign.

I thought about Arnie Felsen who had finally gotten drafted and who wrote to me from Korea where he was an MP, of all things, little Arnie Felsen an MP. Evidently he was still pursuing his writing because he had sent along various clippings from various Army newspapers, little articles he had written. At last he was a published author. He was a tenacious sonofabitch and I figured he'd bust through, too, quietly, in his own way, in his own sweet time.

Big Al Epstein—he had gotten his wife pregnant too late for him to qualify for a deferment, so the Army came by and scooped him up. But it was okay, he ended up in the Signal Corps and was stationed at Fort Monmouth, New Jersey, where he was very much into the making of training films. Big Al had lucked out. He always had and always would.

I thought about Bob Steinman, but not for too long because I couldn't deal with it. So I just relegated it to "things to think about when miserable and drunk."

I thought about Tony and that really did me in. Tony

Wesso, dead at twenty-three, lost his head and got killed. That, too, I was unable to think on for too long primarily because I missed him, but also because that bastard McArdle had me believing that I was more than just a little bit responsible for Tony's death. I didn't want to believe it, but everytime I thought of Tony, I thought of McArdle, and the issue of my guilt came with it. The whole thing was going to take time.

I thought about Johnny Munez and that was good. Johnny was a survivor, a street kid who could take care of himself no matter how tough the situation. Johnny would be all right. He'd come back. Bet on it.

I thought about Pat Jarvas because her I would be seeing again. She had been kind of a random fuck and I had deliberately not written to her because she was in no way the girl of my dreams. But now that I was back, the sudden idea of her seemed very exciting, and it warmed me to realize that she'd be there when I got back to the office. She wasn't all that bad, and with Maggie out of my life—

Maggie. I thought about Maggie because I'd *always* think about Maggie, especially her tears during our last kiss. She had to be the greatest thing in bed that I would ever know—but all the way home I was haunted by the knowledge that, despite her madcap exterior, she smacked tragically of doom, aiming herself at self-destruction while laughing it in the face. Still, if indeed I were to never see her again, I would never forget that chic lady—for she had favored me, introducing me to a brand of sex that, despite its fuck-in-the-gutter overtones, was, all the same, vital and exalting and strangely tender.

Maggie, so candid, so easy in her lovemaking, so pretty, so "older woman," so "back in Boston" that I winced at the missing of her. That face, that tilt to her head when she said the foulest of things, taking the most obscene phrases and speaking them as if they were Elizabeth Barrett Browning. "How do I love thee? Let me count the ways. On the floor, on the ceiling, up the ass, in the mouth." And there she was. Coming up the stairs. Outlined by the hall light behind her. It was her silhouette, her gait, so unmistakably Maggie that I almost called her name. But it wasn't Maggie.

It was Ginnie. Ginnie, my roomie, and what a package she was, dropping all her groceries and throwing herself at me like a medicine ball. She hugged me and welcomed me and called me "Christ" over and over until I almost believed it.

We went inside and she showed me around. She also showed me a body the likes of which no one gets to see except in an erotic dream. Her legs, seeming to sprout from on high, made her look ten feet tall. And her ass—well—her ass was the living end.

Only after recovering from her legs and ass did I realize that there was more to her. She had breasts, tightly packed into her leotards, I'd say thirty-three and counting. And hips modeled, no doubt, on the Venus de Medici, or vice versa. And she had a head. And, goddamnit, it was a beauty. Eyes—watery blue, as though just used for crying. Nose—aquiline, patrician. A slight tilt to the tip but not so's you'd notice. Mouth—mostly lower lip with a built-in pout, turned up at the sides, the quicker to laugh with. Teeth—glaring white, with just enough irregularity to the upper canines to make them interesting without being frightening. Chin—a touch of the jut, cantankerous yet delicate. Cheekbones—Garland. Jaw—Dietrich. Ears—Allyson. Neck—Lamarr. All of it framed within a crop of blonde hair, natural but assisted, pulled back and gathered into the most audacious ponytail since Seabiscuit's.

Still in her rehearsal clothes, she glided rather than walked, moving from room to room as natural and as easy in her actions as a slow-motioned cat. And were it not for the fact that I was so utterly dumbfounded by it all, I would have grabbed her and loved her and asked questions later.

She had kept the apartment nice, a little to the "girlie" but not enough to remark on. My own room was unchanged except that my clothing was arranged neatly, as if overseen by Jeeves. We made small talk through which she revealed a ready wit and a gangly charm. Everything about her was gangbusters, multiplied by Cadillac and mixed with jam. And she was my roomie. Soldier, beware.

After I showered, she bathed. She came out of her room in some kind of clown suit that I properly laughed at. The garment, feathered and beaded and flying a banana, I took as further evidence of her piquant sense of the absurd. To dinner she wore clothes more suited to a fat man who had lost an election bet than to a young girl who had won a dashing roommate. Unsure whether or not I should comment on her odd attire, I decided to say nothing.

Returning to the apartment, I decided to be funny since she had been doing it alone until then. So, playing the young girl coming home from a first date, I left her standing in the hall as I said good night and went inside. Again her flashing humor came to the fore as she quickly assumed the role of antagonized suitor, banging on the door until I opened it.

One word invariably leading to another, she went full into character, shoving her chin out pugnaciously and demanding, as payment for the evening, "a little fuck." Expecting nothing that appalling from my own sweet Ginnie, I found myself dissolving into laughter and

sinking to the floor, my sides splitting with the sudden
incongruity of such an ingenuous middle-class request.

She was laughing, too, and sliding to the floor likewise. And our arms filled up with each other, and our
legs. And there was a ponytail on my shoulder and a
woman at my side. And we were not two people who
had just met, but lovers from before, as familiar with
each other's bodies as we were with our own.

But how could that be? How could I know her so
well that the Chinese puzzle of how a woman responds
in bed was so quickly unraveled? Could fuzzy letters
and sleepy phone calls before the fact have caused traditional clumsiness to fall away? Could they have
turned oafish foreplay into practiced ecstasy, and made
of a first-time loving a series of unerring rockets to the
moon? Or were Ben and Ginnie such inherently skillful
lovemakers that they made no mistakes, required no excuses, and offered no apologies?

Throughout our lovemaking, questions surfaced and
questions subsided, none of them answered so all of them
left. We *had* met, of course, somewhere where perfection
is commonplace and love is the rule. Call it *Casablanca*
and be done with it. Call it Bogey sees Bergman and
Bergman sees Bogey and simply by the way they look at
one another we know that they have loved before. The
where and the when all coming later if we're patient and
if we care and if we truly believe that "a sigh is but a
sigh."

Afterwards, still clinging, the two of us lying together
on that cold, hard floor, as wrapped up in each other as
an eel swallowing its own tail, damned if I didn't raise
an imaginary glass and say to her, "Here's looking at
you, kid." And damned if she didn't cry.

Ginnie—five days and six nights of her. We never
knew what time it was, the days and dates but cross-

eyed approximations. We ate when we remembered to, slept when we ran out of steam, and did not let go of each other except when nature called. We turned on television and then ignored it, our own show more to our liking. Newspapers were anathema, weather beyond our ken, downstairs a place to run up from, and the telephone a thing off its hook. Life was horizontal, the pair of us seeming to fall whenever we touched. Our beds, no sooner made, were rumpled. First mine, then hers, then mine. Switching off like newlyweds, we could never make up our minds—Beautyrest or Simmons? The couch, the chair, the floor, the rug. The shower was kicky, the tub and we almost drowned.

Horizontals used up, we went for verticals—the wall, the door, the armoire, the refrigerator. The closet was cozy, the window was risky (must remember to draw the blinds). We were drawn to each other like magnets and flew at each other like hawks, breaking only for rehearsals because *The Joey Magnuson Show* was drawing nigh.

I went with her. It was a barn of a place and cold. I met Florrie who looked at me strangely, as though I had just flown in from Tibet, on a chicken. Richie Pickering was civil but nervous, more concerned with his routines than with meeting Ginnie's fella. No one else was there. They were rehearsing to a record and had yet to do it on camera.

I watched them and they seemed very good. I couldn't really tell because, first, I knew nothing about dancing. And second, I only had eyes for Ginnie. Whatever Florrie and Richie were doing could have taken place in Pittsburgh for all I saw of it. They could have jumped up and fucked on the ceiling, I'd never have noticed; I was only watching Ginnie. And she was a thing to behold, her feet never seeming to touch the floor, and when she leaped up, she could have stayed up, her only reason for coming down being that it was a dance act and not a glider launching.

They rehearsed for an hour, took a break, rehearsed another hour, took another break (for lunch, which nobody had), rehearsed again for a third hour, and then broke. I know of no athlete who could have gone through all that without incurring a coronary.

Ginnie was drenched, and afraid she'd catch cold. I poured her into a cab and we headed for home. I led her into the shower, first making certain that the water wasn't too cold. Oh, yes—I was in the shower, too.

Not that that was all we did. We did do other things. We did go for walks, and we did take in a couple movies, and we did reconnoiter what was new at the Museum of Modern Art. But all of it became a contest called "How long can we go without making love?" And, all too often, we'd find ourselves racing home because we knew that doing it in the street was frowned upon, except for dogs. And even if it weren't, the thought of someone coming over and throwing a bucket of cold water on us wasn't terribly inspiring.

Once, running home from a Fritz Kreisler concert which drove Ginnie to hitherto unscaled heights of sensuality, we couldn't quite make it to the apartment and began to make love as soon as we burst in off the street. I mean in the downstairs vestibule, and all the way up the stairs, breaking and resuming, fighting it and giving into it—the third floor landing being particularly critical in that most of our clothing was off and the bannister there quite unreliable and we were sure as hell testing it.

We broke clean, making it away from the third floor and were halfway up to the fourth floor when Mrs. Harkaday, a bovine fifty, came out of her fourth-floor apartment and stood staring at us in disbelief.

It was time for quick thinking because, though my

trousers were still on, Ginnie was down to her bra and panties. "Quick," I said to the lady, "take off your clothes and get downstairs!"

"What?" she said, her voice seeming to boom out from between her big brass knockers.

"They've opened up the fire hydrants and all the kids are playing in the water!" I said. "Jinkies, it's fun!"

"Yeah," said Ginnie, quick on the upbeat, "they've put a sprinkler on it! It's sensational!"

Mrs. Harkaday stood blocking our way, seemingly thinking it over, then shrugging it off. "I've better things to do than shower in the street," and she started to descend. We pressed ourselves out of the way because she had momentum on her side.

"Really, Mrs. Harkaday," said Ginnie, inhaling as the barge blew by, "it's just keen. Bring a piece of soap and you can kill two birds with one stone."

"Indeed. Indeed, indeed," she kept saying, as if it had great significance in the scheme of things. She indeeded herself down all the stairs and out of the building. I hated to think of it but it did occur to me that if ever Mrs. Harkaday and dear old Jessica were to hit those stairs at the same time, the building would be a parking lot in no time.

When I looked up, Ginnie was already racing around the fourth floor landing, heading for the last flight of stairs. "Come on! Come on, Ben, I can't stand it!" And she was pulling off her bra, wriggling out of it as she struggled up the stairs, looking like a combination stripper and Harry Houdini.

Halfway up the last flight she paused to step out of her panties and I caught her and wrestled her to the stairs. "Gotcha!"

"You're crazy! On the *stairs*?"

"On the stairs."

"Ben, *no!*"

"Yes, me proud beauty."

"Ben, I don't bend that way!"

"Try."

"Ben!"

"Give it a chance."

"Ben—look—four, five more stairs and we're there! We're almost at the top!"

"Almost is as good as a mile."

"What? Ben, someone can come out of an apartment and see us!"

"Holler rape and you'll be off the hook."

"Ben, *no!* . . . Ben?"

"These steps—fourth, fifth, and sixth from the top—will be sanctified. I hereby sanctify these steps with a glorious fuck."

"Oh, Jesus, you can't. You've got to be—"

"A blessing on these steps. Hereafter, whenever people walk these steps, let them know that—"

"Ben . . ."

"—that here love once lay. Laid? Lain."

"Ben . . ."

"Shut up. Just—"

" . . ."

" . . ."

" . . ."

" . . ."

"Wow."

"Phew."

"Boy do I love you, Ben."

"I love *you.*"

"I said it first."

"I mean it more."

Sunday night we slept in Ginnie's bed because that's where we were at the time. I set the alarm clock for five

A.M. so that we'd have plenty of time to say good-bye as I wasn't due to be in the office until nine.

I arrived at 20th a little before nine, not expecting any great reception and not being disappointed. The first one I had gone in to see was Josh, but at his desk was this man of about sixty, grey-haired, dapper, gaunt, and short. He was wearing a double-breasted grey pinstripe suit with a red flower in its buttonhole. He was also flying a blue necktie of some iridescence so that, on my first look at him, I thought he was on blue fire.

He looked up at me and smiled, fifty-eight brilliant false teeth picking up the glow of his necktie and making him look like he was the cat who had just eaten the inkwell. "You're Ben Webber, right?"

"Right."

When he stood up he was shorter than when he was seated; and, as he came toward me, his hand outstretched in greeting, I could see the cushion on his chair. The man was no taller than five foot two. I could see him handling the advertising for short subjects, but full length films? "I'm Alan Morse. Come on in. Sit down."

"Thank you."

"You've been away how long?"

"Year and a half."

"Kill any Japs?"

"That was the last war."

"I meant Koreans."

"I killed five Japs." Careful, Ben. Watch it. Check the orneriness. This ain't the Army. When they send you home from here it's without a job, baby.

Alan Morse smiled. He smiled a lot. I had the feeling that, with his new teeth, he was making up for all the years he didn't smile because of his old teeth. And I pictured his old teeth, tucked into the breast pocket of his old suit, hanging in his old closet—with his old brains.

"Josh is gone and I'm in charge." He filled his pipe with tobacco that came out a very Abercrombie humidor. The rest of the office was done in that same woodsy style—early Men's Club. There were no ads or layouts pinned up on bulletin boards, no feeling of busy-busy as it had been when Josh was running the show. Instead, beautifully framed pictures, of ducks. Ducks on the wing; ducks on the pond. And what wasn't a duck was a goose. And what wasn't either was a pheasant. Or an egret. Or maybe a platypus. Who gave a shit. The man was a gentleman sportsman, probably shot birds from the deck of the *Mayflower*. Precisely the kind of ad man who sold America the depression.

"Now then, I know that veterans get their old jobs back, so there'll be no problem there. Your old job is waiting. It's all yours." He smiled blue.

"I was under the impression that someone else had my job."

"Oh, no, no, no. That was only temporary, until you got back."

"He's been let go?"

"Not exactly. He's been moved up to Jessup's job. Roland Jessup has left us, you know. He's out there beating the drum for jigaboo entertainers. Represents a whole slew of boogie acts. He's now an entrepreneur. We'll be looking to get two or three new Negroes of our own, so as not to give the company a black eye." He laughed, evidently what he had said being very funny. "Anyway, we moved Sam Gaynor up to copywriter, so—your old job is all yours."

"As office boy."

"Yes. For the time being, of course. As soon as there's an opening—"

"I was writing copy before I went into the Army. I was under the impression that—Josh had led me to believe that—"

"Meyerberg is no longer here. And at the time Jessup quit neither were you. Sam Gaynor was here. Sam Gaynor got the job. Simple?" The gloves were off. He was not going to take any shit from me.

I had to work at sitting on my temper. "Doesn't seem fair."

"Well, maybe not. But Sam is good and there's only just so many copywriters I can keep. And I can't exactly demote him back to office boy, can I?"

"Why not?"

He puffed his fucking duck-shooting pipe. "It's not as though you came back a hero, fella. If you came back a hero you could have *my* job. But you didn't. All you did was kill five Japs and, unless I'm mistaken, that was the last war."

My smart-assedness had boomeranged. Chalk up one for General McArdle and Major Hochman. Still, I knew that, even if I had come in and groveled at his patent leather feet, Sam Gaynor would still have that job. Something else was at the root of it, not my behavior. "Maybe I should take it up with the Guild."

"That's already been done. Your friend, Mickey, he's a real agitator, isn't he? He threatened us with union action but, evidently, your union wasn't all that anxious to go to war for you." He turned on his blue smile again, not in triumph but as some kind of conciliatory gesture. "Ben, you have to hang in. Something will open up and, when it does, you'll have your opportunity. I promise."

"Should I still turn in my copy ideas?"

"Absolutely. But right now my inkwell's empty and, for some reason, the cleaning crew didn't empty my basket last Friday—would you take care of it, Ben? I'd appreciate it."

I filled his inkwell and emptied his waste basket into the big barrel in the corridor. As I was doing it, Mickey Green came by. He saw me, only he didn't want to, not that way, not with my head in the garbage barrel. But he saw me just the same and had to stop to say hello and tell me how glad he was to see me. He motioned for me to follow him on into the copywriter bullpen.

My old desk was there, a couple letters on it—cards of some sort. Mickey's desk was the same trashpile it had always been. Dora's desk had the same vase with the same flowers and the same box of Kleenex. Roland's desk, however, was different because it wasn't Roland's anymore, it was Sam's.

And Sam's desk had all sorts of mementoes on it. Like a foot-high solid brass radio microphone. And some bronzed phonograph records pressed into separate mahogany settings. And on the wall—a cluster of silver framed photos of the immortal Skip Gaynor, songbird of the air waves, his mouth open in melody while four chins that would eventually strangle him gathered over his bow tie like the hand of God.

Mickey sat at his desk, watching me absorb the whole thing, after which he calmly said, "Makes you want to shit, doesn't it?"

"Something like that."

"We tried, Ben. Me and Dora and a couple others. But you weren't exactly popular with the Guild. We tried to tell them not to think of it in terms of personalities but as a union matter. Ben, they're glad to still have their own jobs. We all are. Everything's moving to California. They'd fight for Herman Temple, for Joe Angrisani—they'd walk barefoot through snakes for Danny San Filippo and Lou Shanfield. But for *you* they won't walk around the corner."

"What do I do?"

"I don't know. Give it a try. Look for something else. Kill yourself. I don't know what to tell you."

"What would *you* do?"

"I'd be a good union member."

"A little late for that, no?"

"Maybe not."

"Why don't I kill myself and look for another job at the same time?"

"Might work. I don't know."

Dora came in and gave me a big hug and then ran to her Kleenex and honked into it a half dozen times, signifying nostaglia. Mickey filled her in on the discussion thus far and she could add nothing to what he had already said.

"Who's Alan Morse?" I asked.

Mickey shrugged. "Some old-line ad man. Used to work in the silent era. He's a hundred and eight years old and I think he died at a hundred and one."

"He any good?"

"Not good enough. But neither is he bad enough. We think it's some kind of power play."

"What do you mean?"

"Well, the best he can be is stopgap. We think someone else'll be brought is as soon as they settle on who he is. Meanwhile, old Blue Mouth sits on the throne."

"I thought his teeth were reflecting his tie."

"Maybe they are. All he wears are blue ties. When he starts wearing green ones, I'm leaving."

"Okay. Who's Sam Gaynor and why isn't he in the Army?"

"Sam Gaynor is an egomaniac with a hernia, 4-F. He can't write copy and he don't plant cotton."

"You don't like him."

"Anyone who likes Sam Gaynor has to be all bad."

"When does he come to work?"

"When he remembers to."

Sam Gaynor remembered to come to work that day at ten fifteen. We could hear his clubfooted whistling and feel his off-key clomp long before he ever reached the bullpen. And when he opened the door and stepped in, the door slammed against the wall as if the G-men had burst in. And I knew how the Lilliputians must have felt when Gulliver washed up on their beach. The large ox came right over to me and offered me his paw. It was gigantic and it swallowed mine. "Ben. It is Ben, right?"

"Right."

"Gladda seeya." He said it like Phil Silvers. The man stood about five foot six and seemed almost that wide. And his arms, extending to just above his knees, gave him the stance of an orangutan—the only thing human about them being gold cuff links, items not ordinarily found in the bush country. His face, a perfect moon with the beginnings of a double chin, seemed so round and so large as to better be the side blister of a Flying Fortress than the face of a human being.

And his mouth—ah, his mouth—and the teeth that came with it, they never stopped working, a perpetual spew of words pouring forth as though strung on a ticker tape. I had the image of his testicles unraveling and being pulled up through his innards, his throat, and then spinning out of his cavern of a mouth—thousands and thousands of yards of testicle strand, tripping lightly over his lips, springing alive with incalculable verbiage as if sluiced out of that gargoyle of a maw, splattering innocent bystanders with a Niagara of self-esteem that arrived doused in an ersatz southwestern drool, all of it invisible, of course, unable to be captured even by high-speed lens. But it was audible—shit, was it ever audible. I can hear it now.

"Man, ah have finished my film and it's jes' gonna knock 'em on their butts. It is so wild, I'll want you ta see it, Ben, as ah value your opinion. It's called *The Color Is Red* and it's all about red in our daily lives— red socks, red sweaters, red balloons, red bicycles—ah even have spliced in some footage of a anal operation where red blood just shoots out of this ass! Red phonograph arm movin' back an' forth 'cause the records's playin' out, red fingernails on a cocktail glass so fuckin' phallic, tomato juice pourin', red paint pourin'. It's all called *The Color Is Red,* all silent footage but ah'll play it to some appropriate music when ah show it. Ah'll have a private screenin' to which you are all invited; you all come to it. Shit, ah better arrange for a room." He picked up his phone and dialed while still talking. "You have to do these things in advance before some asshole moves in and—Deon? This is Sam Gaynor. Ah want to book the small screenin' room for tomorrow afternoon about four. Who? Shit, Deon, you jest put him in at five and don't worry about it. You tell him to talk to me and ah will explain it. You do that, Deon, and ah'll take care of you good come the Italian Christmas." And he hung up.

Sam Gaynor was a full-of-shit juggernaut that you either side-stepped or got run over by. He was as likable as ptomaine and as narcissistic as a peacock in a pig pen. They had found antidotes for tuberculosis and diphtheria and small pox, surely they'd come up with one for Sam Gaynor before we all died of his plague.

He left the bullpen without even having sat down, rumbling away like a downhill truck, and when he had truly gone, it was as though the air was breathable again.

I found myself gasping for breath and looked over at Mickey. "I'm not going to make it, Mickey. I'm not going to be able to live through that."

Mickey said nothing because there was nothing to say, no platitude available to cover such a moment. Dora was equally mute. In the merciful silence I opened the envelopes on my desk. One was from Ginnie: "Congratulations on your Academy Award for Best Special Effects on a Flight of Stairs. I love you—Ginnie."

Another was from Pat Jarvas. "Welcome back. You know where to find me. Love—Pat."

And a third was from W. Charles Gruber. "See me."

I figured I'd take care of the last two at the same time. Pat Jarvas was at her desk, looking as good as she skinnily could, obviously having taken great pains to do so. She looked up at me, pretending to be cross. "Bad. You never answered my letters."

"I was very busy."

She puzzled and then smiled. "It's okay, I forgive you. Can we get together soon? I still like you."

"I have to see him first. Is he in?"

"Yeah. He's goin' through his mail."

"How long will that take?"

By way of answering, she buzzed the intercom. "Ben Webber would like to see you."

And Gruber answered. "Send him in."

I went in and he got up from behind his desk to shake my hand. It was the first time I had never touched the man, and, remembering what Maggie had told me about him, I took special note of the texture of his hand, expecting it to be soft and pudgy. It wasn't. It was hard and rough, and I could see that, despite his roundness, old Charlie Gruber was nobody's fag—at least, not to the touch.

"Welcome back, Ben. Here. Sit down. Talk to me. Tell me something about the Army."

I sat. "The Army is made up of fools, idiots, and fags." With that last one I was trying for a reaction.

He didn't bat an eye. "You're describing every army not just the US Army. How come you never dropped me a card or something? I'm the Big Boss, you know."

"I thought it might be a little presumptuous. I didn't want you to think I was—sucking around." Did it again.

"The least you might have done was thank me for sending you a little farewell present the night before you left."

"Thank you. Why'd you do it?"

"Two reasons. First, I figured you could use it. And second, I figured you could keep it quiet."

"Right on both counts."

"How was she?"

"Enthusiastic."

"She took care of you?"

"Nobly."

"Good." He looked quickly at his wristwatch. "Okay, I see that something's on your mind. Spill it."

"Two things are on my mind. Sam Gaynor and Alan Morse."

"What about them?"

"One has my job and the other gave it to him."

"You'll have to let it alone for a while."

"Why?"

"It's too complicated. You'll have to trust me."

"I trusted Josh and he's gone."

He laughed. "I'll be here for a while."

"How do I know?"

"I'll not let you exact any promises out of me. You and I we kind of respect one another. I think you're good and that you'll go far. Not because of any special talent—I haven't seen any of that—but because of your attitude."

"Lately I've been told it isn't too good."

"Not for the Army maybe, but it is good for you. You want something, you go after it, and you still manage to preserve your individuality. You're the only man in this company who is distrusted by his management and hated by his own union. That takes some doing, and it's *good*. We all know you're here. Either you'll go quickly to the top, like cream, or you'll drop slowly to the bottom, like shit. But you've never going to hang around in the middle like most everyone else, pushing for a raise, hanging on with white knuckles until retirement. As such, I'll help you all I can. But right now I can do nothing about Gaynor and Morse."

"They're both idiots. Certifiable. One can't grow and the other won't stop."

He looked at me through his squinty eyes. "You have no problem, Ben. Sam Gaynor is no problem because he's going on to bigger and better things, and the sooner the better. You'll just have to sweat him out. Alan Morse is *my* problem—and that's all I want to say on the matter. So beat it." He was smiling and it buoyed me. W. Charles Gruber obviously knew more than he wanted to talk about, and he obviously saw both of my problems as being highly soluble.

I finished out the morning saying hello to people, able to tell by the way they acted which of them had been for me and which had been against.

I stayed as far away from Alan Morse as I could, running imaginary errands and avoiding his horse of a secretary at every turn. Willa Nichols and her new nose had blown with Josh Meyerberg, and everything seemed out of whack in that people just weren't where I had left them. Except Pat Jarvas, who called me on the phone and sweetly offered to blow me between the hours of three and four because she owed me and that was when Gruber would be out playing tennis and she'd be free. I told her that if I wasn't there by three thirty she should begin without me and she failed to see the humor of it. Still, game girl that she was, she probably tried.

I had lunch with Mickey, after which we went over to McGirr's and played snooker. Mickey was the best snooker player in the world—never lost—and said he was the captain of the 1948 US Olympic Snooker Team and that, as soon as he got a new agent, he'd be turning pro. I loved Mickey Green. We both knew that he couldn't help me yet we both pretended that he would.

The rest of the afternoon I sat at my desk, reading scripts. Mickey and Dora quietly worked. And Sam Gaynor was off somewhere, either talking or frightening people to death. I read three scenarios of upcoming films and began to feel that a caveman could do better.

At three forty-five, Pat Jarvas called to remind me that I still had fifteen minutes in which to get blown. I thanked her for her thoughtfulness, but precisely at five I went home to Ginnie because it was Ginnie with whom I wanted to be. Even if we did nothing but hold hands and hug, Ginnie was my love and I needed the sweet safety of her company—and when was the last time I ever felt that about anyone?

chapter
sixteen

ginnie

1952

Ben got home Monday evening after six. He had walked all the way from 20th to "clear his head" and he had brought with him an armful of movie scripts, at least five of them. He was very down, nowhere near the high-spirited stallion he had been when leaving for work that morning. He told me why and I couldn't blame him. It was hardly a great way to resume civilian life. I hated them all.

I had planned a romantic little dinner—a little chianti, a tossed salad, a beef bourguignon dish, and, for dessert, I figured we'd have each other. But, as it often is with mice and me, I fucked up the beef bourguignon, got cork in the chianti, and had neglected to buy dressing for the salad. So we had ham sandwiches and potato chips, though the dessert (as planned) was delicious and we both went back for more.

He made love with a frenzy, not at all his usual gentle and thoughtful self. But that was alright, too, because it was like being in bed with a different man (my second). He apologized for being a boor, promising that it would never happen again so I scolded him until he promised that it would happen again—and again—and again.

We lay in bed just talking, mostly about things at 20th. I had known that Roland was leaving but had no idea that Sam Gaynor would be taking his place. I knew about Sam Gaynor from Don who also didn't much care for the man.

"It's bad enough he's an egocentric prick," said Ben, "but the sonofabitch never stops talking. If verbosity was a crime, he'd be executed, unless they made the mistake of asking him if he had any last words, in which case the turn of the century would come around and he'd still be talking."

"Other than that, how'd it go today?"

"You—" and he grabbed me.

"No! Ben! I want to tell you about *my* day!"

"And I want to hear."

"Then get your hand out of there! I can't talk when you do that to me and, for God's sake, file your nails."

"Yes, ma'am. Now, tell me. What kind of day did you have?"

"Well, our numbers are getting better all the time. I almost think we can do 'em backwards. I only hope that, by the time we go on, we're not so over-rehearsed that we do do it backwards."

"It's this Saturday, yes?"

"Yes."

"Am I allowed to be at the studio?"

"I'll sneak you in. I want you to be there in case I sprain an ankle or something."

"I don't think I know it well enough to go on."

"You can try, can't you?"

"Oh, I'll try anything."

And we made love again and fell asleep and it was wonderful because it felt like we were married. I don't know why feeling married was so marvelous. I guess maybe it took some of the "evil" out of it. My upbringing again—as if marriage were so great. Judging from *my* family, marriage was exactly the *wrong* thing to inflict on a love affair.

I fell asleep snuggled next to him and I dreamed I was the little flower that miraculously grew through the big rock. It was my room and my Ben. It was my time, Ginnie's time. I had rhythm. I had music. I had my man. You know the rest.

Deep in the night I was awakened by Ben, or rather, by the lack of him. I got up and walked quietly through the hall and peeked at him where he sat, in the living room, poring over one of the scripts he'd brought home. Somehow I knew not to disturb him and I went back to bed. I fell asleep again, more deeply than before. I had worked hard that day and the old bones, pushing nineteen, really gave out. I didn't wake up until almost eleven the next morning.

We ran through the act eight times that day. I thought it was getting terribly automatic but Richie was pleased. It was exactly what he wanted. He felt that the emotionality would come later, when we did it to full orchestra. Florrie and I were too pooped to debate it with him. We hoped he knew what we were doing. Besides, it was his trio. When the day came that we'd call ourselves Florrie, Ginnie and a Guy, we'd debate. Until then, we'd dance.

I got home early, bathed and fell asleep before I could even get dressed. I was awakened by a man lying on top of me whose face I couldn't see because I was lying on my stomach. He was making love to me in a most beautiful manner, gently, delicately, slipping into me slowly like a small burglar, poking around tenderly so as not to trip the alarm, then withdrawing stealthily because why rouse the dog. Then, as if realizing that he hadn't made a complete enough search, he made another illegal entry, and another, and another, each entry followed by a lingering and a withdrawal, all of it so magnificently unhurried and performed with such a jewel thief's perfection that I really couldn't tell whether or not I was being burgled or banged, rummaged or ravaged, filched or fucked.

We ate dinner out——the Sixth Avenue Delicatessen because I felt like a pastrami omelet and Ben said I looked like one. We filled each other in on the day's events.

His second day was no better than his first. Maybe worse. Alan Morse had him rearranging the supply cabinets, running to the drugstore for prescriptions, and was generally making Ben fell sorry that he'd ever come back. At four o'clock he had gone to see Sam Gaynor's film, *The Color Is Red*.

"How was it?" I asked.

"About what I'd expected. He showed the film while playing Stravinsky. *Rite of Spring*. The music was great. The film was an atrocity."

"Did he ask your opinion?"

"Yes. I told him to try another color."

We laughed all the way home, figuring that Sam had about three thousand colors left that he might one day work into a film. But he had used up red. Red was dead. It would never again be the same. Nor would Sam's attitude toward Ben be the same. Up until then it had been condescendingly tolerant, but following Ben's candor it could only take a turn for the worse. Nor would Alan Morse be too thrilled that Ben had taken off without getting his permission.

Ben didn't seen to care. It would just be one more test for his union. I didn't like his attitude because it was the same attitude that Don had manifested before chucking the whole thing and running west. Ben didn't impress me as being a runner, but then, until he had run, neither had Don. I could see that, despite his flippancy, Ben was very concerned. I knew that if he indulged in that kind of depression too long I'd have to say something about it. But it was too soon for that and I was too scared. I hadn't known Ben a week. Too soon, too soon. And too scared.

And too premature a judgment as I discovered when we got back to the apartment. Because Ben had no intention of lying around and letting things happen while he did nothing more than complain. Yes, he was pissed off, and hurt, and disappointed, but no longer depressed. Now he was motivated. And it had to do with a script he'd been reading. With all the scripts.

"They're crap. They're so god-awful, I don't know how they get made. Yes, there's Mankiewicz and Nunnally Johnson and Jean Negulesco and a few others, but the rest of 'em? They write camera angles and 'cut to' and 'dissolve.' They know how to indent, where to line up the dialogue passages, how to number their scenes, but what the hell is that? There's no *people*, no *stories*."

I said the magic words. "Then why don't *you* write a script?"

He hated to be patronized. "You make it sound like I can't."

"I didn't mean it to. I meant it to sound like you can and you should."

He tossed the script at the wall. "It'd be a waste of time."

"Why?"

"First of all, they don't buy many original screenplays. Everything is an adaptation. A book or a play. Unless it's appeared somewhere—in print or on a stage or on a men's room wall—it just doesn't get bought by the movies. Second of all, all the screenwriters are out in California, sitting around their pools. And third of all, even if they weren't, how in Christ's name could I ever get a job as an adapter? I've never written an adaptation. I've never written *anything*."

"Maybe you can find a book you like and adapt it yourself."

"On spec?"

"I guess so."

"Well I thought about it. I mean, it's occurred to me, but I think there's something else that makes more sense.

"What?"

"Television. Just about everything on television is an original. A lot of New York guys are busting into it. Guys who've never written or directed before. Bob Mulligan—Jesus, he started out getting coffee for people. Sidney Lumet, there's another director. They're good and they're not much older than I am. Somebody said 'Hey, anybody know how to direct a TV show?' and they raised their hands—and they were directors. A lot of writers are surfacing. I mean aside from Paddy Chayefsky and Reggie Rose and Rod Serling. A lot of good talent, guys who couldn't get arrested in Hollywood. Tad Mosel. N. Richard Nash. Robert Alan Aurthur. Gore Vidal."

"I didn't know you watched that much television."

"Neither did I. But evidently I did because all those names jump out at me and from before I ever went into the Army. Ginnie, what I have to do is watch the dramatic shows. See how they break down into scenes. See where the commercials go. See how the half-hour shows are constructed, too, as well as the one-hour shows. I don't have to shoot right away for *Studio One* or *Kraft*, I could do a *Lights Out* or a *Suspense*. Most of them are derived from other things if not stolen outright. In a single volume of Edgar Allen Poe there's probably enough material for a hundred television scripts."

"Okay, so what's *stopping* you?"

"What's stopping me is I don't have a fucking typewriter!"

"Get one."

"What's stopping me from getting one is, I don't know how to type!"

"Learn. Take a course."

"Learning to type while I'm learning to write?"

"*I* can type. I learned in school. You can dictate to me."

"How many words can you do a minute?"

"Three. If they're small. How many can you dictate in a minute?"

"Two. But big."

"Let's give it a try."

"You're on."

We got Ben a secondhand typewriter, which the man at the store swore once belonged to a first-rate writer whose name escaped him because the writer died in obscurity. The moral: Don't ever sell this typewriter because it's bad luck, and, if you *do* sell it, bring it back to Handleman's East Side Typewriters where you'll get a trade-in that'll knock your shift-lock off.

Handleman threw in, for good will, a little booklet titled *Typing, Self-taught by Experts*. Ben worked at it as diligently as he could, but between his job at 20th and his script-writing at home, there wasn't much time left for learning how to type. So, after two days of trying to do it all, Ben abandoned the course, choosing to write in a cluttered longhand that I, later, would attempt to decipher and type up.

We managed. It was slow but we managed. The important thing was to establish a routine. Equally as important was for Ben to hang in at the office, even if it meant taking a lot of guff. We needed the income of his

job in case *my* career went ka-flooey. It wouldn't be
easy, especially for someone as volatile as Ben, but it
had to be done—so it *would* be done.

It wasn't easy for me, either, because I had to do all
the shopping and cooking and cleaning, three things I
was as proficient at as flagpole-sitting. But I did it. Together we did it. He would come home at night, we'd
make quiet love (cocktail-hour love, very chic), we'd
have dinner, after which he'd go to his room while I
cleaned up. He'd quit around eleven and go to whichever bed I was in. We'd make love (midnight love, mu-
cho racy), say nice things to each other, and go to
sleep.

He'd get up in the morning and go to work, catching
coffee and a doughnut along the way. I'd get up at ten,
stick some breakfast into me, and type up what he'd
done in longhand the night before.

His first script I thought just dandy, a little horror
story about a sculptress who seduced men in her studio,
poisoned them, and then made statues around their
corpses that she'd then sell to whoever would buy them.
That was Ben's approach, too. He'd kill himself writing
and then sell it to whoever would buy it. The play was
titled "Come Into My Studio, Said the Sculptress to the
Guy," and when it was properly finished it would be
simultaneously submitted to *Lights Out, Danger,* and
Suspense—after which I went to rehearsal.

Florrie was very concerned. "You look lousy."

"Do I?"

"Yes. By fucking him you're fucking us."

"Oh, I don't think so."

"I do. In two days we go on. Richie'll lift you once
and your cunt'll fall off."

"Ought to bring down the house."

"And what'll you do for an encore? Throw your tits

to Baltimore? Listen, kid, there's too much at stake. We've worked too hard. We've got a chance to show-case our act that comes maybe once in a lifetime. Don't fuck it up. Give him a couple hand jobs, all he wants. Give him head, but for Christ's sake, save your body for us."

I guess Florrie was right, but I was so in love that I actually thought I was dancing better than ever before. Still, just to make sure, I told Ben of Florrie's fears. He was very good about it and we agreed to curtail all sex until after the Pickering Trio went on. The agreement lasted one night, being torn into bits when what had started as a neighborly hand job turned into fellatio fab-ulo, followed by coitus colossus, followed by the alarm clock. We were addicts who could not go cold turkey. Whatever was to become of us?

Ben came home Friday having somehow survived the week. He had had to apologize to Alan Morse for going AWOL to Sam Gaynor's screening, and Morse humili-ated Ben by chewing him out in front of Mickey and Dora as if he were a kid who had wet his bed. But Ben took it. As to Sam Gaynor, that sonofabitch was really giving it to Ben just for Ben's being honest about his fucking home movie. But Ben hung in, telling me (oh, so romantically) that it was easy for him to eat crow when he knew he could come home and eat *me*.

Saturday came, and with it a letter from Don, post-marked LA. It came from out of the blue and was wel-come in spite of its content.

Dear Whoever-is-living-in-my-apartment:

I have made a fortune submitting to malaria ex-perimentations while vacationing on Devil's Island. But now that the mosquitoes have gone back to

Capistrano, I find myself a little short on blood and cash. So if you can send either we might at least save the kid. Seriously, folks—I am working in a small TV studio—as a tube, learning to be a director. To date I have directed two 15-minute children's shows which, though mercifully forgotten, did earn me credit—*on camera*. I hope to move on to dogs and then, with any luck, fish. Meantime, as mentioned above—help! I am at the Montecito Hotel where *all* unemployed showfolk hang out, and I will remain here through the end of the month. After that, Schenectady is a good bet—if they'll have me.

Ginnie, if you are still there, please send me $100. Enclosed is my marker for same which can be honored anytime after July, 1980, at 8% per annum, a good deal you will admit. If you are *not* Ginnie and not *anyone* to whom I am known, then just send $50 and there will be no hard feelings.

Where is Ben Webber? The world wants to know. I wrote to him three times for money but I have never heard from him, perhaps because I never had the courage to mail the letters.

I am unhappy to have to write such a letter but there is a gun to my head and the hand that holds it is mine. If you are generous, you will be rewarded a thousand times over. (Remember Jack and the Beanstalk?) Only don't send seeds, when it's shekels what I need.

Yours in dire straits—
The Heart Fund,
Don

We laughed and cried at Don's letter, glad to hear from him but saddened to learn that he was barely hanging on. It was all a little strange in that both Ben and I knew Don so well yet neither of us had known the other when last in Don's company. We sent the money, of course (my check), along with a letter explaining how we were living together in sin and joy; and we put Don's marker in the drawer, not one day to collect on, but one day to laugh over.

It was time for rehearsal and Ben went with me, like a trainer sending his boy in against Gargantua. We took a cab part of the way and walked the rest of the distance to Rockefeller Plaza and the NBC Studios.

At the studio we had an on-camera run-through, blocking everything out and setting our marks so that the director and technical director could pick their shots. Then we ran it for music and it was astounding, all that sound. I felt as though we were dancing inside a tuba. It was also kind of stirring and show-bizzy and I danced well, responsive and strong, great in "Sing, Sing, Sing," fantastic in "Sweet Georgia Brown."

Monty was there, to bolster Florrie who was suddenly so nervous and fidgety that she made me feel like Anna Pavlova. Monty took Ben aside and castigated him for going with Jewish girls. (Me?)

"Benny," he said. "Benny, mine feller, you should get yourself a cute shiksa because shiksas are good for what ails you even if nothing ails you. What are you messing around with that Ginnie Mazeltov?"

"She makes great chicken soup," said Ben, trying dopily to hang in there with the master.

"Is that an answer coming from a sound mind? Did you ever fuck chicken soup? Feh! All those feathers, all that rice. The only thing better to fuck than a shiksa is a blintze. And that is only to a point. Because once you fuck a blintze it wants to marry you. But not a shiksa. A shiksa will be happy if you give her a plot of land in

Palm Beach and keep your mouth shut. But woe be unto the Hebe who knocks up a shiksa because the father of every shiksa is a nine foot, eight inch tall farmer what can hit you over the head with such a cow you'll see milk the rest of your life."

And so on, with the hours ticking away and the show drawing closer and all of us growing more anxious. Ben and I sat off in a corner, holding hands so sweaty that they kept falling out of one another. We had a lunch break but couldn't eat, choosing to stay there and watch the cast run through the rest of the show. Joey Magnuson and his distaff sidekick, Mara-Jayne, were hilarious, their timing flawless, their sketches foolproof. "What the hell do they want with a crummy dance act?" I said to Ben, suddenly wanting to be in Seattle and going west.

"Too much of that stuff is too much. They have to break it. Sobel's very smart."

"Explain."

"So much of that stuff is verbal. Joey's dialects, the silly lines, the foreign movie sketch. It's all very funny but it comes so fast and so unrelieved that the ear needs a rest. Television is a visual medium. If you just fire words at your audience, you wear 'em out. They need something for the eye to concentrate on and enjoy in an hour-and-a-half show, otherwise their ears are going to fall off."

"Where'd you learn that?"

"I didn't. I made it up."

"Sounds right."

"That's the nicest thing you've ever said to me."

Ben was right. That's why the show needed the Pickering Trio. To relax the tourniquet. The trick, though, was for us to be good. Otherwise, more than being relieved, the people would be going to sleep.

As usual, Ben was reading my mind. "Don't worry. You're going to be good."

I was beginning to understand the essence of Ben Webber that even he would require more time to comprehend. I was only a kid but I was in love, and love, I still believe, gives insight to instinct and power to purpose. Ben had an ability that would always cause him to be on fire. He could, and always would, arrive at the core of something long before he'd know he had. And like a genius infant who had yet to learn the dynamics of speech, he would be unnerved by it and frustrated, throwing tantrums and sponsoring rages because if *he* did not yet understand what he understood, how could he tolerate others never understanding at all?

He had a nose for a scene. Even in the little sex skits we worked out on the spot—it was Ben who set the characters and the situation, and Ginnie who sang the Trilby. And he had an innate sense of what was dramatically correct, a born awareness of the size and shape of a moment, a feeling for the form of an action long before it took substance. Others might acquire that talent, but Ben had it going in and, damnit, he would always have it. All of that I knew to be true because I loved him and felt it. And even allowing that love can be blind, then cannot it also be tactile? How else can it survive?

He sat beside me, holding my hand in both of his, as if to keep the wounded bird from flying off prematurely. And he looked foolishly young and naively "Army" in that brushcut of a haircut that so unflattered what once had to have been a bumper crop of Scotch-brown hair. And huddled in the back of the theatre, knees drawn up and shivering in my tights, I had a quick flash-forward to the time when Ben would have arrived, when all of his natural forces would be given full play, when offstage he'd be more powerful than those onstage and onstage they'd know it. And if that didn't describe a playwright then, fuck it, Shakespeare never writ.

And I thought, lovingly, maybe, just maybe, my clacking at that horror of a typewriter, making words out of his alphabet soup boil—maybe that would make me as important to Ben as Boswell had been important to Johnson. It was a good moment and I swam in it, right through the dress rehearsal and up to ten minutes before air time, at which point, wouldn't you know it, I cried.

Florrie saw me and went ape, coming more apart even than me, flying off and all over like a triggered grenade, screeching that it was no time for me to get hysterical, yelling that I should remain calm. Monty had to shoot her down and get her out of there. Poor kid, the pressure was getting to her.

Next, Richie Pickering tried to console me, substituting logic and experience for Florrie's blaring panic, advising me to trust my body because my body knew what to do, that my muscles had memory, that if I just went out and went on all would go well automatically and as predicted. I could hear his calm words but I wouldn't let them into my head, for he sounded like Daddy teaching me how to walk, and I fell many times in those days—everytime he let go of my hand.

Then Noah Sobel came over, peering into my eyes as if to see into my soul. Then he stepped back and sighed and began to look around as if to say, "Call Sullivan and see if he'll give us Hogan's Dogs." I was slipping away, I knew it, a whimpering fog of former girl, dissolving before their eyes—and wouldn't *that* be an act, no?

It was Ben to the rescue, taking my hand and pulling me like a blind mule into Mara-Jayne's dressing room which that lady graciously vacated because she had seen that kind of thing before and knew that it could not be contended with if crowds were looking on. Ben closed the door, sat me in a chair, and proceeded to get very nervous, pacing about, looking at the ceiling, hitting the wall, showing an emotion more akin to frightened truculence than to bubbling anger. "Let's get the hell out of here!"

"What?"

"Let's sneak out, get a cab, and go get a beer. This is ridiculous! Working a month, like a slave, just to go on for what—four lousy minutes? Don't do it! It's crazy! Do something else! Be a nurse, a fireman, sell table-clothes at Macy's! But not this! Ginnie, not this!"

"What?"

"You don't need it! A hundred years from now, who'll care? No one'll remember, least of all you because you'll be buried somewhere near a babbling brook—'Here lies Virginia Troppenheimer.' And on the stone it'll say: 'I won't dance, can't make me.'"

"Troppenheimer?"

"Yes, Jedidiah Troppenheimer. Nice man. Raised pigs. Married this girl, I forget her name—it was a hundred years ago. Nobody cares."

"You don't care?"

"A hundred years from now? You kidding? Fuck it!"

"Troppenheimer?"

"Something like that. Might have neen Doodlemunger—it was so long ago. He married this gypsy. Nice girl but all she was ever good for was farm work. She had nine kids and tits down to here. Breast-feeding'll do that, to *any* cow."

"I was going to do the show. I just wanted to stop off for a little cry."

"Okay, you've had it. Now what do you want to do? Do you want to go on or do you want to go home?"

"Fuck you with your psychology! I'm onto you, you bastard! Doodlemunger?"

"Could have been Schepplebinder."

"Sure it wasn't Findleburger, you sonofabitch?"

"No. Findleburger raised horsies. This man raised pigs."

"Findleburger didn't raise pigs?"

"Move your ass, Swan Lake, you're on."

"Keep a cab waiting. We may be leaving quickly."

"Okay, but a hundred years from now, who'll care?"

"Tits down to where, you quack?"

"Move it, move it."

I came out of Mara-Jayne's dressing room reborn and just fine. They were all looking at me, waiting for me to explode, but I outfoxed 'em. Virginia Troppenheimer was going on.

I looked over at Ben, just to get one last look at him in the event I died onstage and got buried beside a babbling brook. He stuck his tongue out at me, gave me the donkey's ears and the hee-haw that went with it, and finished it all off with the finger. I countered by crossing my eyes, giving him the old half-arm "fuck you" and showing him my ass. Everyone had to think we were obscene deaf-mutes, but I was going on. All I had to remember was not to trip on my tits.

Music up. Lights up. Titles crawl. And we were on, standing before the big eye for a quick stand-up intro, an invisible announcer booming, "And the Pickering Trio, sophisticated dance troupe." That almost busted me up because if there was anything we were not it was sophisticated. I held my pose just long enough, laughing till I coughed once we got off. Florrie would have nothing to do with me, and Richie had nothing left he could say to me. So, I was alone, waiting.

At the twenty-two-minute mark, the Pickering Trio went on. "Sing, Sing, Sing." The music thundered and the beat was wicked and our three adrenalines pumped so forcefully that we never did it as well. All the percussion that Lucas Harrison had woven into the arrangement came pulsing out, driving the number like a locomotive down a ski slope, to the point where I had the distinct feeling that the orchestra was struggling to keep up with us. The studio audience went slightly nuts as we jumped around in our red and yellow baggy sweaters, twirling our dumb derbies, springing up and down in our white sneakers like three bunnies on a hot plate. It all worked. Smasho-boffo.

We came off to big banana smiles from everyone and skipped our way to our dressing rooms because we had over a half hour in which to rest up for our second number. Ben was there and hugged me and was still hugging me when Florrie tore us apart, reminding me that I had a costume change, which I made, getting into my froufrou "Sweet Georgie Brown" outfit, with a little help from Ben. Christ, his hands on my body—I could have outleapt Nijinsky.

Florrie wanted to take a nap, Richie, too. Bless 'em, I had no objections. But I was still on the crest of that marvelous high, still glowing five hundred watts. So Ben and I took a little walk, outside, where it was more June than February. We walked without talking, just holding hands, me in my Gypsy Robe because I had yet to give it up as tradition demanded. I wore it over my "Georgia

Brown" costume but it was debatable which was the more bizarre.

Have you ever walked with someone you loved after something wonderful had just happened? If not, too bad. You've never been alive. Because all you have to do is *touch* and it does away with all need for words; the communication just flowing, one circulatory system whizzing through both bodies, one thought shooting through both heads. We were never closer, Ben and me. Not even in our most passionate craziness were we ever more a part of one another. Nor was there ever a time in my life when I had a greater self-awareness, my brain uncurling and setting everything I knew right out in front of me, so clear that I could touch all my knowledge, all my memories and potentials, all my tendencies and trepidations—which is why I knew I was pregnant.

It hit me all at once, like a saint's revelation. I wanted to mention it to Ben but held back, thinking that by merely holding my hand he'd know it, too. And if he didn't, then why spoil the moment with accusations of insensitivity? I felt the budding life in me—a boy. A most beautiful, wonderful little boy.

We kept walking until one of the stagehands came running up to us, panic smeared all over his face, sweat on his brow, blood in his eye. "You crazy! You're on in three minutes!"

Running, running. Back to the theatre. People getting out of our way. Mostly because I looked like a flapping aberration in my blossoming Gypsy Robe. We dodged cars, sideswiped drunks, side-stepped lampposts, and got back to the stage door, where pandemonium awaited me like a process server.

Florrie was screaming again, fluttering about almost in feathers. She was getting good at it, had it down pat. Richie was, for the first time I had ever seen, undone and indelicate. "You stupid cunt! What the hell's wrong with you!"

"I'm having a baby!" I said, in self defense, and Ben almost fell on the floor. "I am!" I said, turning to him, still trying to shuck off the Gypsy Robe which fought my escape with flashes of static electricity. "Ben I am! I'm pregnant! Look at the—electricity!"

"It's okay as an encore," he said, gently getting me out of the robe. "But first, let's see you do 'Sweet Georgia Brown.'" I guess he figured I was flipping again. Well, I thought, he won't feel that way in nine months, I warrant.

Someone shoved me on and I danced, only later I didn't remember. I do remember hearing the music, though, Lucas' arrangement, fairly bonging with rhythm, jungle and jazz, half cha-cha, half Dixie one-step. I had an umbrella and pantaloons and high heels and an ice-cream cake of a hat that was topped with a three foot feather—everything white except the feather which was scarlet. And I knew it was going alright because all of me was moving with that prior knowledge that Richie had spoken of—muscle memory, so ingrained with total input that I danced as if mothered by Terpsichore and fathered by a computer.

When we finished, the audience went berserk, standing and cheering. I flew into Florrie's arms and hugged her like mad, only she wouldn't hug back. She just pushed me away, large tears in her huge eyes. "*You* are out of your fucking *mind*! Stay *away* from me!"

I turned to Richie and he was staring at me as though I had returned from the dead after *he* had paid for the funeral. "Just be around for curtain call, okay? Can you do that?" I nodded and he walked away, shaking his head. He certainly seemed bothered and I wondered why.

Up until the curtain call, I tried to figure out why everyone had turned weird. After curtain call, even as the studio audience was applauding itself down to its wrists, I looked for Ben. Ben would tell me. Ben was my friend.

I saw him, leaning against some rigging like a French sailor, so cute I could have devoured him where he stood. I walked over to him and hid in his arms. "Please tell me what happened?"

"A hundred years from now no one'll remember."

"My tits fell out!"

"No."

"My ass split!"

"No."

"What?"

"Funniest dance since Salome stuck her finger in the socket."

"What?"

"Come on. Let's take a walk."

It went like so, according to Ben. Florrie and Richie were doing the number to perfection, but not me. Me was staggering around, trying to catch up. It was an old routine, as old as vaudeville, but Ben assured me that it had never been done better.

"The audience loved it. They couldn't stop laughing. You were Nancy Walker and Martha Raye all at once. Greatest piece of comic timing since Buster Keaton." So much for Richie Pickering and his fucking "muscle memory."

"Ben, I want to die."

"You kidding? You're a star. You were doing steps out there—shtik? Is that the word?"

"Yes."

"You were doing such shtik, I thought Magnuson was going to split a gut. Your friend, Monty, he wet his pants. I think he wet Mara-Jayne's pants, too. When did you all decide to put such a twist on the number?"

I started to cry. "I ruined it, didn't I? I ruined Richie's whole show."

"The hell. You saved it. There was no way you could have followed 'Sing' with 'Georgia Brown' done straight. 'Sing' was so precise, so perfect, so all-out that, by comparison, 'Georgia Brown' would have looked like you were loafing. It was inspired."

"And no one's angry?"

"Bewildered, maybe. Stupefied. But not angry. Only problem is, can you do it that way again?"

"I don't even know what I did!"

"That's what I was afraid of. Oh well, it'll come to you."

Back at the apartment, I hit the bed and collapsed, looking up at Ben, I'm sure, like a mortally wounded doll. He began to undress me very nicely. "Ben, what's going to happen?"

"Well, if millions of people were watching like they were supposed to, I'd say you'll be getting more offers than a hooker in a barracks."

"I mean about the *baby*?"

"Oh yes, the baby. I'd forgotten."

"How can you not know? My gawd!"

"Well, for one thing, if you're pregnant it ain't *mine*."

"You're not going to try *that*!"

"I only know you two weeks. And when I met you you were a virgin, unless you've got a hymen you can take out and put back depending on who you're with at the time . . ."

"So I *can't* be pregnant. It's too soon. Right? Right?"

"I don't know. Maybe it's immaculate. You can get a lot of funny things sitting on toilet seats."

"But why should I *feel* pregnant?"

"The word, Miss Nineteenth Century, is *guilt*."

"Guilt?"

"You went to bed with a man and got pregnant. Isn't that the way it works?"

"Wow. So fast?"

"Fastest pregnancy on record. Baby's probably due in twenty minutes. I'd better get some clean sheets and boil some water. Hey—I've got a great name for the kid."

"What?"

"Speedy Gonzales. Speedy Gonzales Burglemeister."

"Whatever happened to Troppenheimer?"

"It was so long ago, who remembers?"

chapter seventeen

ben

1952

After her big hit on *The Joey Magnuson Show*, Ginnie slept a lifetime. I peeked in periodically to see if she was dead or was trying to hatch the mattress, having just come through a rather traumatic false pregnancy. She'd mumble and drop back into her coma but I knew that she was still alive because the little trays of food I left her before going to work were empty when I returned at night, often with a note, like: "Thank you, Mystery Chef, but where's the Pepto Bismol?"

I certainly did love Ginnie Maitland. She was so quick to pick up on me, on what I was thinking or was about to say, that I was convinced that she had occult powers. As to our lovemaking, it was so natural and easy and unembarrassed and funny that it could not be improved upon, though we continually tried because nobody is perfect.

In the office, Pat Jarvas still came at me but each time with less ardor, her passion for me gradually dwindling, slowly and insidiously being displaced by an iciness that turned my fingertips blue. And I remember what Dorothy Parker had once written: "Scratch a lover and find a foe." Not that Pat and I had ever been lovers, it's just that we had the record for the fastest fuck in town and I guess she wanted another chance to improve upon her time.

My life at 20th Century-Fox was horrific but I was able to deal with it because I knew that it would one day end. Sam Gaynor, of course, was insufferable but I managed to handle him by doing everything he asked of me without whimper or complaint. It drove the sonofabitch mad, and once, grabbing me by my lapels, he pressed me against the wall and threatened me with a form of death too indelicate to recount here. I liked that. It meant that I was passively resisting the shit out of him. I did decide, though, never to be alone with him because, if he *was* going to hit me, I wanted some witnesses around—for the law suit and the homicide charges.

As for Alan Morse, I withstood him, too. Needless to say, I was no longer writing copy. I was just an office boy and, as such, wasn't even allowed to attend screenings. Mickey, who saw and felt everything, verbalized his curiosity: why was I hanging on? I told him that I needed the money and that he shouldn't worry because I had a master plan.

My master plan was simple. I would break into television as a writer of original dramas. The plan was more easily formulated than facilitated, especially as my first half-hour script was bombing everywhere, returning to me with the accuracy of a boomerang and always with the same message tied to its foot: "Thank you for submitting 'Come Into My Studio, Said the Sculptress to the Guy,' but we find, at this time, that it doesn't fit in with blah, blah, blah, etcetera and so forth and fuck you."

So I wrote another, about a man who had a camera that could take pictures of the future. I called it "See What Develops" and Ginnie typed it up neatly and we sent it out and back it came with the same cursed rejection attached to its shaft.

A similar fate awaited "Dead As They Come," "Don't Look Now," and "Whisper to Me of Blood." Of the latter script I asked Ginnie if it wouldn't better be done as the book to a musical. She didn't laugh, suggesting only that I stop trying to imitate others and start trying to discover *myself*, which I thought was very sound advice, *if* I was *America*—but since I was not—what the hell did she have in mind? She didn't know but had hoped that *I* would—otherwise she'd never have said it. So we kissed and made love while the typewriter, glad for the recess, looked on without saying anything.

Still, the gist of what she was trying to say stayed with me. The function of the artist is to be heard, and he cannot be heard, truly, if all he does is join the existing chorus. He must step out and solo and make his own noise. All that remained was for me to figure out just what kind of noise I wanted to make. It didn't take long. My noise would be "Tony."

I got home before Ginnie that night. She was rehearsing another two numbers for another *Joey Magnuson Show*. The Pickering Trio had been such a hit that Noah Sobel quickly booked them for one more appearance that season, and Sobel was also talking about next season.

When Ginnie did get home I pounced on her with my new idea. I had told her about Tony and the thought that his story might become the basis of my first really original play really hit home with her. I went to work immediately, setting it all down in the illegible hand that only Ginnie could pry free. I worked nights, of course, but I also worked days, squeezing out of my scullery-maid chores a few minutes here and a few minutes there just to make notes, to record thoughts as they occurred to me. The days flew by, the pages piled up. It would be a one-hour script geared to shows like *Kraft*,

Studio One, Theatre 60, Philco; and it would be important in that it would be important to *me*, for I wanted
Tony alive again. I wanted to make a noise that would
be his as well as mine.

I don't think I slept five hours in five days, and Ginnie was fabulous. As tired as she was, she would type
up my pages so that both of us could see what I had
written. For the truth was that my longhand, performed
so quickly because the mind was quicker than the hand,
was so unruly that I could not read it back. But Ginnie
could. It was typical of the thing that was happening
between us. She could read my writing, and I knew before she did that her period was coming.

That it did come came almost as a relief to both of us
for, as much as we loved making love, there were other
things upon which people can build a relationship. We
simply had no idea what they might be. We had been
burning our candles at both ends as well as from the
middle out, getting precious little sleep and both of us
with so much to do. We had five days off.

More weeks passed. A month. Two months. I kept
writing and she kept typing. She also kept rehearsing.
They were to be on the last *Joey Magnuson Show* of the
season and Sobel wanted it to be the best of the season.
So they rehearsed as though for the last show of their
lives.

The day arrived, a Saturday, and I went with Ginnie
to the Studio. I had no idea what the new routines were.
I had asked Ginnie but she wouldn't tell me, saying only
that she wanted it to be a surprise. They had gotten
Lucas Harrison into it again because his arrangements
were as vital to its all coming off well as was Richie's
choreography. And that's all I knew.

I watched the dress rehearsal. The first number was
kind of soft-shoe, Ginnie and Florrie wearing black pus-

sycat costumes while Richie was dressed as Fred Astaire. It looked silly but they danced as though they
were royalty, all snooty and blue blood, and the entire
effect was one of controlled absurdity, performed to an
aristocratic rendition of "My Blue Heaven" that only
Lucas could have conjured up. It was so good as to be
awesome. Monty Rivers sat next to me and kept quiet
throughout. Only at the end did he nudge me and say,
"I'm sick of pussycats, can you fix me up with that
cutie-pie waiter?"

Their second number was a jazz ballet done to Lex
Baxter's hit music, "Jet." And I didn't know *what* to
think. Florrie and Richie did it while Ginnie sat next to
me and watched. All through the dress rehearsal and
the on-camera rehearsal Ginnie just watched that second number, studying it, taking it all in, learning every
step, every move, familiarizing herself with it but never
performing it. Why? I'd see.

Air time came and, at the twenty-minute mark, the
Pickering Trio did Fred Astaire and the pussycats and
"My Blue Heaven" and brought down the house. At the
forty-minute mark, they did "Jet"—the three of them.
It was the funniest thing I ever saw.

Florrie and Richie, in ballet attire and sober countenance, came out and did the first minute straight, like
Russians afraid to be shot. Then Ginnie wanders on,
this incredible blonde thing slung into black tights, this
willowy waif, looking on as the other two dance. Then,
shyly she does it by herself, off to the side, tentatively at
first because she's never done it before. Then, confident
that she *can* do it, she joins the duet of dancers and
hilariously fucks up the whole thing.

Richie's and Florrie's approach to the number was to
survive the intruder, to hang in like serious artists, class-
ical troupers if you will. Ginnie, the clown wanting to

belong, gave the routine its counterpoint. Gorgeous in her innocence, ablaze with the insouciance of *I Love Lucy,* Ginnie kept shaking them up, ultimately busting in so that Richie, not knowing how or why, was lifting Ginnie and leaving Florrie out in the cold. And up there, at the highest point of the lift, Ginnie registered such facial horror that the audience toppled out of its seats. The crusher came at the end when Ginnie attempted to lift a trembling Florrie while Richie, defeated, sulked off the stage.

To Richie Pickering's everlasting credit, he was aware of Ginnie's inborn sense of lunacy and he trusted it, knowing that she could do it to perfection *once* but that if she were ever to have *rehearsed* it, all the spontaneity, all the risk and surprise so necessary to the comedy's working would disperse, leaving the number to collapse under its own apparent ineptness.

And out of it a character was born—the leggy blonde, the dauntless clown who simply had to dance no matter how the world turned and who she interrupted, the half-woman-half-child who didn't seem to know whether she should be jumping rope or hopping freights. What Ginnie had done in "Sweet Georgia Brown" was an accident. What Richie Pickering had done in employing that accident as part of "Jet" was genius. It is a process repeated over and over again by men with enough sense to leave room for happenstance and thus harness the unexpected.

Things proceeded to happen quickly and well for The Pickering Trio. Agents poured out of Sardi's as if Toots Shor had yelled "fire!"—all the Lennys and Bernies, plus a few Shellies and Arnies, plus two Kevins and one Percy. They had all read the reviews, smacked their lips and come at the kids with pens poised, but to no avail. For Richie had signed up with Barry Nadler, a little guy in his sixties who operated out of a little office on West Forty-sixth Street with nothing in it but a telephone, a coffee pot, and a 150-year love affair with show business.

The power of television in those days was devastating, and Barry Nadler had no trouble in booking The Pickering Trio into good clubs and for good bucks. Ginnie, of course, was delighted. The summer, conservatively, would earn the trio $15,000, and Barry was already weighing television offers for the fall. Richie's cut was fifty percent with Florrie and Ginnie splitting the other fifty percent, which was more than fair. Ginnie's share, less ten percent to Barry, came to well over $3,000, and she told me to quit the chain gang at 20th so that I could write full time.

It was very tempting but I had yet to sell anything and feared that I might never sell anything so why give up my only source of income even if a coolie earned more? Ginnie's feeling was that the only way I'd find out if I could write was to commit to writing totally. The compromise position, of course, was for me to quit the moment I sold my first script but to hang on until then.

The night before she left for a six-week tour with the act, she typed up "Tony" so that it was presentable for submission. Then we made love as if we never would again, lying in each other's arms as though she were the only girl in the world and I were the only satyr.

She left in the morning, first stop Chicago, and I was never more alone in my life. I slept in her room that night where the smell of her cologne was so prevalent that I could pretend she was still with me. Two nights of that and I couldn't stand it so I went back to my own room and abstinence. She called on the third night, or should I say morning—it was three thirty A.M. Chicago was a smash. We talked for an hour—so long that I half believed I was speaking to her from Fort Devens.

I sent the original copy of "Tony" to *Philco* and the first carbon to *Kraft Theatre* because I felt that those two shows represented my best chances of a sale. I had two other carbons which just weren't legible enough to inflict on any reader. It occurred to me that I was paralleling what Ginnie was doing in her act. Just as she stood and watched and then jumped in, so was I. All my life I had been a reader, an observer of writers— now I was jumping in in hopes of becoming a writer. It had worked for Ginnie, maybe it would work for Ben. For nowhere is there a rule that states that to be a writer one must do it from birth.

I didn't want to sign with an agent just yet, mostly because I didn't want any of them reading my script and telling me I was lousy before I could have it demonstrated that such might well be the case. Barry agreed with me but still wanted me to show it to this one agent, a woman, for whom he had great respect. Only because I liked Barry, and his cigars, did I bring my script to Helen McIninny at the Morris office.

She called three days later, having read it, and asked that I come to see her. I hadn't heard from *Philco* or *Kraft* yet, so I went into Helen McIninny's office knowing that hers would be the first professional opinion of my script.

She was a nice enough lady, sort of dowdy and thirty-fivish. At first she did try to be kind, which I guess is what you do with someone who is obviously terminally ill. Still, inside of five minutes, during which time her phone rang eleven times, I was getting the message loud and clear that she didn't think too much of my play. Finally, unable to pull her punches any longer, she smiled at me, very motherly, and said, "You're no Henry Denker."

I must confess that, at that time, I had no idea who Henry Denker was, that he was then (and still is) one of the more versatile writers on the scene; that he wrote books and plays that, if not always financial hits, *were* always skillfully written and highly praised. I knew none of that which is why I hope you will understand why I responded to Helen McIninny's statement as follows:

"Fuck Henry Denker!"

"You don't even know who he is."

"Fuck him anyway!"

And I could see her hackles rise, though the tone of her voice denied it. "Henry Denker is a writer whose pen you will never be able to lift, let alone carry."

"And so that's your opinion of me?"

"Yes."

"That I'm no Henry Denker."

"Yes."

"What do I do, put it on my *tombstone*? 'Here lies Ben Webber—he was no Henry Denker.' What does he put on *his* tombstone, that he was no William Saroyan?"

"He has a better chance of becoming William Saroyan than you have of becoming Irving Tannenbaum."

"And who the fuck is Irving Tannenbaum, if I may make so bold?"

"Irving Tannenbaum is the worst writer since hieroglyphics, only he doesn't know it, won't quit, and is going to be very miserable unless he goes back to his original profession of dentistry."

"And he's a better writer than me?"

"By far."

"And what goes on his tombstone, pray tell?"

" 'Here lies Irving Tannenbaum, Pulitzer Prize-winning orthodontist.' Now get out of here. You're as rude as you are untalented, and I'd rather answer the phone knowing it's someone telling me that my house burnt down than spend another minute of my time speaking to you." She turned away and answered her phone. I didn't wait around to see if it was her house but I like to think that it was.

The woman, of course, had originally planned to set me down easy, why else invite me up for a friendly chat about how untalented I was. But upon being confronted with my overreaction, she became equally overreactive, and because she had been doing it for much longer she did it much better. I skipped dinner completely, spending the rest of the evening with Johnnie Walker.

In the office things proceeded as usual, but without Ginnie to go home to, it was becoming increasingly more difficult for me to cope, especially with Sam Gaynor continually on my back. I wasn't sure how much more of him I could take. I knew not to get into any kind of fist fight with him, but, maybe, maybe if I came up behind him, with a stiletto, a gun, and a bomb . . .

Pat Jarvas wasn't helping my morale either, for she had gone completely the other way, calling me "office boy" and making me run errands that I knew could not be of Gruber's design. The atmosphere was clumpy. I seemed to have more enemies than friends, though I could not object to my co-workers lack of affection for me since I had earned that enmity (though not by design). What I questioned was the imbalance of my own relationships. As friends I had Mickey Green, with Dora Leindorf a kind of nonbelligerent. Gruber? Tough to figure. Certainly I couldn't go to him with my troubles. What it added up to was one friend, one neutral, and one enigma.

As enemies I had that anatomical trio: Sam Gaynor,

Pat Jarvas and Alan Morse—a prick, a cunt, and an asshole. The rest of them, as I said, were indifferent to me. Adding to the mix, both of my scripts were returned to me on the very same day.

Philco had sent me a form letter thanking me for my submission and hoping that, perhaps, another script etc., etc. *Kraft* was a bit more personal: "We do not find the material to our liking and, in the future, please submit through a recognized literary agent . . ."

What *is* a recognized literary agent? Does anyone really know? To this day I am uncertain what that phrase is intended to connote. At that time the image I had of a recognized literary agent was of a well-read fellow whose socks matched, who worked for a percentage, and to whom, if one recognized him on the street, one would say hello and feel the better for it because class had passed him by. Today I think otherwise. Today I think that a recognized literary agent is a man who sells books, can easily be picked out in a police lineup and readily be identified as a purse snatcher.

I shined up my two returned scripts and, before they had even caught their breath, sent them out again, one to *Studio One*, the other to *Theatre 60*. If they came running home I'd call up Irving Tannenbaum and perhaps the two of us would get together and collaborate on a tooth.

I was feeling wicked and evil the next day. No word from Ginnie beyond a picture post card of the Wrigley Building upon which she had written "Did you know there are no stationery stores in the Wriggly Building?" It took me a half hour to figure out the joke and even then I wasn't sure it was funny.

I went to the office with a premonition of doom. It wasn't a specific feeling, it was more of an uneasiness. And I decided that, if doom was really afoot, I did not want it to be of my making. Or if it was to be of my making, then I hoped to exercise enough restraint in the provoking of it to still be able to bail out without getting the axe.

Since I'd rather have been in Philadelphia, I managed to arrive at work ten minutes late and was instantly informed that "He wants to see you."

I strode into Alan Morse's office and he was in his puffed-up chair, swiveling around so that he was looking out the window, his back to my face. He was a detestable runt, still rubbing my nose in it even though he had all the weapons and I had hardly a nose left at all.

"You wanted to see me?"

He didn't move and didn't speak. He just sat there, the top of his head barely visible over the back of his chair, gazing out of his stupid window which commanded a view of a brick building that had no windows with which to look back.

"Your secretary said you wanted to see me."

No answer.

And I blew. No script sale, no money in the bank, nothing between me and the poorhouse but the generosity of my out-of-town girlfriend, and I blew. "Listen, you little blot—" Even as I was talking, I wished that I wasn't, that it was my thoughts I heard and not my voice. ". . . let me give you the word. I don't want this fucking job! I wouldn't work for you if you paid me a thousand bucks an hour! What you know about movie advertising wouldn't fill your fucking inkwell! So shove it, Mr. Morse! Take a hot ramrod and shove it!" And before he could turn around and raise as much as an eyebrow, I stalked out, slamming the door on him, causing his secretary to jump three feet straight up. Had she been under the ceiling fixture at the time of her ascendance, she'd have impaled herself.

I stormed down the corridor to the bullpen, slamming the door to that so hard that the entire plate glass fell out and crashed into the corridor. Dora screamed but Mickey looked at me with a mini-smile. "You did it, didn't you?"

"Yeah! And it's a far better fucking thing than I have ever done before." I was packing my things, throwing it all into the waste basket that I'd eventually use to haul it all away.

Sam Gaynor was at his desk and was laughing, "You stupid shit. That's what he wanted you to do. You walked raht into it. Man, you are some kind of a simpleton, you know that? He hands you the loaded gun and you go and blow your own balls off. He can't fire you because of the fucking union so you go and fire yourself—to Mars! Webber, you have got all the intelligence of a freshly laid buffalo turd in the Sahara sun. You are as stupid as—"

That's all he got to say as I had picked up my metal stapler and fast-balled it at his head. Unfortunately for the glass partition behind him he ducked, and more glass flew. And Dora screamed anew. And Mickey moved to restrain Sam because that King Kong lump of crap was coming at me and it wasn't to wish me good luck.

I didn't know whether to run for my life or wait for the sonofabitch in a field goal-kicking position from which I might send his balls over the wall to Grandmother's house—three points for my side at the final gun, even though I'd lose the game by a hundred. Mickey couldn't restrain the lummox for more than five seconds because Mickey didn't weigh as much as Sam's arm, but *in* that time another scream was heard from up the corridor, from Alan Morse's office.

It was his secretary, hysterical. "He's dead! Oh my God he's *dead*!"

That set everything moving in a different direction. Sam Gaynor was standing and looking at me, his red-faced anger turning to bald-faced triumph. Mickey looked at me as if I had suddenly grown another head. And Dora collapsed into her chair, clutching at her heart and reaching for a life-saving Kleenex.

Footsteps. Doors opening and closing. Other people arriving to investigate the situation. And Sam Gaynor leering at me. "I hope you did it, Webber. Man, how I hope you did it." And he flicked Mickey off and swept past me, clomping up the corridor to see for himself.

Later, after the police and the ambulance had arrived—because, yes, Alan Morse was dead, he had died just before I'd gone in—I was in Gruber's office and that man was explaining it all to me.

"He had terminal cancer. He knew it and we knew it. When it got to be too much for him, he popped a dozen sleeping pills and closed the book. He was an old buddy of Skouras's. Strange man, Spyros. With Josh having walked out so suddenly, he told me to put Morse into the job, that Morse couldn't live longer than a couple of months and that all the man wanted was a chance to die in the saddle. Don't ever try to read Skouras, Ben. He's been known to destroy people simply for the way they looked at him, yet he'll turn around and make a gesture for an old friend that no one else in the world would make. Anyway, that's what I couldn't tell you and why I asked you to hang on."

"I've already quit."

"The man was dead. He never heard your resignation speech, though his secretary did. I hear it was a beaut."

"It was—heartfelt. I'm sorry the guy is dead, but a

lot of Skouras's loyalty came out of my hide. If someone had told me—"

"Sorry, kid, nobody tells office boys nothing."

"Why was he such a bastard to me?"

"You were Josh's boy. You reported for work all
teed off. You never gave him a chance to like you. Anyway, it's over, and I think you should stay on. Don't
worry about the glass. We've been planning to do that
whole place over anyway."

"Who gets to be ad manager?"

"Buddy Connors. He's *my* man. He's been waiting
since the day Josh walked. He knows you're to be
moved up to copywriter status."

"What happens to Gaynor? Won't we have one copywriter too many?"

"Sam moves to Special Projects."

"What's that?"

"Who knows? Whatever he wants. Best thing to do
with Sam is to get him the hell out of the way."

"Isn't he Skouras's boy, too?"

"His father is. I promise you, Ben, it'll be the way
you want it, the way it should've been."

I stayed on at 20th. Buddy Connors walked in almost
before Alan Morse was carried out. It was as though he
were waiting downstairs in the lobby. It was an aspect
of daily life that I knew I had better get used to for it
was happening continually, almost cyclically. I had seen
it with my stewardesses and I had seen it in the Army;
people were interchangeable and replaceable. Like
leaves on trees they could fall off and be substituted for
even as they were falling. There was always someone in
the wings, waiting to go on. All I wanted then was *my*
turn, one shot at the world before I too fell into the
compost heap.

One thing Gruber had said, albeit in passing, was that

I had not given Alan Morse a chance to like me. Again it was being suggested, however obliquely, that thanks to my aggressive temperament, I had made a bad situation worse, made a dying man grieve, and brought dishonor upon my name. Well, I was getting just a bit tired of that shit. I had tried to keep my pugnacity in tow in every new relationship, but it never seemed to work out in my favor. And all I was ever left with for my efforts was a form of Hebraic guilt that, if I was not careful, was going to cause me to take on, as a second nature, a negative personality that would soon overpower the one God had given me. Though far from perfect, it was at least a positive personality, one I could build on and move forward from without forever wondering what bug I had offended or what cloud I had dislodged by simply attempting to establish my own tiny territorial rights.

Why should I have given Alan Morse a chance to like me? What would have been so bad if he had given *me* a chance to like *him*? Why was I always being asked to give up the Sudetenland, to offer the first olive branch, to bake the first bread? Why was I always expected to be the Little Red Hen? I hadn't killed Cock Robin. I didn't even see him die. It was the sparrow who did it. He even admitted it. The sparrow had a bow and arrow. Me? I didn't even have a pot to piss in.

A conclusion and a new self-evaluation was cauldroning in my mind. For it was beginning to dawn on me that perhaps aggressiveness was not such a bad thing, that maybe it wasn't aggressiveness at all but only ambition, and that maybe no one had the right to point fingers at anyone other than one's own self. If one's self thought one's self bad, then one's self was. But if one's self didn't, then one's self wasn't. And if one's self didn't do it anymore, then one's self didn't have to feel guilty anymore. The prime obligation of one's self was *to* one's self. And that applied to me just as it applied to little winter animals foraging for roots. I was foraging, too, and in the foraging I determined to God damn not feel guilty anymore. Mea Culpa get off my back!

Back at my apartment I found two things in the mail: my script returned from *Studio One,* with the usual letter of rejection, and a letter from Don asking for another hundred dollars.

I was not of a mind to send Don any more money, mostly because I didn't have it to send. But even if I had, I wouldn't. Who knew if I'd ever see him again or if he'd ever pay it back? Why should the Little Red Hen send bread that nobody had helped her bake? Fuck you, Cock Robin, you're getting to be a pain in the ass, and I have miles to go, miles to go—mixing my metaphors all the way.

I thought of writing to Don to explain why I could not send him more money, but I just didn't feel up to either lying or spleenventing. So I just tore up his marker and placed his letter in the drawer.

No letter from Ginnie and that was depressing, but she called an hour later and I lied to her on the phone, telling her that my three rejections were all very encouraging, that all three shows wanted to see more of my writing, that I had sent "Tony" to *Theatre 60,* and had a strong feeling I had a sale there because they were taking so long to decide.

What I didn't tell her was that Alan Morse had died and that I wanted to forget he ever lived. She filled me in on the act which was really going great. She was calling from Cleveland and next stop was Pittsburgh and did I want her to call my folks? I said yes, if she had the time, and no, not to tell them that we were living together.

We swore eternal love, fidelity and celibacy, plus abstention from masturbation for as long as we both could last. When I hung up the phone I had no idea where I was in time. I took Don's letter out of the drawer and figured what the hell, I'd send him the hundred dollars. But all I had in my checking account was $83.60, so I put his letter back into the drawer, thinking that maybe I should write to him and ask him for money because maybe he'd find it funny and wouldn't it be better than not replying at all. So I did.

Then Johnnie Walker and I went to Ginnie's room, going to her closet and touching all her things and wondering what that was all tied up in brown paper, leaning against the far wall. But it really wasn't my business and, excruciatingly tired, I fell asleep—in her bed, in her arms, in my dream.

The phone was jarring, ringing as it did so middle-of-the-night that I thought the noise was inside my head and how do I answer that? Stumbled into the living room and got it. Somebody from NBC calling all day. Why hadn't I put a phone number on my script where they could reach me when I wasn't at home? What? Who is this? Jerry Kaplan, NBC, *Theatre 60*. Frank Brokaw's office. Have your play. Can you come in to discuss? Who? Please take this number down and call at ten A.M. Jesus Christ. Goodbye.

I woke at around seven, knowing that I'd spoken to someone on the phone during the night and wondering if I'd managed to write anything down on the subject. I had, on a bit of paper, on the table by the phone, two names and a phone number: "Julie Klimplin—Frankbroe Craw—Plizzy 630-999-256342-8808088808-8." Which made about as much sense as having a hangover in the middle of the week.

I made coffee and studied my scrawl as I sipped.

Only Ginnie could have deciphered what I'd written. I got dressed, stuffed the bit of paper into my pocket, and bussed myself off to work.

Buddy Connors was nice to me. He wanted my approval on the new office boy, Arnie Felsen—Corporal Arnie Felsen, back from Korea, honorably discharged, no battle scars, and anxious to go to work in the ad department if a transfer could be arranged.

I was very glad to see Arnie because, due to circumstances over which I had only minimal control, he had become just by showing up my dearest and closest friend. I approved of him immediately and, suddenly, we had a nice group going—Mickey, Dora, Arnie, and me—all under the benign direction of Buddy Connors, not a great ad man, but in favor with Gruber and that's what dreams are made on.

Alan Morse was buried somewhere upstate, and Sam Gaynor was buried in an office on another floor, in another world, where later that day he would ask to have Arnie to run him some errands but would be turned down by Buddy because Arnie could not be spared until August of '73. Buddy was applauded for his actions, after which we all went to a screening of a film that I don't remember seeing because, ten minutes into it, I realized what the names and number in my pocket meant and ran out of the screening room and called NBC.

I sat opposite Frank Brokaw in his dandy functional office that was strewn with photos of prior *Theatre 60* productions, plus a few Emmy Awards and a thousand empty coffee containers. The man had to be the tallest, skinniest man alive—if he *was* alive, for there was some doubt in my mind because he hadn't moved and hadn't spoken and had been for ten minutes doing a superb imitation of Alan Morse the last time I saw that man.

The talking had all been done by Jerry Kaplan, a young man in his early thirties, darkly handsome and carefully dressed. Kaplan had been telling me of all the problems they had with my play—that it was too long, depressing, had too many sets, and was guaranteed to unhinge the US Army because it was so blatantly anti-. Other than that, the play was fine.

Brokaw spoke, in a raspy voice as if pushed through a pencil sharpener. "Do you see the validity of our comments and will you make the changes because, if not, on our last play of the season we don't need this kind of a headache." He was clearly disturbed at having to interpret the rules to me and I half expected him to say, "Watch the low blows, no rabbit punches, and go to a neutral corner in event of a knockdown."

"I'll make changes."

"I'm not anxious to murder your script, but the way it is now, I'll never get it passed Network Continuity. And even if I did, the sponsor will kill it. Kemper Aluminum is very conservative. Who's your agent?"

"Barry Nadler." Why in the world had I said that?

"Who?"

"Barry Nadler. Mostly handles performers. I'm his first writer." And last.

"Tell Jerry where the man can be reached. We pay $2500 for a first script. After that, if you do more with us it goes up."

"Yes, sir."

Brokaw drew himself to his feet wearily. "Look, you two work it out. I've got to get down to stage four. I've got Paddy waiting and—"

"Paddy Chayefsky?" I asked.

Brokaw smiled at Kaplan as he headed for the door. "Get him some aspirin, and a contract."

Kaplan sat on the couch, lit a cigarette and spoke slowly. "Ben, if I could write like you, I'd tell 'em where they could put this job. Still, I can do other things, okay?"

"Okay."

"First off, I think you ought to know I was with the 35th Division in Italy, and, though I share a lot of your opinions about how the Army can fuck up, I'm not anxious to do a hatchet job on them."

"Yes, sir."

"And don't call me 'sir,' because all I was was a PFC. Your script is too partisan. The trick is to do it in a way where the audience can make up its own mind. Otherwise it's liable to boomerang, and they'll end up liking the Army and hating you. The way it is now, it's too loaded. And, frankly, I resent a lot of it."

"Okay. I'll look at it again."

"Have you thought about who might direct your play?"

"No. I really haven't."

"Ben, go home. Think about the things I've just said. See if you can find a way to make it more impartial. Your view *and* the Army view. It's the only way it'll work. Also, write down the names of actors you see in the roles. Meantime, tell me where I can reach Harry Sadler."

"Barry Nadler."

"You sure he's a recognized literary agent?"

"I'd recognize him."

Kaplan pretended to boot me in the ass and I left the office and the elevator and NBC feeling as if I owned it all, feeling like the hick hero in those old movies who stands on the deck of the Staten Island ferry and shakes his fist at the New York skyline while saying, "I'll beat you yet, New York!"

I went back to the apartment and looked for Ginnie's itinerary. I wanted to call her but couldn't find the damned thing. I didn't know, offhand, what hotel she was at or where she was playing. I could only hope that she'd call.

No dinner. Just three apples and a jug of chianti. And I went to work on the script. It was easy to make it "less partisan." All I had to do was remember some of the things that McArdle had laid on me. Then, a couple speeches changed around so that they'd be less pointed, one scene eliminated because the author's point of view was too on the nose, and I had it in line. Then I went to work on the casting and here's what I came up with after my last swig of chianti:

BEN	Montgomery Clift
TONY	Charlton Heston
JOHNNY	James Cagney
HOLDOFFER	Jack Palance

Others in the cast were: Audie Murphy, Tony Curtis, Jeff Chandler, Billy De Wolfe, the Marx Brothers, and the Chianti Brothers. For directors I had: Joseph Mankiewicz, Frank Capra, Cecil B. DeMille, Billy Wilder, Buz Berkeley, Elia Kazan and Emilio Chianti.

I threw it all away and laughed and laughed and then went back to work on the script, tightening it, polishing it, shining it up. I'd let NBC worry about casting as I had obviously gone way over budget in my hallucinatory ideas, though, I must say, the idea of Montgomery Clift playing me did seem perfect casting.

Ginnie—bless her—called at around eleven thirty. She had arrived in Pittsburgh and sounded a little remote, as if something might be wrong. I let it go because I was in no shape to make any such judgment.

She said that everything was going well, that she had called my folks and was going to drop by to say hello, and then the conversation switched over to how things were going with me. I told her. And she got so excited that I could actually hear her jumping up and down on her end of the line. We sent kisses and love and, before I remembered to get her itinerary again, we'd hung up. Still, I slept very well that night, "I'll beat you yet, New York" playing over and over in my head, a song sung by John Garfield to Ann Sheridan, as Henry Armetta played the concertina on the moonlit upper deck-a-reena.

Next morning I made a triumphal entrance into the office, calling a staff meeting in Buddy's office and telling them all. They couldn't have been happier for me—even Arnie, who had been trying to sell a script for as long as I'd known him. He asked if we could have lunch during which I might give him a couple of pointers. I said it would be fine.

Barry Nadler phoned.

"Ben, what the hell is this with NBC?"

"It's crazy, that's what it is."

"You sold that script?"

"Don't sound so surprised. Anyway, they still want some changes."

"What do you need with *me*?"

"I don't know. You're an agent, aren't you?"

"What do I know from scripts?"

"What do you have to know? Just see that it's all legal."

"I'm trying. They sent it over. If you were a juggler or a comic, I could help you. But this? Re-writes? Polishes? Writers Guild? The Writers have a Guild? Is that like a Cousins' Club?"

"Barry, just do the best you can."

"Listen—congratulations. And what does that stupid Helen McIninny know from good writing anyway? Good-bye."

Two days later, Jerry Kaplan called. Said there was a small problem and that, if I wanted to make the sale, I'd better get over to Brokaw's office post fucking haste. Buddy gave me permission to go so I canceled my lunch date with Arnie and cabbed to NBC pronto.

The following people were in Frank Brokaw's office when I got there: Frank Brokaw, Jerry Kaplan, Harvey Epstein, and Jason Kimbrough, the latter two being introduced to me upon my breathless arrival.

Harvey Epstein was a small, almost minuscule man in his late thirties. He had no shoulders that I could see and wore a pullover sweater as if a circus tent had collapsed on him. He also wore thicklensed glasses in heavy black frames that continually kept sliding off his nose. He had hair like a shrunken bath mat and a pair of black sneakers that once had been white only don't bet on it. He was to be my director. He had done a dozen or so well-received shows and was very much in favor. But to me he looked like someone who didn't get picked for a choose-up stickball game, even though it was most marvelous how he could catch his specs just before they hit the floor.

When I say that Jason Kimbrough was the client, I don't mean that he handled the Kemper Aluminum account for the agency. I mean he was the *client*! He was Kemper Aluminum! Of medium height and build, he looked to be no more than fifty though his hair was so white that it was almost blond. He was so damned American in his chiseled handsomeness that, had he been introduced as Jack Armstrong, I would have immediately shat Wheaties. And, if ever I were redrafted into the Army to defend that man's front lawn, I would have considered it my duty as a citizen to do so.

We began chatting, gradually coming to the subject of my play, nobody really showing either affection or disgust though the teams were lining up more or less as follows:

Jason Kimbrough had serious doubts whether Kemper Aluminum should have anything to do with my play. He meant no disrespect for my writing, which, he was quick to say, was quite superior. That was the thrust of his position: good script but maybe too hot to handle.

Frank Brokaw was kind of on Kimbrough's side but was hard to pin down, hard to define. He seemed to be willing to go whichever way the wind blew, but *un*-willing to take an affirmative stand on either side of the issue, and un-anxious to go to the wall for my play because, to use his words from our first meeting, "we don't need this kind of headache."

My two allies were Kaplan and Epstein, and all through the discussions I had the feeling that any two men with two such names should be making me a suit and not fighting for my script. I'd much rather they'd have been Solomon and Disraeli, or, more realistically, Kaufman and Hart. But even as Kaplan and Epstein they weren't bad.

Jerry Kaplan, wearing his ruptured-duck discharge button in his lapel, was lawyeresque, well spoken, logical and clear, pointing out the quality of the writing, the maturity of the audiences, and the need for America to face up to and deal with its own imperfections. He thought that, with proper changes in the script, the play could help Kemper add to its image as one of the nation's leading corporations and shapers of public opinion. He was pretty fucking eloquent.

Jason Kimbrough remarked that all that was well and good, his only question was would they all not be acting a bit prematurely in jumping into the conflagration so soon? Yes, the Army should be held up to inspection just as any other arm of the government, but was it necessary for Kemper to assume the risks that always came with being first? Kaplan countered by saying that if and when somebody ever ran the mile in under four minutes, no one would ever remember the man to do it second.

Frank Brokaw wondered if Kaplan's comparison had validity in that men were forever trying to break the four-minute mile, whereas no one had theretofore evidenced any great interest in besmirching the reputation of the US Army. He seemed to be saying things that reinforced Kimbrough's stand—my first producer and he was made of pudding.

Kaplan respectfully allowed that his sports analogy might not bear up under all that scrutiny, but he still insisted that new times were upon us and that corporate giants such as Kemper *had* to assume certain obligations because if they didn't, who *would*?

Kimbrough asked Kaplan if he could be more specific, and Kaplan was in the process of doing just that when Harvey Epstein rose from his chair, catching his glasses as if he were W. C. Fields catching his straw skimmer. Then he stuck his arms out like Durante and carried on like Aimee Semple McPherson. "Gentlemen, please! I ask you—what the fuck are you talking about?"

That stopped the discussion, hushing everyone in mid-flight and giving Harvey Epstein the floor. And his marvelous New York accent, half emotion, half profanity, filled the room with evangelistic zeal, almost rattling the photos off the walls. "I *mean*," he repeated, "what the *fuck* are you talking about? No one's going to the moon and no one's going to the gallows. There's a play here, written by a man who, on first appraisal, seems to be passably sane for one so eager to write for television. Mr. Playwright, is this a true story or did you just make it up just to hand out a couple heart attacks?"

"It's all true," I said, stopping short of adding "your honor."

"Good," said Epstein. "That's what we thought. And even if we didn't, that's how it reads. It reads real. The dialogue bites clean. The characters know who they are. In a one hour drama you have to have all that going for you before you start or you'll have a cadaver before you're halfway through. Mr. Kimbrough, I now address myself to you, sir: why are you breaking my balls? This is one helluva play. Dramaturgically it works. You like that word? Okay, so you're concerned with its politics, to which I say so am I, because, as a veteran of the US Army, and having sustained two very severe cases of the clap with oak leaf clusters, I don't want the world believing, not for one minute, that ours is the only army in the world that fucks up regularly."

Kimbrough roared. Brokaw smiled. And Kaplan winked at me, as if to say, "Don't worry, your suit will be ready this afternoon."

Harvey Epstein was racing for the paddock, coming down the back stretch with nothing but finish line in front of him. "The object of this drama is to keep the audience from falling asleep. That is the object of all drama. Not to kindle conscience or make political merry or duck pertinent issues—no, *that* is the job of musical comedy."

Kimbrough roared again. Brokaw lit up a cigarette in comfy triumph. And Kaplan sat back as though he had four aces, having drawn three.

Epstein jogged over the finish line juggling his glasses like a hot potato. "This play is not perfect. The writer is still at work on it. I want all names changed because I didn't come this far in life—by subway—to risk being a defendant in a lawsuit. You say you're concerned, that your concern is for the Kemper Aluminum Company. Well, let me assure you that those of us in The Epstein Bullshit Company are no less concerned. There will always be aluminum. There may not always be an Epstein. In closing, I say to you, Mr. Kimbrough, if you like the way this play 'reads,' you will love the way it 'plays.' But, if you're afraid of it and want to water it down, take my word for it, if you water it down, all you'll have left is 'Francis the Mule Pisses on his Hoof.' Sir, add *no* water. Season it with intelligence, bake for one hour of prime time, and you will have a dish that can be set before a king."

Kimbrough stood up. "Harvey, most of what you say is such a lot of shit that I marvel at how the air is not polluted within five minutes of your opening your mouth. But, so is most of what I say, so—do your play. All I ask is that you keep my reservations about it in mind and that you act accordingly." He came over to me and shook my hand. "Young man, thank you for your very fine play. I just wish that you never wrote it." Then he left, followed by Frank Brokaw.

Jerry Kaplan congratulated Epstein on how well he had tailored the suit, after which Epstein came over to me. "Schmuck, have you checked with your lawyer?"

"About what?"

"About if you can still get the firing squad even though you're no longer in the Army."

"Yes. He says I can, and will."

"Then you've got a smart lawyer." And he started out.

"Hey—don't you want to see my rewrites?"

"What rewrites? There are no rewrites. I don't want a thing changed other than the names of the characters. Except 'Tony.' Keep that. He's dead and can't sue."

"Yes, but—"

"And stop with the 'yes, but.' You sound like Jack Benny." And he started out again, tripping over his untied sneaker laces and catching his glasses on the fly two feet in front of him. "Christ," he said, "who the hell waxed this carpet?"

With Harvey Epstein gone and all his insane logic with him, I looked over at Jerry Kaplan, who was lying on the couch, smiling at me. "What do you think, Ben? You have just seen a drama that we play here, oh, maybe three times a month. Your mouth is hanging open. Are you catching flies or is there something you want to say?"

"I don't understand about the rewrites."

"Nothing to understand. No rewrites. Happens maybe once a century." And he sat up straight. "The show will only work as written, from your gut. Any changes and it risks flying apart. And if that were to happen, Kimbrough would have a conniption fit. So no changes."

"You so sure Epstein is right?"

"Epstein? What does *he* have to do with it?"

"He's the one who said 'no changes.' "

"He's the one who said it to *you*. The one who said it to *him* was Frank Brokaw."

"But, he was—"

"Sucking around Kimbrough?"

"Yes. Exactly."

"Is that the way it looked to you?"

"Yes."

"Looks can be deceiving. Ben, Frank Brokaw is two

things. One, he is a superb actor. And two, he has more raw courage than any producer in the business. He would have fought harder for your play than you would have. The trick was to not let it come to that. Jesus Christ, are you going to faint?"

"I already have."

"Frank can play Kimbrough like Evelyn plans her magic violin. But, there's one more thing you should know. Kimbrough knows it and allows it."

"So it's all a game."

"It's a game for as long as we continue to put on good shows. Once we stop doing that the game is over."

"And Kimbrough never gets his hands dirty."

"You got it. He always keeps himself in a position to say that he was against something but that we insisted. And so it becomes our asses and not his—because ours are flesh and blood, and his is aluminum."

"Do you think he likes the play?"

"He never read it. We sent him a synopsis."

"How the hell do you guys function?"

"Nobody knows."

It was midafternoon when I finished up at NBC, or should I say, when NBC finished up with me—and I just didn't feel like going back to the office. Kaplan had told me to shake myself free for casting and for rehearsals, which would begin quite soon. I said it might be difficult. He said that I could skip casting but that Epstein would insist that I be around for rehearsals. I said I'd have to quit my job or take a leave of absence. He said that I was every inch a writer and that I had better stop straddling the fence, and that, should I jump off onto the writer side, he was pretty sure that NBC would guarantee me at least three or four scripts on the come, for the fall season, and that I could begin writing them over the summer. I felt good about that.

I called Arnie Felsen and told him to drop by my apartment after work and I'd fill him in. He was frothing at the mouth to do just that. When he came up he was so fascinated with the whole story that he prevailed on me to read a script of his that no one on earth had as yet seen.

I was depressed after Arnie left because I knew instinctively that the guy couldn't really write. I just didn't want to be the one to tell him that he was no Henry Denker. I had a drink and then, feeling better, called Ruby Foo's and had them send up a Chinese dinner that would have made Marco Polo's eyes slant.

An hour after consuming that dinner I was depressed again. I had all that success going for me, all those vibrations on the wind, and nobody to talk to about it but Arnie Felsen—and I had already talked to *him*.

I thought of Ginnie. She'd still be in Pittsburgh. Maybe she'd already seen my folks. Maybe I should call my folks. Maybe they'd be glad to hear the news.

I called and they were both at home. They were delighted with the news. Surprised, too, for they had had no idea that I wanted to write. Yes, Ginnie had dropped by—nice girl. Made a nice impression. I told them to watch *Theatre 60* on Sunday night because at the end of each show they announced the next week's show and mine would be coming up soon. My father, who liked to watch Fred Waring and his Pennsylvanians, said he'd forgo that pleasure and I thanked him. I told them to allow for the one hour time difference between New York and Pittsburgh and my father, insulted, asked if I thought he was a moron. We all tired of talking and said good-bye and I was really depressed.

I knew to stay away from the booze because I had been doing too much of that since Ginnie left town I was mad at Ginnie for not being somewhere where I knew I could call her. I knew I could get her number from Barry Nadler but that would be the next day. Besides, I didn't want to talk to Barry Nadler, I wanted to talk to Ginnie.

I wandered into her room and it drove me crazy. I guess I was a little tipsy because I felt some tears on my cheek and I was not known to be a crier. I touched her clothes again, in her dresser, dungarees and leotards, funny blouses, underthings—silk and maddening. And some better class things with Bloomingdale's labels, and Sak's Fifth Avenue. My photo was on her night table. Me, in uniform. It seemed a long time ago, as if that soldier was a stranger because *I* was a *playwright*. And how could anyone who looked that stupid be a playwright?

I touched the clothes in her closet, those Ginnie things hanging with no Ginnie in 'em. I saw that thing again, pressed against the far wall of the closet, wrapped in brown paper, tied in string—a picture of some sort. Just as I reached for it the phone rang.

I ran to answer it because maybe it was Ginnie, and I grabbed it as if it were oxygen and I were a dying man. "Hello?"

"Ben?"

"Ginnie?"

"Who?"

"Who's this?"

"Maggie."

"Maggie?"

"Yes. I'm in town. Come see me."

"Maggie?"

"Yes! Ben, is that you?"

"Yes."

"I just flew in. Please come and see me. I've been

thinking of you all the way down from Boston. Got a pencil?"

"Yes."

"Take this down. St. Regis Hotel. You know where that is?"

"Yes."

"Room 735. Got it?"

"735."

"When will you be here?"

"Well—"

"Oh, Ben for Christ's sake, I'm on my way to Europe and may not see you for a year. And I won't be in New York for more than two days. Are you coming over or do I have to call Rock Hudson?"

"Maggie, I've been seeing someone."

"Wonderful. You can tell me all about it when you get here."

"I don't know if—"

"Ben, I'm seeing someone, too. Stop being so fucking bourgeois. This is *Maggie*. Get over here and—we'll talk. We'll just talk, okay?"

"Okay."

I hung up the phone and was surprised to find that I was trembling. I thought about calling her back and telling her that I couldn't make it. I mean, how could I go see Maggie after Ginnie and I had taken a vow? I pulled myself together. Of course, I could go see her. Maggie and I were friends. We'd talk, I'd tell her about my play. It would be harmless. Ginnie wasn't around, and at least with Maggie I'd be with someone on a night I just *had* to be with someone. Nothing would happen, I'd see to that. We'd just talk. I took a fast shower, got dressed, and took a cab to the St. Regis.

Alone in the elevator I determined not to let our reunion get out of hand. We would meet as old friends, or former lovers—same thing. We would have a few laughs, hoist a few daiquiris. I'd stay maybe a half hour and that would be it. We'd see each other again—next time the Red Sox came to Yankee Stadium.

Still, I knew that if Maggie was of a mind, I'd be stripped and screwing inside of thirty seconds. At least, that's how the old script went, the one we broke in in Boston in its pre-New York run. So I prepared some excuses. Sprained back, migraine headaches, acid indigestion, painful arthritis, bent cock. Any or all of them would have Maggie so hysterical that she simply wouldn't be able to concentrate on making love. So I thought of more excuses as I walked down the seventh floor corridor: torn knee cartilage, deviated septum, embarrassing dandruff, the heartbreak of psoriasis, dislocated scrotum . . .

I knocked on the door of 735, as close to death as I had ever come, a doddering old man with debilitating diabetes, chickenosis, halitosis, galloping crud, encroaching senility, and an erection so outrageous that I had to raise a leg and shake it, like Fido at a hydrant, to calm it down.

Maggie came to the door and took immediate note of my condition. "Why, Ben, how nice of you to bring me such a lovely present." And she hugged me very close and the game was over.

She let go, turned, and went back into her suite. She was magnificent. A black dress up to the chin, so form-fitting it looked as though it had been painted on. High-heeled shoes so provocative that I could suddenly understand why certain men liked to be walked on by such seductively shod ladies. "Ben, it's a disaster. I don't have more than ten minutes. I tried reaching you but you'd already left."

"What's the matter?" I asked, suddenly as disap-

pointed as a man finding out that his beautiful mail-
order bride had to be sent back for additional postage.

"Oh, it's this charity. I don't know what it is. Angela
Corrigan got me involved in it and I have to meet with
their fundraisers and at *this* hour, my God, is it really
eleven thirty? And I so wanted to be with you. I don't
suppose you'd care to wait here until I got back."

"What if you come back with a sailor?"

"If I knew you were here, I'd come back alone." She
was in front of me, her arms about me coquettishly, her
perfume seeping right through my skin, paralyzing my
capillaries. "Whaddya say, big boy? And my, but you
are big." She reached down, fingering me, then finding
me. "Have you grown since last I—sucked this?"

"Jesus Christ, Maggie."

"Jesus Christ, yourself," she said, seeming to come
all undone. "When the day comes that I don't react this
way to hard meat, that's the day I want to be dead."
She was using both hands. "You're back to zippers, are
you? In the Army you had buttons. Zippers are faster
but they're also more dangerous. Don't want to get
snagged. Ah, there he is, my old champion. And ready
to pop, too. Well, let's see what we can do for him."

"Maggie, I really don't think—"

"I know you don't. That's why I'll do all the thinking.
Come with me." Again, as in days of yore, she was
leading me by the pecker, to the bed.

"Maggie, you'll miss your appointment."

"So what?"

"It's an important charity."

"Charity begins at home. Take your things off, darling, or I'll rip 'em off, and I'd hate to do that to your
nice sports jacket. Gentree or Tripler's?"

"Broadstreet's."

"Swell, but off it comes."

And off it came, plus everything else I was wearing. She undressed, too, and we were on the bed in seconds, banging away at each other like knights in combat. The acrobatics that Maggie performed would have won the United States an Olympic medal had there been a competition in free-form fucking. She could have made love on the parallel bars, the uneven bars, the rings—the hammer throw, the long jump, and especially the pole vault. The marvelous thing was that, no matter what she did, she was graceful and lovely. Positions that might have made an ordinary woman look like a slut so flattered Maggie that she appeared as some kind of sylvan creature, clad in webs, wafted on zephyrs. And she enjoyed it so. Even the profanities that she bit into my ear went into my head as sonnets and came out of my penis as passion.

"Maggie, Maggie, you are a fucking wonder."

"I know."

"You're too much."

"I never charge."

"I won't be able to walk for a week."

"Anybody can walk."

There was a knock on the door and Maggie looked up at me. "Who the hell is *that*?"

"Beats me. I'm new in this neighborhood."

Maggie called out. "Who is it?"

"Chambermaid!"

"Come back later, I'm fucking!"

"Maggie!" I gasped.

"It's okay. They love it. Makes their day."

The voice from the corridor again, slight French accent. "But, madame—I'ave fresh towels for you."

"Later! I'm sucking this big cock!"

"Jesus Christ, Maggie! They'll throw you out of the hotel."

"Never. I give it an air of class."

The knocking again, and the voice. "Please, madame—will only take one minute."

Maggie looked up at me. "Go answer the door, love. Give the lady a thrill."

"She'll faint."

"She's *French*, darling. She'll probably applaud."

I grabbed a towel and wrapped it about my waist. "Maggie, one day they're going to lock you up."

"Never. There's not a jail that can hold me."

I walked to the door, careful to keep the towel over my privates. I was unaware that Maggie was tip-toeing behind me. I opened the door, and, as I did, Maggie pulled the towel away from me, reached around, grabbed my cock, and began jerking it from behind, a hundred strokes to the minute, while shouting over my shoulder, "Vive la France!"

I stood there like a fool, looking into the face of the chambermaid, and my heart stopped—and Maggie stopped. And all life as I knew it, and all the planets—stopped.

It was Ginnie.

She froze for a moment, poised as if in midair, a pretty, blonde hummingbird just minding her own sweet business. Then she turned and flew, disappearing around a bend in the corridor. I kept standing there, seemingly for hours, hoping for some kind of comprehension. Was it really Ginnie? Ginnie?

I turned to look at Maggie who was sitting in a chair, shakily attempting to light a cigarette that never did get lit. "You're not going to believe this, Ben—but—that was my daughter."

There are no words.

chapter eighteen

ginnie

1952

The night before I left to tour with the Pickering Trio, I typed up Ben's play so that it would be clean, legible, and saleable. It was so good. He had so captured all the joy and pain of Tony's life and death. Damn, but Ben could write. No, I was no judge, not of writing, per se, but I knew when something reached me, when it touched me. I knew when there were tears in my eyes and lumps in my throat. I didn't have to be a critic or a producer to know that my emotions had been wrung so much that there was nothing to hang out to dry. There was no doubt in my mind but that someone would buy "Tony." It was just a matter of Ben's patience and the world's waking up. The former worried me more than the latter.

We made good love that night, total, insane, physical love. I don't think we spoke a word until we had finished. If Henry Ford had given his first tin lizzies the tests we gave to our beds, they'd still be on the road. We sashayed from bedroom to bedroom, like strolling troubadors, and each time we did we'd pretend to be two other people. I made love to seven different men that night—no, eight—mustn't forget the polo player from Grosse Pointe who scored three times in the very first chukkah.

I left in the morning. It was a merry parting but sad.

It was, "Here I go, when you see me again I'll be a star." But it was also, "Good-bye, darling, and if I never see you again what a lousy trick that'll be." Anyway, I was off, Midwest, ho.

It was our first separation, and, as I got into the cab, my stomach felt as though I'd left my insides upstairs. Florrie had been waiting. The meter already showed over a dollar. I cried all the way to the airport. I cried in the waiting area. I cried when Barry Nadler showed up with the sleep still in his eyes. I cried when Richie showed up with seven valises and a fifty-fifty chance for a hernia. I cried when the old lady came up to me and told me not to cry. And when the little girl gave me two Tootsie Rolls if I'd stop crying, I practically had to be carried onto the plane.

During the flight I thought of Mary Ann and Walter. They lived in Chicago. Should I go see them? Had they seen me, on TV? Did they have any children? Were they happy? Did I care? No. Would I call them? Never.

In Chicago we stayed at the Hotel Morrison— comfortable without being posh, relatively inexpensive, conveniently located in the loop, and within walking distance (three blocks) of the Palmer House, where we would be opening in two nights in the Empire Room. Not bad. Jane Morgan was headlining. Then there was us, "Sensational dance trio from *The Joey Magnuson Show.*" And an MC, a comic, and Eddie O'Neal and his orchestra. Barry hadn't quite been able to swing us free rooms at the Palmer House because of some kind of convention being held by the National Association Of Soft-Water Service Operators, if you can believe that.

Still, it wasn't bad. Florrie and I shared a nice room, Richie had his own, and the Palmer House paid for it all. We checked in and unpacked, and, before going to the Palmer House to check the stage and hand over our musical arrangements to the orchestra, Richie took us to dinner. The Boston Oyster House at the Morrison.

Over a bowl of chowder, Richie let us in on something that had been bothering him. He was concerned that, despite our ability as a "straight act," we had made our reputation on my always coming in late, busting in, and all of us kind of working our way out, which was swell. Only this wasn't television where you do a routine once and forget it. This was night clubs where we'd be doing our routines twice a night, six nights a week, and the issue was: could we still make it all look funnily spontaneous?

Richie laid out our strategy. We had four numbers, two of which we had performed "straight," and two of which I "screwed up." We would open with our two straight numbers ("Sing, Sing, Sing," and "My Blue Heaven"). The problem was that we only had time for one more number. That meant that we'd have to cut either "Sweet Georgia Brown" or "Jet." Only it wasn't a problem, it was simple. Since there were two shows a night, we'd close the first show with "Georgia Brown" and the second with "Jet." That way we'd never be improvising either of those two routines twice in one night. And, with any luck, we might just get the same effect we got on television. We just might look totally spontaneous in our closing routine's madness.

The stage at the Empire Room gave us more room to work with than we had on TV, and that was a plus. And the orchestra was literally right behind us, which was another plus because we could feel the percussion coming right up through the floor. And the fact that we didn't have to play to the camera was a plus because it gave us one less thing to worry about. The comic, Ricky Davis, was *not* a plus. He was a double minus, homing in on me like a bloodhound.

I had learned by then to accept a certain amount of that stuff as coming with the territory. Where once I might have leveled the guy with some choice bombast, I let Ricky Davis just bounce off me. So nobody got angry and nobody got hurt. He came at me for just two nights, which was all the time he could devote to the sport since his wife showed up from LA on the third night. Sally Davis, an ex-showgirl with cherry hair and three chins, was not to be fooled with, and Ricky, though all cock, went limp when that lady blew into town.

The man who really disturbed me was Johnny Farrar, and most of the disturbance was the result of his looking so much like Ben, except that he was about ten years older, a touch taller, and a helluva lot less emotional. Johnny had money. Old money. Family money from way back. In World War II he had been some kind of hero, and, when he got out of the Navy, it was with a flock of decorations and a seat on the board of directors of Daddy's company, which had to do with electronics and the millions of dollars that it manufactured.

Johnny had a style. He had a repose and an intelligence and a quiet kind of veneer; and when he came up to me after our first rehearsal, I did a double-take because he looked like Ben only without the fire.

"I didn't mean to make you jump up in the air like that," he said. "I wasn't going to bite you. I just wanted to say that I think you're lovely—and a fantastic dancer—and that, if you have the time, I'd like to buy you a sandwich."

The sandwich turned out to be something flaming at the Pump Room. I was vulnerable to Johnny and I knew it, and so I told him immediately about Ben, describing Ben as a playwright and my fiancé. Johnny smiled and said he was flattered that I was so afraid of him. I tried to deny his observation but it did me little good because both of us knew he was right. So I laughed and agreed and enjoyed the dinner.

We walked back to the Morrison and he left me at the elevator and I knew I'd better be wary because there was a smoothy at work. He asked if he could drop by the next day at rehearsal, that his office was nearby and that he often wandered in because one of his friends had to do with the management of the Palmer House, and I said it would be fine, providing he'd tell me again that I was lovely and a fantastic dancer.

The next day he did just that. Dinner was at The Buttery where we got to know each other bettery, telling each other about each other and enjoying each other's company very much. It was staggering how Johnny was the extension of Ben—without the rough edges. Ben with style and maturity. And the whole Johnny Farrar package I found to be irresistibly fascinating.

In the course of our candid conversation he told me that he was married but not too happily and that though hopeful of getting a divorce it was presently tangled and gluey. He "played" occasionally but never to a point where he thought himself a bounder. Stuck in a hopeless marriage, he had certain options for satisfying certain drives—and that that's the way he was living his life.

"You kind of have it all your own way," I said.

"To some degree. Yes, I suppose so."

"You want to go to bed with me."

"Doesn't everyone?"

"Some. But they're not so—sneaky."

"Am I being sneaky? I thought I was being straightforward."

"It translates as being sneaky because no one is straightforward."

"I'll make a deal with you."

"Don't."

"Here's the deal. If and when you decide we should go to bed, you just let me know. And if you don't, then this is as far as we go."

"That's what I meant by being sneaky."

"Then sneaky it is, but the offer still stands."

"And in the meantime, you'll just take me to dinner and leave me at the elevator."

"Unless you invite me up."

"That is *so* sneaky. You mean, you won't even ask to come to my room?"

"No. You have to ask me in. However——"

"Uh-oh."

"No uh-oh. The 'however' is that you understand, from this point on, that I have made my pass at you, okay? The pass has been made and will not be made again. The next move, if there is one, will have to come from you."

"How long do I have till your offer runs out?"

"Forever."

"That's a good deal."

"Think so?"

"Yeah. How many great restaurants are there in this town?"

"Well, let's see. There's the Balinese Room at the Blackstone, the Camelia House at the Drake, the Beach Walk at the Edgewater. There's my room at the La-Salle."

"Sneaky."

"There's Le Boeuf, L'Aiglon, the Cameo, Citro's, Henrici's." Johnny Farrar would bear watching.

We opened the next night at the Empire Room. Jane

Morgan was just great—a great singer, a great lady. And she did it the hard way, having to go to Paris to become a star as an American then returning to America as the French hit of Broadway. All through rehearsals she had been very supportive. She could see how nervous we were and she did everything she could to lessen our anxiety. Marty Kerman, the MC, introduced her, and the show was on.

Jane sang in French and in English. Then Ricky Davis regaled the audience with thrice-warmed-over yoks, and then the Pickering Trio was on.

And we were damned good. Eddie O'Neal gave "Sing" such a beat that it was all the audience could do to keep from jumping up and dancing with us. We followed "Sing" with "Blue Heaven" with Richie tapping like Astaire, all loose and flowing, and me and Florrie as the two sexiest pussycats what ever slunk over a back fence. And we finished with "Georgia Brown" with me coming in on the middle of it and the audience falling off their chairs. It couldn't have worked better. The applause was a cannonade and was still firing after five salvoes. Even when we were in our dressing rooms we could still hear the applause, and only after Jane came on to do her closing numbers did it stop, that nice lady telling the audience that it was our first nightclub appearance and that, if we didn't cut it out, she'd have to go back to Paris and get some new material.

There were flowers from Johnny—a dozen red roses—and I could feel Florrie's eyes on the back of my head. Though she had no special affection for Ben, she saw him as my fella, and me as his girl. It upset her to think that maybe I was playing it a little loose, especially since, in all the time I'd known her, and despite that foul mouth of hers, she had always been faithful to Monty. Florrie believed in one-to-one relationships but rather than butt in with one of her patented caustic comments, she just went to sleep on the dressing room cot until the second show. The note on Johnny's roses read:

> "Le Petit Gourmet, Imperial House, Fritzel's, the Cape Cod Room, and my room at the LaSalle"

—Good show—
Johnny

I got one of the boys to put the roses in water and stuffed Johnny's note in my bag because somehow it seemed incriminating. And I got an old flash: There was Florrie, thinking the worst of me, as had my father, my sister, and my teachers, and all I had done was to have dinner with a man whom I was rebuffing at every turn. So why the Scarlet Letter, gang? Why the heavy silence? In any case I didn't want to discuss it, especially not with Florrie who was already fast asleep.

The second show went as well as the first, "Jet" working as beautifully as had "Georgia Brown." And when I got back to the dressing room there were another dozen roses from Johnny, this time yellow. And this time Florrie felt compelled to comment on it.

"Next time, fuck a diamond miner instead of a florist and we can quit showbiz and open a Tiffany's."

"It's not what you think."

"I know it's not. I share your room, remember? I know where you are every minute of the fucking day."

"Then don't be so nasty. Nothing's happening."

"Something *is* happening. You just don't seem to know it. He's got your panties halfway down. Can't you feel the breeze?"

"I'm in love with Ben."

"Yeah? Then pull up your bloomers, kid, because in Chicago you could get pneumonia."

Richie came in, filled with admiration and compliments. The two closing numbers were paying off in more ways than one. The press, it seems, was fascinated with the way our act was constructed, the interchangeable ending seeming to them to be so original as to be worthy of all the newsprint they could give it.

Richie left and Johnny appeared, knocking on the opened door and offering us a lift back to our hotel. Florrie demurred, saying she'd rather walk because a girl could get pneumonia in a cab if she didn't keep her legs crossed. Then she walked out.

"She doesn't like me," said Johnny.

"You could have sent her some roses, too."

"I did. They're in your room, addressed to her."

"Jesus, you are so goddamned *sneaky*."

"Hungry? Want to eat?"

"No. I just want to get some sleep. Also, I want to call Ben."

"Why tell *me*?"

"I wanted you to know, that's all."

"That you love Ben?"

"Yes."

"I know you do. But what does it have to do with the price of tomatoes?"

"I'm not a tomato."

"Sorry. Poor choice of word."

"Freudian slip."

"Bullshit. Come on, I've got a cab waiting."

A cab ride from the Palmer House to the Morrison is over before it starts. And it leaves very little time for chit-chat. Aware of that, Johnny got immediately to the point.

"I'm leaving tomorrow. San Francisco."

"Oh?"

"Should've gone yesterday but I wanted to see your opening night. You were marvelous."

"Worth your having stayed over?"

"Absolutely. But I don't know when I'll be seeing you again—if ever."

"Sneaky."

"My bag is in the trunk of this cab and after I drop you off, I'm on my way to the airport. Plane leaves in less than an hour."

"Oh."

"So I hope you're satisfied. Or would *relieved* be a better word?"

"*Disappointed* would be the best word."

"Who knows—maybe we'll bump into each other in Siam."

"We don't play there till next year. Burma, Malaya, Siam—all the big eastern cities."

"I'll miss you, okay?"

"It's okay."

"There's been a tentative agreement on a divorce. Don't say anything, it's not required. Just know that the next time we meet, I'll be out of it." He pulled me over and kissed me, so suddenly that who knew what. We never said good-bye—but then, we'd never really said hello. The whole thing had a middle. No beginning, no end, just this little middle. Johnny Farrar, who had put the ball in my court and left it there, had gone. What would I do with the ball? Drop back and punt.

The cab pulled away and I felt stupid and incomplete, like I almost had had the answer to some big important question but hadn't raised my hand to volunteer.

Florrie, still walking, had yet to get back to the Morrison, so, up in the room, I phoned Ben. It was two thirty A.M., Chicago time—which meant that it was three thirty A.M. in New York. Fuck it. Wake up, Ben, for I have things to tell you.

We gabbed forever. It must have cost a fortune but it was worth it. I had spoken with Ben and my love for him was reaffirmed and never-ending. As nice and as provocative as Johnny Farrar had been, he was no longer a factor in my life, just a neat breeze that had blown by and flattered me and picked me up and given my ego a nice ride. And when Florrie walked in, I told her that her worries were over, that I loved Ben Webber and always would, and what did she think of *that*?

Of that she thought nothing because all she could see were the two dozen red and yellow roses from Johnny, addressed to her, and with a properly tidy card attached:

> Applause it pours,
> Torrents for Florence.
>
> Love, Johnny

Florrie harrumphed. "My name's Flora not Florence."

"Florrie!" I was aghast at her insensitivity.

"He took the easy way out. All he could rhyme with Flora would be schnorer, the fink."

"Florrie, don't you like the roses?"

"What'd you do, bring 'em back with you from the dressing room and stick a new card on 'em?"

"You dummy! They're for you!"

"From Johnny?"

"Yes!"

"Why?"

"Because he wanted you to have them! Because he knew that both our fellas weren't here and that—"

"Wrong. Because he's still pulling down your bloomers."

"Oh for Christ's sake!"

"When the fuck are you gonna learn?"

"He left tonight, you jerk. I'm never going to see him again."

"Oh, you'll see him again."

"Yeah?"

"Yeah. No one who is not going to see you again ever sends four dozen roses—unless the reason he's not gonna see you again is that you're *dead*—and in that case he sends you lilies."

"You're a goddamned cynic, you know that?"

"Yeah, baby, you got it. A guy is marking you with his scent, staking out his claim on you and *I'm* a cynic. Well, do you know what you are?"

"No, but I think I'm about to hear."

"You're fair game, baby."

"What does that mean?"

"It means that it's open season on your box and this is only Chicago. We've still got Cleveland and Pittsburgh and St. Louis. By the time you're finished with this tour, you'll have twenty-three Johnny Farrars, fourteen Irving Friedmans, eleven Terry O'Rourkes and six or seven Nick Pasquales. They're gonna flock to you like bees, baby, because the word is out that you're packin' the pollen!"

"My goodness, Flora, how you do talk. Tsk-tsk-tsk."

"Tsk-tsk-tsk, my ass, baby. No, make that tsk-tsk-tsk, *your* ass."

Whoever's ass it was that got the tsk-tsk, Florrie wasn't all that wrong. We played a week in Chicago, during which three other men came at me with a variety of approaches, none of which got any of them past the elevator. I couldn't keep calling Ben because it was so damned expensive. I mean, with Johnny gone and me turning down dinner invitations, if I wasn't more frugal, I'd end up owing money instead of banking it. I sent Ben a dopey post card of the Wrigley Building and then went about the business of being a professional dancer. And when we left Chicago we were all feeling pretty good about the way things were going.

Cleveland was Chicago only spelled differently and not as pretty. We were on the bill at the Landmark with Joe E. Lewis ("America's most beloved comedian") and Sophie Tucker ("The Last Of the Red-Hot Mamas"). He was mostly drunk but always funny, singing, "Show me a home where the buffalo roam, and I'll show you a dirty home." She no longer sang as well as I'd been led to believe she could. Still, when she belted out "Some Of These Days," I felt all the magic that had made her famous.

We played just three days in Cleveland, during which I was hit on by a shoe manufacturer, an optometrist, a trumpet player (in the orchestra), and a descendant of Daniel Boone who, though he wore no coonskin hat, did take dead aim at my ass, grabbing me there with what seemed to be six bear paws. Richie had to call the cops to get him out of the dressing room. Florrie, watching, clucked like a wise old owl and I told her to go fuck herself because my ass was being very tsk-tsked and I didn't need any cluck-cluck to go with it.

I called Ben from Cleveland and, because our next stop was Pittsburgh, I asked him if I should look up his family. He said yes but that I shouldn't go into any great detail about our relationship. Ben told me that "Tony" had gotten three rejections but that he felt he might have a sale at *Theatre 60* because they were holding the script for so long. But I could sense that he wasn't all that confident and that he really didn't want to talk about it, so rather than make any noises of phony reassurance I let the conversation go quickly to how much we loved each other.

Before parting, we had joked about resorting to masturbation if the pressure of not seeing each other got to be too much. On the phone we assured each other that it hadn't come to that as yet but I hoped he was lying because I knew *I* was. I had done it twice in Chicago and twice in Cleveland and I think Florrie was doing it, too, because there was no other way for either of us to remain all that faithful and still get to sleep. I had always been told that masturbation was sick, evil, and physically destructive. I had also been told that babies came from department stores and that Santa Claus was real—so what was a girl to do? Well, I did what I knew Santa Claus did when out of town on a cold winter's night and what all those people in department stores did when the demand for babies dropped off and they had to do something with their overtime—I reached down and found myself and took care of myself and got to sleep. And that is why, to this day, I still believe in Santa Claus and have charge accounts at department stores. Fairytales and fingers, and nobody gets hurt.

We exchanged Cleveland for Pittsburgh—Joe E. Lewis for Jackie Miles, and Sophie Tucker for Beatrice Kaye. Names and faces began to slide around. The orchestra was either Barry Brown or Wally Green and I'm not sure that either of them knew. The club we played was either the Arena or the Premiere Room. All I knew was that the MC's name was Hayden Shepherd and that he was coming on like War Admiral—not at me, but at Florrie.

Hayden Shepherd was one of those fat, jovial types who had hit fifty-five and, surprised at still being around after a lifetime of nothingness, began drinking to whatever life he had left. White-haired and peach-cheeked, he floated around backstage like the local hippo. He never shook anyone's hand but that he didn't also pound that person on the back, as if he were trying to see if the other person had a weapon or cared to arm wrestle. And he was always laughing, a watery laugh that ended as a wet cough. If he said good morning to you he laughed. If he picked up a phone and said hello he laughed. He pressed Florrie's titty, said, "Ooh—cute," and laughed. And when she told him where he could stick his tool, providing it still worked, he laughed. The only thing was, he wasn't funny. Not to us, at least, and certainly not to Florrie.

But I enjoyed the spectacle of his puffy passes at Florrie because it gave me the opportunity to go cluck-cluck and tsk-tsk at her. I certainly didn't think he was anyone that Florrie had to worry about or be on her guard against—and, frankly, neither did she. The truth of it was that she had just wished that the first guy to make a pass at her hadn't been such a faded fuddy-duddy. She'd much rather it had been some big stud. Not that she'd have done anything about it, but just so's she could feel properly appreciated. As she put it, "He makes me feel so fucking last resort, like Sophie Tucker had turned him down and it was either me or the knot-hole."

We had begun rehearsing the day we arrived in Pitts-burgh and it was all getting very routine and Richie warned us not to let down, not to lose our animation and spontaneity. He was right, of course, and we put ourselves through a very rough rehearsal. The stage was smaller than the other two stages we'd worked on so we didn't have all that much room to jump around in. Also, I had a feeling that the air-conditioning wasn't up to snuff and that we might want to kill a few lights during our performances.

With Richie and Florrie going over "Georgia Brown" and "Jet," neither of which I ever rehearsed, I slipped out to a phone booth and looked up Ben's family.

They were both at home because Ben's father had a virus and wasn't working. Ben's mother answered the phone, saying that any friend of Ben's would be more than welcome to come by and could I stay for dinner? I thanked her but said I couldn't possibly because my schedule was so tight but that, yes, tea would be fine, providing she didn't go to any trouble. I knew as soon as I hung up that I'd be stepping into a hotbed of middle-class mores and that I'd have to watch my language, my cleavage, and the way I moved my ass.

Later, after a great hot bath, I phoned Ben. He was a little coy at first, kind of holding back, steering the conversation always back to me what was I doing? how was the show going? Had I called his folks? Then, when I finally asked him point blank why the hell he was being so damned cutesy, he told me that *Theatre 60* had bought "Tony" and I got so excited, I started jumping up and down like America had won another war. I yelled at him that I knew it would happen, and that I loved him, and that I couldn't wait to see him again, anb that I was masturbating all over the place. We went on and on until we both agreed we were beginning to sound like a couple of simpletons, and so we said good-bye a hundred times, lacing our adieu with kisses, sprinkling it shamelessly with phrases like "until then" and "only you" and "I'll see you in my dreams—and you'd better be there."

I hung up just as Florrie came in, with Hayden Shepherd in hot pursuit, laughing and coughing and generally slobbering his fat way right into the room, refusing to take no for an answer. So I had to line up alongside Florrie, presenting the oaf with a united front, and it still didn't stop him.

"Oh, come on, girls," he laughed. "I'm old enough to be your daddy—both of you. Nothing's going to happen. All I want is a little affection in my old age."

With me beside her, Florrie got brave. "Listen, slobber-puss, if I really balled you you'd be dead in ten minutes and how the hell would I get your carcass out of the bed before the police came in?"

"Try me," he laughed.

I nudged Florrie. "Tell him you have the clap."

Hayden laughed, his pudge of a tummy avalanching.

"Tell him you have syphilis," I said.

Hayden laughed again and coughed. Florrie turned on me. "Listen, you're not helping!"

"Oh, tsk-tsk," I said. "And a cluck-cluck."

Hayden had his hands on Florrie and so she punched him in the belly. It wasn't much of a punch and I could see that Florrie wasn't worth a shit in a fight, so I punched him, also in the belly but with much greater authority, feeling my fist go into the glub almost to my wrists. It was like punching a cushion—and all he did was laugh.

We tried to push him out of the room but he wouldn't budge. Again he grabbed Florrie, one hand on each of her tits, and he wouldn't let go, standing in front of her like he was trying to bring in Albany on his television set. His eyes blinked and ran and his breath stunk of booze, and Florrie just froze where she stood, letting the bastard dial her tits.

Me? I jumped on his back, got him in a hammerlock, and began choking him for all I was worth. He was beginning to gurgle and stagger. Then, preposterously, leaping ten years back in time to when I used to kick the crap out of my sister Mary Ann, I spoke the triumphant command into Hayden's ear. " 'Uncle.' Say 'uncle.' "

He wasn't of a mind to say "uncle." Instead, running backwards, he slammed me against the wall. We both fell, kind of sideways, but still I wouldn't let go. "Uncle!" I yelled. "Uncle, you sonofabitch!" And I put everything I had into the crunching of his neck. Florrie just lay on her bed through it all, watching us as if maybe we were all in her imagination.

"Uncle," he said. Barely, because he didn't have much breath left. I let go, rolled away from him, and sprang to my feet like a wrestler. I had an ashtray in one hand and a bigger ashtray in the other.

He was rubbing his neck. "You've got some grip there."

"Anchorman on the tug-o-war team at The Stokely School for Girls," I said, still brandishing my ashtrays.

"I believe you," he said. Then he turned to Florrie and smiled. "Sorry, kid—I had a few drinks and—"

"Will you just get out of here?" she said, drawing herself together and massaging her boobs, mostly to see if she still had them.

"Some pair of pussies," he laughed. "Betch you've never seen a real live prick."

"We're lookin' at one now," said Florrie, and Hayden left the room, laughing, limping and coughing.

I closed the door, locked it, and looked at Florrie. "You all right?"

"Yeah. I just hope my left tit snaps back. I'd hate for it always to be five inches lower than the right one. Won't be able to wear a bra anymore. Have to wear a slingshot." She began to laugh. "Do you believe that guy?"

"I believe anything."

We laughed. Florrie soaked her tits in epsom salts and I washed my hair. In the shower I could only think of Ben. It was a long shower and I only hoped that he was doing likewise and that he was enjoying his soap as much as I was enjoying mine.

Next morning, before rehearsal, I cabbed over to visit Ben's folks, meanwhile wondering why I'd ever suggested it in the first place. It was the act of a dutiful future daughter-in-law, and, as such, it was stupid. And transparent, and bound to be embarrassing. Ben obviously had no more in common with his family than I had had with mine. We had both broken with our former lives so what the hell was *I* doing poking around in *his*?

It was a nice house in a not-so-nice neighborhood, and before I got out of the cab, I made as certain as I could not to look like a flashy chorus girl. I had no makeup on other than a little eyebrow pencil because, without it, I had no eyebrows to speak of and I certainly didn't want to look as though I'd singed them off while baking a batch of Betty Crocker brownies. I wore a kerchief around my hair and a dull sweater and a duller skirt and flat shoes, and I looked more like a Croatian domestic going on a job interview than the hotsy-totsy cutey who was sleeping with their only son.

They were very nice, very cordial, and I could see that Ben favored them both, built like his father but facially resembling his mother. They really didn't know what to do with me other than to pour tea at me and push cookies on me and ask the usual stifling questions about my family. Ben's mother was verbal and intelligent in a most basic way. His father was reticent and fidgety. They didn't seem to match but maybe that's because I was so out of water with them.

Ben had called the night before and had told them about selling his play. They were delighted, of course, but were more surprised than anything else. They asked how I had come to meet Ben, and I told them of the apartment and how I had moved in when Ben went into the Army, adding that I had moved out upon his return, but there was a self-condeming pause in the middle of my statement that Mr. Webber never picked up on, though Mrs. Webber did. She didn't say a word, didn't rustle a hair, but I knew that she knew.

They showed me Ben's room but spared me his baby pictures, and, all things considered, it was a pleasant enough interlude if not altogether thrill-packed. Ben's father said good-bye but stayed inside because of his virus. I guess he didn't want it to get away. But Ben's mother walked me down to the street to where I might better get a cab, neither of us speaking for almost half a block.

"How old are you, Ginnie?" she asked rather motherly.

"Twenty-two."

"Ben is twenty-four."

"Yes. I know."

"How long did you say you knew him?"

"Not very long."

"Are you sleeping with him?"

"Yes."

"You could have said no."

"You would have known. I'm not twenty-two, either. I'm going to be nineteen."

"I can see why he likes you."

"Thank you."

We walked a little further and she seemed to think a long time before getting to what was really on her mind.

I watched her face. It was so much like Ben's that it was almost spooky. "You must be careful, Ginnie."

"About what?"

"You know."

"Getting pregnant?"

"Yes. Sometimes young people let it be the reason for their getting married, even though they're not really suited to each other and they don't realize it until much later."

I went fishing. "Like you and Mr. Webber."

"You're very direct, aren't you?"

"Well, you don't exactly come at a person from out of left field."

We kept walking, down the street of Ben's boyhood—Ginnie Maitland and his mother. She spoke again. "His father and me, neither of us ever understood Ben. But he's good. A girl could do worse. Still, you should try to be certain that when you marry you do it because you want to and not because you have to. I'm not just talking Ben. I'm talking any man."

"Ben is the first man I've ever gone to bed with."

Her words came attended with a most meaningful smile. "His father was the first man I ever went to bed with." She kissed me on the cheek. "Good-bye, Ginnie. Thank you for coming by." And she turned and walked back to her house in that not-so-nice neighborhood.

Sitting inside my cab I realized that Ben's mother was quite a lady. Not the "my son is perfect" type I had half expected, but rather a sensitive and thinking woman who, in her own way, was trying to tell me that love did not reside solely in the genitals and that those who believed it did were courting a lifetime of paying the piper. all for a couple of quick shots in the dark.

I thought about Ben and whether I truly loved him. After all, we had really been with each other for a very

short time and under the most romantic of auspices—
the returning soldier materializing into the budding
playwright, and the dancer stepping out of the chorus to
glorious stardom. Well, maybe not "glorious," and
maybe not "stardom," but a helluva big step toward
both.

Did I love Ben? Yes, I loved him. But weren't there
other things I should be taking the measure of besides
his penis and the duration of his orgasm and how long it
took his to reload? Shouldn't there be more to my
thoughts of him than the way he moved nakedly, and
the things he said to me before, during, and immediately
after our copulations? Oughtn't there to be more to our
relationship than groping and grabbing and lusting and
sexing and fucking on stairs and sucking in tubs? Nope,
I couldn't think of any. Not at that time. Maybe when I
got back to him we'd talk philosophy and politics and
the price of rhubarb in Saskatchewan and the changing
course of the Gulf Stream and the Last of the Mohi-
cans, but, for the moment, nope, there was nothing of
any significance, nothing that could dislodge his penis
from my vaginal mentality. Nothing at all.

So, get thee behind me, Mrs. Webber, with your warn-
ings and your wisdom. If your husband fucked then like
your son fucks now, you have no right to complain. The
merchandise was good when you got it; when you took
it home it worked. That there are no exchanges and no
returns is of no concern to me because, you see, Mrs.
Webber, I'm nineteen tomorrow. Nineteen and I like
what I see turning this way and that in my mirror, bat-
ting an eye, leveling a breast, cocking a hip at the
world. Don't bother me with cautions, Mrs. Webber,
when it's love songs I want to hear.

That night we opened. The first show went very well.
We finished with "Georgia Brown" and it never was

better. The second show was going just as well. We
would finish with "Jet"—or so we believed. But Hayden Shepherd, that laughing lout, told the orchestra that
we'd be staying with "Georgia Brown," just as in the
first show, and that's what they were to play.

He did it to get even, of course, to embarrass us and
make us look bad. But the stage was short and a little
too high, and, when Richie and Florrie came out in
their "Jet" costumes, only to hear the orchestra playing
"Sweet Georgia Brown," Florrie got rattled and mis-
stepped and went over the side, off the stage. And she
broke her ankle. And that was the end of that. The
Pickering Trio was out of business.

The three of us sat in the dressing room looking at
the cast on Florrie's leg as if it were about to hatch and
the three of us would be its mother. There was nothing
much to say, we had said it all. Richie was suing the
hotel but we knew where *that* would get us. As to
Hayden Shepherd, he said that it had all been a mis-
understanding, an unfortunate accident. He had gotten
our music confused. Period. It hardly constituted a
criminal act. Yes, we had insurance but not nearly
enough, especially when you considered that we'd have
been better off working for nothing and getting all that
experience than sitting home and collecting the insurance millions, which it never came to anyway. It came
to five hundred dollars.

Monty flew out immediately, as soon as I called him.
The hotel would give Florrie a good room until the doctor thought her well enough to go back to New York,
which he guessed would be in about a week. As to Richie and me, there was nothing for us to do but cancel
the rest of our bookings. The Pickering Trio Minus One
was like Larry, Curley, and——or Patty, Maxine,
and——or red, white, and——.

We said cheery good-byes to Florrie, telling her stiff upper lip and all that shit and kidding Monty not to make love to her until her plaster cast had properly hardened. And then Richie and I shoved the whole act into a cab and headed for the airport.

On the plane to New York, Richie told me that the doctor had told him that the break in Florrie's ankle was very serious. It would take a long time to heal and, even then, it might never be a hundred percent. Bye-bye that fabulous instep. Bye-bye career, dear Florrie. Hope that Monty will marry you, or you'll be working a switchboard for Linens of the Week.

With the act in mothballs, with Florrie wounded in action, Richie had no time for sentiment. He figured we'd better get to work immediately on getting ourselves a replacement. I resented that and asked him why he didn't just *shoot* Florrie and be done with it. Richie thought otherwise, saying that Florrie might have some value as a brood mare and that, with a little push from Monty, maybe in about twenty years, her daughter could take her place. I told Richie that he was a cruel sonofabitch but I knew he wasn't. He was just a thirty-year-old dancer who'd waited a lifetime for his big chance and wasn't of a mind to quit just because one of his two horses shattered a foreleg. I put my head on his shoulder and cried all the way to LaGuardia.

Sweet Barry Nadler was there to meet us, filled with words of encouragement, most of them profane but all well-intended. We piled into a cab and headed back to New York City, Richie and Barry in the back, planning strategy, me up front thinking only of Ben. He was all I had going in life and I would be seeing him soon.

How I wanted to be with him in that, my darkest hour. How I needed him. My insides almost hurt at the thought of him. Ben would make me feel better. He would wave his magic wand and all the pain would turn to passion. He would hold me and let me cry all I wanted for as long as I wanted. He would be my daddy and my buddy and would dry my eyes and buy me ice cream and tell me I was pretty. And then he would be my lover and the rest of the world would drop away and we'd be at the core of the earth, making lava and causing tremors, waking up Australia with twelve-foot waves, the tidal aftermath of our doing the Oceanic Roll.

They let me off at the apartment, both of them winking paternally at me and telling me to get lots of sleep. I raced up the stairs, my dumb bag clanging every bannister rail, bringing people out of their doors to see what was the clatter. All I could think of saying was, "The British are coming! The British are coming!" after which they all shut their doors, happy to know it was the British and not the Atchison, Topeka, and Sante Fe.

I got to our door and fussed for my key. It was late—almost midnight—and if Ben was asleep, I wanted to wake him in my own way, not with a knock on the door.

I found the key, opened the door and sneakered in. It was dark, just one light on. I put my bag down quietly, as if it were filled with explosives, and, fluffing my hair and straightening my boobs, I went to Ben's room. It was darker there than in the hall. I felt my way over to his bed and was startled by its emptiness. I switched the light on—no Ben, just his unmade bed that looked as though it hadn't been made in a year.

I went to my bedroom, maybe he'd be there. He wasn't. I turned that light on—no Ben. Just *my* unmade bed, looking like *two* years. I turned on all the lights. No Ben anywhere, not in the bathroom, the living room, the kitchen—not even in the refrigerator. I was troubled, insecure, betrayed, humiliated, angry. What the hell was he doing out at such an hour? Who was he with? Had one of those stewardesses returned? Had Ben weakened? Would he do that? Ben? My Ben?

I immediately became frightened. Call the police, the hospitals, the morgue. Would I come down and identify him, they had nine bodies that fit that description.

Something on the table, by the telephone. A bit of paper. Writing on it. St. Regis Hotel. Room 735. It bothered me. Who was in room 735. Were they holding some kind of meeting there about Ben's play? How long had that bit of paper been there? A week? Today? Tonight?

I called information and got the number of the St. Regis Hotel. I called and asked the name of the person registered in Room 735. Mrs. Barringer. I hung up. Mrs. Barringer? Who was Mrs. Barringer? I began to tremble. Should I call that room and ask for Ben? If Ben were there with Mrs. Barringer he'd hardly answer the phone. Nor would she put him on if asked to. *Miss* Barringer might, but *Mrs.* Barringer? Not likely. I left the apartment.

The doorman held the taxi door open. I had no change so I gave him my million dollar smile. He accepted it. To the elevator, my temples thumping, perspiration at the roots of my hair. Seventh floor. Down the carpeted corridor. Room 735. I stood before it, wanting to run, but I had come so far. From Pittsburgh with love to the St. Regis with fear. I knocked on the door.

A woman's voice. "Who is it?"

"Chambermaid!" I said, opting for my French accent, unused since Chips.

The woman again. "Come back later, I'm fucking!"

Not to be believed, but I continued with the scene. "But, madame—I'ave fresh towels for you."

"Later! I'm sucking this big cock!"

I knocked again, going with the flow, thoughtless inertia. Boneless amoeba pressing on. "Please, madame—will only take one minute."

Nothing from inside. Not a sound. Just the booming in my head and the firing across my bow. Then—the door opening—and Ben. Naked. The woman behind him, pumping him, her lips laughing, "Vive la France!"

Mommy? My mommy? Nightmare in the doorway. Phantasmagoria—was there ever such a word? I stood there, looking—again and again, over and over—to make certain. I knew it was them because they knew it was me. Everybody knew everybody and nothing had to be said.

Run, Ginnie, run. Feets, do your stuff. Elevator, down. Lobby, stand back. Door, revolve. Taxi?

The taxi took me to Forty-nine West Sixty-third Street. I had never been there but I knew where he lived. I pressed the buzzer under his name and the buzzer buzzed back. I opened the door and went up the stairs. Richie stood in his doorway, in his pyjamas, watching me climb toward him. "Ginnie?"

"I think so."

"What's wrong?"

"Well—" I reached him and cried and he led me inside. He wanted to make me coffee but I wouldn't let go of him because I couldn't. He took me to his bed and got me to lie down. He placed a cold washcloth on my forehead.

"Want to tell me what happened?" he asked.

"No."

"You're on the verge of hysteria. I think you'd better let it out."

"Can't."

"Can't or won't?"

"Can't." I wanted to talk but the words were log-jammed in my throat. Big bites of them. Chunks. All balled up, choking me. Gum globs and peach pits.

"Ginnie, you have to talk."

I couldn't.

"Is it Ben?"

I nodded.

"Had a fight?"

I shook my head no.

"You found him with someone."

I nodded.

"With who?"

"My mother." And the boiler blew. And the words, jarred loose, came out babbling, over the rush of tears and the wrack of sobs. And if Richie hadn't held me I would have detonated from within.

"Your *mother*?"

"Yes."

"And *Ben*?"

"Yes."

"Jesus Christ!"

"Mommy's dead."

"What?"

"My mommy is dead."

"Ginnie? You—killed her?"

"I'm killing her now. She's dead. Mommy is dead."

In the middle of the night it grew calm. The bed was big and Richie lay beside me, not touching me. I tried to stitch it together in my head. Had I really seen the two of them together? I had. Would I be able to tolerate the reality of it without going bugs? Perhaps. Two questions. One, did Ben know she was my mother? Two, did Maggie know I was Ben's girl? If both answers were yes then the pair of them were irredeemable and would burn in hell. But what if it were all coincidence? Certainly, stranger things had happened. No, stranger things had *not* happened. Not to me. Not to me.

I touched Richie's arm and he propped himself up. "You okay?" he asked.

"It's my birthday."

"Happy birthday."

"I'm nineteen."

"Happens to everyone. You'll get over it."

"Richie?"

"Yeah?"

"Will you make love to me? It's my birthday and—I need a present."

"You know, I've always wanted to. Make love to you."

"Here's your chance."

"I don't think so."

"No?"

"Piss-poor timing, Ginnie. Right now you're too—"

"I really need a present, Richie." I found him in the dark, erect before I'd even gotten there.

"Jesus."

"Richie?"

"I'm only human, Ginnie."

"I know. And you need a present, too. It's been such a lousy twenty-four hours. Let's give each other a present, Richie. No strings attached. Let's just be two very nice, very hurt people who need a little present. Please, Richie. Please?"

"Happy birthday, Ginnie."

ben

1952

There were no words. Not for me. What had she said?
Ginnie was her daughter? Her *daughter*?

Maggie kept talking, so unsettled that she had to put
her cigarette aside. "What the hell she's doing knocking
on my door in the middle of the night—I thought she
was in some girl's school in New England somewhere.
What was that nonsense with the chambermaid and the
towels? How did she know I was here?"

"She didn't know you were here. She knew I was
here." She looked at me, understandably confused. "I
must've written the hotel room number on some pad,
and she found it. Only thing is, she's supposed to be in
Pittsburgh. Oh, shit, Maggie—Ginnie and I have been
living together."

My announcement should have stopped her cold. It
didn't. It just seemed to fortify her. "I told you I had
children. Ginnie's the youngest. Must be eighteen—
no—nineteen, by now. And isn't she pretty? She used to
be such a scrawny little thing. We could almost carry
her around in the glove compartment of the car. My
daughter and your girlfriend—one and the same. How
baroque."

I started to gather my clothes, determined to keep my
head because, wherever Ginnie had gone, it was a good

bet that she had lost hers. "I'd better go after her. Try to explain."

"Her mother jerking-off her boyfriend—right in her face. Vive la France. How are you going to explain *that*?"

"Well, I think I'll start out with the truth and work up. Right now, I just hope she's all right." I glanced over at her as I slipped into my trousers. She seemed to be shoring up, getting back into control. "Doesn't any of this bother you?"

"I'm not going to let it. I made my decision—my move—a few years ago, knowing full well that—"

"That was your *daughter* running off into the night! Aren't you worried about her?"

"Yes. Yes, I am, but the terrible truth is, she's your worry, not mine. I can't do anything about it. You can. That is to say, my friend, that my image in her eyes—if it ever *was* good—has now had the crap kicked out of it forever. Whereas yours, yours still has a shot. How long have you been living with her? Is she good in bed? Her mother, I hear, will fuck anything that moves. And her father's a faggot only he doesn't know it yet. When he finds that out, anything can happen."

"Maggie, you are some cold cookie."

It seemed for a moment that she might care to protest that designation. But she let it slide by. "I guess you won't want to be seeing me again." Her hand flew up, as if to stop traffic. "Don't say anything. Just—leave it at that."

"Come on, Maggie. I never meant anything to you."

"Past tense already."

I was shouting at her. "Why do you demean yourself like you do? Why do you fuck around so indiscriminately?"

"Tell me about Ginnie. What does she do?"

"She is a brilliant goddamn dancer!"

"Ah. Of course. The Ugly Duckling to the Dying Swan. I should have known."

"I've got to go. Your daughter may be lying under a car somewhere."

"Yes. She's going to need you."

"Maybe she needs her mother."

"She never had one." She placed her arm through mine and walked me to the door, as if we were strolling in the Easter parade, except that my clothes were askew and hers were on the floor.

She had the door opened and kissed me on the cheek. "Take care of my little girl, Ben. It pleases me that she has such good taste. Now get out of here."

And I was standing in the hallway looking at the closed door, about as confounded as I'd ever been in my young and idiotic life.

I cabbed immediately to the apartment. Cabs are the red corpuscles in New York's bloodstream. They carry energy from one part of the city to the next. Without them the city dies. With them the city clots. Choose your poison. I didn't expect Ginnie to be in the apartment, but that was the only place I knew to go to. I found her bag in my room, where she'd left it, still locked, the airline luggage sticker still on it.

Over on the table, next to the phone, I saw my scribble: "St. Regis Hotel. Room 735." In the ashtray beside it, three snuffed-out cigarettes—Ginnie's brand, Ginnie's lipstick on them. I wish she'd have thought a carton's worth before knocking on that hotel room door. I was becoming quite the detective. All I had to figure out was where she had gone at half past midnight and where she was then at well past one.

I didn't care to start telephoning people at that hour so I just lay down and tried to think it all through. If

Ginnie was back from Pittsburgh, then so were Florrie
and Richie. And flying from the St. Regis as she did,
Ginnie could only have gone to Florrie, unless, of
course, Florrie had earlier gone directly to Monty. And
if Florrie had gone to Monty, would she have found
him with her mother? After all, if Oedipus slept with
Jocasta, could Betty Boop and Pope Pius be far behind?

There was nothing for me to do with the rest of the
night but be miserable, and I was determined to do that
without any reliance on the bottle. I lay on my bed in
that half-sleep—half thinking, half dreaming. Maggie
and Ginnie, mother and daughter. Maggie was right, it
was baroque. And what if Maggie hadn't called that
night? What if she had never called at all, never again?
Would Ginnie and I have ever learned that I had once
been sleeping with her mother? Would I one day, on
our tenth anniversary, have told her of this woman, this
"Maggie"? And would we then have figured the rest of
it out for ourselves? And how would we have reacted to
the news so many years after the fact? Would we have
laughed and attributed it to life? Or would we have
been mutually shocked, revulsed, destroyed, and would
we have argued in front of the kids?

The next thing to cross my mind was the similarity of
the two ladies. Now that I knew of their kinship, those
resemblances fairly jumped up and punched me in the
brain. Only the twenty or so years between them had
masked them. And suddenly I could see how Ginnie,
older, and Maggie, younger, could easily have passed
for sisters. The smile. The set of the head upon the delicate neck. The lithe walk. The whacky wit. And the
way they made love—the all-out passion combined with
the offbeat humor. How many stories I had heard of
young men who had bedded both a mother and a
daughter, lascivious stories, exaggerations and down-

right lies. But there it was, having happened to me, only I wasn't laughing, and I didn't feel like bragging. I was only staggered and shaken, and worried for Ginnie wherever she was in the dark.

And if *I* was shocked at the sight of *her,* imagine her surprise at the sight of me and Maggie, the pair of us like lewd Cranachs cavorting in a Cruikshank alley. Even if I were to find Ginnie, how does one explain the inexplicable or apologize for the unforgivable? Easier to take to the moon. Better to go out the window.

Morning came. I had watched it every inch of the way. Would it be a good day? Would it give me answers and help me find my love? It was five A.M. and it no longer paid to try to coax any sleep from the little time till dawn. I had yet to touch Ginnie's bag, allowing it to stand just where she had left it, as if it might suddenly open and out she'd dance, singing "Oh, You Beautiful Doll" while spraying me with a Thompson submachine gun. I walked around it respectfully, knowing that I had no right to touch it. I had no right to touch anything of Ginnie's and less right to touch Ginnie herself.

Guilt, my old friend, had come to town and I was the first one he called. He had only wanted to say hello, but while I was telling him that I was away for the weekend, the sonofabitch had set up house in my head, putting his feet up on my conscience and smoking my best cigars.

"Ignorance of the law is no excuse," he said imperiously. "The fact that you did not know Margaret to be mother to Virginia and Virginia to be daughter to same does not mitigate against the jurisprudence involved; i.e., you fucked them both, which is a double carnal sin with a half-twist, for which you must hang by your cock until dead, and may the Lord have mercy on your appeal."

I got into the shower and upchucked therein, and the coffee would not stay down, and the mouthwash was as effective as spit in the ocean. I paced, I sat, I smoked, I conjured, all the while watching the hands of the clock. And at seven thirty A.M., I called Barry Nadler at his home.

He filled me in on what had happened in Pittsburgh, that Florrie was still there but that Ginnie should be with me because that's where Richie and he had dropped her. Worried, he gave me Richie's phone number.

Richie told pretty much the same story. Also concerned, he said he'd call me if Ginnie either showed up or called him.

I called Maggie at the St. Regis. Surprise. She had checked out almost as soon as I left her—at two A.M. So long, Maggie, don't suck any wooden cocks.

I had no one else to call.

My feeling of helplessness was overwhelming, burying me. Then I thought to call the various YWCA's. Ginnie Maitland? No, nobody by that name. None of them had heard of her. Nor had the Barbizon or thirteen randomly selected hotels. Wherever Ginnie was was unknown to me. I could only hope that she was well and safe. If she was still in New York, I'd find her. If she had left New York—I dared not wrestle with that alternative.

I walked to work. It took almost an hour and a half. Ginnie was the most vital thing in my life. If I were to establish priorities, Ginnie would be first, my play second, my job a distant third, breathing an out-of-sight fourth.

I was late getting to the office and went directly in to see Buddy Connors. He smiled at me and I wondered how such a boob, as nice as he was, could ever hold

down such a job without worrying that the law might
one day catch up with him. A few months later I found
out that Buddy had married Skouras's niece, had con-
verted to Greek Orthodox, and was safe from all travail
for the remainder of his days. Good boy, Buddy. If you
can't do it with talent, do it with your cock. And wasn't
it Napoleon who said that the best way to the boss's
stomach is through his niece's vagina? Maybe it was
Norman Thomas.

I told Buddy that, with my play going into rehearsal,
I'd like to take a couple weeks leave of absence—
without pay, of course. Or, if that couldn't be arranged,
I'd take whatever vacation time I had coming; or sick
leave; or time off.

Buddy said it would be fine, that he'd take care of it.
He slapped me on the back and wished me well. I liked
Buddy Connors. He knew where it was at. Unlike so
many others who had married into wealth and power
only to become all-time pricks, Buddy simply relaxed,
serviced his wife, and became a friend to all mankind.
Buddy. He was well nicknamed.

I told Mickey and Dora that I'd be out for two
weeks. Mickey wished me well and Dora blew her nose,
which meant the same thing, only louder.

I went in to tell Gruber but he was in London so I
told Pat Jarvas to tell him. She thawed a little and
wished me luck, running her tongue around her lips
then smacking them as though she had just eaten something delicious. One thing about Pat Jarvas, she let you
know just where you stood with her. In my case, I stood
with my belt buckle against her forehead. All I had to
do was tug her earlobe and heaven was mine.

I went over to the Fraternal Clubhouse on West
Forty-eighth Street where they were holding readings
for "Tony"—in the Brandeis Room—from eleven A.M.

to six P.M. As the author I had been sent a mimeographed schedule, though I was not personally invited. If Harvey Epstein was insisting on my presence, he certainly wasn't insisting to me. I went anyway, feeling that I would not get kicked out if I showed up unannounced.

I knew no one there other than Harvey Epstein and his baggy sweater and his slidey eyeglasses. He didn't seem to recognize me so I didn't bother to go over and say hello. Besides, he seemed very busy and I didn't know what the protocol was. Certainly, as uninformed on the matter as I was, I was not of a mind to interrupt the director with a "Hi, Harvey, baby, how goes it, kiddo, whaddya say?"

I had not been consulted about casting and it was just as well, as I never would have agreed to any of the all-male cast, even if it meant the play's not being done. For the role of Tony they had come up with a thin, dark fellow who looked about as physical as Margaret O'Brien. For Johnny they had a heavy, freckle-faced redhead. For me, a handsome aryan who I'd have died to look like—but not in my play. For Holdoffer they got some kind of scar-faced club fighter whose nose was in his ear. And so on and so forth, with nobody looking at all the way I had described them. Nor did any of them speak their lines as I had heard them in my head when setting them down on paper. The part of Deyo was played by a chubby, forty-year-old, balding homosexual, with a lisp. Kuyper was played by a wavy-haired twenty-year-old with an even lispier lisp. All of the names, with the exception of Tony, had been changed, and it seemed to me that I should go the necessary one step further and change the name of the playwright.

The imminent death of my play, coming so closely on the heels of the disappearance of Ginnie, raised a fury of frustration in me so great that on the first break I practically leapt at Epstein and herded his nonbody into a corner.

"That's not my play," I said.

"Swell," he said, "but who are *you*?"

"The fucking author!"

"Oh," he said, catching on quick, and he took me into another room, smaller, with urinals. "Listen, kid, I know it must look and sound awful to you, but—"

"It looks and sounds disastrous!"

"It's only the first reading."

"The casting is ridiculous! It's all wrong!"

He stiffened and his back arched. "That may be. But I'm the director and that's the way I see them."

"Each character was carefully and clearly described—"

"Look, you want to stay for the reading? Fine. But just stay the fuck out of the way, okay? I've got ten days to get your masterpiece on and I *don't* have any time to pander to your ego."

"I'll take the play off."

"You can't. It belongs to Kemper and NBC. Now you either sit down and behave yourself or don't hang around. I've got enough trouble with actors without having to explain myself to writers."

"You've got two guys so queer—there's no subtlety! Where's the subtlety? They lisp! The both of them! They get too near the camera and it's gonna look like we're shooting the whole thing under water!"

"That's the way they see it, and that's the way they want to read it. When the time comes, I'll bring 'em down."

"With what, a torpedo? They've got speech impediments!"

He pushed his way around me, catching his eyeglasses as they skied right off his nose. "I've got no time for this bullshit. If you create any disturbance, I'll have you thrown out. Excuse me."

Epstein returned to the Ping-Pong table; his serve. He called the cast to order and they resumed reading, only worse than before. And all through it he never said a word, never made a suggestion or gave a direction. I knew I was in deep and grievous trouble and that there was nothing I could do about it. I left, as unnoticed as I had entered. Maybe I *could* change my name. Better still, maybe I could get hit by a car—a glancing blow. Not fatal, just enough to bring about total amnesia.

I went to a drugstore and called Barry Nadler. If Richie was working on getting a replacement for Florrie, Barry would know about it. He would also know where Ginnie was.

He knew but he wasn't telling me.

"Listen, Barry, regardless of what you've heard, I still want to know where Ginnie is."

"I haven't heard anything, except—she don't want you to know where she is. So what can I do?"

"Is she all right?"

"Yes. Though I got a feeling, we'd all be better off if *she* broke the ankle and *Florrie* came home."

"Where is she?"

"I don't *know*."

"She's in New York, yes?"

"Somewhere. Yes. They're looking for another girl. The quicker they find one, the sooner they're back in business."

"Barry, if you know where she's staying, you have to tell me. I have to see her."

"I don't know where she's staying. They don't tell me either."

"Barry, please. Does Richie know where she's staying? He *has* to know, damn it! He has to know where to call her!"

"So ask him. I'm not Information."

"Okay, I will."

"Listen, before you hang up, what's with the play?"

"The play stinks!"

I called Richie. No answer. I called my own apartment on the chance Ginnie might have gone back. No answer. I went to see a movie. Halfway through it it dawned on me: If Richie and Ginnie were auditioning girls, they'd have to be working in a rehearsal studio somewhere. I didn't know them all, but I knew most of the studios they used.

Variety Arts, Showcase, Dance Players, Carnegie Hall, Steinway Hall—I checked out every room in every one of those places, without success. Obviously it had occurred to both of them that I might come looking for them so they were undoubtedly auditioning in a place so remote that not even they could find it without a guide.

It was after seven P.M. when I got home. There was a package for me downstairs. Arnie Felsen's script. He had dropped it off with a little note asking me to read it at my pleasure. It was the last thing I wanted to do.

I called Richie again. No answer. I called Barry again. Nothing new. I read Arnie's play. No talent. I had a sandwich and a beer. Two beers. I called Richie again. No answer. I called Richie every fifteen minutes. At nine forty-five he answered; I had worn him down. He knew it was me and why I had been calling so I went right at it. "Okay, Richie, enough farting around. Is Ginnie with you?"

"She's the guts of the act, Ben. More important even than me. I can replace me. I can't replace her."

"I asked if she was with you."

"She's not."

"But you know where she is."

"Obviously."

"And obviously you're not going to tell me."

"She's a half inch away from flipping. Neither of us can risk that. So, you have to stay away from her. You have to—give it time."

"If I give it time the whole thing'll set and I'll *never* be able to explain."

"You mean you can *explain* that?"

"She told you."

"I practically had to pull it out of her. It was like defusing a bomb."

"Is she all right?"

"She functions."

"What the hell does that mean?"

"If you leave her alone she can make it back."

"Is that your diagnosis, Herr Doctor?"

"You sound like an idiot."

"Richie, I have to see her. I can explain—"

"No."

"What if you're wrong? What if, by keeping me away, you're doing more harm than good?"

"I don't think I am. Whatever your explanation— She's in lousy shape, Ben, okay? That was a helluva surprise you gave her. She's only a kid. You and her *mother*? It's a miracle she didn't flip right on the spot. Why can't you accept the fact that she's on thin ice and that I'm the only one who can get her across—at least for the moment. It's not even twenty-four hours."

"I told you, I'm afraid to wait."

"And I'm afraid not to. It's a standoff. And the way it sets up, I win all ties. You still there?"

"Yes."

"She says she never unpacked, that she left her bag there. Can you bring it over to Barry's office?"

"Yes."

"I'll pick it up there and get it to her."

"Okay."

"Not now. Do it first thing in the morning. Just leave it with Barry."

"Okay."

"You'll have to stay away from her, Ben. She's not ready."

"Who decides when she's ready?"

"Hopefully, she does. Okay?"

"I don't seem to have much choice, do I?"

"I'm afraid not."

"I'll bring her bag over in the morning."

He hung up but I held the receiver for a few moments, afraid to hang up, afraid that, once I did, it would break my connection with Ginnie for all time. Eventually I hung up. And, out of sheer exhaustion, I fell asleep.

I woke up because the sun was in the room. I looked at my rehearsal schedule. Ten A.M. to five P.M. Upstairs at the St. Nicholas Arena on West Sixty-sixth Street. I had almost two hours.

I dressed and took Ginnie's bag down. I sat it on the seat next to me in the cab, with my arm around it. It was as if Ginnie were inside, dead. Worse, I felt as if I were the one who had killed her. I took it to Barry's office. Barry was there, looking sheepish. Richie had called him, and so he was expecting me. I left, feeling as though my insides had been vacuumed out. I waited in the cigar store on the corner because it commanded a perfect view of the entrance to Barry's building. When Richie showed up, I was going to follow him. He never showed. An hour of waiting and I went over to rehearsal. Sam Spade I wasn't.

The whole building stunk, as befit my play. Jock straps, armpits and oil of wintergreen—the smell of the ring, the mythical squared circle in all its putrescent glory. When I had boxed in high school I thought then that the gym smelled offensive. But next to the St. Nicholas Arena, my old gym smelled like Snow White's prom. This was the stench of an unearthed grave, stale and acrid and mossy, of things mummified and better burnt, like plague garments. It was the smell of defeat. Winners smelled of Aqua-Velva and orange slices. Losers smelled of St. Nicholas Arena. No play rehearsed in that building could go three rounds.

I went upstairs and found them still at it, my director and my cast. I couldn't see any improvement, only that they were beginning to memorize my lines—lines *I* wanted to forget, lines that sounded as though Cheetah the chimp had written them while falling from a tree.

Harvey Epstein ignored me until the first five-minute break. Then he introduced me to the cast, and they all told me how much they liked my play. If they were as convincing in their roles as they were in their praise, I had the first play ever that was going to close in a locker room.

I left at four and walked through the park, hopscotching dog turds, passing people in love. It was the weekend and rehearsals would not resume until Monday. I did nothing that weekend beyond calling Richie six hundred times. It had crossed my mind that Ginnie, in all likelihood, was staying with Richie, especially if her psyche were that fragile and Richie was all that concerned. Actually, it was the best and most logical place for her to stay. She'd be with someone who was vitally concerned for her welfare, if for no other reason than that his welfare depended on hers. Were they sleeping together? Not likely. Like most male dancers, Richie was probably gay. And if he wasn't, he'd have too much sense to complicate matters by embarking on a sexual relationship with a girl in his employ, especially a girl whose stability was suspect.

I decided against pushing Richie too much, choosing instead to call periodically and unemotionally just to get a kind of weather report on Ginnie. Surely Richie would tell her I was calling and she'd know that I was concerned. What I didn't want was for them to get a new girl so quickly that they'd be back on the road before I had a chance to see Ginnie. On that issue Barry kept me well informed. No, they hadn't found a new girl yet but they did have two good prospects—one in particular, only she wanted too big a slice of the take. They were negotiating.

Arnie Felsen called and I told him that I still hadn't read his play because I was so involved in my own. He was quite understanding, asking that I give him a call my first opportunity. I said I would.

On Sunday, Richie called. Could he come over and get the rest of Ginnie's things? I said he could. I had by then determined to cooperate with him in every way I could, to demonstrate to both him and Ginnie my willingness to go along with anything that might help straighten her out—after which, hopefully, she'd give me my day in court.

I was taking a condescending position and it troubled me. Though logic told me to give the situation time, a little voice was telling me that the longer I waited the fewer were my chances.

Richie came over in the afternoon with two empty valises. We were very civil, very matter-of-fact as we packed her things (everything but the Gypsy Robe, which I put in my closet before Richie came up and back in Ginnie's closet after he left). I asked if they'd found another girl and he told me exactly what Barry had told me, which I took to be a good sign. Richie was being honest with me. He told me that Ginnie was working especially hard but was, each day, gaining greater control over the situation. Still, she didn't want to see me or talk to me on the phone. Richie promised to remind her that my play would be on next Sunday night.

Richie promised that, if and when they found another girl, he would not leave town without telling me where they could be reached. Under the circumstances, it was about the best I could hope for.

He left with both bags. Ginnie in luggage. Love dismembered and carried off. The killer playwright still at large, somewhere in New York. Caucasian, mid-twenties, deep scar over his heart. Dangerous when challenged, inept when in love.

I watched Richie leave and, somehow, he seemed more straight than gay. For obvious reasons I'd have much preferred it if he had bleached hair, rhinestone earrings, and a walnut in his navel. That the matter was entirely out of my hands did not brighten my outlook, for I was never good in a situation over which I had no control. I bit off a nail, down to the quick. I chain-smoked cigars. And I looked into the mirror at the dissipated man therein and wondered where, oh where, had the little boy gone?

The week eased on, my routine established. I'd check with Barry in the morning, go to rehearsal, check with Barry in the afternoon, finish rehearsal, go home and have dinner, call Richie at eight, and fight for all the sleep I could get.

On Friday I received the following letter from Don. Attached to it was a check for a hundred dollars.

Dear Ben—

The day after your letter arrived my luck looked up. And so I'm returning your lousy hundred dollars because who needs it? Thanks anyway. It got me over a couple of rough spots. I'm directing here in LA at KTLA-TV. It's a little dramatic workshop. Professionals out of work and amateurs who don't know better. But I'm on the payroll, sort of director-in-residence. I don't really know what I'm doing but neither does anyone else, so why worry? I'm living with a very great gal who is thirty, beautiful, no money and no tits. It must be love.

Hang in. If things can break for me, they can do likewise for you.

Love to Ginnie,
Don

I felt like an ass. I didn't even remember what I'd written to Don that he should have so quickly returned my money. It must have been some real, loud cry for help. Still, the news of Don's luck was great and I realized how much I missed the crazy bastard. I hadn't seen him since before I went into the Army, and that was too long for a man to have to go without seeing his best friend—only friend.

Saturday, according to my rehearsal sheet, rehearsal was from ten until two, and from three until five, studio 8G in the RCA Building. I got there early and saw, for the first time, the six sets we would be using. They looked authentic. The barracks, the command post, the PX, even the infiltration course had a ring of truth all about it. The barbed wire, the mud, and that bloody, bloody machine gun.

The show would be shot with three cameras, each one on a dolly that an assistant would push and pull according to some kind of invisible marks on the studio floor. The whole thing reminded me of how, when I was a boy, my two cousins and I, each with a toy metal truck, would run them at each other in hopes of a simultaneous three-car, head-on crash. The three cameras looked like they could do it. Lord knows, *we* never could.

Then there were the miles of electrical wires, squiggled about on the floor like snakes without beginnings, and huge lights and circuit boards and plugs and switches—a cobweb of equipment, crisscrossing the floor, ceilings, and walls, making the entire studio look like the nether side of a Jackson Pollock splat. I was impressed, awed, and terrified. My little play had spawned all this. Would that it might prove worthy.

Harvey Epstein was once again at the throttle. He was neither confident nor anxious, merely businesslike. Somehow it all made sense to him. Somehow he saw a way into and out of it, like a surgeon, or a burglar who had been there once or twice. And I had a momentary feeling of confidence. It vanished when Epstein's glasses slid off his nose and, because he failed to catch them, shattered on the floor. Someone brought him another pair almost as soon as the first pair had killed itself, all of it perfectly performed as the passing of a baton in a relay race.

How many pairs of glasses had slid off Epstein's nose in the course of his career? And what did it portend that he failed to catch them? If the glasses broke did it mean failure? If he caught them three times running, did it mean we'd be a hit? What if *one* lens broke and the other survived? What if the left one broke and the right one received only a hairline fracture? What would happen to Epstein's career if he switched over to a monocle and directed like Von Stroheim? What Delphic Oracle could explain the significance of Epstein's slidey glasses and still hang onto his union card?

The cast knew their lines but the show was eight minutes long. Harvey Epstein grabbed a script, made five slices on five separate pages and—voilà—the show was the prescribed forty-seven minutes. Was I consulted? No. Was I upset? No. I would have cut the whole thing and then cut back to the studio for organ music. Studio 8G did not smell like the St. Nicholas Arena, but something did and it could only have been my play. Oh, that I had never written it and that Tony had never died. Perfidious friend, had you been standing ten inches to either side, I wouldn't be on the air and you wouldn't be in the ground.

There was dinner in there, somewhere, but Saturday still slid into Sunday without my much noticing. After rehearsal I walked the city, all night, getting to bed well after three. Ginnie's image still hung around, leaning on my conscious yet lying back just enough so that I could still go about the business of being alive.

From one to two thirty Sunday afternoon they blocked it and did a run-through. From two thirty to three fifteen Harvey Epstein gave them notes. Some of the cast seemed interested though two of them were inconspicuously asleep. Had they been in the 42nd they'd have made Draftee of the Week.

From three fifteen to four thirty they had a coordinated run-through—camera and cast. From four thirty to six twenty-five was dinner and makeup, and I was involved in neither.

Barry dropped by the studio to see how I was holding

up. He brought me a bag of salted peanuts, which I ate one at a time, popping them like arsenic tablets, wishing they were, waiting to die, failing in even that. Barry shook my hand and went home. He'd be watching with his wife and he knew it would be great. But even as he said it, he shrugged in his own Semitic way, as if to say, "And if it isn't, so fuck 'em, you'll do another. What do they know from playwrights?"

Gethsemane was drawing closer and I would soon be up there on the cross. I straightened my crown of thorns so as to look good for the cameras, and I watched the dress rehearsal from six twenty-five to seven twenty-five P.M. I watched in the private viewing room, just me and the cleaning lady. Her only comment on it was a deep and meaningful belch, filling the air with the scent of garlic, after which she flounced her dust mop and left.

The dress rehearsal was an unqualified disaster, which, I was told, boded well for the actual performance, only I couldn't see how. I had counted twenty-eight things that went awry, after which I stopped counting. Lines were blown. Cameras filled the screen with stagehands picking at their underwear and probing their ears. Props fell. "Holdoffer" snagged his feet on a wire and took a header. "General McArdle," during the scene in which he reads me out, forgot that most important speech and filled the time with "The Boy Stood On The Burning Deck," which I thought most applicable.

And in the big scene, the closing scene, the scene in which the entire play comes together to pose the issue of who is guilty for Tony's death—the Army or me—two lights fell over and a camera dolly pulled the plug on a microphone and all the sound went out and nobody knew who said what and nobody seemed to much give a shit.

From seven twenty-five until nine P.M. (air time) Harvey Epstein and his giggily goggles went over his notes. He had fewer than I had. Obviously his glasses had tried to escape and he had missed the entire second act. Of the two actors who had fallen asleep before, only one fell asleep again, for which Horrible Harvey gave it to him pretty good. "Maxwell, since this is the last fucking show you'll ever do for me, I suggest you stay awake for your own sake. You were late on your cues four times and were facing the wrong way twice. If you do that on the air, your next show will be radio—in Finland. The rest of you—okay; it's pulling together. Just remember to keep it pumping. Don't let any air in. If it's running too fast I'll tell you at the commercial breaks."

I couldn't believe that Epstein really believed that the show was pulling together. To me it looked to be flying apart. He must have said that to give the poor bastards courage to go on—to Akron, where the local Lions Club would do it because their cubs had eaten all the scripts of *Philadelphia Story* and it was either my play or *Captain Jinx of the Horse Marines*.

Again I moved into the viewing room. It was eight forty-five P.M. I didn't want to talk to, see, or be with anyone. It was something I wanted to do by myself, like an old cat going off to a corner to die. I knew that by ten fifteen the word would be out on me and I would be stoned wherever I went thenceforth, serfs and peons appearing in the doorways of their hovels to shout, "Let him write greeting cards!"

At five minutes before nine, the door to the viewing room opened and in came Frank Brokaw, Jerry Kaplan, Jason Kimbrough and his smashing-looking wife, and four middle-aged couples smacking of such wealth that I knew them to be the Kemper family. I was introduced and everybody smiled like sunshine on aluminum. Then my show stupidly went on the air.

The announcer spoke over my screen credit. "Tonight, *Theatre 60* proudly presents the work of a provocative new writer—Benjamin Webber." After that, everything was a merciful blank. I knew that my show was on, I could see it, hear it. I just didn't comprehend its place in the world, why it was on, what it was meant to say, who gave a crap.

The hour transgressed, the lights in the viewing room came on, and everyone there sat around and talked about something else. Then the door opened and Harvey Epstein came in, preceded by his flying eyeglasses. Without getting up they all told him that it was a fine show, only they said it with the same emotion they'd expend in ordering a can of sardines over the phone.

Harvey came over to me and asked me what I thought of the show. I told him I thought it was a fine show. A photographer took some flash photos as we all stood around and babbled in Sanskrit. The room cleared, only Jerry Kaplan and myself remaining. He sat down next to me, the both of us looking at the silent monitors.

"I was worried," said Jerry.

"So was I."

"With the dress rehearsal going so well, I figured, for sure, we'd bomb on the air."

"The dress went well?"

"Weren't you watching?"

"I got here too late. I was having dinner with some friends."

"It went great. But when the cast peaks for the dress, they usually collapse on the air."

"Yeah. We have to be careful about that."

"Harvey did a fine job."

"Yes, didn't he?"

"Want me to be honest with you?"

"Sure."

"He was better than your script. We offered it to five other directors. They wouldn't touch it."

"Too hot to handle?"

"No. They just didn't like it. Harvey thought he could make it work. I tell you this so's you won't get a swelled head when I also tell you that Brokaw wants to contract you to write three more originals for next fall. Will you do it?"

"Okay."

"You'll get a little more each script. Anyway, if I were you, I'd make certain to thank Harvey. I'd also give him first crack at your next scripts. The two of you work well together, don't you think?"

"Oh, yes. Hand in glove."

"I'll call your agent. We'll set up a meeting. Talk over subjects that might interest you. I think we should get started right away. It'll fill out your summer."

"Check."

Kaplan left and I was alone in the viewing room, wondering where my play had gone and how come I hadn't seen it leave. I sat there until someone came in and said that the studio was closing up. I left the RCA Building and I was shaky. The show, I guessed, went well. They weren't jumping up and down yelling "Emmy!" but I gathered that they were satisfied. Also, they wanted me to write more. Fantastic.

I walked back to my apartment, a million miles, wondering how many of the people I passed had seen my play, wanting to ask them, "Sir? Lady? Doggie? Did you see my play? It was about my friend, Tony, and how he got killed. Some people think I killed him like they think I killed my girl. Her name was Ginnie. Danced like a cat. Moved like a dream. I'm going to do three more plays for NBC. Do you think I'll get away with it?"

The apartment was barren. I had survived the show, would I survive the night? Doubts flew in through every window, rabid creatures sucking on my confidence. The provocative playwright was at home, entertaining his vamoosed friends, toasting them *in absentia*. A glass to Don Cook in California, another to Jessica in flight. A snifter to Alice, a jigger to Susan, and a bottle to Maggie from Boston. And to sweet Ginnie, a magnum of kisses and a case of what might have been. For the Great Traffic Cop in the Sky had fucked up our stars, colliding them with the comet that was her mother, and the firmament would never again be the same.

When I was halfway between Schlitz and Dewars, the telephone rang. I groped for it and fell into the table, but I had the damned thing by the throat. "Yeah?"

"Ben?"

"Yeah?"

"Great show. Arlene and I loved it. You're on your way." It was Barry.

"Really like it?"

"Like it? I even understood it. No shit, it was great."

"They want me to do three more."

"You're kidding!"

"No. Jerry Kaplan'll be calling you."

"My first writer and he turns out to be George Bernard Shore. I sure can pick 'em."

"Wouldn't happen to know if Ginnie saw it, would you?"

"Well—I don't think so."

"You mean you don't know, don't you?"

"No. I mean I don't think so. They left for St. Louis today. I don't know what time."

"You said you'd tell me."

"They didn't tell *me* until late last night. They found a girl to take Florrie's place and the Bryant Hotel was still holding their booking, so—"

"Richie said he'd tell me when they were leaving. The sonofabitch lied, Barry! Why'd he lie?"

"I don't know. Maybe he didn't think it was time."

"He's sure been doing a *lot* of thinking when it comes to Ginnie. Barry, what the hell is going on?"

"What the hell is going on is life. I can't keep up with you young people. You tell me what's going on, okay? So then maybe I'll understand."

"You're sure they're gone?"

"Yes. Positive."

"Okay."

"Don't get depressed. You should be on the top of the world. Don't let a little tiff with your girlfriend ruin your evening. Ben? Ben, you listening! Ben?"

I hung up and dove for the bottom of the world. Not only had Ginnie left me, but she hadn't even seen my play. She had typed it. She was as much a part of it as I was. She had midwifed it and nursed it, and she was gone. Cleared out. Lock, stock, and Richie. Christ, I hated that bastard. My first instincts had proven correct: he was worried about Richie and not Ginnie, and he certainly didn't give a damn about Ben.

I drank more, mixing my drinks and not caring. Anything in a bottle or a can was a target for my despair. I played the radio, getting a station as depressed as I was. Delius, "Two Pieces For Small Orchestra." Then Mahler, "Second Movement of Symphony Number Seven"— "Lied Der Nacht." After that, "The Lark," by Vaughn Williams, properly ascended only I didn't see it because

I was in Ginnie's room, parading my misery, wallowing in the absence of her and, I think, crying just a little— as she might have done, had the situation been reversed.

Shit, but I wanted her with me. And, shit, did I hate Maggie, for the irresistibility of her cunt and the inconceivability of her being Ginnie's mother. Her mother! Christ, was there ever a more implausible wrinkle in the unraveling of a tragi-comic love story? Why couldn't Maggie have been Ginnie's cousin, or even her maiden aunt? Or how about her wicked stepsister, going out to ball while Ginnie had to stay at home and sweep the hearth? Her *mother*?

I stood in the middle of that room that was empty of everything but curtains. All things Ginnie I had witlessly allowed Richie to cart away. I had nothing of hers. Nothing but a number to call in St. Louis that I didn't have yet but that Barry would give me on the morrow of my life, provided God picked up my option and allowed me a morrow because, despite the anguish, I did *not* wish myself dead. I did not wish myself unborn and unknown and therefore unremembered. I wished myself hanging in and pressing on and scaling heights—and showing them all that I was of substance and had a talent and could fill a place and make a name.

Fuck 'em. Fuck 'em all. Fuck the unreachable and the unattainable. Fuck Elizabeth Satterly in sparkling yellow, forever adrift in my uncompleted youth. Fuck the invisible Alice, balancing my balls before taking my innocence. And the fattish Jessica, bigger than Oklahoma and housing the loosest box to ever host the Pittsburgh Kid. And Susan, the orange-squeezer, who could squeeze more juice out of the man of the hour than Bing Crosby could squeeze out of a regiment of Minute Maids. And fuck Pat Jarvas, the Brooklyn Bang, fastest fuck in the East. Fuck her even as she called on the phone to tell me how much she loved my play, even as I ripped the brown paper off the "thing" in Ginnie's closet and found Maggie Barringer smiling me in the face.

"Hello? Ben? It's Pat, okay? I know it don't mean much to you but I loved your play, okay?"

"Pat?"

"Yeah."

"Get over here and bring your cunt."

"Pardon?"

"Get over here—please."

"I want you, Ben."

"Yeah?"

"Remember I told you I was gonna give you French?"

"Talk, talk, talk. Jesus Christ, Pat, when are you gonna come through?"

"I'm on my way."

She was there in under a half hour. Almost before she could catch her breath from all those flights of stairs, I had her clothes off and her on her skinny back. And, pretending she was Ginnie, I went at her as if it were my last turn at bat and I was shooting for the Hall of Fame.

Her words, so Brooklyn, came out all broken—no sentences, not even phrases, just obscenities and directives, imperatives and utterances, and descriptions of what she felt and what she wanted to do and how she wanted it done.

We fucked upside down, banging against the wall, eating on the kitchen table, bellowing in the hall. Gutter talk and animal moans, a balancing act in the center ring. Bang, bang, bang, the confrontation went. Labia major thwucking, labia minor clutching like a milking fist. Penis drilling for oil, buttocks hammering home. I started out screwing Ginnie but ended up nailing Richie, and Pat was bloodied and bruised because I was using my fist as well as my phallus.

And when it was over, when it was packed in and zipped up for the night because to go further would have been to kill her, neither of us knew the time or had a hint as to who the other one was. The bed was soaked and tilted, one leg coming undone beneath its task. Pat had orgasmed so often and so mightily that she could no longer abide my touch. I had deliberately bent my lance on her, clanging it continuously against her thin flanks and pointy bones, hoping to dent it irreparably, to splinter it beyond restoration. I didn't want it anymore and wished it would go away.

The phone rang but I was fast asleep, so Pat answered. Whoever it was hung up. It happened again fifteen minutes later, with the same result. Somewhere—in the morning, who knew when—the inane chatter began. Peculiar to the female, incumbent upon the male—we jousted verbally, because Pat felt loved and I was too much of a gentleman to tell her she'd merely been fucked.

And when she had gone, stuffed into a cab like a laundry sack by yours truly, I looked again at that portrait of Maggie. Ginnie had brought her mommy to New York with her and I composed a greeting card to honor the occasion:

> *Mommy in the closet,*
> *Baby on the bed;*
> *Bang the two together—*
> *And wish that you were dead.*

> Best wishes on your nervous breakdown—
> Ben

And now the both of them were gone from my life, Maggie humping in hotel rooms, the quintessence of Room Service, and little Ginnie—

> *Somewhere in St. Louis,*
> *Dancing in the sky;*
> *Laugh the wildest laugh,*
> *Wink the bluest eye.*

Congratulations on your triumphant
return to the Midwest—
Ben

Next morning I looked for the reviews of my play. There were none. Channel Five, WABD, a local New York channel, had carried the presentation of the coveted Antoinette Perry Awards "for creative excellence in theatre" opposite *Theatre 60*, so that, as far as New York was concerned, my play had been wiped out in the ratings.

Oh, they had seen it in Dayton, Toledo, and Dubuque; and maybe some viewers had seen it in New York, but no critics. The critics had all watched Channel Five and their columns said as much. I had climbed the highest mountain but no one had seen me plant my flag. No one had seen Leif Ericson either, or Abner Singleday or the Left Brothers or Mae East. All that there was of my play in the morning papers was a photo of "playwright Ben Webber and Mrs. Jason Kimbrough"—a swell thing for Ginnie to have seen had she been in New York, and a mean jolt for Jason Kimbrough who had been neatly cropped out of the photo by some zealous newspaper makeup man.

NBC and Kemper Aluminum were quick to make a deal with Barry Nadler. It occurred to me that that could only mean that my play had gone well and that I should have held out for more. But I was so happy to not have been thrown out on the street that I accepted their offer before a cigarette had been flicked. It was $3,000 for the first of three new scripts. $3,500 for the second. And $4,750 for the third. $11, 250 for the lot, almost as much as it would have taken me three years to earn at 20th. And so, with a minimum of fanfare, I phoned in my resignation to Buddy Connors and everyone was happy for me for a variety of reasons.

I met with Brokaw and Kaplan to discuss subjects that might be of interest to the client. And then I began to work with a rage. One of my objects was to avoid, for as long as possible, calling Ginnie, hoping that before it would ever come to that, she would have already called me. Surely she knew that I'd tried to reach her. If Richie hadn't told her then Barry certainly had. And if she chose not to return the attempted contact, then she was very sick and simply couldn't or very well and simply wouldn't. In either case, any further moves by me in her direction could only weaken my cause and diminish myself in my own eyes. And I did not care to be diminished in my own eyes as I needed all the assurance I could assemble if I was to truly develop into a Number-One TV Playwright.

I realized how much of my life was accident and how little prepared I had been for any of it. A few months before, writing was as foreign to me as Pago-Pago, and Ginnie Maitland was as much in my thoughts as Vasco Da Gama. You walk down a street and make a left turn instead of a right and you're a dentist instead of a lumberjack. Had I never worked in Patterson's tobacco place in Pittsburgh and stolen 100 fine cigars and walked down a certain street in New York smoking one of those stolen stogies, Don Cook would never have walked up to me to guess at the cigar's brand, and nothing that had happened to me from that point on would ever have happened at all.

Life was not preordained. It was not scripted and cast ahead of time and allowed to play out to predictable reviews. Au contraire, it was a blind crapshoot with the dice having been rolled years before, in Cuba, in a field where Maugham's tobacco grew, the dice-roller being a cordovan-skinned man in a straw hat and wicker sandals, who lived in a hut with his wife, Maria, and seven babies and who picked leaf for Alfred Dunhill, who, himself long dead, had no idea that I was alive.

Brokaw, Kaplan and I fixed on the three subjects for my three plays. One—"The Magic Horn"—would be a jazz fable in which the leads would be played by jazz musicians and during which jazz would play continuously. The second, "The Fair-Haired Boy," would be about internecine politics in the advertising department of a pseudonymous movie company. And the third, "The Lonely Look," would be a love story about a young writer and a young dancer.

I began work on the first, establishing a routine, writing in long-hand in the morning, typewriting self-taught from twelve thirty till two thirty, and back to writing for the remainder of the day—or until I ran out of ideas, dialogue, and steam.

I phoned Arnie Felsen to tell him that his script was good. He was such an odd little guy and so eager to be praised that I couldn't let him down. If God had been watching and listening he would have had to have given me good points for my bad lies to Arnie.

Pat Jarvas became a regular thing. She was a most avid lover, always coming to the apartment whenever I called, no matter the hour, which was invariably after midnight. We'd make love. She'd tuck me in. And she'd disappear—I never asked to where.

I began to use the anguish of Ginnie as a negative drive, a desire to punish her for having left me without facing me building up in me to the point of its taking over. It drove me to my work earlier than scheduled and kept me there later than usual. "I'll show her" became the legend on my banner. Not "In God We Trust" or "Don't Give Up the Ship!" but "I'll Show Her." I truly believe that such negative drives are always more powerful than the so-called positive ones, that men driven by rejection, revenge, and injustice go further and accomplish more than men motivated by such generic propulsions as success, fame, and happiness. All the girls you may fuck tomorrow are not as strong a goad as the girl who fucked you yesterday. Not something you'll find in a book of proverbs but valid nevertheless if you are of a mind to wrest triumph from despair and turn manure into melody.

My work was proceeding well. I had established a good regimen to go along with my passion. The times I discussed Ginnie with Barry became fewer, and usually the discussion was in a professional sense, about the Pickering Trio and not about Ginnie and Ben. It was clear that Barry had no taste for the subject, though I did, on one occasion, point-blank ask him if there was another man in her life. After taking a long time to answer, he said "Yes." And I knew that I had lost her and that I would continue to use her as negative fuel to power my rocket. I could understand the way she felt— I always could. My problem was that she had never faced me, which, in my then condition, translated into "She never loved me" and from there into "And I never loved her."

My schedule was my own. No one was around to

crack a whip or point to the descending sands in the hourglass. Brokaw and Kaplan were somewhere out on Long Island for the summer. Occasionally one of them would call, never really inviting me out for the weekend, only suggesting that if I was ever out on the island I should drop in. Drop in what—the ocean or their lives? It didn't matter as I never found myself out on Long Island and therefore never had to tangle with the Sphinxian riddle.

I was a hermit in Manhattan, wandering out of my cave only for food and drink, exercise, and a newspaper. The television was rarely turned on and the electric fan rarely off. I worked on my three scripts in sequence, doing a first draft on all before doing a second draft on any. "The Magic Horn" was fun, all Dixieland and Southern, with my dialogue (at least to me) sounding like Tennessee Williams on a New Orleans zephyr. "The Fair-Haired Boy" was intriguing, populated with characters derived from the people I had worked with at 20th. Pat Jarvas was in it, and Bob Steinman, and myself, of course. But the one I most wanted to write about was Sam Gaynor because he was bigger than life and ten times more intolerable.

"The Lonely Look," about me and Ginnie, came out of my gut and hurt like hell. But by turning that lost love affair into something as alive as a newborn play, the pain slowly dispersed, scattered by dialogue through which I reshaped remorse into the stuff of love. Lies, all lies, of course, but what a way to beat the blues and sweep away bad dreams.

Every word I wrote put Ginnie further and further behind me. And if one play about her would not do it, then the next one would. I would write about her forever if it took that long to forget her. And if it took longer than that, then I'd strum it on my harp or twang it on my pitchfork, for I was a one-man band playing a one-note tune—Ginnie in the morning, Ginnie night and noon—an endless aria da capo, until I'd get it right.

On one of my nights with "The Lonely Look" it all got terribly oppressive and I had to stop. I had to get out, take a walk, kick a can, fly a coop. I was about to do just that when the phone rang. It was Pat. She was sorry to interrupt me but would I like to come over to her place for a late dinner? She had never made dinner for me and would just love to as she was a very good cook and had come into possession of a duck or something that her brother had shot so many of that he'd dropped one off at her doorstep—so I said I'd love to.

Walking over to Pat's place I felt like a man who knew he was walking into a trap but who couldn't turn back. Poor Pat was making dinner for her boyfriend. Where I came from that meant the ringing of church bells and the immediate stitching of a wedding dress. It would never come to that, of course, but Pat didn't know it. I considered telling her, the only question being before or after we'd made love. A gentleman would tell her before. I would tell her after, for I had reached a point in my life where I placed my own well-being ahead of the well-being of others. It was a simple jungle approach, predatory to a point except that I was not quite a vicious carnivore, merely a leaf-eating cad who, if he killed at all, did so only to stay alive. I would take from Pat, but I was also giving. And if it reached a point where I was giving more than I was getting, then I'd be off to a different pasture, leaving her to the jackals. I would feel badly, of course, because I rather liked the girl and her obscene innocence, but a good animal takes to the high ground at floodtide and to the river during drought.

It was candlelight and Kostelanetz, and the duck

never had a chance. I had thought to pick up a bottle of wine and that was gone in a few clinking, lying toasts. For the evening Pat had dressed primly, something gingham and high-necked. It was endearing, almost poignant, and we sat opposite each other at the table, peeking at each other from around the candle she had set so close to dead center that it looked to me to be up her nose.

The chit-chat was impossible and unendurable, about everything and nothing at all. And I wasn't sure that the eventual love-making was worth the price of the banal preamble. I knew I was being a prick because, at least for that one evening, Pat most certainly deserved better from me than grudging endurance.

Dessert was something fluffy and coffee was something espresso with a lemon floating on it. Pat did the dishes, singing "America the Beautiful" while I put my feet up and smoked a good cigar. She came out of the kitchen with nothing on but high heels and a garter belt, thinking that that would turn me on. She was right. The interesting thing was that, all through the lovemaking, my main concern was not with keeping my pecker up but with keeping my cigar lit. I managed to do both very nicely as Pat cursed and moaned in her usual manner and groaned and screamed and came, always in that sequence.

For the highlight of the evening she had decided to go with her own special brand of fellatio, or "French," as she so darlingly put it.

"Ben, I'm gonna give you French like you never got it before."

"Be my guest."

"You just lie back and I'll—that's right, get comfortable. Oh, Jesus, but you are beautiful. It's like—I just have to—" Then she stopped.

"What's the matter?" I asked, lying sultanic on my back.

"I want all the lights off. I want it so dark that—" and she turned off all the lights. "Don't go away, darling."

"I ain't goin' anywhere, sweetheart."

"Be back in a minute. Don't move. Ben, just stay there."

I stayed there as I had no other plans at the time. The only light in the room was the orange dot from my waning cigar, and I lay on my back making orange circles in the air with it, marking time till the return of my gal, Frenchie Marseilles. I heard her in the doorway. "Pat?" She didn't answer. "What're you up to?"

"Shhhhhh."

"Shhh, yourself. Where are you?"

"Shhh."

"Pat?" I could hear her getting closer and I could feel her weight on the bed. Christ, I thought, little skinny Pat—had she eaten that much for dinner?

I felt her hand sliding up my leg, at my knee, moving up my thigh. It seemed a little coarse, a little sandpapery. "Pat?" I asked. The hand found my penis and grabbed it. It wasn't Pat. It was a man—and he was diving for my cock. My right hand shot down and found a bald head and I knew who it was. I smashed at him with both fists but still he wouldn't let go. I could feel his head, his face, his mouth, trying to draw me in.

"You sonofabitch!" I shouted, all the while hitting him, gouging at his eyes, trying to get a grip on them as if his head were a bowling ball. Finally, his head bent backwards and his fingers let go of me, the bed sagging to one side with the bulk of him. "God damn you, Pat!" I yelled. "You're in here somewhere! Turn on the light!"

The light went on and the following people were on-stage and in the following manner: Pat was standing at the wall switch, one hand covering her face. She was sobbing, frightened, bordering on shock. She was in a plain robe and wasn't skinny pretty anymore. She looked like a faded whore, tubercular, waning.

W. Charles Gruber was naked right down to his chubby toes, his flabby Santa belly hanging over his sex so that he looked to have none at all. He sat on the edge of the bed, his face bloodied where I must have hit him a minimum of fifty times. It was swollen and off kilter. It was a mess.

I sat against the headboard, my legs drawn up like those of a caught-red-handed tart, both my fists smarting, both my hands searching the sheets—for I had lost my cigar and, on top of everything else, I didn't need a fire.

"Ben—" Pat was gasping, fighting for air as she spoke. "He made me do it. I swear. Please. Oh, Jesus."

"Shut up, Patricia," said Gruber, surprisingly calm despite his bloodied condition. "Don't be toady." He looked at me and tried to smile. "I thought you'd be more a man of the world, Ben."

"No, you didn't," I said, getting up and scrounging for my clothes. "If you did, you'd have propositioned me directly instead of sneaking abound in the dark, using her as a shill."

"Please, Ben—I had to do it." Pat was a wretched, sexless thing, pitifully irretrievable and knowing it.

"What a fucking waste you are," I said to her, "setting me up for the phantom cocksucker."

"No need for that," said Gruber, finding a towel witn which to mop his face.

I challenged Gruber. "What do you do, use her as bait to smoke out the fairies?"

"You'd be amazed at how many are glad to come out of the closet. She warms up the audience for me, gets them receptive."

"You thought I'd be receptive?"

"Well, I hoped so. Nothing ventured and all that. I think you may have broken my nose."

Pat was raging. "I'm not gonna do this anymore, Charlie! No more! Never again, you shithead! I'm never gonna do this again!"

"Yes you will." And he looked over at me. "She gets three hundred a week, under the table—plus her salary. Plus a lot of cock. All she wants."

"No overtime?" I asked.

Gruber laughed. "Ben, I hope you're mature enough to keep this to yourself."

"Actually, I'm thinking of taking out an ad. I'll bring it to you for your approval."

And he laughed again. "God damn shame that you're so—provincial. Nobody has to know and—I can give you favors."

"I don't need favors. I don't work for you anymore. I quit."

"Some day you may need backing for a play or influence in setting up a film. You're a good writer but it can still take you years. Why don't you just look at me as being a short cut?"

"I hate to tell you what I look at you as."

He drew back, annoyed. "It's one thing to reject, it's another to insult. Don't flaunt your heterosexuality so strongly. It suggests that maybe you're a little afraid."

"Not afraid. Just disgusted."

"As for Patricia, don't be too harsh on her, either. She's only a poor working girl. Besides, it isn't as if she hasn't been fucking you royally. Only let me assure you, I do it better."

"Is that supposed to tempt me?"

"You're not required to do anything but lie back and let it happen. No big deal. What are you afraid of?"

"I'm afraid I'll make you pregnant and that I'll have to marry you."

He didn't laugh. "Better men than you have let it happen and have reaped the rewards without feeling compromised or soiled or threatened."

"Yeah? Name five."

"I can name fifty."

"At 20th?"

"At 20th. At NBC. At Kemper. Not everyone is as square-assed as you are."

"Why don't you go for broke and make a pass at Rocky Marciano?"

"Best I ever had."

I had all my clothes on and Pat looked at me sadly. "I love you. I'll never do this again. Even if you never call me again, I'll never do this again. I'll love you, Ben—till I die. I swear." She reached out to touch me.

I pushed past her, not angrily, just a sidestep. "Th-that's all, f-f-f-folks," I said.

I went out and walked home. Nothing surprised me anymore. Not even the next afternoon's newspapers which said it all.

MOVIE V.P. STABBED TO DEATH
IN LOVE NEST WITH SECRETARY

Mogul's wife shocked and distraught.
Unknown assailant sought.

W. Charles Gruber, V.P. of 20th Century-Fox Films, was found naked and stabbed, in the East Side apartment of his secretary, Patricia Jarvas,

aged 20. He had been beaten about the face and
head and his nose was broken. Miss Jarvas claims
that, while they were together, a man whom she
described as black and about 40–45 years of age
came in through the fire escape window. Gruber
attempted to fight him off but was evidently not
strong enough. According to Miss Jarvas, the man
stabbed Gruber, took his wallet and fled via the
fire escape. The police found the wallet in the
courtyard below. It contained over $200. They
also found Miss Jarvas's fingerprints on the knife
handle. The young woman claims that she tried to
pull the knife out . . . etc., etc.

Dear, sweet, Brooklyn Pat Jarvas, trying desperately
to save her skin, had not implicated me in any way. Nor
could she without having the whole thing look as though
she had murdered Gruber herself which, no doubt, had
been the case. As far as the world was concerned, the
entire matter added up to just another lecherous old
man having dinner with his secretary—a little soiree
which they had probably done many times before—only
to be interrupted by a burglar. The police were troubled
that the burglar had dropped the money and run off
without retrieving it. Still, they were inclined to believe
Pat's story because, obviously, only a man could have
inflicted such a beating upon Gruber. And even if a
woman could, Pat's unbruised hands put her above suspicion. Also, the coroner stated that the beating occurred before the stabbing, that the victim was not
drunk or poisoned, and that Pat was, according to the
police, guiltless.

I stayed out of it, of course, for it was mutually ad-
vantageous to both Pat and me to let things be. No
charges were filed, though there had to be a legion of

men in town who knew that sharing a candlelight dinner with a girl was hardly Gruber's style. In any case, he was dead and in death had become a kind of tarnished hero. For though he had been cheating on his wife, he *had* attempted to fight off a much larger man. The black man was never apprehended. There was a play in there somewhere—as soon as I had the time.

ginnie

1952

Waking up was awful and I avoided it for as long as I could, thrashing about on Richie's bed in a last valiant effort to stay asleep. As long as I could convince myself that I was asleep, that's how long all that had happened could pretend to be a dream. But the sheets were pythons, and the sun had no respect, and already the dark bats in my head were fluttering to get out. I couldn't hold them back and out they flew, chased by the morning, but not far enough. They didn't go away like bad dreams should, they just sat on the bedpost and wiggled their veined wings and screeched at me, "True, true, true." That's how you know you're in trouble—when the bats don't leave. They all scattered when the door opened and Richie walked in, not out the window or into the closet but back into my head, where their caves were, and where all the leases were for ninety-nine years.

Richie had a cup of coffee for me and was being very gentle. "Good morning, pretty girl."

I sat up and took the coffee. "Thanks. What year is it?"

"Hard to tell. You've been alseep so long. All I know is it's three in the afternoon."

"What afternoon?"

"My guess would be Thursday."

"We made love last night, didn't we?"

"I'd hardly call it that."

"Was I awful?"

"Just a little crazy."

"Yeah? Lucky you."

"Not that way. I don't think it should count. I don't think it should go on your record."

"If you're really my friend, you'll tell me that I made it all up. Everything that happened. Are you my friend?"

"Yes. Which is why I have to tell you that you didn't make it up."

"How do you know I didn't?"

"Because Ben called. And Barry called. And everything they said backs up what you told me last night."

"What'd I tell you?"

"That you found Ben with your mother."

"How do I not let it get to me?"

"Accept it. Accept it as being real and having happened, and go on from there. You're nineteen. There's a lot of living behind you. What you have to do is use those nineteen years to deal with the next ninety."

"You mean I have to die at a hundred and nine? Trees live longer—and turtles."

"But they can't dance a shit."

"Such wisdom."

"I have a plan. I want us to put it immediately into motion. I want us to find a replacement for Florrie and then get our asses back on the road. Ben's been calling."

"I don't want to talk to him."

"He says he can explain."

"I don't want to hear it."

"What about your mother?"

"She's dead."

"Ginnie—come on."

"She is God damn, no fooling dead. I mean, she could show up and stand right where you're standing and she'd still be dead. She'd just be wasting her time."

"There's got to be an explanation somewhere, don't you think?"

"I don't think anything. Nothing. Zero. Let's dance."

We auditioned girls, which I found grisly. Florrie still hurting in Pittsburgh, and there we were in New York, looking to write her off. We found an out-of-the-way rehearsal hall to avoid Ben's finding us—provided he was really looking—Meridian Hall, way on the West Side, with a floor so tilty it was like dancing on the deck of a sinking ship. None of the first batch of girls was good enough—giving us a new appreciation of Florrie—but we kept plugging. Maybe Ruby Keeler would come out of the chorus, or Carol Haney, all sloe-eyed and yellow-banged, an imp to set off my kook.

I gathered that Ben was calling and that Richie was fending him off. But as much as I wanted to see him, I couldn't bring myself to even talk to him. I knew I'd get so furious that it'd blow all chances for a reconciliation. The idea was for me to slowly come down to earth and then, with both feet on the ground and the shock and hurt worn down at least a smidgeon, be better able to hear his explanation. For, surely, there was an explanation. There had to be. Though I could believe anything about Maggie, I couldn't think the smallest evil of Ben. Yes, I'd speak with him, of course I would. Yes, I'd see him, you bet your ass I would. And, yes, it would have to be soon because I just wasn't making it without him. Sleeping with Richie was to have someone to hang onto when the world was falling away, and after that one time, I slept single-o. In the spare bed. Claudette Colbert to Richie's Clark Gable.

I never knew what day it was, not really. All I knew was that, on Sunday night, Ben's play would be on and that would mark the beginning of his bound-to-succeed career. I looked forward to seeing that play, wanting desperately to be at his side when it went on but knowing that it was out of the question.

My plan was to call him right after the play to tell him it was brilliant and to assure him that, even if we never saw each other again, I was pleased that he was on his way to adoration and riches (fame and fortune seemed too hackneyed). I liked that plan. It was corny as hell, right out of a movie that only an audacious Katharine Hepburn could carry off, but it had a cold dignity and a snooty style. And, more than anything else, it might just mark the resumption of diplomatic relations, showing Ben that I had an open mind and was willing to hear his version of the St. Regis story, after which we might meet on neutral ground for an adult discussion of that painful breech in our affair. The truth was—okay? —the truth was I was ready to forgive him anything because to go on without him was to court insanity, something I was not crazy about doing.

That afternoon Richie showed up with the valise I had brought back from Pittsburgh and left at Ben's. He said that Ben had dropped it off at Barry's, which I thought was very nice of Ben. But Richie was acting strangely and not caring much to talk about it, so I let the matter drop.

I unpacked, and because most of my duds needed washing that's what I did. Up till then I hadn't needed any workout clothes because Richie was doing all the auditioning while I took notes on how each girl did. But since that was getting us zilch, Richie figured that he and I should do the numbers together, the better to show the girls how we thought it should look. As to all my other clothes, they were at Ben's, wondering whatever had become of me and why they had been so dreadfully abandoned.

The idea that Ben still had my belongings was something I rather liked. It gave me another reason to call him if calling him after his show didn't work. Lord knows, I wanted every opportunity to contact him, and I was not averse to dropping in on him to read the electric meter or lay down a spray against termites. It was beginning to look to me that I was a lousy hold-out, that if a dumb breeze blew the smoke of one of his cigars into my nose, I'd go running into his arms, begging forgiveness and hoping he'd take me back.

The world and all hope ended when Richie came back with all of my belongings. I asked him how come and he stalled around for an answer. So I asked him again, "Richie, how come?"

"He called and told me to come and get them. I'm sorry, Ginnie, but the guy's a prick. You caught him cold and he's not even embarrassed. What I don't understand is how you could have loved him in the first place. For Christ's sake, couldn't you *see*?"

"No."

"Well, maybe now you can. I went up there and— damn it!"

"What?"

"Ginnie. There was another girl there!"

"An airline stewardess? Because if it was, it's all right."

"I don't know who she was. Ben introduced her but the bitch was walking around half naked."

"Was her name Alice, or Susan, or Jessica?"

"No. Her name was Marjorie. Marjorie something."

"And she wasn't a stewardess?"

"If she was a stewardess it could have been on her

own airline. She had a ring on that'd knock your eye out. And a necklace—Ginnie, she was not a stewardess. She was too old."

"Maybe she was my mother."

"Does your mother have platinum hair and tits down to her knees?"

"My mother has brown hair and no tits at all."

"Then she wasn't your mother."

"Did Ben say anything? I mean, did he give you any message for me?"

"Yes."

"What? Richie? What'd he say?"

"He said to tell you he was sorry about your mother and that, even though he could explain it, it was just as well that it happened because—"

"Because what?"

"Because—for the time being, if you don't mind, he'd like to leave things the way they are. And that maybe, at some other time—Do you want me to go on with this shit?"

"No."

"Good."

"Because I don't believe it. I think he's making it all up."

"He didn't make up Marjorie. I saw her."

"She's a stewardess. They drop in from everywhere."

"For Christ's sake, will you wake up and face life? The guy's a prick. He's going big time. He doesn't want to hang around with chorus girls anymore. As for Marjorie—here—her picture's in yesterday's paper. 'Mrs. Jason Kimbrough, the former Marjorie Robertson, is in New York City for the telecasting of Sunday night's *Theatre 60* show to be aired at nine P.M. over NBC.' Ginnie, she's the wife of the client. Your beloved Ben was not only screwing your mother, he's now screwing the client's wife! And if you can't figure out what kind of man that makes him, then you deserve everything that happens to you!"

"Oh. Wow."

"What you have to do is be tough. Figure you've learned something—and get on with your life."

"Some pretty lady, isn't she?"

"If you like that type. Who you calling?"

"Barry."

"What for?"

"To see if he knows anything about this."

"You don't believe me."

"I just want to see what Barry knows."

"Barry knows everything. He was with me."

"Barry went with you to carry two little bags?"

"Ginnie. Call him."

I called Barry with Richie standing right alongside me and asked Barry if what Richie had told me was true. Barry took a long time in answering but finally said that it was true, that he was with Richie and had seen the Marjorie woman, that he was sorry, and that he was so disappointed in Ben as a man that he was going to drop him as a client. I firmed up and told him it wouldn't be necessary, that his was a business relationship and that he should make his money wherever he could, and that it would be dopey to resign Ben over me. Barry said he loved me and we hung up.

Then I apologized to Richie and he huddled me in his arms and I cried—because I hurt so bad, so blues-in-the-gutter bad that if Richie hadn't been there to hold me, I'd have crawled down a sewer and died.

I managed the next day—barely. Something was bothering me. All that Richie had told me and that Barry had corroborated—it just didn't sound like Ben. And yet, neither would I have expected the Ben I knew to be in my mother's hand in a hotel room doorway. So those two canceled each other out.

As to Richie's motive for lying, he had one—the preservation of his act, the survival of the Pickering Trio. If Richie thought that my reconciliation with Ben would destroy or even delay the act's chances of getting back on the road, yes, Richie could lie, probably would. He could easily have come across Marjorie Kimbrough's photo in the paper and made up the whole story just to keep Ben and me apart, perhaps thinking that if we got together, I'd quit the act. But then how did he come by my luggage? And Barry? Would Barry Nadler be a party to a lie like that, knowing how deeply it would hurt me? I didn't think so. Barry reminded me of Sy Fein, and Sy Fein would never do that. Never.

Still, the doubt persisted. I knew that there was only one way for me to find out just what the truth was, and that was to call Ben. And I did. I called him I don't know how many times over that Friday and Saturday, the weekend of his show, using the same dime from the same pay phone outside the ladies' room at Meridian Hall. There never was an answer. He never was in. Probably was at rehearsals. I'd have to keep trying.

And I would have kept calling forever, but Fate reared her ugly head because Saturday we found the girl——a sensational dancer named Sheila Sawyer. She was about twenty-five and had that society gloss that could augment the act so well. And she learned fast. The truth is, she was a much better dancer than me. If her dancing lacked anything, it was humor. And that made her just perfect for the way our act laid out. She'd be the square, I'd be the dip.

Richie negotiated with her in no time. Then he called ahead to St. Louis, to the Bryant Hotel, and told them that we were on our way and could open on Wednesday as originally scheduled. We were on a plane at ten A.M. Sunday morning.

We were in our hotel by three thirty in the afternoon. I hardly knew Sheila and asked Richie if it would be all right, at least in St. Louis, if I had my own room—staying with neither him nor Sheila. Richie said it would be fine but that, if I wanted to do that throughout the remainder of the tour, it would have to come out of my own pocket. He was being tough with me, and I knew why and respected him for it.

I took a walk around St. Louis and then tried phoning Ben again, knowing full well that he'd be at rehearsals. I phoned Florrie in Pittsburgh to see how she was, telling her that we had a passable replacement for her for the time being and not telling her about Ben and me, just reminding her to watch Ben's show, which she said she would. During our talk I discovered that Monty had had to return to New York and that Richie had yet to call her. That was a bad mark for Richie. He was beginning to get me nervous.

At seven P.M. I was in my hotel room in front of this terribly small television set, so small that it looked as though it should only carry fifteen-minute shows. Television was not yet a very big thing in St. Louis, and I was lucky to have had a set, however small, at all.

The picture wasn't the best—sudsy with periodic waves—but the sound was fine. And I fussed with the controls from seven until nine, New York time, at which time the announcer said that "Tony" was on, written by Benjamin Webber, and I went numb.

Ben's play was on and I was watching it in St. Louis. It was all wrong and I felt unreal and immobilized. It was good. Very good. At first I had trouble with some of the casting because many of the players were not as Ben had initially sketched them. But the lines came out

right, just as I had typed them after first having interpreted Ben's paleolithic scrawl. I found that I knew every line of dialogue of every character. And when an
actor floundered or groped, I fed him his line—from St.
Louis. And it worked.

It was all there. The whole play. The whole idea of
"Tony"—the tragedy of it and the questions it raised of
guilt and doubt, comedy and despair. Ben could write
drama and in the middle of it have the funniest things
going on. I didn't know of many writers who could do
that without subverting their whole statement. All of it
poured through the tube and spilled out into my little
room in St. Louis. We had done it together, Ben and
me, the pair of us. We had sweated it out and sent it in,
and there it was, for all the world to see. A fine play,
taut and comic, yet making you very nervous because
death was always hanging about.

When it had concluded, I switched off the TV set and
sat staring at the grey-empty tube. For one hour Ben
Webber had commanded the air waves. *My* Ben. No
matter that we no longer were together. We were together then, in the fashioning of the play. If we were
never to be together again then that one hour out of
the world's history forever belonged to us. Nine P. M. to
ten P.M., June 11, 1952—Ben and Ginnie Time. Our
time.

It was so quiet in my room that I didn't know what to
do with it. So I stood up and applauded, the tears coming down my face as if Caruso had sung *Pagliacci* for
me and me alone. I applauded Ben's talent and the
short time we had spent together. And I applauded my
decision to stop the crap and call him, and have it out,
and see if we couldn't get together again.

Sometime after eleven, New York time, I phoned his
apartment, knowing damned well that he couldn't be

home yet. But I wanted to establish in my brain that I was capable of calling that number. No answer. I phoned again at around one in the morning. A woman answered and I hung up. To make sure I hadn't dialed a wrong number, I waited fifteen minutes and called again. The woman answered again. Marjorie Kimbrough, no doubt, screwing her young playwright on his home field. And that was the end after the end that should have been the end. C'est fini, cheri. Vive la France and fuck you.

And in my head I heard the rumble of moving vans, carting off all the pretty scenery of my short-lived love affair, packing it away in a warehouse for which there was no key and to which no road led. All the laughter of our short run was stuffed into trunks and stifled, all the happy hopes and passionate speeches torn from the script so that nothing remained but the characters' names and some brief passages describing where the ancient action had taken place.

And any doubts I may have had as to our love affair's being over, they vanished with the arrival of the next morning's New York newspapers. No reviews of Ben's play in those papers. They had reviewed the Antoinette Perry Awards instead. But there was a picture in the *Daily News*—"Mrs. Marjorie Kimbrough and playwright Benjamin Webber"—a swell kick in the head and a fine launch into my nineteenth year, which, I vowed, would not find me as trusting as I had been a million years ago, when I was eighteen and the world was my oyster.

There's always a next morning. It does always come. Even though the night is endless and the clock doesn't move and the pills have no effect, the next morning always does arrive. It doesn't necessarily sweep clean but it does, in its own way, shuffle the cards for another go at a new ante.

I am not a strong person, never was. I might bluff people into thinking that about me, especially with my shocking language, I might even bluff *myself*, but my underpinning is all wobbly despite my superstructure's seeming solid. That's the way I have always seen my ship. From the water line up—a dreadnaught, and you'd better give it room when it sails past your dinghy. But below the water line the timbers are weak, the bolts slipshod, the ballast sliding, and the bilge continually slapping at my hammocked ass.

Still, if the captain stands firm and steers well, he *can* navigate the Good Ship Lollipop and make it through the storm. I was that kind of captain—still am. And it isn't all self-deception. A lot of it's a pragmatic awareness that, if the ship flounders, the crew skips and the captain's left alone on the bridge, saluting like hell as down goes Lollipop, into the briny. And that stuff in your lungs ain't rum and nectar, swabby, it's salt and shit. And the song they're playing ain't "Over The Bounding Main," it's "Nearer My God To Thee."

So, okay, I firmed up for the rest of the voyage. If Ben Webber was a disappointment, I would not allow him to sink my ship. How he and my mother came to be in that room, with me at the door, was no longer the issue. Nor was Marjorie Kimbrough or all his women before and after me. The issue was me. And the question, and only question, was how much fresh canvas could I unfurl to get my ass out of those stagnant waters?

And stagnant they were, starting from the moment I realized that Sheila did not have her own room as I had but that she was shacking up with Richie. I discovered that by picking up the phone and asking for Sheila Sawyer because I felt we should get to know each other and what better time than breakfast. The hotel operator said they had no Sheila Sawyer registered but that perhaps she was Mrs. Pickering. I was surprised but by no means shocked, for that seemed to be the way Richie worked. He had made love to me once to keep me whole and the act together. He would make love to Sheila for similar reasons and save room money in the process.

Interesting man, Richie Pickering, a shark to be sure but not without talent—and the nautical opposite of me. When he swam, only his dorsal fin protruded the surface, slicing the water passively, in no apparent hurry. His course was happily circular, docile, and meandering. But below the surface he was all teeth, an insatiable killer without conscience and harboring no remorse, driving steadfastly through schools of itty bitty fitties, his theme song, "Dinner For One, Please, James," his warning, "Get the fuck out of my way."

It was okay, I understood. He was not unlike Ben except that maybe he was a little more out in the open and, no doubt, more rapacious. I didn't think that Ben ever intended to hurt, whereas Richie couldn't have cared less. As to which was the more dangerous to Sally the Salmon, Ben got the nod because, though you always saw Richie coming, you never saw Ben until after he'd gone.

I was determined to be mature about things. After all, Richie had all the rights of a free man and Sheila was 100 percent cunt. I wasn't even jealous. The one time that Richie and I had made love was little more than therapy for me. He had a beautiful body and it did everything a girl could want done, but it was all too thought out, like his predictable choreography, whereas my forte was spontaneity and passion.

Sheila, I just couldn't warm up to, especially since it turned out she was married. Her husband, an actor, flew in from New York for our St. Louis opening, for which—one night only—she had her own room.

The act went very well. And if Sheila didn't dance with the honesty of Florrie, she did dance with a regal haughtiness that worked beautifully when I, the clown, came on to mess up the act.

Men came at me continually. I needed it but did nothing about it. I knew I should, and there were times I wanted to; but somehow I knew that that would be the beginning of slutdom, and I wasn't ready to sally into that territory. St. Louis was therefore dreary. As were Cincinnati and Minneapolis and Dayton and Louisville. Florrie had by then gone back to New York, where a specialist told her to take up basket-weaving. It never came to that as she and Monty got married. And if she limped down the aisle, I didn't see because I couldn't get to the wedding.

They loved each other, Florrie and Monty. The both of them thorough crazies but they did love each other. And it was good for me to know that it could happen as it gave me a nickel's worth of hope in a world I'd begun to think was totally filled with slugs.

In Louisville, on a rainy Sunday, Richie kind of asked me if I'd like to join him and Sheila in an afternoon *menage à trois*. He said it would be fun and that Sheila, though not a dyke, did have eyes for me. I thanked him for his kind invitation but said that I'd sewn up my box for the duration. Richie laughed, and it rained like hell.

The summer went. Draggingly, but it went. The only news I had concerning Ben's career was a syndicated column in the *Cincinnati Enquirer* in which it was mentioned that NBC had signed him to write three new original dramas. So he was on his way.

Each day that passed made it a touch easier for me to be away from him. Still, he was never completely out of my thoughts. I knew it would all take time and that it would be better if I could take another lover. But somehow I couldn't. All the men I met on tour did not want intellect or companionship or even a fun evening, they just wanted to get laid and how come I didn't understand them? That's what comes of wearing scanty costumes and a yellow pony-tail. Such riggings evidently do not speak well of a girl's character.

My belligerent attitude was not lessened by the fact that, when I got back to New York, I went straight to Barry Nadler, as he was holding the money, and there learned the following: one, Sheila had gotten more money than I had gotten. And two, deductions were taken from my salary to pay for my room, whereas Sheila, who had been shacking up with Richie, had no room deductions at all.

I screamed at Barry, my voice rising like a fishwife's. I told him what they all could do with the Pickering Trio. He said that it was a definite and flagrant inequity and that he'd take the matter up with Richie. He also pointed out, as nicely as he could, that we had more bookings coming up—good ones—and that rather than quit, I'd be better advised to start looking for an apartment. And that's when it hit me.

I had no place to stay. Sure, I could move in again with Richie. After all, Sheila would be going back to her cluck of a husband and Richie's bed and board would be available. I had a delicious thought—to call Marty Sawyer and tell him about his beautiful wife and Richie Pickering—but you know what? I couldn't do it. Some kind of tradition, don't ask me what. I could kill

Sheila; I could pour acid up her cunt and sell the sound effects to a horror show, but I could not tell her husband that she'd been sleeping around. It was the one taboo, the one action I was not allowed to take. It was stupid, like applying Marquis of Queensbury rules to a gang bang, but that was the unwritten law and woe be unto the gypsy dancer who broke it.

I asked Barry if I could stay at his office as he had a room in the back, with a cot, where he often took naps. I told him it would only be for as long as it took me to find myself a new apartment. He said it would be okay and, at six thirty, he went home, saying good night and departing in little pirouettes, like a Jewish Jimmy Durante.

And so there I was, my first night back in New York, and I was as alone as I'd been the night of the big fire in my pretty little Greenwich Village apartment. Immediately I thought of Roland Jessup and called him. Some very genteel faggot answered the phone and said that Roland was out of town, Xanadu or something. I thought about who else I might call, as it was getting dark and Barry was two hours gone and I didn't really want to be alone with the telephone for the remainder of the night.

Who else could I call? Florrie? She was on her honeymoon—the Virgin Islands, yet. I had already tried Roland. Don Cook was somewhere in Los Angeles. Alan Braden? He was probably still in knots from his one night fling with Ginnie the Jerker. Girlfriends? I had none. It was a sorry mess.

How about Ben Webber? He used to be a nice guy. Maybe *he'd* like to hear from me. Trembling, I dialed the number. It rang twice and then he answered. And I hung up immediately, terrified. I had heard his voice. It was like listening to God. I still loved him. It was a curse.

I hated myself for having called him but I liked the fact that, anytime I wanted to, I could dial his number and hear his voice. That was neat. That would always keep him near to me, the sonofabitch. When would I stop behaving like that? When would I be mature enough to accept the fact that I had loved and lost, and been used, and cast aside, and traded in for something of greater value?

I heard a hand on the outer door, turning the knob. Stupid, I had forgotten to lock it. I stood there as the man came in and I could see the next day's headlines—"Dumb dancer found mutilated and tortured to death in agent's office. Police suspect foul play."

It was Richie and he smiled at me, stickily paternal. "Barry told me you'd be here."

"I was, but I left."

"He says you're unhappy with me."

"Shouldn't I be?"

"I have your money. I'm surprised Barry didn't tell you."

"Explain that, please."

"The money deducted for your room. Plus the money to bring your pay up to Sheila's. Here. Comes to over three hundred dollars. Ginnie, I had to do it this way, Sheila insisted."

"Why?"

"Because she's a bitch. She didn't like you. Actually had to see all the contracts, exactly the way she wanted them, or she'd have walked out on us as soon as we hit St. Louis. Without her we'd have had no act."

"She moved in with you, right off."

"That was her idea, too."

"You asked me to join the both of you on that rainy Sunday."

"Also her idea. Among other things, she's a voyeur. Thought it would be cute to watch us at play."

"And now that she's back with her husband you want me to take over."

"Not exactly. I want you to have a place to stay. If you don't want to get in bed with me, that's okay. I just can't see you sleeping in this crummy office."

"And when we go on the road again? What happens then? Does she move back and I move out?"

"She's out. Out of the act."

"Why?"

"Because her husband found out and kicked the shit out of her. Her face is a mess. No makeup will cover it. And she's got a couple busted ribs. Called me less than an hour ago, so much gauze in her mouth I could barely understand her."

"Who told Marty?"

"You kidding? I thought you did."

"Thanks a lot."

"Listen, Ginnie, think anything you want about me, I'm a realist. I can replace Sheila but not you. We've got almost a month to find somebody. Noah Sobel wants us for two more shows this fall, and Barry's got us into the Riviera for three weeks, on the same bill with Howard and Birch. I took Sheila with all her nuttiness because she was the only girl we saw who didn't have two left feet, and you know it. Now, when we audition, we not only look for a good dancer but for one who doesn't have scrambled eggs in her head."

"I don't want to move back in with you, Richie. You have answers for everything. You make me unhappy."

"Okay. I understand. But staying here is stupid. Stay with me until you find another place, okay? I'll continue with my 'handsoff' policy. Okay? Now, come on."

He picked up my bag and I followed him into the

elevator, where he stayed pressed against the far wall, smiling, as if to say, "See how far away I can stay from you?"

In the cab he sat practically on the running board, which the cab didn't have. And he carried my bag up to his apartment as if that's what he did for a living. But once inside he tried to make love to me but I wouldn't have it. He was annoyed but then shrugged it off, figuring he'd get me when I was hotter. But he was wrong. I never made love to him again. Never. Ever.

I always watched the newspapers, looking for word on Ben's plays. One of them was on—"The Magic Horn." It was kind of marvelous. A Jazz Fable. Sal Mineo played a deaf and dumb kid who was left this magic trumpet that would only play if he believed it would play. Ralph Meeker was his older buddy, a piano player. And all the other parts were played by jazz musicians like Vic Dickenson, Milt Hinton, Ernie Caceres, Pee Wee Russell; and Jimmy McPartland, the great cornetist, as the heavy. It was beautiful, really touching. The reviews were generally good but only Bob Salmaggi, the music critic of the *New York World Telegram and Sun*, really understood it, saying that music played the lead and that the humans were only secondary. I called Ben's apartment, heard his voice—and hung up. I was having the crazies again and had to know he was nearby.

We found another girl, Dolores Murphy. She was perfect. Pale skin, black hair, blue eyes—Irish and basic. And she had the flaming personality of a grape. But when she danced, she was quite something else. She had incredible legs, a body made of rubber, and a stage presence that, if you're not born with, takes ten years to develop.

Dolores was quick to fit in. Our only problem was

that Noah Sobel was concerned that the TV audience would see that one of the girls had been changed since the Pickering Trio last did *The Joey Magnuson Show*. So, no sooner was Florrie back from her honeymoon than she was asked to come in so that the makeup men could try to make Dolores look like her.

We had to develop new numbers, of course. But we'd have to have done them anyway because, by then, all the improvisation had gone out of our old numbers and I just wasn't a good enough actress to come on stage and make like I had never danced them before. Also, for the Riviera, for Howard and Birch, we *had* to look bright and fresh and new. As a matter of fact, Richie was so leery about opening there with numbers we would have first done on television that we worked out additional numbers just for the Riviera.

We did the first of our *Joey Magnuson Shows*. Two numbers, as before. It went smoothly, the newness of the material making it easier for me to come on and do my bit. The first number was straight, of course, but the second number relied on my ability to break up the act. And I did. Even the orchestra broke up and the director had the good sense to throw a camera on Joey and Mara-Jayne, who were collapsing in the wings. Anyone watching on television would just have to know that the whole thing was spontaneous, unrehearsed, and hysterical.

Ben's next play went on, only three weeks after "The Magic Horn." He was getting to be a celebrity and there was a lot of stuff in the papers about his show even before it aired. It was called "The Fair-Haired Boy," and it had Jackie Cooper playing Ben in a kind of behind-the-scenes drama of a movie company's advertising setup. The reviews were all respectful if not out-and-out raves. And all the critics agreed that Ben was a writer to watch. One man, though, had to be pretty ticked off about that show and that was Sam Gaynor, whom Ben had redubbed Ron Garner and presented as the villain of the piece.

I called Ben again, of course, after the show and hung up as soon as he answered. And then I cried and felt better, and felt worse, and wished I was dead, but knew enough to go on. One day, I thought, and soon, I'd have to answer when he said hello. One day. Very soon. Maybe after his next play. Maybe not, but maybe so.

We began rehearsing our Riviera numbers and were very busy because we still had another *Joey Magnuson Show*, to do in another few weeks. Work, work, work.

The way it worked out, as soon as we'd done our last *Joey Magnuson Show*, we went right over to Fort Lee, New Jersey, where the Riviera was, and began rehearsing there on their very large stage. Noah Sobel wanted to sign us for another show, maybe two, but Richie was playing it cool, taking it slow, giving it thought.

Let me tell you, Normie Birch was a crazy nut. A comic, he threw plates around the stage and danced on the outsides of his ankles and made faces and could make a condemned man laugh. Gary Howard, the other half of the act, was basically a romantic singer but had a streak of pure insanity running through him. Rehearsals were a ball because nobody seemed to take anything seriously except Richie, and after a while even he got into the swing of it.

Ben's third play of the season went on and it clobbered me. It was a love story—"The Lonely Look"—and it was clearly about Ben and me, with Jack Lord playing Ben and Janice Rule playing me. The only thing was, it had a happy ending, with the playwright marry-

ing the dancer and the whole world wrapped up in roses.

Before I called him after that show, I had determined
to tell him who I was, sticking two Scotches in me to
help me do the deed. But the operator came on and told
me that they no longer had a listing for Benjamin Webber at that address. Nor did they have a listing for Benjamin Webber at all except Benjamin J. Webber, in the
Bronx, a plumber, and Ben T. Webber, a shoemaker in
Queens.

So my little attempt at reunion had gone awry. Too
little, too late. Ben had changed his phone number and
had possibly even moved. That fun apartment, that love
place—he might no longer be in it. If so, then I had to
view it as no longer being there. It would be less painful. All my bridges back to Ben were being burned, and
I hadn't even struck a match. Spontaneous combustion,
or time and tide not waiting—whichever it was, the past
was fading and my idiot heart was breaking. Oh, where
was the little girl who rode ponies on Sundays and sat
on her daddy's knee?

The reviews on "The Lonely Look" were sensational,
and Ben was heralded as a writer who could do it all—
comedy, drama, love stories, fables, fantasies—the
whole bag. And two of the critics wondered just when
television would lose him to Hollywood. Soon, they suspected.

We opened at the Riviera and—ho-hum—we were a
smash. And I mean *really*. It started out okay. After the
Don Arden dancers opened the show, we came on. We
did our first number straight, were applauded, and got
off. And then came back. That is, Richie and Dolores
came back. I was still offstage, waiting to go on with my
improvisation. But, before I could, crazy Normie Birch

came out in a tutu, tentatively watching Richie and Dolores (like I was supposed to be doing) and then joining in, grabbing Richie and dancing off with him, spinning him off the stage and out between the tables in the audience. Richie knew enough to go with it, to follow Normie's lead, because what else could he do? But Dolores, left alone onstage, dissolved into hiccoughing hysterics, practically wetting the floor as she sank to her knees, trying to keep her legs pressed together.

Me? I'm standing in the wings like a lox because what do they need *me* for? Only out comes Gary Howard, dressed up as either a Hawaiian warlord or a large chicken. He grabs me by my arm and pulls me onstage and tries to lift me only he can't. By now Dolores is lying on the stage in a fetal position, laughing her way through very heavy labor. Richie and Normie are waltzing all over the Riviera, and the orchestra, quick to pick up on the nonsense, goes into a Strauss waltz.

Gary next pulls me over to the stage mike where he starts throwing one-liners at me and I try desperately to respond. I guess I was good because Gary was breaking up. At first I thought my costume had split (shades of *Guys and Dolls*), but no, it was just me, standing up there with Gary, trading ad libs with him. And it was all working, everything of-a-piece. Finally, when it looked like we were hung up for an ending, I tap-danced on point, watching out of the corner of my eye as Dolores, completely bonkers, rolled off the stage, landing on one of the ringside tables and lying spread-eagled on the tablecloth, where those Philadelphia Mummers might eat her (one of them actually trying—with a spoon).

There came upon us the loudest burst of applause I'd ever heard, and all of us took bow after bow. And when the curtain finally closed on us, we lay on the floor in hysterics while out front the orchestra played "Onward

Christian Soldiers." We managed to crawl offstage though we couldn't stand up straight for a half hour.

When I was sprawled out in my dressing room, a waiter brought me a blotty note that had been hastily inked on a paper cocktail napkin. It read: "You were great." It wasn't signed so Dolores insisted that it was from Sol Hurok and that we were stars. Gary and Normie came in to see if we were alright. They apologized for destroying our act and then asked if we couldn't do it as a regular thing throughout the run. Richie thought it was a great idea if we could at least do our opening number straight. After that, anything that happened was fine with him.

The toughest assignment was mine. I had no idea what Gary would be talking about because neither would he; it would all be ad lib. The upshot of it was that the dopey girl dancer I had played until then emerged as a dopey foil for Gary Howard. And I wasn't bad. I was more verbal than I thought I'd be, quick on the uptake and brightly inventive (I'm told). Also, Gary was easy to work off, and, whenever I got stuck, I just tap-danced until Gary stopped me.

Amazingly enough, even though we did it every show, Dolores got sincerely hysterical every time. Richie and Normie became very adroit at dancing all over the Riviera, one night even coming out of the ladies' room on roller skates, flinging toilet paper as the orchestra played "Rule Brittania."

The whole gig got to be the talk of the town. *Life* magazine did a spread on us—"The Riviera Rowdies"—in which they said that Richie and I were an "item" and would be married in the spring. It didn't bother me because it was too funny and Richie laughed, too.

I even appeared on *The Stan Arlen Show*, playing off

him as I had played off Gary, being the dumb blonde who somehow wasn't all that dumb. And after our run had concluded at the Riviera, Stan Arlen asked if I'd consider becoming a regular on his late-night TV show. I said I might, providing it didn't interfere with the regular bookings of the Pickering Trio, and we left it at that.

Richie wasn't happy and he took me aside and told me so, pointing out that we were a dance act and that I owed him some loyalty and that, though it was all right in a club, working off Howard and Birch, I'd be getting in well over my head if I began seeing myself as a stand-up comic. I assured him that I had no such view of myself, letting him know in the process that I was a free woman and could damn well do what I pleased.

I didn't intend for it to end in a fight but that's what it did, with Richie calling me cunty names and me asserting my god-given right of free choice. And so there I was again, in Barry Nadler's office, facing another night alone on the cot.

Barry, thinking that Richie and I were lovers, was reluctant to take sides, saying only that he hoped we could work it out. He left at about six P.M., giving me permission to sleep on that lousy cot of his. He'd have invited me to sleep at his place, but his brother and his wife were in from Albany and there wasn't any room. I told him not to worry, that I'd be perfectly comfortable and that I preferred to be alone.

I sat at Barry's desk, wondering if Ben had seen me on TV or had come across the spread in *Life*. The usual phone calls came, about a half dozen from various clients in distress. I told them all that Barry would be in in the morning and that they should call then.

One of the calls, however, was from Sheila Sawyer. I identified myself and she was very pleasant, glad to be speaking to me and to have read how smashingly the act was going and all that. She seemed very sincere and not at all consistent with the image I had of her, so I probed.

"Sheila? You all right now?"

"Sure. Why shouldn't I be?"

"Well—the bruises and the ribs?"

"What're you talking about?"

"You know."

"Look, Ginnie, I called Barry to get some information for my taxes. I need some W-2 forms or 1040's. I don't know *what* the fuck I need."

"Marty didn't beat you up?"

"What? Why should Marty beat me up?"

"Richie told me that Marty beat you up."

"Yeah? Well, if you want to believe that sonofabitch. He told me a few things about you, too."

"Like what?"

"Like you were dykey and wanted to do a scene with me and him. I didn't believe him but that's what he told me."

"Weren't you sleeping with him?"

"You kidding? I'm a married lady. I slept on the fucking sofa. He said if I wanted my own room I'd have to pay for it, and listen, kid, I needed the money and still do. Marty hasn't worked in six months. I know it didn't *look* good—and Richie sure tried—but you go sleeping with your boss, baby, and that can only lead to bad news."

"You were getting more money than I was."

"Right. So what? Richie was over a barrel and I took advantage of it. And it wasn't as if I was a bad dancer. I was damned good."

"Why'd you quit?"

"I quit, dear heart, because I'm having a baby."

"What?"

"I was in my third month when I signed on with you guys. I didn't want to tell that to Richie, and I didn't want to push it much beyond my fourth month because I've had two misses already. Jesus, kid, what the hell has he been saying about me?"

"Nothing good."

"Yeah? Well, if he tells you we were making it, don't believe him. We weren't. Anything else he says, I don't give a crap."

"Okay."

"And would you please ask Barry to call me about the fucking tax forms? I don't want to have my baby in jail."

"I'll tell him."

"Bye, kid. Take care of yourself."

"You, too—and the baby."

I hung up, things awash in my head that I didn't like. Okay, so Richie had lied. I knew he could lie. I had often been around when he lied. Often he had lied to me, as was obviously the case with Sheila. But the big question, the nervous question, was had he lied to me about Ben? Because if he had, if he'd lied to me about Ben, and about Ben's not wanting to see me, and about Ben's being with Marjorie Kimbrough, then he had fucked up my life and deserved to be dead. I could kill him and get away with it because no jury would convict me. I could claim to have done it as a public service and they'd give me a medal instead of a prison term.

Richie's accomplice in that act, if he had lied about Ben, would have to have been Barry Nadler. Barry had backed up everything that Richie had told me about Ben. It wasn't yet eight P.M. Barry wouldn't be in until nine the next morning. Though I wasn't hungry, I went downstairs for a hamburger and coffee, and I came back with some magazines because there was no TV in Barry's office that I could waste my mind on. It was going to be a long wait between trains.

You know how things get exaggerated in the night, how fevers rise and toothaches get worse. Well, so do doubts. They rise and get worse, and by dawn mine had completely enveloped me in a kind of anguish I'd never experienced before. It gathered in my head, stabbed at my soul, and got up a Greek chorus so loud that it was a wonder the neighbors didn't complain. By midnight the doubts were gone, displaced by facts, awful truths so bald that I hated my stupid self for not having noticed them sooner. Of *course* Ben had tried to reach me. Of *course* he wanted to at least try to explain the Maggie scene. Of *course* Richie had lied for his own self-serving purposes. Of course, of course, of course. Stupid, stupid, stupid. Schmuck, schmuck, schmuck.

I paced about like a picket, going to the john every five minutes because the urge to pee was uncontrollable. I looked out the window and counted cars. I counted people walking dogs, dividing them into men and women and subdividing them into big dogs and little dogs. Colors became apparent at four A.M. Garbage trucks came with the news trucks at five. Derelicts were visible in their doorways at six. Rolls and pastries were delivered to restaurants at seven. School kids poked up at eight. Barry Nadler came in at nine, carrying two containers of coffee and a pair of Danish as large as horseshoes. The night had passed. The inquisition would begin—but not quite.

He pushed my share of the breakfast across the desk at me. "You look awful. You didn't sleep. Me neither. So it's a draw." He tried to get comfortable but couldn't quite do it. "I want to tell you a story. Would you like to hear a story? Doesn't matter, you'll hear it anyway.

It's about a man who all of a sudden grew old. He was doing okay. Wasn't sixty and felt maybe forty-five. But he got to be seventy in a flash. Anyway, once upon a time, so the story goes, this man was minding his own business which wasn't much—he was an agent, making ends meet with a list of clients that wouldn't interest *Our Gang*. Anyway, he chances upon a couple magical acts that are real winners, gold mines you might say. One is a dance team and the other is a writer, and by now you know of whom I speak or else you're a dunce, yes?"

"Yes."

"As it turns out, one of the dancers, a girl, is in love with the writer, a boy; only lo and behold, a crazy thing happens and everyone is upset. The dancers are barely dancing and the writer is barely writing and the gold mines are leaving town. And because the agent is either a weak man or a crumb, he lets Richie Pickering talk him into a story that would grow a nose on Pinocchio the size of Dumbo. Am I going too fast for you?"

"Richie lied and you backed him up."

"Correct. And I'd do it again because I've got nine dollars in the bank and why turn gold to shit to bring two lovers together who don't know baloney from salami?"

"Did you go to Ben's apartment with Richie to get my things?"

"No."

"Richie went alone."

"Yes."

"And was Marjorie Kimbrough there?"

"Marjorie Kimbrough was a picture in a paper. Richie made a story out of it. He told you one story and Ben another—and you both fell for it. Some suckers."

"Did you ever speak to Ben?"

"All the time. Lying every inch of the way."

"He wanted to see me, didn't he?"

"Of course. I told him you didn't want to."

"You knew that wasn't true."

"True-shmue, so what? I *owed* Richie. He gave me the Pickering Trio and he gave me Ben Webber. For the first time in three years my head was above water—and I was not of a mind to bite the hand that was holding me above water."

"Then why are you biting it *now*?"

"Because ya got me, baby. Because I'm caught. You think I'm suddenly noble? That I see the error of my ways? Again you show what a sucker you are. Sheila called me last night, at my apartment, breaking a cardinal rule and also blowing my cover. So now I'm making a clean breast of it as what else can I do, especially with Arlene ready to leave me. And it's not that I love her either—it's that the nine dollars is in *her* name. I'm really a terrible person. So terrible that I'm ready to say, right now, if you leave Richie not only will I understand, but I'll handle you. How do you like *that* for a final touch?"

"Richie has the talent. Stay with him."

"Dance acts have had it. I know. I was there for Tony and Sally DeMarco, and for Grace and Paul Hartman. It ends with them. But it begins for *you*. I haven't been telling you, but—I get five calls a day for you. Stan Arlen calls so often I think maybe he's the UJA. So wise up—let's both of us dump Richie and go on to greater things. At least I'll have one gold mine for my troubles."

"You have Ben."

"Ben has signed with William Morris which I knew he would one day do."

"God, I don't *believe* this."

"You mention God—I'll tell you something. If God came back, and Moses with him—and the other guy, too, the fat one—*Buddha*? I'd sign all of 'em, bill 'em as The Three Stooges, and let 'em tour Africa. That's the kind of man you're talking to. My cupboard is so bare, I'd sign *Hitler*. So, if you're through being hysterical, finish your coffee and get out of here. I'm expecting a call from Jack the Ripper and I'm going to send him Dolores. It'll only be for one night but, what the hell, a buck's a buck."

"Good-bye, Barry."

"You're going to look for Ben, yes?"

"Yes."

"What do I tell Stan Arlen?"

"Tell him I'm available."

"Will you work for scale?"

"Yes."

"Can I have your Danish?"

"Yes."

"I'll make a fortune for you."

"Jesus Christ, Barry . . ."

"Him, too."

In the cab on my way to Ben's apartment, I didn't even *try* to make myself look good. After a night of nonsleep my face was as puffy as a soufflé. Still, I had my dark glasses, and if I pulled my collar up, maybe Ben wouldn't notice. Maybe he wouldn't even notice it was me. Maybe I wouldn't notice *him* because he wasn't living there anymore. Certainly he had a different phone number; maybe he was living over at Sutton Place somewhere.

When the cab pulled over and I saw the dear building, I almost cried. My building. My apartment. My Ben, goddamnit. I looked at the names on the registry.

"Cook/Webber." And beneath it, where I had inked it in, "Maitland." Maybe. Maybe, maybe.

I climbed the stairs hoping I wouldn't make it, wondering what I'd say if I did make it. What could I say? "I'm sorry but everyone lied to me"? "I'm sorry you and my mother caught me in the hallway"? The situation was impossible and I thought of turning back and going down and sending him a post card from Peru, and signing it "Inca-Dinka-doo."

The hell. I continued. The whole five flights. And I stood before the old door. Open Sesame—and turn my life into a burning fucking miracle. The prodigal daughter has returned, heart in hand, foot in mouth, cigarette trembling. Knock-knock.

The door opened and a girl stood there. Pretty, in a nice robe. Ten o'clock in the morning and the girl was pretty and she was wearing a robe—need I know more? "Excuse me," I said. "I think I have the wrong apartment."

"No, you don't," she said, with a small sigh of resignation. "This is it. You've got it." And she held the door open for me as if I were the cops and had a warrant.

"I'm looking for a Mrs. Prendegast. Dolly Prendegast."

"Oh, stop it and come in."

I went in, absolutely blotto, not knowing what to say or what to expect. I could hear the shower running inside. I desperately wanted to run.

"Hey," she said. "It's all right. What airline you with?"

"What?"

"What airline do you fly?"

"Oh. Peruvian."

"Where you coming from?"

"San Fran. Just in for the day."

"There's room. Don't worry."

"Oh, I'm not worried. I just don't want to inconvenience either of you."

"Forget it. It's no problem. Do you know any of the other girls or is this your first time?"

"I know a couple of 'em."

"What's your name, kid?"

"Debra Dubonnet."

"I'm Candy Carson."

"You're kidding. That's better than Debra Dubonnet."

"You don't have a bag or anything. How come?"

"Well first of all, I'm not a stew. And second of all, I'm not staying."

"What?"

"I'm sorry. I don't know why I thought—I'll come back some other time. Better still, if you'll give me the number, I'll call. You're very nice. Just tell him that Ginnie came by."

"You're Ginnie?"

"Yeah. Bye."

"Hey! Wait a minute!"

"No, I don't think so." I zipped out and started down the stairs. Would I always be running for my life?

She was calling after me. "Ginnie! Don't go! It's alright! Honest!"

I didn't answer. I just wanted out. Also, I wished she hadn't been so nice. I hit the street on the fly. No cab so I just hiked. He caught up to me, looking like a flasher in his bathrobe, running up the street after me, finally catching up to me, grabbing my arm, and spinning me to a halt.

"Ginnie! What the hell you doing?"

"Huh?"

"Where the hell are you running?"

"Don? Oh—Don!"

We hugged and kissed on East Eighty-third Street, drawing a small crowd of mostly kids, the flasher in his robe, the blonde in dark glasses. Then we went back, arm in arm, to the building.

Candy was Don's girl. She had been living with him in Los Angeles and came back with him to New York. Ben had shared the place with them but only for a while, then he moved—not to Sutton Place but to Hollywood. And he had turned the apartment back to Don from whom he had gotten it in the first place. As I had no other place to stay (my usual situation) it was determined that I could have my old room back at the inn. I called Barry and asked if he could get my clothes back from Richie's place. He said he couldn't as Richie had called and, when told where I'd gone, had thrown every stitch I owned into the incinerator, swearing that he'd kill me on sight or, at the very least, break both my legs and mess up my vapid face.

So, as on the night of the big fire, I was once more down to nothing, except for the Gypsy Robe which Ben had left in my closet. Oh, yes—he'd also left my portrait of Maggie. What a lucky child I was. My mommy would always be with me.

The clock was turning back but it was also spinning ahead. I was in Ben's apartment but Ben was away, further away than ever before. And though I could touch his bed and sleep in it whenever I wanted, we were light years apart. He being Mercury on the air waves. Me being Venus in the dumps.

ben

1952

I worked like a bastard on my three plays for Frank Brokaw. And with every page I learned a little more about myself as a writer, about what I could do well and what I had trouble doing at all. I continued to write the three plays simultaneously, jumping from one to another so that whenever I returned to any one of them it was newly fresh in my mind. It was a good way for me to work. It smacked of mass production but the plays were so different from one another that the designation could not properly be applied. I was, by then, typing fairly well. I still made mistakes but my work was comprehensible. I didn't let it worry me because NBC would have it all multigraphed later on.

As to Ginnie Maitland, I was coming to terms with the idea that ours had been an affair of intense but short duration, a firecracker in a tin can—loud but quick, and with nobody getting hurt. It had been weird, Maggie and Ginnie, but it had to be taken in stride. To pursue it beyond its natural conclusion would be to ask too much of it. Stretching a crazy minute to an hour's length would not multiply the craziness by sixty, it would only divide it by a million. All things have a beginning and an end, even though the geometry of it may not be immediately apparent.

I had loved my three stewardesses and Maggie and

Pat, and I could see all those endings as clearly as if I had written them myself. I had loved Ginnie, and, though I had fought the ending of it kicking and screaming, the end had arrived all the same. The idea, then, was to not be bitter at the affair's conclusion, but grateful that it had taken place at all. Nor should one look to place blame or seek exoneration when it all does fly apart and go boom. One must leave when it's time. One must tip his hat and thank the lady for her time and her tears, knowing all the while that everything that goes up has to come down—that axiom applying to moods, stocks and elevators, balloons and passions, aviators and erections.

And yet, I continually asked Barry about Ginnie. Though he was reluctant to keep me plugged in, he did tell me about her upcoming appearances on *The Joey Magnuson Show*. I was pleased for Ginnie, truly, pleased that she had landed on her feet and had come out swinging. In a way I was also pleased that I had been spared having to explain that night in the St. Regis. It would not have been easy.

And, if Ginnie and I ever met again, I could be as annoyed with her for not having allowed me to explain as she might be with me for the incident's ever happening at all. Things were evening out. Time was doing its job. It would take more time, to be sure, but the girl was fading. One day she would be part of the wallpaper of my life, occurring and recurring at specific and well-defined intervals, part of an overall pattern that I would learn to live with because, in the final analysis, I would have picked it out for myself.

I delivered all three of my scripts to Brokaw in one trip, ending my months of monastic living and stepping out into the world only to realize that all of the summer and much of fall had slid past me and that it was late

October. So, like the pilgrim of old, I revisited the Museum of Modern Art, again studying the girls therein and wondering which of them might fall in love with me if I asked her to.

I went to Saks and bought some shirts, and in Dunhill's I picked up three boxes of Monte Cristos plus another three of Uppmanns. I smoked one of them while walking down Sixth Avenue, half expecting to conjure up Don Cook and his magic nose. I went home and waited for Jerry Kaplan's call—two days.

But he did call and he loved my plays, as had Brokaw, and he was sure that Jason Kimbrough would love them, too. I would not have been surprised if Kimbrough hadn't wanted *any* of them, as I had caused a tiff in the Kimbrough family, albeit innocently, by having my picture in the paper with "the Mrs." Kimbrough hadn't much cared for it, he and his wife evidently juggling an uneasy marriage at the time the photo appeared in print. It was all easily explained but the man did look at me slightly sideways from then on, as did his wife, though, I suspected, for another reason. But I knew to steer a course wide of her—to Madagascar via the Cape of Good Hope—for I had had enough of women in their tardy thirties. I didn't need another Maggie, expecially if it turned out that the Kimbroughs had a daughter like Ginnie.

Ginnie. I had thought of Ginnie. Obliquely, offhandedly, but of Ginnie all the same. She was there faintly, lightly—still on my shoulder, still on my mind, but in silhouette, not solid. And further away. Each time further away.

"The Magic Horn" swung into rehearsals, Norman Felton directing. Sal Mineo was a nice kid, very young and into lifting weights, but decent and learning in every way he could. Ralph Meeker struggled to get to rehearsals on time. He always came in carrying a container of milk and looking as though he had slept under a bear. But he did a good job, as did the rest of the cast, all of them jazz musicians. I got some nice reviews and some more phone calls in which people on the other end hung up as soon as I answered. Jerry Kaplan told me that the stuff came with fame and that I should get an unlisted number. But I wasn't quite ready for that because, who knew, maybe someone might call me from out of the past, someone I might like to speak to.

NBC, via Brokaw and Kaplan, had begun to make noises about a long-term contract, to which Barry was very receptive but on which no one had as yet asked for my signature. Another agent was seen hanging around. He was from William Morris—tall, bluesuited, grey at the temples, and very presidential. The few times we chatted he told me not to sign with anyone too hastily. His name was Vernon Stacey and he impressed me. Though I suspected that he was soliciting me, he was so low-key that I often was unaware that he'd been around until I saw him leave.

I watched the Pickering Trio on television. They were good enough in their first number but were fantastic in their second. The tall blonde in particular, naively sexy, was in such control of what she was all about that even Joey Magnuson and Mara-Jayne came close to dissolving in laughter. It was Ginnie, I could tell by the ponytail; but the old TV had seen better days, and its seven-inch screen was greying around the edges and the whole thing was coldly two-dimensional, whereas the girl *I* knew had been most decidedly three. When the show concluded, I suspected that I didn't know her anymore. And when I turned the set off, I had to wonder if I'd ever known her at all.

"The Fair-Haired Boy" went on, directed deftly by

David Greene, a Canadian. Jackie Cooper played me, and the nearest actor we could get who was large enough to play Sam Gaynor was a half-ape, half-Viking named Ulf Redmond. If Sam Gaynor had been an indifferent adversary before that play, he had to be a blood enemy after. Yet all I had done was to put him up there in all his boring splendor, designing his three longest monologues so that they were interrupted by commercials—and were still going on after the commercials had concluded. The effect was astounding, making the character look as though he never stopped talking, which was the essence of Sam Gaynor and was why I doubted if he'd heard the show, let alone seen it.

When I got back to the apartment that night after having chatted briefly with Vernon Stacey (who was about to make his move), I received another of those prank phone calls. It was unsettling because I knew who I wanted it to be. Anyway, on the following day I arranged to get an unlisted number. So ended an era, finally, and by my own hand.

The reviews were fine and Brokaw and Kaplan and two NBC vice-presidents came at me with visions of glory and offers of the moon. But Stacey had advised me not to commit, and, as nicely as I could, I didn't.

The Pickering Trio did another *Joey Magnuson Show* and were once again funnily great. But someone in the control booth had chosen to train the camera almost exclusively on the blonde ponytail, superimposing her face over a full shot of all three of the dancers. It was a brilliant move, for the ponytail's face was a perfect mirror of the trio's dancing, reflecting innocence, then interest, then confidence, then bliss. And even when the whole number came apart at the seams, the ponytail never knew that it was she who had caused it. The camera work gave the choreography elements of

Chaplin, Mary Pickford and Pearl White. And damned if that leggy blonde wasn't Lombard incarnate.

My third and final play of my NBC contract was "The Lonely Look," directed by Harvey "Slidey" Epstein. It could not have gone better. Though Janice Rule did not much look like Ginnie, she did have that dancer's grace and a spooky kind of repose that made her wonderful in the role. As for Jack Lord's playing me, that was a stretch. He was better-looking, more intelligent and less obtrusive. But, because he was also a helluvan actor, I could not object to his being cast as the writer. He gave the part a sympatico that even I hadn't realized was a prerequisite to the play's working. And I was pleased to see what a nice guy I actually was underneath all that sturm and drang. I had taken liberties in the scripting. It wasn't exactly Ginnie and me. And it had a happy ending because, in the fifties, that was more often than not required. But in its own way it worked better than had any of my preceding plays.

We had our meeting in the Oak Room of the Plaza Hotel, Vernon Stacey and me. It was the first time we had really talked. All the other times we had merely touched elbows and grazed conversations. That night he was not one for beating around the bush. Even before our first drinks had arrived, Vernon Stacey had already come to grips with the reason for our being together.

"Barry Nadler is a nice man," he said. "And NBC is a nice network. And Kemper is a nice aluminum company—but you've already outgrown all of them. And to saddle yourself with any of them would be to stunt your career before it had a chance to get properly started."

"Barry's been good to me."

"Really? Did he waive his commission?"

"No."

"Then he wasn't being all that good."

"Will the Morris office waive their commission?"

"No. Not because we're not nice but because it will be too large a figure. If you were starting out, and we believed in you, and our commission was fifty dollars, we'd waive it if you asked us to. But you're not starting out, you're cresting. And you're worth a lot more than NBC is offering."

"Do you know what they're offering?"

"I don't have to. No matter what they're offering, it would be wrong for you to accept. It'll tie you up, keep you in the corral when you should be allowed to roam. I can get you more for one movie assignment than they can pay you for all five of those plays."

"How do you know it's five?"

"I guessed. Ben, NBC is hung with a weekly budget. If you want to limit yourself to television, stay with Barry Nadler and with Brokaw and be happy. But a film studio has a different budget for every film, and it's big. And screenwriters get a big hunk of it. Warner Brothers has already called Barry Nadler. Twice. He's turned them down."

"How do you know?"

"I know."

"Why would Barry turn them down?"

"Because he knows that once you leave New York you leave him. He can't possibly handle your career from here. It'll be but a matter of time before *some* big talent agency convinces you to join them. The Morris office thinks the time is *now*. We want you, Ben. We think we can help your career and make big money for ourselves in the process."

"Does Helen McIninny still work for you?"

"Yes. Do you know her?"

"Yes."

"She's very good. Would you like her to be assigned to you?"

"I don't know. I'm no Henry Denker."

"You lost me."

"No. I would not like Helen McIninny to be assigned to me."

"Barry Nadler handles comics, acrobats, jugglers, and dance teams. He's strictly Borscht Belt. How he talked you into signing with him—*Are* you signed?"

"No. It's verbal."

"And you feel you have to honor it."

"To some degree, yes."

"I'll take a guess right now that it will cost you fifty thousand dollars this year to have Barry Nadler represent you instead of us. Ten percent of fifty thousand dollars is five thousand dollars. Give him the five thousand dollars and call it quits."

"Where do I get the five thousand dollars?"

"From your first movie assignment."

"I don't have it yet."

"You have it the minute you sign with us. Do we have a deal, Ben?"

"Can I take a couple of days to think about it?"

"Take all the time you want. Just don't sign anything without letting me know what you're signing. Even if you don't sign with us, I'll help you in your deal with them."

"Why would you want to do that?"

"To impress you. So that next time we come back at you to sign, you'll think of us kindly and remember what a schmuck you once were—and you'll sign."

"I'd like to think about it."

I thought about it. And while I was thinking about it I received a long distance call from Don. Said he was coming east and was there room in the old pad—for two more. I said yes but that he'd better hurry as I might be going west. He said he'd hurry.

Jerry Kaplan was being very solicitous of me. He asked if I'd like to join him and his wife for the opening of the new show at Bill Miller's Riviera. He said I could bring a date but I simply couldn't think of anyone so we went as a threesome. Karen Kaplan was a smashing-looking girl who just couldn't bring herself to fawn over me as her husband was doing, and I liked her for it. Our table was not the best, about midway. But it was the center table of a dozen that sat on a one-foot-high raised landing, thus affording us an excellent if somewhat distant view of the stage.

The dinner was passable. The Don Arden Girls did a nice opening number, strutting about in floral array to a "Lady In The Dark" medley. Then—a big surprise to me because I hadn't even looked to see who was on the bill—out came the Pickering Trio and it took me a few moments to accept that it all was happening. They did their first number straight, with Florrie's replacement doing just fine. But it was the blonde ponytail who caught my eye, as she always had and always would.

They danced in meticulous synchronization, sort of a modern version of "In A Country Garden." It was precise, stylish and clever and the audience ate it up. Their second number never got started, at least not the way I thought they must have intended it. Because out came Normie Birch, on point (on *ankles* would have been more correct), in some frilly ballet get-up—and it was mayhem. Everyone knew that it was ad lib because it was a show-wise audience and they knew what could happen on opening night with Howard and Birch. But I don't think they knew how funny it was going to be until that leggy blonde stood up there with Gary Howard, feeding him straight-lines and often topping him. By the time it was over, some guy was pulling the other dancer off a ringside table where a drunk had already begun to dig his way into her with a spoon. The rest of it segued into a kind of pandemonium that hadn't been since Olsen and Johnson's last production of "Hellzapoppin'."

I looked over at the Kaplans and they were as out-of-their-minds hysterical as everyone else. I scrawled a hurried note on a cocktail napkin, and gave a waiter five bucks for making sure that the blonde dancer got it. Unfortunately, I gave him that fiver before I'd signed my name, and the oaf took off with both, practically tearing the napkin out from under my autographing fingers.

The Kaplans dropped me off at my building. I thanked them and then proceeded to fake the next few days, avoiding everyone and gathering my courage so that I could tell NBC and Barry that I'd be going with the Morris office. Barry took it very well. He also took the five thousand dollars I offered him to break my non-existent contract. Jerry Kaplan sighed and said he hoped I was ready.

Don called again. He and his girl were flying in the next day. There was a cover story in *Life* magazine entitled "The Riviera Rowdies." The photo on the cover was of Gary Howard, Normie Birch and the Pickering Trio. And inside there was one of Ginnie alone that looked so good that I almost ate the page. In the text was a passing reference to the fact that "Miss Maitland and Mr. Pickering, long an item, are to be married in the spring."

I called Pat Jarvas but she was no longer at that number. I called a spade a spade, consumed half a fifth of Scotch and fell asleep on Ginnie's bed. I didn't dream. I didn't dare.

chapter twenty-two

ginnie

1952

Again, I bought enough clothes to get by on, to go alongside the only garment I had left beyond the stuff on my back—the Gypsy Robe. Still, I just couldn't get comfortable living with Don and Candy. They were wonderful, truly, but there were so many memories of Ben ghosting about the apartment that, even when I was alone, I wasn't alone. Then there was Maggie in the closet. Often I thought of slashing that portrait of her, or burning it, and, in so doing, ridding myself of the Curse of the Maitlands. But I never had the couarge to do it, fearing that it would be interpreted as an act of matricide and that the heavens would open and the hand of God would reach down and flick me off the earth.

Don had no information for me as to how Ben felt about our breaking up. Evidently Ben had simply told him that it hadn't worked out and that it was better left undiscussed. Needless to say, I didn't care to have them think I was carrying any kind of torch for Ben, so we all forgot about it like the third chorus of "Just One of Those Things." I was being very adult about it, which was fine with Don as he didn't care to take sides. But Candy, being a girl—and a sensitive one—knew there was more to it. But I never let her in and, finally, she stopped trying.

Candy had been a model in Los Angeles but without

much success. About thirty, she had those great facial bones, and her body was as angular as a maze. But it just hadn't been enough and she never got to be top-flight. Also—oddly—she was quite Catholic and couldn't get herself to do the things that many girls had to do to become successful in sunny California. How she could live with Don in an unmarried state and still toot to church on Sunday was, of course, none of my business. But I think it was all made easier for her because she and Don were planning on getting married as soon as things properly broke open for him. In the meantime, they had no choice but to stretch the scriptures a little.

Don had returned to New York in hopes of breaking into TV as a bona fide director of dramas. New York was where television was, and, though Don knew it all had to move west eventually, he also knew that the best way for him to make it in the West was to make it in the East first.

Ben had lived with Don and Candy for only a brief period before he himself went west. That way they all got a chance to get to know each other—again for Ben and Don. Barry Nadler became Don's agent. Some guy, that Barry. If you were breathing he'd sign you. I, of course, never mentioned his involvement in the breaking up of me and Ben. I simply figured it was habitual and that he couldn't help it. Still, I'd keep an eye on him in case he tried to pull something on Don. Somehow I felt he wouldn't.

Meantime Candy was able to pick up some jobs modeling lingerie because none of the really successful models would be caught dead in a girdle or bra ad. Stewardesses and such dropped in on us but none of them were old-timers, just a whole new generation of kids whom Don and Candy felt obliged to put up whenever they stumbled in.

Barry handled my deal with *The Stan Arlen Show*. It was a fair deal. Barry was negotiating from strength because Stan Arlen really wanted me.

The Pickering Trio immediately fell on hard times. Richie tried to replace me and, according to Barry, actually found a girl. But the whole routine was wearing thin and playing out. And with the original kooky blonde now a regular on *The Stan Arlen Show*, Richie never had a chance of climbing out of the pit. I think, too, that dance acts had just about had it. Just like the nightclub business, they had slowly gotten pummeled into oblivion by TV.

I felt sorry for Richie, I really did. As angry as I had a right to be with him for deliberately keeping Ben and me apart, I understood him all the same. He was just another shipwreck victim trying to hang on, just another gypsy playing his tambourine, hoping that someone might see him and give him a dollar for his dancing. Eventually he just kind of faded from the scene, choreographing a few flop shows, directing a couple industrial shows, and generally falling off the world.

So there I was, on network television. And a helluva show it was. I would have to vote for Stan Arlen as the quickest mind on earth. He was so fast that sometimes I couldn't believe he was unrehearsed. The retorts and rejoinders came out of him with such velocity that you had to wonder if the man was human. He never paused to think. He never reached for words or asked to have something repeated so that he'd have time to frame his ad libs. He just fired them off almost before whoever was talking had finished, and the results were nearly always staggering.

What *I* did was sit in the audience every night, and

Stan would see me and recognize me and say hello to me (my name was Ginger) and invite me to come up and sit next to him and chat. I'd be wearing something very slinky but not too revealing—none of that low-cut Faye Emerson stuff—and when I got up on stage I'd do a little timestep before sitting down next to Stan. (I always did my timestep before sitting down. It was my trademark and was hokey-cute and everybody loved it.) Then we'd chat, neither Stan nor me knowing in advance just what we'd be talking about—and that was the fun of it. He'd open with whatever line came into his head and I'd try to hang in there with him. It didn't always work and, whenever I got stuck, rather than sit there with egg on my face, I'd stand up and go into my timestep. After a while it got to catching on all over. Comics on other shows, whenever they'd bomb, they'd go into my timestep. It was becoming a showbiz tradition.

It all made me pretty well known. I couldn't walk down a street without someone saying, "Hiya, Ginger." They knew me in stores and restaurants and I received mail from all over. Much of it wasn't anything you'd want to write home about, though, a lot of it just filth and propositions, and a photo or two. And always a handful of viewers wanted to know whether I was Ginger Rogers and what was my beauty secret that I could stay looking so young while Fred Astaire was getting older and older.

I still lived with Don and Candy because the pair of them kept me sane. They also kept me company because I just couldn't apply myself to serious dating. Besides, my hours were so crazy that I seemed to attract only crazy men. So, when I did go out, we went as a threesome, to some dinner spot, with me happily picking up the check because Don's money was running out and because I loved them both. Actually, it was good for *all* of us, our names getting into the columns without our even trying—such as:

> Ginnie Maitland, Stan Arlen's "Ginger," sampled the steak last night at Manny Wolfe's Chop House. With her, as usual, were TV director Don Cook and fashion model Candy Carson. A most beautiful *ménage à trois*, eh, Lucky Don?

Happily, all that publicity helped get Candy's New York career off the ground. One of the larger modeling agencies, Plaza Five, called her and signed her and pegged her price at seventy-five dollars an hour.

The publicity didn't hurt Don either as Barry Nadler parlayed Don's ricochet notoriety into an assignment at CBS. Don would direct a *Studio One* drama. My good fortune was rubbing off on my friends, which I thought was just dandy. So how come I wasn't happy?

I wasn't happy because the Good Lord never intended me to be without a fella. It didn't have to be Ben Webber —those days were over—but it did have to be someone and soon. I was pushing twenty and crowding loneliness. Right there in the middle of New York, fame and fortune in my pocket, my face and figure without peer, I was, as Barry had put it, "as lonely as an Arab in the Catskills," and I was reading more books than Clifton Fadiman would have if locked in the British Museum.

I was all sixes and sevens—as at odds with the world as I had been the day I landed at Grand Central having run away from Connecticut. And being known as the dumbest girl on television wasn't exactly helping to round out my life. So I decided to take some of that time I had on my hands and find out whether or not I could act.

I asked Barry who he knew who could help me. He knew Helga Nathan. Would she see me? Yes, but she might not notice me. With that as the only ground rule, I went to see Helga Nathan.

Her studio was just over a funeral parlor, which is why she was never noted for comedy. It was a big room, bare and poorly lit with thin overhead lighting. For a minute I thought I might be on the wrong floor. I looked around to pay my respects to the family of the deceased when I realized that the people in the room were alive, and one of them was Helga Nathan. "Selma," she said, to a mouse of a secretary, "would you bring me some tea?"

Helga Nathan was about sixty. She was formidable both in physicality and in bearing. Buxom and matriarchal, she was also queenlike and serene, sitting in a carved wooden chair that was covered with worn red velvet and hugged her like a throne. All the other chairs were wooden, the kind you see at a church function— foldable, stackable, and uncomfortable. The stage was two steps off the floor and had one bulb hanging on a thin strand of wire. The light looked like a fat spider that had fallen asleep while trying to spin an electrical cord.

Helga Nathan continually ran her hands through her hair, like rakes. She took long pauses when she spoke and fiddled with the buttons on her blouse, minutes sometimes going by before she would actually say anything, even though her mouth was moving all the while, shaping words but making no sounds. Suddenly, while she played with her buttons, her breast popped right out of her blouse, like a cuckoo out of its clock looking around as if to ask, "Hey, what time is it?" I must have been staring at it because Helga Nathan looked at me and then at it, and, stuffing it back into its housing, she gently admonished me, "It's a *tit*, darling. You have them, too, don't you?"

I nodded at the truth of it and she went on to ask me what I did to survive. I couldn't quite bring myself to tell her that I was a comedienne on a late-night talk show. I didn't have to tell her—she knew.

"Why did you do that, Virginia?"

"Well, I have to earn a living."

"Why?"

"Why?"

"Steal, darling. Burglarize. Pick pockets. Do anything you have to do to keep the bulk of your time your own."

"Oh."

"Then, once you have it, *give* it. Every moment of it. Give it to *acting*. Can you do that, child?"

"Yes."

"Devote yourself to words not of your own creation, but words so shining that to speak them is to flatter your larynx beyond all human cackle. Yes?"

"Yes."

"Here is a play. Eugene O'Neill. *Long Day's Journey into Night,* yes?"

"Yes. Thank you."

"Page eighty-eight. Mary's speech. Are you familiar with it?"

"Yes. No."

"The middle of the page. Where she says, 'It's a lie. I did want him.' "

"Yes."

"Read it violently, Virginia. Violently."

"Yes." And I read it violently, storming about the stage, suddenly as emotionally Russian as the czar and as raging as the Volga. I couldn't believe it: as she was watching me, her tit popped out again, as if to listen.

And again she was unaware of it. But I couldn't continue, not with the damned boob staring me in the face.

"Is there something wrong child? Why did you stop?"

"Well—"

"Is it my tit again?"

"Well—yes."

"But why are you watching *me*?"

"Well—"

"Very well. So my tit is out. Someone in your audience has popped her tit and is playing with it and it's very distracting. Virginia, audiences play with many things during a performance. Why else do men wear hats? When it happens what do you do?"

"Well—" I knew she wanted me to say that I would ignore the tit and go on with my reading. But that was not my instinct. I also knew that she wanted me to be honest, and that's why she was popping her tit in the first place, to see if I was up to continuing.

"Virginia, what would you do?"

"Me? What would I do?"

"Yes."

"I'd go into my timestep." And that's what I did. And Helga Nathan just loved it. And she applauded and yelled for more, and stamped her feet. So I finished with trenches and went cake-walking off into the wings while waving an imaginary hat. And I stayed there, hidden, waiting for the world to end.

"Virginia?"

I peeked out at her. "Yes, Miss Nathan?"

"Please come back."

"Yes, Miss Nathan." I walked back onstage, still holding onto the script. It was wet and warped from my body heat. Also, it was tired from my big dance because it had also been my imaginary hat.

"That was very good."

"Really?"

"Oh my, yes."

"You think I'm an actress?"

"No. I think you're a madwoman."

"But not an actress."

"No. But it's a prerequisite to being an actress. To be an actress you must first be mad."

"Oh. Then—may I study with you?"

"No. But I'd like you to teach me how to do that—what you just did."

"I don't understand."

"Syllogisms. All actors are mad. But all mad people are not actors. Some are dancers."

"No talent, huh?"

"Much worse. A sense of humor. Very destructive onstage. Quite necessary offstage, but destructive onstage. You would laugh at anything. At the lunacy of what you were doing. You would realize how absurd it was to be onstage while people were watching you, and you would laugh. You would laugh through *King Lear,* would you not?"

"I don't know, but—yes. I think it's better than leering through 'King Laugh.' " What the hell, I thought, might as well be hung for a Bob Hope as for a Henny Youngman.

She was smiling—maternally but with the smugness that comes from the knowledge of being correct. "Making people laugh is much more difficult than making them cry, don't you think?"

I stamped my foot in petulance. She was right, God damn her. "But I don't *want* to make people laugh!"

"Then why do you do it?"

"I don't *know!*"

"My darling, you do it to keep *yourself* from *crying,* which is the essence of comedy. Come back to me when you're not so sad. Right now you are too sad and you will make everyone laugh. And I teach drama. Did I offer you any tea? Oh, Selma? May we have another tea for Virginia, please? Thank you, darling."

Helga Nathan had me cold. She knew me inside out. She knew, just as I had always known, that whenever I was funny it was because I was sad. As funny as I was as Ginger on *The Stan Arlen Show*, that's how sad I was as Ginnie in The Ginnie Maitland Show. Egads, Yorick—and I thought I knew her well.

I went back to the apartment totally devastated. Yet, when I went on *The Stan Arlen Show* that night, I was the funniest I'd ever been. Somewhere along the way I had turned into Pagliacci, only prettier, better paid, and with better legs. But I couldn't sing, was not allowed to act, and was unable to cry at the end of my aria; so the applause was hollow and the fulfillment lean, and handsome tenors never wanted to sing with me.

Don was in rehearsal at CBS on his first show, and I could tell from his attitude at dinner every night that he was in total command of it all. Candy could see it, too, and the pair of them were so happily confident that it often made me ill. Also, they then had money coming in and no longer had to depend on my generosity for food and expenses. They started going out on their own, asking me along, of course, but I preferred to stay home and be miserable—and then go on as Ginger and be hilarious and break up America—and then come home and cry. A-ha-ha-ha-ha (that's Pagliacci).

Don's show was on a Monday night, the usual *Studio One* time, and it was quite good. The script had been good from the outset and Don's direction only made it better. CBS was pleased, and Westinghouse, the sponsor, just loved it. They all came at Don with offers of more. He was one of the bright young directors. He had earned it and he enjoyed it.

Don would have loved to have done a Ben Webber script, but Ben Webber was in Hollywood—doing what, we really didn't know. He had been big in New York, a vital and highly touted young writer. But out there, in California, he ran the risk of being just another body in the pool. Barry defended Ben, saying that he did what he had to do. Also, it seems that Ben had given Barry five thousand dollars to get out of a contract that never existed in the first place, at least not on paper. The truth was, none of us could knock Ben, least of all myself, who, though duped by Richie, should still have known better and might have granted the poor sinner an audience before consigning him' to Purgatory. It might have changed both our lives had I done that. No, it *would* have.

Arnie Felsen came around a lot, his script under his arm. He had worked it and reworked it into about ten different versions. And every time he came in he looked like he was delivering the Sunday *Times*. He asked Don to look at it and Don, as busy as he was, did take time out to work with Arnie on it.

Singly, I continued my duality, sad by day, locking myself away from my adoring public, then appearing on the tube at night, five nights a week, to help make the nation a better place to laugh in. Often, though, upon getting home at two or three in the morning, I'd upchuck out of sheer misery, telling Candy that it was the flu or athlete's foot or false pregnancy. But she knew otherwise.

Then, one day, when I was deep into my daily noontime despair, I got a phone call from Johnny Farrar. Chicago Johnny Farrar, calling from his suite at the Delmonico. He was in town, on his way to Paris, and had gotten my number from Barry who had happily broken my edict of giving my number to no one. It was Saturday; could we have dinner that night? "Shit, yes!" I thought, though what I said was, "Johnny who?"

He picked me up at eight and was as beautiful as I had remembered him. And courteous and thoughtful, and as fly-by-night as a bat. He was leaving at midnight, Paris or bust, and timidly he asked me if I'd consider going with him. If so, he'd see to it that I'd be back in New York in time for Monday night's show. Also, as promised, he was divorced.

We had dinner. His car picked us up at the restaurant, and we drove directly to Idlewild. We flew first class to Paris and checked in at the Ritz, which is where he always stayed when in Paris. I had no idea what time it was, or the day, or the year, or the eon. Paris was a tonic and Johnny Farrar the somalier who poured it. Nor did I have any clothes, only what I wore to dinner in the previous century. It was my usual trick—running off with the parade and never looking back. I was a gypsy, heart and soul, tambourine and golden earrings.

We made love on silk sheets, madly yet gently (yes, it's possible) and we did it a number of times, with time out for dinners and for waltzes along the Champs-Elysées. And I stocked up on fashions in Parisian shoppes that Johnny had somehow gotten to open even though it was Sunday.

And I was on the Monday plane back to New York, in time to do the show and feeling so marvelous that I just wasn't all that funny. But no one was really funny on Mondays so nobody noticed or cared.

I did a week of shows, getting unfunnier each time. And, following Friday night's show, I was back on the Paris express. Johnny lived regally, money at every turn, electronics—whatever that was—apparently being a good thing to be plugged into. If he worked hard throughout the week, that's how hard we played on weekends, and my twentieth birthday was celebrated as if I were a dying child given one last Christmas a few months early.

I was building an entire Paris wardrobe, stashing it at the Ritz. My American wardrobe was in my apartment in New York. I had clothes on both sides of the Atlantic—so many that I could have been all of the Gabors. As a result of two such well-stocked closets, I was able to fly light, back and forth, a crazy kid in jeans and dark glasses, flying first class, you bet your ass. I looked carefully at the stewardesses, wondering if any of them had ever stayed at the apartment. But the girls were French and had such cute accents and asses that if they stayed at anyone's apartment it could only have been Howard Hughes'.

Johnny did the continent during the week but would always be in Paris for our weekends. We did the environs, the Wine District, the three-star restaurants. I tried to learn French but frankly couldn't handle it. I would do a phrase and then laugh, and the natives didn't care for it. One weekend I met him in Rome where we bought more clothes and stayed at the Hassler. Then we did Venice, then Vienna, then London, all of those wardrobes being sent back to my apartment in New York, where Don and Candy had to wonder if I was opening my own shop—"Ginnie's of Europe—y'all come."

It was crazy and endless and unreal and passionate. I knew it had to end yet refused to give the thought an ant's width in my mind. If Europe be the food of love, then play on, oh Columbus, and never leave Genoa. That Ferdinand and Isabella had sent you can only mean they were having too much fun to go themselves.

In New York Stan Arlen took me out for a drink and the conversation went something like this:

"Ginnie, you're not as funny as you used to be."

"I know."

"What's wrong?"

"I'm happy."

"I see. And when you're happy, you're not funny, right?"

"Right."

"You're only funny when you're sad."

"Right."

"Okay—you're fired. Does that make you sad?"

"Yes."

"Good. Hang onto that sadness. We've got a show to do in an hour."

"In an hour I'll be happy again."

"Wears off that fast?"

"I'm afraid so."

"You're in love."

"Yes."

"That's not funny."

"I know, but it's happy."

"Very unprofessional for a clown to be happy. Ruins your timing."

"I know. That's what Helga Nathan told me."

"*That's* funny."

"What should I do?"

"Take a couple weeks off. Go out and have yourself a terrible time and get all that happiness out of your system. Don't come back to work until you're pale, sickly, depressed—and funny. I don't care if you have to get terminally ill. All I want is a few laughs."

I took a two-week vacation from *The Stan Arlen Show*, and I never went back.

chapter twenty-three

ben

1953

I flew to Hollywood with lots of money already in my kick. Aside from what I still had left of my TV earnings, I had $25,000 as half payment for a novella I'd be adapting for Warner Brothers. The other $25,000 I'd be getting in various stages through rewrites and up to commencement of principal photography. Less ten percent commission to the Morris office and I would have, within eight weeks, something like $48,000 in hard cash.

I was flying out alone, all my belongings crammed into two bags and my typewriter stowed under my seat. Someone named Steiner would be meeting me at Los Angeles International Airport and I would be in his hands from then on. The flight was almost eight hours, and I passed the time with Scotch and soda and thoughts of where I'd been and where I'd be going.

From Pittsburgh to New York to Los Angeles—it had all happened relatively fast. Four years in all, including a wasted year and a half in the Army. Not bad. From selling greeting cards to writing screenplays—not bad at all. Odd jobs, pretty girls, a few knocks, a few kicks—and at twenty-four, moments away from becoming twenty-five, I was flying high. And, thanks to the Scotch, higher even than the plane.

Though I had yet to read it or even learn the title, the

novella that Warners had asked me to adapt was, as I understood it, well-plotted but rife with stick-figure characters. Since I was a playwright, it was assumed that I would know how to make those people more compelling and less static. Because of the success of my TV plays, I was considered a good dialogist. All I had to do then was to apply my so-called expertise and—voilà—it would all pull together like steel shavings to a magnet, and a movie would emerge.

I knew, however, not to be overly confident—not to be the cliché hotshot young writer with nothing but contempt for the old pros. After all, film was a medium that called for a technical comprehension as well as a sense of scene and a nose for action, and I was aware of it—even reading a few books on the subject before flying out. I felt additionally secure in the hands of Vernon Stacey who was already in LA, having left a day ahead of me to attend to other matters first.

Hollywood being the stuff of dreams, I had a few dreams of my own that I wanted to script, shoot, edit, and release—and then stand back and enjoy as the world acclaimed them to be the greatest dreams ever dreamed and *me* the greatest dreamer, and the nicest person, and the best athlete, and class president, and most popular, and best loved, and most revered, and the second coming, and the first in the hearts of his countrymen. That's how drunk I was by the time the pilot circled the Grand Canyon so that us yokels could get a look and realize how fucking insignificant we were after all.

By the time we touched down in LA, I didn't know whether or not the name of the man who was supposed to meet me was Steiner or Stoner or Steber or McGillicuddy. Fortunately, he knew my name and had me paged in the baggage section.

The sun was blazing on my bare little head, my brain trying to curl up inside my ears so as to avoid being broiled. Steiner (I never got his first name) was about forty, with the hollowed-out eyes of a skull and the frame of an elongated Ray Bolger. His hair was every which color and flew every which way as he drove the open MG over the Santa Monica Freeway.

I hadn't quite expected a limousine and a Japanese chauffeur, but neither had I foreseen being picked up by a prewar MG and a consumptive driver. Both vehicle and driver sounded to me to be tubercular, with the car a better bet to make it to the hotel than the wheezer at the wheel.

Steiner drove up and stopped at the entrance of the Hollywood Roosevelt and watched as I wrestled my bags to the street. A bellhop came to help me. He was as sickly as Steiner, but I allowed him to take my bags anyway since it seemed so important to him.

"You have to be at the studio at nine thirty in the morning," said Steiner, gunning his car or clearing his throat.

"Who do I report to?"

"Someone'll call you. Don't worry."

"Thanks for the lift, Schreiber."

"Don't mention it, Werber."

I had a room like nothing I'd ever seen before. One whole wall was a glass door that opened to the swimming pool. Since I was on ground level, I could take a swim by simply stepping through my wall. It was a grand idea except that I didn't have a bathing suit. No matter, I had a pair of Scotch-plaid BVD's—so I dove into the pool.

I got back to my room just as the phone began to ring. First it was Vern Stacey—was I all right? How was the flight? Was the room okay? Did I want to go to dinner with him? My answers were, "Yes," "Good," "Yes," and "No." And I agreed to call him from the studio the next day, to report.

The next call was from Mike Abel's office, his secretary. Just wanted to know if I had arrived safely, and was I comfortable, and they'd be expecting me the next morning at nine thirty. To which I said "Yes," "Yes," and "I'll be there." And I hung up, wondering just who the hell Mike Abel was.

The next call was from the front desk. My car would be there at eight forty-five A.M. Good. The next call was from the hotel manager because any friend of Warner Bros. was a friend of his, and I should not hesitate to call for any reason whatsoever. To prove his sincerity he sent a basket of fruit to my room, and I wondered if my masculinity was being compromised. The next call was from Joe Blyer at Warner Bros. Could I find time the next day to stop by his office for purposes of publicity? I'd try.

I loved it. I loved it all. I really did. Everything I'd ever heard about Hollywood was true. Palm trees pushed up between moving cars. Telephones never stopped ringing. You could fall out of your bed into a swimming pool. And people from New York were treated as though they knew some fantastic secret.

Still to be experienced were smog; freeway driving; canyon driving; projection rooms; script conferences; starlets; and weekends in Mexico, Palm Springs, and points south. And I wondered aloud as I plopped myself into my bed, "Where have I been all my life?"

Through the miracle of room service I had a filet mignon, a bottle of California red, and then a fine night's sleep. When I awoke it was ten thirty A.M.

I flew into the shower, then shivered upon getting out because I hadn't stayed in long enough for the hot water to come on. And I was dressed and in the lobby inside of twenty minutes.

I asked at the desk about my car. Where was my driver? The desk clerk gave me a ticket and told me to give it to the doorman. The doorman gave it to a parking attendant, and my car was brought around—a white convertible Buick with red leather upholstery.

I got behind the wheel and asked how to get out to Warner Brothers. The attendant seemed unsure. So I gave him the dollar he'd wanted since birth and he told all and I was swiftly on my way.

It was a near disaster. I got onto the freeway via a feed-in from the left that put me immediately into the speed lane. Leaning over my steering wheel and squinting at the signs, I could see that the next exit was the one I wanted. And it would be on the right. All I had to do was get over to the right within a quarter mile, six lanes, heavy traffic, average speed—seventy-five miles per hour. And everyone daring me to try.

I managed to get off and aimed myself at the studio, passing Forest Lawn Cemetery. It was a most inspired spot for a cemetery, very strategic. Conveniently located between the Hollywood Freeway and Warner Brothers Studio, thousands of people being murdered daily at both those locations.

I got to the main gate and it was eleven fifteen A.M. eastern standard time. Los Angeles time, as the guard at the gate fleefully pointed out, was eight fifteen A.M. "Don't worry," he laughed, "everybody does it."

My car sniffed out a space, and I parked, sheepishly. I had an hour and fifteen minutes to kill. I also had a watch I could kill because it had so misled me.

I sat in my white Buick and smoked six cigarettes until nine thirty came around. I wanted to make it in Hollywood, and I wanted to be a nice guy. Why did those two objectives seem so incompatible to me? And, if allowed only *one*, which would I choose? No contest. I'd choose to succeed first—after which, if I could swing it, I'd be the nice guy. Somehow I knew that doing it in reverse was bad thinking, that better writers than I would ever be had ended up invisible and on the dole, and that, conversely, poorer writers had managed to carve out cozy careers early enough so that they were able to live off their reputations and withstand the cold snaps that come to even the hottest writers.

I got bored with all the soul searching. I had worked hard, had earned my success, and should be permitted my excesses at my moment of triumph. And if I needed further proof, I had to look no further than the last twenty-four hours of my life—during which time I had been flown to LA at studio expense, and had taken the parking space allotted to Joe Mankiewicz, author and director of *All About Eve*, my all-time favorite film. So get thee behind me Modesty and Humility and Sensitivity and Charm. I was throwing in with Arrogance, Ego, Aggressiveness, and Gall—the Four Horsemen of that metropolis and the daily diet of giants while all the nice guys lived on hope. In other words, I didn't believe for one minute that I could write so much as a greeting card and that everyone at Warner Brothers would shortly know it, proving once again that braggadocio is the last bastion of the fearful.

A boy on a bike told me where Mike Abel's office was, and I went up to see him. It was nine forty-five. I was late but not late enough to volunteer an explanation.

Mike Abel had an impressive office and an impressive tan though his peeling nose was as raw as if it had been sucked on by a piranha.

"Ben! Come in! Come in! Good Christ, have we

ever been waiting for *you*! Nancy, see if Mr. Webber
would like some coffee."

"No, thanks," I said. "I'm fine."

"Sit down! Sit down!" Mike Abel said everything
twice. It made it sound as though there were an echo in
the room.

"Thanks. Thanks," I said, sitting down and wondering if I was going to behave or not.

He tossed a small book at me. "That's the book. That
is the book!"

I looked at it. It was very thin. A little over two
hundred pages. The title was *Another Chance at Jenny.*
"Nice title," I said, the big title expert.

"I think so too. We all do. But what it lacks is the old
Ben Webber touch. The characters have to jump out.
They have to sing!"

"Ah—it's a musical."

He laughed. Then he got grimly serious. "Ben, if we
do it right as a drama, there's no reason it can't be a
musical four years later. No reason at all. Look at *Anna
and the King of Siam.* It was a book first. Then a
straight drama—Irene Dunne and Rex Harrison. Then
a musical on Broadway—Yul Brynner and Gertrude
Lawrence."

I was aware of someone behind me and I turned. It
was Big Al Epstein. I jumped up and hugged him—not
easy because he was heavier than ever.

Mike Abel kept talking. "Al is the reason you're
here, Ben. He's your biggest booster. The biggest. What
the hell do we know from television out here? To us it's
minor league. Still, it's also where all the majors should
have farm teams. Thanks to Al, we're bringing you up,
Ben. Some of our people don't think you're ready—but
I do. I do."

"Thanks. Thanks." I felt Big Al wince when I made my double thanks.

But Mike Abel could not be stopped. "I want you to read the book, Ben. Won't take more than a couple hours. Read it, make notes—and we'll discuss. There's an office for you. A phone, a john. Go in there, take the phone off the hook, take a crap, and read the book. Then we'll talk about it over lunch."

"The crap or the book?"

"Sonofabitch, Ben, that's exactly the kind of sharp dialogue we need. Exactly. Al, show him his office. Pick me up at one. Nancy'll get us a table in the exec dining room."

Big Al showed me to my office. When we were both inside, he closed the door and quietly read me out. "They don't know it themselves, Ben, but out here nobody has a sense of humor. You keep doing that and you'll be on a plane back to New York in no time. Not only that, but the plane'll be shot down before it reaches Nevada. So watch that shit."

"Yeah. I guess I'd better."

"I mean it. This isn't the Screen Publicists Guild. My ass is riding on this film, and I've got a pretty big ass. I got Warners to buy it and Mike to make it. And I got them all to buy you."

"Vern Stacey had nothing to do with it?"

"Vern Stacey, my butt. We didn't know who your agent was so we took a shot and called the Morris office in New York. We got Stacey. He said he was your agent. Isn't he?"

"He is now."

"See how it works, Ben? See?"

"I think so."

"But it's okay. Stacey got you a good deal. Fifty

grand. A little more than you were making in the mail-room, eh?"

"Al? You ever see any of my plays?"

"No. But Laura has. All of them. She loved them."

"And on the strength of your wife's opinion you picked me?"

"She's never wrong."

"You're crazy, you know that?"

"Everyone's crazy. There's three hundred guys out here who can adapt that book. But the fucking studios are always yelling for new writers. So? You're a new writer, aren't you? Ben, I have to tell you something. If I could've gotten this picture made with a seasoned pro, I'd have done it. Who needs the risk? I mean—you're a risk. You've never done a movie in your life. But, no, the studio's on a new talent kick. Laura suggested you. It wasn't my idea. I'd never have thought of it."

"Well—you're honest."

"So you be honest with me and turn out to be a great writer. Because if you do, I can live off my discovery of you for five more pictures. Maybe by then Laura'll discover William Inge."

"I'm parked in Joe Mankiewicz's spot."

"Park behind his typewriter and I'll feel better."

"Why don't you get *him*?"

"Because he's creating the world this week, and Sunday he's resting. Listen, Ben, do me a large favor—stay in here and read the book. It's really good and it'll make a helluva film. What I'm trying to say is, try very hard to like it. Because, even if you don't you've got to make a screenplay out of it. Otherwise, you have to give the money back, and I'm off the first picture I've ever been on."

"I got it."

"See you for lunch."

"Right."

I read the book and it was good. As I had expected, some of the characters were standing around, calling on deaf heaven to help them when it was they themselves who ought to have been doing the work. But I could fix that. I knew what to do and how to do it, and all of it would be relatively easy.

We had lunch, during which Mike Abel did all the talking—so he never got to eat. They took his plate away, untouched, and he thanked the waitress twice because it was so delicious. It was amazing that the man was so heavy—almost as heavy as Big Al. Sitting between them, even though I had space on each side of me, was like being crushed between a streetcar and a steamroller.

We agreed on a time schedule. I would deliver the first draft in six weeks. I could have done it in three but was afraid to tell them, thinking that they might think that I was sloughing it off. We agreed on the major points that the screenplay would have to embrace. The rest of it—the doing of it—would be solely up to me.

Before leaving the studio I dropped in on Joe Blyer, the publicity guy. We talked briefly and I filled out questionnaires and allowed them to put into my biography that I had been "—a middleweight contender prior to turning his fists to the typewriter." It sounded good even to me, and for five minutes of my drive back to the hotel, I actually believed it, losing to Ray Robinson on a TKO at Barham Boulevard.

I had dinner with Vern Stacey and another man, Jack Rush. And I was informed that Rush would be handling my career as Stacey had to return to New York, his home base. I was a bit miffed and acted the part of the bruised young writer, but that passed quickly because I knew that it didn't matter who handled me as long as I delivered.

I spent the next day with Jack Rush, buying me a red Porsche and checking out the Hollywood Hills for digs. Living in "the Valley" would be out of the question, too "plebeian." That was Jack's word, not mine.

Jack Rush was alright, a nice guy if a touch nebulous. Chunky and condescending, he knew enough people to serve his clients well, if not flawlessly. He had set up appointments with real estate brokers well ahead of time, so as not to steal from my working time. He was efficient, pleasant, erudite, and decent. But he had the smell of fear about him, forever wiping the palms of his sweaty hands on his pants—especially before shaking hands. I hoped to outgrow him. Otherwise, I'd have to wear gloves.

We found a house. On Outpost Drive, near Mulholland—Mulholland being the road that ran practically the entire crest of some mountain that separated Hollywood from the San Fernando Valley. The house was redwood and glass and self-consciously Californian, which is why I liked it—because so was I. It was open and had lots of crawling greenery hugging it to the steep hill. Built and formerly owned by some producer who never quite busted through, its present occupant was only renting and was required to move out as soon as anyone came by to pick up the mortgage. It looked good. Thirty thousand as is, furnishings included. Four grand down and the place was mine. No pool, but you can't have everything.

Jack thought it would be a good move—easy to unload if I got big, easy to hang in with if success proved a sluggard. I signed some papers, and the Morris office handled everything else. I must say, they were great. I lost no time in moving in and getting to work.

I did my shopping in the Valley because, what the hell, it was cheaper and just as easy for me to get to as was Hollywood. I loaded my freezer with enough steak for a year, stocked up on beer and wine, bought reams of paper, dozens of typewriter ribbons—and directed all of my energies at *Another Chance at Jenny*.

It was a lonely existence, but I wanted it that way. Also, I was used to it. You want to be a writer, you'd better like your own company, otherwise nothing gets done. Big Al and Fat Mike called on occasion and were always glad to find me in, working on their project. They reminded me of Jerry Kaplan and Frank Brokaw calling in from Long Island to make sure that I was still shackled to my typewriter. Jack Rush dutifully called from time to time, spurring me on with tales of how other producers were lining up for my services, and the sooner I finished the Warners job, the sooner I could take on the rest of the world.

But I knew not to rush. My first film assignment was important and my first draft crucial. I wanted my two fat boys to like it. I wanted the word to get around that I was good. To accomplish all those ends, I became as devoted to my typewriter as I would have been to a beautiful mistress. I seldom bothered with the time of day. I shopped only when the fridge and the freezer told me to. I took my laundry out only when the hamper overflowed. I slept no more than two or three hours at a time—but I did that two and three times a day.

But the script was coming. It was really coming—all the characters taking form and dimension, lining up on my pages to do as they were told. It would be good.

One evening I received my first visitor: an Irish setter, his wagging tail almost too big for my house. His name was Redwood, so his license indicated. And as I patted his head, his owner appeared before me—not the beautiful girl I would have written for that specific situation.

Fred Horner was a fifty-year-old drunk, plain and simple, big and soft. None of the words he spoke had any consonants. And when he first spoke I suspected that maybe the dog was a ventriloquist, and a lousy one. He regaled me with nonsense and hospitality, advising me that one wrong step and I'd be on his roof, as his house was around the curve and just below mine. He sold motorcycles and drank gin; the immediate atmosphere about him smelling like a mixture of both. He sat down, throwing his shoe across the terrace so that Redwood could fetch it back. It was Redwood's big trick. Fred Horner looked at my typewriter and asked the brilliant question: "Writin' somethin'?"

"My memoirs."

"You ain't old enough."

"I will be by the time I finish."

"I'm in cycles."

"Listen—I've got a lot of work to do."

"Don' let me stop you."

"I won't." And I led him to the street. He threw his shoe a mile and Redwood disappeared after it. Then, limping, Fred Horner walked away from me with a wave and a burp. I had a neighbor. I had better put up a fence. Electrified.

Big Al invited me to dinner. He had a nice Tudor house in the poor section of Beverly Hills, southeast of the Beverly Wilshire Hotel. Two kids came with the house. One of them was a boy. The other was up for grabs. It was nice seeing Laura, and I thanked her for haying put in a good word for me. She said, "You're welcome." It was some enchanted evening.

I drove home properly depressed. I could see right away that Big Al had outgrown his spouse. Old adage: "Marry in haste; repent in Beverly Hills."

I funneled all of my emotion into my script. What I had left was hardly worth taking out of the house, especially in a Porsche. I had the highs and lows of a turtle. I wasn't eating, could not abide the phone—and if that idiot dog came around once more, I'd piss on it, just as it had been pissing on the artificial plants in my ersatz garden.

Redwood came around again, fifth time, and I threw a large rock at him, hoping to miss him but to scare him. It hit him and he was not seen on my doorstep again for a week.

"You shouldn't do that." It was Fred Horner's wife.

"He comes around again and I'll tie a tourniquet on his pecker."

"He's only a dog."

"I meant your husband. You are Mrs. Horner, yes?"

"Yes." Harriet Horner was an ex-Follies tomato in a pink satin slack suit who looked as though she had remained on stage and rotted there following the final performance of *George White's Scandals of 1931*. She was about fifty trying to look twenty—so she looked ninety. She was tall and bulging, like a pinched balloon. She had carrot hair, eyelashes so long that when it rained, her nose never got wet. And she had ruby lips so greasy that she had to give up smoking, as the cigarette would keep slipping out and into her cleavage, where it did nothing to brighten her day. All of her stood on plastic wedgies so high that her nose had to bleed the moment she climbed up onto them. "I came to fetch Redwood." Her voice was an amalgam of Betty

Boop and Zasu Pitts, and she seemed the ideal wife for her booze-bellied husband. She didn't walk—she wobbled and swayed. It was supposed to be sexy, but to me she looked like a ride at an amusement park.

As my concentration was already broken, and, as I hadn't been to a circus in years, I became uncharacteristically gracious. "What would you like to drink? I have orange juice and beer."

"That would be fine."

Maybe she was being funny but I didn't think so. In any case, it didn't matter. I just wanted to see if she'd drink it. She did. Orange juice and beer. I silently dubbed it a "schmuckdriver."

"Where's old Fred?"

"San Diego."

"He can throw his shoe that far?"

"He went on business."

"Would you like another drink, Mrs. Horner?"

"No, thanks. And my name is Harriet."

"Mine's Ben."

She looked at my typewriter. "You a writer?"

"I like to think so."

"What're you writing?"

"A suicide note."

"Ever take a break?"

"Sure. What time?"

"I got a couple errands. But I should be back at four."

"Where do I find you?"

"Doesn't matter. Your place or mine?"

"Let's make it yours. Mine's a mess."

"Six o'clock. I'd like to freshen up." She turned, took off one of her wedgies—and threw it. "Fetch, Redwood!" Redwood ran off to fetch it, and she limped away, a decaying rainbow.

I don't know why I made the appointment. I certainly wasn't panting to bang that barrage balloon. I think that after being locked away as I had been, almost a month, I was ready for any kind of diversion. It would be interesting. Like screwing some kind of sideshow act. Actually, it would be like fucking a pink couch. The idea became more fascinating as the day wore on, and I couldn't work. I had a date with Harriet Horner, wowee, gang. And before I left my wee house, I clipped some flowers from my garden to bring to Harriet, the girl of my nightmares.

I walked down the winding road whistling "Here Comes the Showboat." I knew the house because it was, indeed, directly below mine, but also because there were five motorcycles chained up out front. Redwood chained up out front, too, so apparently Harriet meant business—she didn't care to have to throw her dog a wedgie while in the middle of a sex act with a gentleman caller.

I went into the house. It was still light, but the sun was quitting, already on the Valley side of the hill. The hi-fi was playing mood music—"Music to hump Harriet by." It was a small house, not unlike mine, but done in chartreuse and mauve. It was good that the sun was setting, very wise of it.

The bedroom door was open and I saw her spread out on that baseball diamond of a bed. She was all orange and pink in her yellow nightie. And the bedspread was green and the shag rug was violet. The woman was either color-blind or whimsical. She was smoking a cigarette, and when she saw me, she coolly ground it into a nearby ashtray and shifted her weight. The bed creaked, as if it knew that it was in for a rough time.

I lay my flowers aside, indicating that they were for her, and she blinked her eyes like a geisha. She watched as I removed my clothes, kind of rocking herself from side to side, exposing a fleshy thigh, wiggling a nail-polished toe. All I could think of was the phrase: "Abandon hope all ye who enter here." But enter I did—a new low, but not bad.

If a fella closed his eyes, if he didn't look and didn't think and just went along for the ride, Harriet Hot-Hips Horner had to be the greatest game in town. She lobbed me from side to side like a kid unthinkingly playing with a ball, caroming me off thighs that were doing the carioca eighty-eight beats to the minute. Then, with lower legs working like the swatters at the base of a pinball machine, she gathered me up and slapped me in, sealing me in her great beyond with everything she had going. I bounced against the squishy tummy, pushed by the spongy ass—all of it like lifting off and then descending upon a pizza-pie trampoline. Beneath me she was an earthquake, on top of me a volcano. On the side, she was a tidal wave, and from the rear—a roaring spa. She monsooned me, typhooned me, cycloned me, and tornadoed me. And when I was nothing but a drizzle, when all the convulsions had subsided, when the universe had ceased its shaking, and when I lay there like that sole survivor, Crusoe, she patted me on the back and whispered, "Okay, kid, you can go home now. Don't step in any dog shit."

Later, lying in my own bed, feeling to see if all my ribs were still evenly distributed, I realized that everything that old drunken Fred Horner knew about horsepower he had learned from his Percheron wife. I would have at that mare again—as soon as I was well enough to leave the barn. I didn't much like myself, as a matter of fact, I barely recognized myself. I just couldn't help myself.

My first draft was ready and I dropped it off at Mike

Abel's office myself, where Big Al seized it and pressed it to his breast. He would read his copy that night—as Mike Abel would read his. If I came in early the next morning, we could all "get to work on the rewrite."

I didn't care for that remark, but said nothing. Everyone is out to justify his existence, I thought. How dare a writer turn in a shooting script first shot? It reminded me of the old days at 20th, when we saved our first ideas and brought them in last, showing them to Gruber only at the eleventh hour when he had no choice but to accept them. W. Charles Gruber, killed by an unknown black assailant named Pat Jarvas. And where was Pat Jarvas? What had become of her after leaving her job at 20th? Like Lizzie Borden she had given her victim forty whacks—only no one knew it but me. Well, I was a good repository for that knowledge. Your secret is safe with me, Sweet Patricia—but I do miss your scrawny body and your cute little animal ways.

I drove all around. Out Sunset to the beach at Santa Monica, because I had never seen it and it was supposed to be really something. It was a grey day at first, but the jocks were out on Muscle Beach all the same— pumping up their oiled bodies, building their biceps, triceps, and deltoids to garish proportions so that when the predicted earthquake came, all three hundred of those bleached blondes could hold onto California and keep it from falling into the sea while Cecil B. DeMille took all the shots he needed.

I did the Farmers Market and the Hollywood Bowl, and I went up and down the mountains—over Laurel, Coldwater, and Benedict Canyons—until even after my car was tucked into its garage, I couldn't walk a straight line without fearing I'd hit a house.

I dined alone, listening to Sinatra, eating steak, swigging beer, and feeling as mellow as a cheddar. I knew that my script was good but was fearful that they might not like it. I'd find out the next morning at ten.

I parked in the space marked "B. Webber." It was an eerie feeling since I knew my name had been painted over another name. How many times had my parking spot had its name legally changed? Who had been there before me who no longer was? T. Edison, D.W. Griffith, T. Mix, F. S. Fitzgerald, W. Faulkner? And who would come after? M. Mouse, D. Duck, H. Doody, J. Stalin?

Mike and Big Al were ebullient, both of them already there by the time I arrived. We had coffee and doughnuts and shot the breeze for a few minutes before Mike stood up and began the festivities. "Ben—it's good. Awfully good. Not that we're surprised. We knew it would be. Al and I discussed it on the phone last night and again this morning. We wanted to coordinate our reactions, so as not to confuse you when you came in."

And Big Al moved in. "We like it, Ben. Please understand that we like it. But—it's not a shooting script."

"What's wrong with it?" I asked.

And it was Mike's turn. That's the way they worked it. First one and then the other until I felt like a tennis ball. "It's a touch static, Ben. The dialogue is great, all of it, really is. But there may be too much of it. It's just a question of cutting. No big deal. No big deal at all."

"Cutting what?" I asked, directing my question at Big Al because it was his turn next.

"A lot of it," said Big Al.

"How much is a lot?" I asked of Mike.

"Most of it," he said, sighing, his disappointment finally pushing through.

"How much is most of it?" I asked of Big Al.

"All of it," he said.

And I said, "What?"

"It's in the wrong idiom," said Mike, the gloves removed and the white knuckles showing. "Those people wouldn't talk like that."

"They'd think like that," said Big Al, "but they wouldn't talk like that."

"Listen," I said, "my head's gonna unscrew. Why don't you guys drop the sister act and just one of you do the talking, okay?"

And Mike Abel chose to do the single. "They're simple people. They think well but they're basically simple. You have them sounding like they're applying for Princeton. We think you should take the edge off that and rely more on the book."

"The book was all action and no talk," I said. "Why don't you just do it as a silent movie?"

Mike was striving for patience. "Ben—we didn't buy the book because it was a great book, but because we thought it would make a great movie. We needed a writer who could fill it out with the right dialogue. The characters are farm people. They raise cabbages and shovel manure. They're not intellectuals. They're not intellectuals."

"What makes you think farmers are nincompoops?" I challenged. "Farmers talk. They say more than 'fetch the bucket, Maw—looks like Jodie Lee's gonna have another calf.' "

Big Al slumped into the most distant chair in the room, leaving the contest to Mike and me. I could almost feel all the air going out of him. Fuck him, I didn't care.

Mike was talking. "Ben, you're ignoring the camera. Sometimes the camera can say more than any dialogue.

You've written a fucking radio show! This is supposed to be a movie!"

"Movies talk. Jolson proved it."

"And where is Jolson, now?"

"Oh, beautiful." I was losing my control. I could feel it going. I would try to hang onto it, but—

"Ben. Ben. For Christ's sake, listen to what I'm saying. If I show this script to the studio, they'll pass on the whole project."

"Be specific. Where is the dialogue too much?"

"Everywhere! Jesus, ain't you listening to me?"

"It'd be hard not to."

"You wanna know where? Okay, I'll tell you where. From page one to fadeout—how's that? You've got these people talking so much they wouldn't have time to plant weeds!"

"Okay,"—because he was screaming, I tried not to— "what is it that you want me to do?"

"Take another whack at it. You've still got over two weeks. Take four. There's no rush."

"I'm not interested in making it my life's work."

"Four weeks does not a life make."

"You're not talking a rewrite. You're talking a whole new script!" My voice was rising.

"I don't want a new script. I want the old script that you never wrote."

"Well, you know what you can do—" Which is what I was bound to say from the moment I came in the door. Stupid boy. Frightened rabbit.

His voice dropped. "I can't submit this script. It'll kill the project. The only reason the studio ever went along with it was because you were going to be the writer. If you can't do it—"

"I did do it, you idiot!"

He let it go, continuing softly. "If you can't do it,

they won't even go for another writer. They'll kill it where it stands."

"I said I did do it! If you're such an asshole that—"

"None of that, kid. That I don't need."

"Yeah? Well, that's what you got. I don't believe the studio's as stupid as you make them out to be."

"I will not submit this piece of shit!" He flung it across the room. It hit the far wall like a wounded bird. "It stinks! I'd rather tell 'em you got hit by a truck a month ago and that we didn't find out about it till now!"

"Tell 'em whatever you goddamn please. This is as far as I go."

Mike Abel was almost smiling. "You don't know how right you are. If you walk—if you walk, baby—you might as well keep walking until you hit Hawaii."

"And if the natives are as stupid there as they are here, I'll keep walking until I hit Japan!"

"Okay. Okay, hotshot. There's the door. You can start now. Get your canoe and shove off. And pack a lot of limes, sweetheart, because you're gonna be out there one long fuckin' time."

"Crazy. I'll discover Australia." And I walked.

Big Al caught me as I was getting into my car. He was very direct. "I'm not going to ask you to reconsider because I know you won't—because you're the same cocksure sonofabitch I remember from your union-baiting days. All I want to tell you is that Mike Abel is going to survive, and I intend to survive *with* him. You're going to be the loser, Ben, because you insist on losing. It's your style. You've got some kind of fucking death wish, and believe me, this is the place where death wishes come true. Go on—get the hell off the lot. Take your fucking ego and your fucking Porsche and go drive off a mountain. You won't be the first guy to do it and you won't be the last. Go on. Make a hard right at Forest Lawn. I'll call ahead and tell 'em to reserve a spot for you—in the writers' section. You'll get two lines in *Variety* and *we'll* get another book."

He slammed the hood with both his hands and I kicked the car into reverse, backing it out of my parking space. I shifted into forward and hit the accelerator— stopping just short of hitting him. He didn't budge. Instead he just leered at me. "If you change your mind, let me know. We've still got some time."

If Big Al Epstein had not delivered that last line of dialogue, I just might have called him within the hour— and come back for a rediscussion. But by saying what he did, when he did—by extending that feeble invitation, by keeping that small door open, I knew that he was as unsure as I was about the whole damned calamity. And I therefore drove off, consigning him to hell— producer's section, third Cadillac from the left.

Back at my house I phoned Jack Rush and told him what had happened. He wished that I hadn't gone off so half cocked because, in so doing, I had blown my second twenty-five grand. He asked if he should call them, since they'd be sure to understand and anxious to get on with it. After all, I'd worked so hard and all that. I told him that if he called them, I'd be on the next plane to New York. And he took a moment's pause before telling me that there was something for me at MGM.

I called Harriet Horner and asked if I might drop by. She said I could, and I was in her bed within fifteen minutes. She bounced me around good, just what the doctor ordered—but my mind wasn't on it. It was only on the things that Big Al had spewed at me. If they were true, then I was in deep trouble, and by my own grand, if unconscious, design. But they weren't true because they couldn't be true. And I'd prove that to be the case with MGM.

Harriet Horner and I said good night, each of us trying hard to remember the other's name. She sent me home because old drunken Fred might be stumbling in at any minute. Lying on my patio, sipping beer and acknowledging my twenty-fifth birthday, I heard his motorcycle pull in. Redwood barked at the sight of his master. Fred Horner would have no idea that I had fucked his wife. Nor would he know that on that fine California day, I had fucked myself as well.

ginnie

1953

Johnny Farrar was not to be believed. He was handsome, intelligent, thoughtful, and loving. And he took me just about everywhere he went—and he went a lot of places—like Spain. Olé. Spain was a knockout. Under Franco and all those guys, it was stark in spots. And the people wore black and didn't know how to smile, and all the women were a hundred and five and squat and had chickens, and I never saw any children, none at all. And I never heard any laughter.

Still, for the most part, blame it on my youth, I felt like Ava Gardner. I felt crimson and orange and flamenco and gypsy—not the Broadway gypsy, but the Castillian kind—wet, parted lips and castanets and tortoise-shell coronets. I felt tempestuous and Latin and seductive. And I wanted to live in a cave, and not bathe, and let the hair grow on my legs, and read tea leaves, and roll sailors. The only reason I didn't do any of those things was that we stayed at the Palace Hotel, in Madrid, in the Velasquez Suite, and if the management didn't throw me out, Johnny would have, so I bathed, and shaved, and wore perfume, and smelled like a tourist, and saw the Prado and the bullfights, and bought luggage at Loewe's that was so "leather" that it mooed. We ate at places like the Jockey Club and Las Lanzas, and we drove out to Toledo (not Ohio) and saw all the old ruins of whatever once was there. We kept the Mercedes limousine and did Cordoba and Cadiz and the Alcazar—and Seville. Ah, Seville. A double olé for Seville.

I fell in love with Johnny Farrar in Seville, at the Hotel Alfonso XIII. I had made love to him all over Europe, but I fell in love with him in Seville, on the Costa del Sol. I'd have fallen in love with Quasimodo on the Costa del Sol. I'd have fallen in love with Hayden Shepherd. (Remember him? Pittsburgh?)

And in Marbella, at the Marbella Club Hotel where we were the only two Americans, I knew that if my life ended then and there, I would have seen enough of heaven to know my way around, if and when I ever got there. Marbella was too much. A triple olé for Marbella—two ears and a tail.

Though a minor, and with no passport or birth certificate, I still got around because Johnny was forever greasing the right palms. It was giddy. I had no identity and no responsibility. I was a balloon, confetti, tinsel. And I was never happier in my life.

We were traveling with some English business associates of Johnny's. Their women were illegally gorgeous, only I don't think any of them was married. One girl was French and the other Swiss, and they had as little to do with each other as possible. It was as though they always showed up at the same places—but in separate cars. I was prettier but they were grander. It was okay. I'd be grand, too, one day. Maybe any minute.

The Marbella Club Hotel was run by Count Rudy, some kind of Austrian prince who had lost his ass and his title somewhere along the way. A descendant of Franz Josef and a whole mess of Hapsburgs, he was a neat man—cosmopolite and cordial, and he knew every language because he had to, because people of every nationality stayed at his hotel. The Germans were always the first to the beach, either making sure to get beach chairs or rendezvousing with some U-boat. The French were always the first into the dining room, mostly because they never left it. The British, Wimbledonians, played tennis on the mosaic-tiled tennis court and said "bully" and "rather" and "shit." And the Scandinavians took thermometers down to the Mediterranean and would not go in if the water wasn't cold enough.

Inland, behind the hotel, was Monte Blanca—the "white mountain"—and Johnny and I climbed a lot of it one day, and when we stopped because we were pooped, we looked out and could see Gibraltar and North Africa and the rest of our lives.

"Ginnie—do you know how old I am?"

"Seven and a half."

"Close. I'm forty. Twice as old as you."

"You won't always be twice as old."

"No, but it'll always be twenty years."

"I won't hold it against you."

"I'll never marry you."

"Who asked you to?"

"You did. Last night."

"I did?"

"In bed."

"Don't listen to anything I say in bed. I'm not to be held responsible . . ."

"Just the same—"

"Why would I want to marry you? You're twice my age."

"This isn't *The Stan Arlen Show*. So you don't have to be funny."

"Whoops. Sorry."

"I'd like you to stay with me, travel with me—for as

long as you like. But I won't marry you. Do you know what I'm saying, Ginnie?"

"Yeah. You want me to be your mistress."

"In the terminology of the times—yes."

"Aren't I that already?"

"No."

"How do I get the job?"

"You stop working altogether. That means no more *Stan Arlen Show*. No more television or nightclubs. No more nothing."

"Okay, I've blown *The Stan Arlen Show* anyway. I've been away for almost three months. If they ever took me back, it would be a television first."

"I'm being serious, so pay attention."

"Yes, sir."

"Much of my business is in Europe. Much of my success is the result of social maneuverings—appearing in the proper places with the proper people."

"With a mistress?"

"Yes. It's all right for me to have a mistress—as long as she's beautiful and charming. But—"

"Aha!"

"She must belong solely to me. Not to Stan Arlen or Richie Pickering. And she must have style. She must have—grandeur."

"Shit, I think I've got a whole lot of grandeur."

"I think you have, too. A little whacky, but grandeur just the same, of a type."

"Then screw this mistress crap—let's get married."

"I am married."

"You said you were divorced."

"I had to. When I saw you in Chicago, I told you I'd be getting a divorce. I knew that if I called you this time in New York, you'd have nothing to do with me if I told you it hadn't come through."

"You lied. The world is filled with liars. Hot damn."

"Ginnie—if that bothers you, you've got to get out of here. I'm not big on white slavery or deception. I'm still married. Here's your chance to run."

"You're making it impossible for me to run, and you know it, you sonofabitch!"

"Ginnie, she made it impossible for me. I can't go into it. If you were a lawyer you'd still have trouble understanding. I could have let you go on thinking I was divorced. But, damn it, I love you too much to do that to you."

"Oh, my, here's a howdy-do, isn't it?"

"Don't make any decisions just now. Think about it. We'll talk about it again in a couple of days. You're a beautiful woman and—"

"Oh, sure."

"And that's part of it—the fact that you don't know it."

"Then keep telling me."

"I'm telling you that you can do just about anything in life that you want to. And I'm saying, if you don't want to stay with me, I'll help you. I'll buy you *The Stan Arlen Show*."

"Yeah? Buy me NBC."

"I've got to go back to New York. Just a few days. You'll go with me. And when I leave, I want you to stay there, at my suite in the Delmonico, and think about everything I've told you."

"I've got an apartment—with my friends."

"No. You have to stay at my place."

"So the world'll see you're keeping me?"

"And you can't do any shows. You can't work. You're on call, okay? That's the way it has to be."

"Why?"

"Because that's the way I want it."

"Do I have to sleep with friends of yours?"

"What? No. Where'd you get that idea?"

"I don't know. It just seemed like the next thing you were going to say."

"You don't have to sleep with any friends of mine. But neither can you sleep with any of yours."

"How would you know?"

"*You'd* know—so *I'd* know."

"Boy. All of a sudden we're so fucking European. Is that grandeur or is that grandeur?"

"I'm sorry, but that's the way it has to be. If you want to end it—"

"It's unfair of you to keep saying that. So just cut it out. Jesus, it's like you give me a toy and then you take it back."

"Come on. Let's go back to the club. It's getting dark."

"When are we going back to New York?"

"Tomorrow."

"And how long do we stay?"

"I stay maybe three days. You stay till I send for you."

"Do I get chained to the radiator?"

"Yes."

Johnny Farrar did something to me that no man I ever knew could do. He made me feel like a little girl. I don't think he meant to—he just brought it out in me. I mean, I was always a little girl but had learned how to fool people into thinking I wasn't. You fool people with things like tits. Little girls have no tits. You fool them with knowing how to make love. And "knowing how" doesn't mean skill—it mostly means showing up, and saying "oooooh," and smoking a cigarette while not answering the phone.

But Johnny Farrar somehow seemed to see right

through all that. And I wouldn't have been surprised if, in the middle of the night, if the lights suddenly went on—I wouldn't have been a bit surprised to discover that it was a teddy bear I was hugging and a lollipop I was licking.

Anyway, I did what Johnny told me to because I always did what Johnny told me to. Because, if I didn't, I'd get no allowance, and wouldn't be permitted to use the phone or stay up late or wear a training bra, so—

I was back in New York—three days with Johnny. Then he was off somewhere he couldn't take me because it was Alaska and he was hunting elk with the president of General Motors, or Africa where he and the head of the New York Stock Exchange were on safari, or, would you believe it, Russia because the US government had sent him there on something so hush-hush that not even Eisenhower knew what it was about.

When Johnny left for Moscow, he left me with credit cards, two bank accounts, and enough cash to bail out India. I was alone—but I could have bought New York.

During my three days with Johnny, I didn't call Don or Candy because I figured there'd be plenty of times when I'd be doing that after Johnny had taken off. I did, however, call the Stan Arlen office to tender my apologies for never having given them official notice. But there was a new girl answering the phone and she didn't even know who I was. Sic transit Ginnie.

Another thing I did was change my hairstyle, figuring maybe that would make me feel more grown-up the next time I was with Johnny. I didn't mess with the color but I did get rid of the ponytail, swapping it for something that came all the way around from one side and ended up on the other. It looked very Grecian. I thought it was definitely Grecian. It also looked like an earmuff because it covered my right ear completely. It

was also a pain in the ass because it required so much
time and attention. Every other day I had to spend an
hour at the hairdresser's, Mr. Calvin. He never talked
to me—just to my hair. Very weird. Took me an hour
every time I left his salon to convince myself there
wasn't a midget in my hair, under my earmuff, whispering little nothings.

On the fourth day, my first without Johnny, I called
Candy and she yelled at me for not writing and then
invited me to dinner. Spaghetti Ypsilanti or something,
her specialty, which she was trying for the first time,
and she needed, as she so chauvinistically put it, a
"guinea" pig.

It was good to see Don and Candy again. They were
so in love. Better than that—they had gotten married.
That Candy was older by a couple years didn't matter
because I never knew two people more suited to one
another. Both of them were making real good money
and Don's reputation as a TV director was peerless. He
had resisted a few feelers from Hollywood because he
wanted to make certain he was ready. Very mature of
him and, on the surface, much smarter than what Ben
had done.

No, they hadn't heard anything either about Ben or
from him. Hollywood seemed to have swallowed him
up, though Barry had heard that Ben was acting somewhat the prima donna and just wasn't doing as well as
all his talent indicated he should be doing. Still, it was
early in the game and none of us had any doubts that
Ben would rise to the top.

Candy loved my hair and immediately called Mr.
Calvin for a consultation so that he might conjure up
something equally as wild for her. Don thought we were
both being dopey, that sophisticated, aristocratic women
did not need all that overstatement. We told him to

mind his own fucking business and dove into the spaghetti.

They were careful in what they said about me and Johnny, but I could tell that they didn't exactly approve. I wouldn't have expected them to. I didn't approve of it either. I just loved Johnny and he was good to me and none of it was frantic. Somewhere in the back of my head I somehow knew that we would one day be married. It was just a matter of his wife coming to terms with life. It was just a matter of time, and time was something I had plenty of. I was twenty and unemployed. I could wait it all out without getting hysterical about giving up the best years of my life. Candy was at least ten years my senior and it had worked out for her. I didn't want to think too much about the immorality of it all. The band was playing "Blue Skies." Who was I to sing "Stormy Weather"?

Arnie Felsen came over and I gave him a big hug. He thought I looked wickedly wonderful—a poor choice of words but heartfelt nonetheless. Oh—he came over with his fiancée, Marilyn, a very nice girl, but that's about all I could say about her that was positive. She was intellectual and a little creepy in that she followed him around like his shadow, agreeing with him, flattering him. You'd have thought Arnie had just come into a huge inheritance the way she glommed onto him. It was nice for Arnie, though. He did enjoy it. There was a time when I thought he never had a shadow—all of a sudden he had two.

There was a lot of talk about his play. I gathered that he and Don had done a lot of work on it and that some producer was really hot to get it on. I was very impressed with Don. He had talent and patience and seemed to have a good fix on where he was going. I guess what I'm trying to say is I was jealous of him and

Candy. I didn't love Don. I didn't want to switch places with Candy. It was just that they were doing things together—fun things, creative things, things that were growing and taking shape. Whereas I, for all the clothes and money at my disposal, I was a hanger-on—Johnny Farrar's lady (I couldn't think "mistress"), a glorified camp follower, one more company in his conglomerate. Still, as I said, there was no rush, no need to panic at the thought that the warm wax was hardening and that's what I'd always be. It was all there to be experienced and enjoyed. If it turned sour, I'd know it and I'd get out. By the same token, if it stayed sweet and got sweeter, we'd be married and get on with the rest of the good life.

The nice evening over, we loaded all my clothes into a cab like the Salvation Army leaving the Rockefeller estate. It took two Delmonico bellhops to bring it up to my suite. It was some suite. Five rooms and two bathrooms. But Johnny wasn't there so it was like living alone in Shangri-la.

I tried to walk around Manhattan without buying anything and that took some doing. I would have preferred the old ponytail and sneakers and jeans, but it would have been bad for my image so I went around all gussied up and people looked at me because I sure as hell stopped traffic. Only no one knew who I was, like in the old days on *The Stan Arlen Show*—and I missed that. That was another thing that was going to take time.

One day I ran out of cigarettes and ducked into a little store on Lexington Avenue that had everything a drugstore had except a pharmacist. The man behind the counter—gong—he struck a familiar chord. Gong. Bald to the top of his head, after which all that red hair made him look like a lion.

"Sy?"

"Yes. Can I help you?"

"You don't remember me."

"Blondie?"

"You *do* remember me."

Sy Fein came out from behind the counter and gave me one of his patented rib-splitting hugs, pulling my Guccied feet right off the floor. "Blondie! Oy, is this a Blondie!" He released me and stepped back to size me up. "So let me look. Woo-ee, some business! What happened to you?"

"What do you mean what happened?"

"What happened to your ear?"

"What?"

"It's all covered. A dog bit you?"

"Sy! It's the style!"

"Some style. What's in it—a telephone call?"

"Oh, Sy—it's so great to see you! You look so good!"

"I *am* good. How do you like my shop? What do you need?" Hershey bars? Lipstick? Tampons? You name it—I got it."

"It's marvelous."

"I'm here almost eight months. It's number fourteen on my Hit Parade. What number was I up to when you last laid eyes on me?"

"I think it was seven."

"Seven. Hmmmm. Well, there's a lot of water over the bridge since seven. Also—two bankruptcies."

"But you're all right?"

"Am I all right? In less than ninety-nine years this place will be all mine. Free and clear. Like the Suez Canal. But look at you. Who'd you marry—the Sultan of Swat?"

"I'm not married."

"Oh. So you struck oil. Some duds you're wearing. Hardly a *shmatta* from Klein's."

"It's a long story."

"It usually is."

"Don't sound so disapproving."

"Me? Disapproving? A girl I used to know from torn sneakers comes in wearing a golden earmuff—why should I disapprove? It's none of my business. You a call girl? Don't answer."

"Sy, I'm not a call girl."

"I only ask because it's some neighborhood for call girls. This is the Call Girl Belt. You could make a fortune. You could also get syphilis if you go in for that sort of thing. You can get a *lot* of things but married."

"I'm not a call girl."

"Your word against mine."

"Sy—shut up. You're being silly. How's Iri?"

"Who knows? I haven't seen him since last week. For all I know he's bombing Pearl Harbor again."

"Is he all right?"

"I should be so all right. He's got another restaurant. Just Japanese."

"It's not kosher?"

"What he does with his books is his own business. All I know is that he's making money hand over glove. It's on the West Side—in the twenties. He cooks right out in front of the customers. Wears a white suit and yelps when he chops a shrimp's head off. It's some show. If he knew I saw you, he'd send his best. He's funny that way. You sure I can't give you a little trinket? A ballpoint? A flashlight? How'd you like a deck of cards?"

"I really came in for some cigarettes."

"Name it, I got it."

"Rothman's?"

"Rothman's? What is that—a Jewish cigarette? When did that happen?"

"Oh, Sy—it's an English cigarette."

"Pip-pip—an English cigarette. Well, I'm fresh out. You're such a big shot you can't smoke Lucky Strike?"

"I'd *love* a pack of Lucky Strike."

"So what's wrong with Old Gold? You're wearing it—why can't you smoke it?"

"Sy—I'll smoke whatever you say."

"Here. Lucky Strike. And I don't want to hear anymore about it. How come you're not on *The Stan Arlen Show* anymore? Can't hold a job, Miss Ritzy Rothman?"

"Sy—will you take me to dinner?"

"Yes. But we'll rule out Maxim's, okay?"

"Anywhere you say."

"Charmed. I'll be down to get you in a taxi, honey. But first I'll clear it with my wife as she's a killer at heart."

"I live in the Delmonico."

"Of course, you do. Where should you live—in the Hotel Dixie?"

"Penthouse B."

"I didn't think it would be behind the boiler."

"Sy, cut it out."

"Better be ready 'bout half past eight."

"I'll be ready."

"And dress like a human being because all I got is a sport jacket from 1938."

"I'll be expecting you."

"Hey, Blondie?"

"Yes?"

"You have made my whole day. Keep the cigarettes."

"Oh—I didn't pay you!"

"It's all right. I just wanted you to know you didn't

slip a fast one over on me. Also—it's a thrill to see you again and looking like you do. I only hope it's on the up-and-up."

"I'll tell you all about it."

"And I'll tell you mine."

I knew Sy wouldn't let me pay for the dinner so I let him pick the restaurant. He picked a very quiet place way over on Second Avenue in the Fifties—Sendetti's. And I brought him as up to date on my life as I could without going into too many details because I didn't think he was ready for it. But he was very good at filling in the blank spaces, and though he didn't get heavily paternal, he did kind of intimate that Johnny Farrar was "no one you should hang your hat on."

I invited him up to my suite for a nightcap but he was afraid that people might talk, that he had a clientele that frequented the Delmonico and he didn't want to be seen with a blonde chippie because "even the Wohls have ears."

I stopped by Sy's place almost every day. And every day it was the same. "Have a bubble gum." "Do you need an aspirin?" "What do you hear from the playboy of the western world?" If Johnny and I ever got married, I'd want Sy Fein to give me away. And I can hear him now—"Give you away? Maybe I'd give a forty percent discount, but *away*? Never!"

Johnny called from Lisbon. He'd be in New York the next evening. It had been a successful trip, and they'd worked something out with the Russians—he and IBM. We'd celebrate when he got in. Maybe the Russian Tea Room and I laughed long distance.

The night he called I invited Don and Candy up to my suite for dinner and had it all sent up via room service. Over coffee they gave me the news. The producer had committed himself to Arnie's play and Don would direct. The producer was Daniel Van Sumner, an old pro and very active of late, having brought in three new plays over the last two seasons. One of them, *The Widow's Mattress*, was a smash and still running or, as Arnie put it, "still layin' 'em in the aisles."

Arnie came up later, followed a step behind by his Marilyn. So we were five in all when Johnny walked in. The louse had called from Idlewild Airport, already in from Lisbon. Though he was very civil, it was obvious to all that he wasn't delirious about seeing four strangers eating up a storm in his mistress's suite. Needless to say, they all hustled out as quickly as they could without looking even ruder than Johnny.

Johnny was short with me as he unpacked. "I thought we had an understanding?"

"Johnny, they're my friends."

"They're not *my* friends."

"We were celebrating. Arnie's play is being produced and—"

"And you know how I feel about show business."

"I'm not show biz, *they* are."

"I don't want to see them here again. Is that understood?"

"It is understood but I don't understand."

"I'm seeing the vice-consul of the Russian embassy tomorrow morning—early. So I don't want to discuss it now. Right now all I want to do is take a shower and go to sleep."

"Does that mean I sleep alone tonight? In the Tower of London? Or how about Devil's Island? I hear it's very nice this time of year."

He turned, smiled, and pulled me to him. "You can get away with just about anything with me, can't you?"

"Can I? I hadn't noticed."

"All I ask is that you show me a little mercy."

"Why should I? You're unreasonable, ridiculous, stupid, and prejudiced."

"Ginnie—"

"And you didn't even notice my hair. We might just as well be married."

"I did notice but I thought it was an accident."

"What?"

"It's beautiful."

"It ought to be. You paid enough for it."

"Good. What else is money for?" He headed for the shower, and from inside the bathroom, he continued to speak to me. "Met some interesting people in Lisbon on the way back. Thought you might enjoy meeting them."

"Who?"

"The Barringers. He's in oil. Up to his ass in it."

"Who did you say?"

"Kevin and Maggie Barringer. You'll love 'em."

chapter twenty-five

ben

1953

They were as dense at MGM as they had been at Warners, and I marveled at how those companies could remain in business and still turn a profit. I assumed that
at Columbia, Paramount, Universal, and United Artists—and good old 20th Century-Fox—it was no different. Lunatics and con men were at the various helms.
And only creative bookkeeping could get those companies to show any moneys on the credit side at the end of
a fiscal year.

It had gotten grim. Months had passed and I had no
friends other than Harriet Horner, and she was beginning to grind me down like an old stone mill. The
woman had the intellect of a thimbleful of cornflakes,
and on two occasions I actually did step in dog shit
upon leaving her place. And, in my then state of mind,
that's what the lady began to smell like in the midst of
our amours.

The MGM deal had been simple enough—a small
rewrite of a script that two previous writers had worked
very hard at mangling into oblivion. One look at what
they had done and I knew instantly what the problem
was—the hero was never in jeopardy. As a result, no
matter what kind of predicament he was in, we always
knew that he'd get out of it. It was a dramatic lack that
the screenplay could not tolerate. I fixed the whole

thing up in under five weeks—and don't you think those mini-minds were unable to comprehend what I'd done?

They thought that I'd rushed it, that I owed it more time, that "fast" was bad and "slow" was good, and that it was the tortoise who always won the race. They said "haste makes waste," and I said "a stitch in time saves nine." They said "anything worth doing is worth doing well." And I said "shove it up your ass" and got into my Porsche and drove out Sunset to the Pacific.

A little white Mercedes passed me going in the opposite direction. A blonde girl was driving. She looked so much like Ginnie that I found myself turning around and following her. The traffic was gummy and she was driving fast, as if intent on shaking me off. I stayed with the white Mercedes for as long as I could, even running a couple of red lights to stay on its tail. But it rid itself of me by the simple expedient of turning invisible. So I continued on back to Hollywood, to my house, where I called Harriet. I went to see her. We chatted. We balled. And I went home, not liking myself much but not knowing what I could do about it.

Jack Rush called. He had been nagging me for having blown the MGM assignment and wanted to drive over to see me. I told him that I didn't feel up to it, but he said that it was important and that he was on his way.

I heard his car pull into my most limited driveway. It was a Porsche driveway, not a Cadillac driveway, and my garage door complained when nudged by Jack's Coupe de Ville.

He came in, saw I was at work on a can of beer, and went inexplicably for my jugular. "You're screwing up a beautiful career. Laying around, drinking beer—that proves nothing."

That took me aback, and whenever I'm that way, I get smart-assy. "Well—I'm fresh out of champagne."

"I'm trying to be helpful."

"Then don't come here in a Cadillac. Come in a Studebaker. You guys can't even write your names, and you're driving boats I couldn't even pay the insurance on."

"Ben, please, I know it's upsetting. You come out here and all you get for your efforts are agents and producers who give you platitudes and criticisms—and you're right. Nobody knows what he's talking about. No argument on that. All I'm asking you to do is acknowledge the fact that certain people out here have the clout to make things happen, and even if they're imbeciles, you can't tell them that and expect to work for them. I'm sorry, but that's the way it is."

"No, *I'm* sorry that's the way it is."

"Then you accept my point?"

"What the hell is this, a fucking debate? No, I don't accept your point! Not if it means my writing down to the level of those in charge! I can't do that! All I can acknowledge is that the higher the man, the lower the intellect. That's the great big Hollywood axiom. That's 'Zanuck's Law,' 'Skouras's Law,' 'Warner's Law'— they're all in it together."

"Okay. Call it a law. You're right. It *is* a law. Now, as a citizen of the filmmaking community, are you prepared to obey that law? Because if not—you're not going to survive out here. You're going to drop into a bottomless hole of self-righteousness, all the way— splat—so long and *au revoir*."

"Shit. I think I may vomit."

"You already have. All over yourself. That's the sadness of it. You like my Cadillac? You know why I have one? Because I obey the law. I don't try to change it. I don't even question it."

"Listen, Jack, you're a nice guy and you mean well, but if you don't get out of here, I'm going to have to throw you out."

He took a long time before speaking, as if deliberating the fate of the condemned man—noose or garrote. Whichever—get on with it. "Okay, I'm leaving. But not until I tell you the real purpose of my visit. The real purpose of my visit is to present you with this bill. It's all itemized. Read it over. Comes to a grand total of $11,990.62."

"What the hell is this?"

"Read it."

"One Porsche—$6,533.32. One down payment on house—$4,000. Gas, electricity, and telephone installation—$457.39. Miscellaneous, itemized on request—$1,000. What the hell is this?"

"$11,990.62. That's what you owe the Morris office. If you were earning any money, we'd be happy to lay back and deduct it a little at a time, with no interest charges. But you're not earning any money, and it doesn't look as though you ever will—so the agency doesn't want to be on the hook for it. We've deducted our regular ten percent on your $25,000 from Warners and your $15,000 from MGM. That came to $4,000—leaving you $36,000. From that we're deducting the $11,990.62—plus what the governments of the US and California get, plus Social Security, which you're going to be glad you have one day—all of which leaves you a total of $19,226.09, which is the amount of this check that I now hand you. And which ends our relationship with you because we can't afford to waste our time with clients who continually tell our customers to go fuck themselves. And don't bother to throw me out because I'm going."

"Vernon Stacey assured me that—"

"No, Ben, he didn't. And if he did he was not empowered to. As your agents it was our responsibility to help you in every way possible. It was *not* our responsibility to pay for your dental work, or your foster children in Pakistan. If you want to get a lawyer on the thing—go ahead. Also, you should check it out with the Writers Guild. But, as a friend, I have to tell you you don't have a leg to stand on. Good-bye, Ben. Believe it or not, I wish you luck."

Hollywood was beginning to crowd me. It was ganging up on me. My agents had fired me. When those wily predators resign a client it's only because they know they'll never make a buck on him. They could be wrong, of course, and I was sure they'd been wrong with other people, but I still didn't care for it. It was not a good omen. All was not right with the world. How could I get work if I had no screen credits and no agents? Who'd know I was alive? Still, I would not berate myself. All I had done was to act with some integrity. Yes, I had a short wick. Yes, I had been ill-advised to read out anyone and everyone who disagreed with my own evaluation of my writing. But if I didn't establish my individuality and independence very early on, then there was no way in which I wouldn't end up as a hack writer with some money in his kick but no pride in his vault.

Another disturbing aspect of my clash with Jack Rush was that he had arrived at my house with that check already in his pocket. Was he so certain of my reaction? What would have happened had I meekly agreed with him and promised to be a good boy? Would he still have resigned me? Had I been baited by Jack

Rush so that the Morris office could resign me while making me feel that it was of my own doing? Had they so given up on me as a writer that they were willing to cut me loose no matter how well I played that scene with their emissary?

It was a bum rap—like having your father throw you out of the house before you had a chance to run away. I knew not to lose confidence in my ability. Whatever their opinion of me, it was my opinion of me that counted. And I had a high opinion of me. Four original television dramas done network in a period of just months. Maybe it was a testimonial to the quality of my writing that I couldn't make it in Hollywood. And that's where I left it—at least for the time being. I had enough money not to go hysterically off the deep end. Something would happen. There were other agents. The word would get around that I was no longer with William Morris and someone would call. They were all birds of prey, flying the same feathers, circling the same territory. If a squirrel got away, another hawk would spot it and go after it. Someone would call and I'd present a more conciliatory ambience. Another assignment would come up and I'd try to be a better American, a gamer whore. It was too early in the game to accept a couple of minor setbacks as being anything but nothing. Fuck 'em—I'd outlast 'em and outfox 'em.

I pretty much pissed the time away. Months and months of it. Lying in the sun. Reading. Drinking. Driving around. A couple trips to Vegas. Christmas day in a movie house. New Year's eve on my own. Dissipation. Corrosion. Nothing happening. No one calling.

When I went to sleep, I would seldom get there, odd things loose in my head. Vague suspicions. Violent shifts in direction. Road signs once clearly marked, fading. Weather vanes and wind socks, sedentary. No breeze on the tundra. Popeye becalmed. Achilles heeled.

The phone did not ring once in January. Nor did the doorbell. Nor did Redwood Horner prance by to drop a load. February and March came served up as four-beer nights and three-Scotch dawns, my colors still ahoist but not smartly, not straight out and flapping, but flaccid. And my music, once brassy, was Sousa displaced. Monkey on the flagpole jigging the danse macabre.

April and it had to be faced: things were not good in the West. It was then that lethargy left the house because anxiety was at the door. And the lad who had once played anthems on his Smith-Corona was stirring again, goaded by the juices of spring.

I lay on my sun deck, framing strategy. It would be self-defeating to let many more days go by without making a positive move. Perhaps I could call the Writers Guild and ask if they knew where I might find employment. And I wondered—was the Guild a hiring hall? Should I arrive for the shape-up with my typewriter in my arms, like a longshoreman with a hook? Maybe I should take out an ad in the Yellow Pages:

> East Coast writer in town.
> Presentable and multi-faceted.
> Screenplays and other
> odd jobs.

There is a terror to being alone in a city with no one to call. It is not new. It happens to many people. But it should be good for writers. An imposed solitude. No distractions. No intrusions. The trick is to have something to work on. A suicide note; a mash letter; a telegram to the White House demanding that Alaska, Hawaii, and Ventnor Avenue be admitted to the union. Or a novel. Unemployed writers are always working on a novel—ask 'em. Pap for the outside world. A euphemism for starvation.

I thought about getting a dog. Then a parakeet. I thought about Tony and Johnny. Then I stopped thinking about things that were over and done with and began writing a screenplay—an original. A love story.

Of all my plays, "The Lonely Look" had been the best written and the best received. The screenplay would be simple enough, with enough cinematics to please those who believed that a movie wasn't a movie if a car did not hurtle over a cliff, or slaves did not revolt, or locusts did not devour the spaghetti crop. But it would also have two people with whom an audience could identify, whose dialogue would be a shade or two deeper than "Look out, Rusty, he's got a shiv!" or, "You may have the gold in the morning, Don Sebastian, but tonight you will help us celebrate the fiesta."

I stocked up on paper, typewriter ribbons, and beer and wine and Scotch—and went at my writing with the burning zeal of a Tom Paine. Sitting at the old Smith-Corona, I became aware of a little roll of fat that was hanging over my belt and hiding my buckle. It bothered me. I had never seen it there before. At first I laughed, telling myself that it was a money belt. But you can't laugh at fat or hide from it, especially when it reproduces and overpopulates and drags down your whole abdominal society. I looked in the mirror to see what else had been going on with my anatomy that I had been too busy to take note of. There were a couple of small bananas under each eye, and some buzzard scratches at the corners. Maturity or dissipation? My hair, abused by the sun and shampooed with whatever soap was in the shower stall, had taken on the consistency of a dead broom. My cheeks were a little puffy, a couple of jowls blossoming below my jaw like embryonic barnacles. If I were to let my beard grow like untended ivy, and if I were to sit at my typewriter in a ragged undershirt, I would quickly look like Monte Cristo writing to Judge Crater, requesting a pardon on purely humanitarian grounds. For it would be obvious to all that I had terminal dry rot and would not last another six-pack.

Ignoring my declining physicality, because what was more important than art, I pressed on with my script. It was called "Let There Be Love," and briefly, since you ask, it was about a young writer who created a girl and then believed that she was real. Each time they quarreled he would rewrite her, even though she protested that they should try to work out their differences and not just throw them away. He was nuts, of course, and in the end they locked him up. But as long as he had his typewriter, she was always with him—one day as a nurse, another day as his lover come a visiting. And within the confines of his room, away from harsh reality, he eventually creates the most perfect love story, one in which the lovers remain eternally young, until he dies at ninety-three. He's buried in a pauper's grave but his story is published. A half century later, a young girl reads it—and guess who *she* is? The whole thing was about love everlasting, spanning time and crossing space, and linking lovers together even though *he's* dead behind the nut house and *she's* never alive in the first place.

Harriet came around, pathetically, but I could not service her. She was angry even though I tried to explain that I either must work or die. I was sorry about that, truly, for I was beginning to see her as a creature in need whom I was not helping.

A month and it was finished. I had it. One hundred nine pages of solid scenario. I felt like celebrating. I had earned it. My beard had grown from my nose to my collarbone, and I had to scissor most of it off before my razor would risk going in there. I hadn't eaten much or well throughout my scripting and was surprised to learn from my scale that I had put on another eight pounds, again around the middle. Beer will do that. An occasional two dozens cans of beer a day will do that.

I went over my script again and again, reading all the dialogue aloud. It flowed. It held. I called Harriet because I wanted to read it to her, but she told me to stuff it. I took that as an indication that my script was no good and I became depressed for three full days. It took a night filled with music supplied by the London Symphony to rekindle my faith in my script. And at three A.M. that night and morning, I knew that it would not die aborning.

The next morning I called Jack Rush at the Morris office. He was very pleasant and asked how I was doing. I told him I'd finished an original screenplay— would he like to see it? He told me that he was no longer my agent and couldn't get involved. I pointed out that the script was good and salable and low budget. He said he had no doubts that the script was good, but that there were a lot of good scripts around and that all of them had been written by much nicer people than myself. Therefore—why would any studio want to get mixed up with me? I told him that I realized my mistakes, that I was a changed man, and that my script could speak for itself. He said he hoped my script *could* speak for itself since William Morris had no intention of speaking *for* it—and he said he was at a meeting, and he hung up.

I called Vernon Stacey in New York and gave him essentially the same pitch. He gave me essentially the same reaction, adding that they had all bent over back-

ward to help me and that I had hung myself with my
own petulance and immaturity. He said that the only
way I'd get a studio to read my script was to slap a
pseudonym on it because the name "Ben Webber" was
all used up. He said he couldn't talk with me any longer
as he was in a meeting, and he hung up.

I was blacklisted. No communist ties, nothing I'd
ever signed, no "Benefit for Bolsheviks" I'd ever appeared at—but I was all the same blacklisted, for conduct unbecoming a writer. I had dared to stand up to
them, and exile was my fate. Cut loose in the Hollywood sea with not even an agent to siphon off ten percent of my last bucket of fresh water. Okay, I figured,
very well. I would do what Vernon Stacey had smart-
assedly suggested. I would send out my script with a
pseudonym on it.

I sent one to Warners, one to MGM, and one to Paramount—all of them with the name Jackson Dowe on
them (J.D.—Juvenile Delinquent). They all came homing back. Unopened. Each of them more or less attended with the same letter:

> Sorry, but for our own protection, we do not read
> material that is not submitted through a recognized
> literary agent . . .

I was back to that bullshit again, back where I had
started. And it was infuriating. I was down but, goddamnit, not out. I took an ad in both *Variety* and *The
Hollywood Reporter*:

> I am sorry for the trouble I have caused my
> friends in the motion picture industry. And I apol-
> ogize for my behavior. Nonetheless, I have com-
> pleted an original screenplay and find that, be-

cause I am persona non grata, no one will read it.

I think it is worth the reading and well worth the making. Is there anyone out there willing to invest two hours of his time on the odd chance that I may be correct? . . .

Ben Webber
639-9844

PS.—For my own protection, my script cannot be submitted to a recognized literary agent.

The day my ad ran I camped by my phone as if it were the Hope Diamond. I did not leave the room to *pee* but that I hauled the phone along with me. It never rang. I couldn't believe it. I didn't even get a call from the people in charge of Mexican Relief and they usually called five times a week. Being the period of McCarthyism didn't help. People were afraid—of everything. Especially movie people, because they were *really* blacklisted. I began to wonder if maybe my little postscript hadn't been too clever—if I wouldn't have been better advised to allow an agent—any agent—to see it and then have it submitted to the studios under his auspices. That conclusion became more and more obvious as the day wore on.

But at eleven thirty P.M. I received a phone call that was to change my life dramatically. It was from Sam Gaynor. He had seen my ad.

"Ben, you fucker—that's the funniest ad ah ever did read. Sure put a lot of people in their place."

"Think so? Then how come nobody called?"

"How could they? They think you're nuts, out of your fuckin' gourd. Runnin' that ad maybe got you some jollies, boy, but it ain't ever gonna get you any results. Those idiots read that and they are gonna steer as fah away from you as they can. Man, that was a fuckin' suicide note! You mean nobody called?"

"Not a soul."

"Nobody at all?"

"You called. First and only. And that's a bigger surprise than if nobody called. The way I worked you over in my play—?"

"You kidding? Ah loved it! Gave me notoriety. Laughed so hard ah almost mussed my pants. And callin' me Ron Garner? Sheet—that was fuckin' inspired. And as to me talkin' a lot—ah do talk a lot. It's better'n listenin' a lot, 'specially when the mothers out here got nothin' to say and take all day provin' it. Mad at you? Hey—ah am not mad at you. Ah think you are one helluva writer. Ah think you're so good that even if ah was mad at you ah wouldn't let on because you'd only do it to me again—in your next script. Is that not raht?"

"I've got a sneaky feeling there's not going to be a next script."

"Naaaaah. You just have to roll with it. They got a different rule book out here, kid. And they stick it to everyone, every chance. Fuckin' bunch o' frightened sadie-masochists. Sheet, you know it as well as me, there's nothin' of any quality comin' outa this town. Only trouble is, they don't know it until after the fuckin' films are released. Anyway—ah just called to see how you were doin'. Ah mean—ah heard about your little experiences at Warners and MGM because that kind of stuff gets around. Also gets exaggerated."

"Whatever you heard was no exaggeration."

"Good. Ah love it even more. Ah don't know whether you got guts or are just nuts, kid, but if you're dead, at least you went down fightin' and that's more than the other corpses lyin' around out here can say. Anyway, like ah said, ah just called to commiserate

with you, for old times sake. Ah mean, we've had our
differences but we did kind of come out of the same
litter. If you got nothin' to do, why don't you drop by
mah office and ah'll buy you a cup o'coffee. Ah'm in
the book, just off Beverly Boulevard. Ah've got a couple things going at Columbia, couple little flicks. But
ah'd like to see you and give you the benefit of my expertise, as ah have been fucked about with too, and
know what you're goin' through. Okay?"

"Sam? Do you think you might find time to read my
script?"

"Yeah. Ah suppose so, but not raht away. Ah mean,
ah'm not stallin' you, kid, but don't bring it over if you
want me to read it overnight because ah can't. Ah
mean, ah just fuckin' can't. Ah don't know why you
need mah opinion anyway. You know it's good. You
know your problem is not your talent, it's your fuckin'
big mouth. Bigger than mine even, eh, you mother? Ah
mean, ah remember you when, boy, and ah don't figure
that success has exactly turned you into a deaf-mute."

"Success has come and gone."

"Then get up and do it again. Listen, kid, ah gotta
hang up. Got a girl here, you know? Hey, bring your
script around, ah'd be happy to read it. Really would.
Just give me a call when you're comin' over so's ah can
make sure to be here. Give 'em hell, Ben. If ah don't get
to see you—fuck 'em all."

Sam Gaynor's number was in the book, and I called
him the very next morning. His secretary said he was at
Columbia and didn't know when he'd be back. I drove
around, feeling cowed but less angry. Talking with Sam
had somehow brought me down to earth and I realized
that I'd been fighting windmills when what I should
have been doing was mending fences. And I thought, if
a guy with the negative personality of Sam Gaynor

could have work in progress, then he either had more pull than the magnetic poles, or he had truly learned— the hard way no doubt—how to keep his poisonous personality in tow.

I could hardly look upon Sam Gaynor as a friend. I had never liked him and probably never would. But somehow, out there in Fantasy Town, things could go topsy-turvy at any minute, resulting in something as astounding as Big Al Epstein becoming my antagonist and loud Sam Gaynor my ally.

The next morning, feeling more insecure because maybe Sam really *was* ducking me, I called him again, first thing. He was in and expansively told me to come over. He didn't tell me to bring my script and I didn't ask him if I should—I just brought it.

His offices were pleasant and unostentatious. In a small four-storey building, Hollywood modern, in which he occupied most of the second floor, there were the compulsory mementoes of Skip Gaynor plastered onto walls and strewn upon tabletops. But beyond those, the place was no more garish than any other offices one might find on the outskirts of Pompeii.

A receptionist who looked as though she had been slept in by the Los Angeles Rams also handled a small switchboard. She announced my arrival. The door opened and Sam came out like a lion at a bishop. He seemed so much bigger than I had remembered him that I actually stepped backwards, the prescribed action when being charged by a wild animal.

"Ben, you fucker! Ah oughta drop you with a hard raht for what you did to me in your fuckin' play!" Instead, he pumped my hand as if inflating a zeppelin.

"You said you wouldn't."

"Yah, yah. Come on in. Oh—this is Althea. She's our receptionist. And, as you can see, she's still a virgin.

Movin' right along—in here we have Gloria, my private fuckin' secretary. Say hello to Ben Webber, Gloria, and then get back to whatever dirty book you're readin'."

Gloria and I exchanged hellos. She was reading James Joyce.

"This is *mah* office," said Sam, "and next to it is mah partner"—he opened the door to an adjoining office and pointed at the man behind the desk—"Randy Hampton, who, in reality, is a snake and a golf hustler. Randy, say hello to Ben Webber."

Randy Hampton stood up like a mongoose fixing on a target. He was a thin, shoulderless man of about thirty-five, with a head so outsized as to border on being macrocephalic. "Heard a lot about you, Ben. Don't believe what he says about me. I'm in charge of the money and, with him around, if I didn't ride herd we'd be broke in a week."

Sam bellowed. "Don't listen to him, Ben. He's so busy fuckin' Columbia out of their lunch money, he has no *time* to watch what *ah'm* doin'! Come on, come on. You've spent enough time with the riffraff."

Sam and I went back into his office, where he closed the doors and buzzed the intercom. "Gloria, who am ah havin' lunch with?"

"Charlie Brackett."

"Shit. Ah can't break that, can I?"

"Why not? You broke it yesterday."

"Yah, yah. Ben? Coffee and doughnuts?"

"No, thanks. I'm—"

"Gloria, you sweet-titted thing, get us a dozen doughnuts. Assorted. Four or five containers of coffee. Milk and sugar on the side." He switched off, sat back in his chair with his hands behind his head, and he smiled at me as he looked me over. "Yep—ah really oughta punch you out. Ron Garner. Sheeeet. Weren't you afraid ah might one day catch up to you?"

"I never thought about it."

"Fearless fucker. Listen, kid, as long as you're not doin' anything." He opened a door and riffled through it like a steamshovel. "Ah got a couple scripts here which ah'd appreciate you're lookin' at. Ah'd like your opinion of 'em."

"Okay."

"Ah mean, they both need strong rewrites and ah'll pay you if you're really interested. What do you get for a rewrite?"

"I don't know."

"You don't have an agent anymore?"

"Nope."

"Yeah. Ah heard that, too. Well, you're better off without them blue-suited fuckers. We'll work somethin' out. Ten grand. Fifteen. Twenty. Whatever. I don't give a shit, it's Columbia's money. Will you read these?"

"Yes. But will *you* read *mine*?"

"Brought it with you, I see."

"Just in case."

"Okay. Soon as I can. But it won't be tonight. Ah can't get out of this dinner, and ah know it'll go on forever."

"Doesn't have to be tonight. Whenever you can."

"Fair enough."

We swapped scripts. "Let There Be Love" for "Hellbent for Leather" and "Dynamite Truckers." And it was immediately apparent to me where Sam Gaynor's interests lay. The doughnuts arrived and he dispensed with six of them. I had two. Other people would have the leavings. We had coffee, gabbed about the old days. And he left for his lunch date.

I drove back to my place, went out onto my deck,

and read both of his scripts. Each was worse than the other. Take your pick. "Hellbent for Leather" was hopeless, some kind of Western in which there's a horse race from Tucson to Phoenix, winner taking all, including the marshal's idiot daughter. "Dynamite Truckers" was about truck-drivers who schlepped dynamite—in this case, over the Hump in Burma, with Japs shooting at them all the way. Both scripts were authored by Sam Gaynor. I wasn't surprised.

Of the two, believe it or not, I preferred "Hellbent for Leather" because, though derivative, it was not baldfaced plagiarism as "Dynamite Truckers" was. (I had seen it under various titles such as "Over The Hump," "Roaring Wheels," "Truckride to Tomorrow"—like that.) I made some notes on it, how the characters could be reshaped and filled out. I wanted a job, plain and simple. Not for the money but for the screen credit. A chance to show the film community that I was not the unbalanced hothead the Morris office was painting me to be. Also, judging from the two scripts I had just read, it was not likely that Sam Gaynor would leap at "Let There Be Love." All that I had going was what *I* might be doing for *him*.

I called him the next day to tell him that I thought I could do a strong rewrite of "Hellbent for Leather." He was delighted. He told me to come in and speak to Randy and work out some kind of deal and that the Writers Guild could help me in the framing of the actual contract.

And the following morning I sat opposite Randy Hampton as we worked out the bare beginnings of a deal. The man never stopped smiling and never once pondered. There was a touch of the mafioso to him, and I made a mental note to never let him kiss me full on the mouth.

I would get ten grand to start, another five upon the delivery of the rewrite, another five upon delivery of a polish, and another ten, deferred, out of first profits. I was guaranteed twenty grand even if the picture wasn't made—plus another ten if it was made and paid off. Considering that it was only a rewrite and my first assignment, it was not a bad deal—providing I could hang onto my temper. Randy said that their lawyer would draw up the contract but that, before I signed it, I should have the Writers Guild look it over. Meantime, he didn't think that I should start doing any work until it had all been straightened out. He didn't think the contracts would take longer than five days—ten at the most—as it was a pretty standard thing.

I began work anyway, mostly because I had nothing else to do and was fighting to maintain a hold on the strings of my sanity, but also because I knew I could do it. Sam had not yet been able to get to *my* script which I thought was just as well since all it would do would be to convince him that I had no business rewriting *his* script. I began to hope that he'd never read it and I regretted ever having given it to him.

I worked continuously and was glad to do so, and Sam's dumb script actually began to look as though it might just work. I called him and told him that I had begun the writing and that it was proceeding well. He said that he wished I hadn't because no one should work on the come. He offered to pay me five grand up front, right away, in good faith, but I told him that money was not my problem and that I was having such a good time with the script that I thought I should be paying him. He thanked me for my attitude which he described as "admirably professional," and said that he hoped to get to my script by the next night. Afraid that he *might*, I told him not to rush it, that there were things still wrong with it, etc., etc.

It was a lonely life, and yet it was great. Nothing was in my way. It was a time of pure creativity, total and all-consuming. Eating, sleeping, writing, and that's all. I even curtailed my drinking, which I knew was close to getting out of control. The script would never be of Academy Award calibre, but it could be the basis for a tidy, low-budget sleeper. And suddenly I began to see that, in his own obtrusive, elemental way, Sam Gaynor had authored a script that had more good things going for it than I had first believed. I wondered about screen credit. After all, it was Sam's original script. Still, without what I was doing, it was *no* script. Would Sam try to screw me out of screen credit?

Ten days had come and gone and I had yet to see a contract. It began to worry me. Maybe the sonofabitch had finessed me. Maybe the Sam Gaynor I remembered and despised had not changed at all, but was counting on my writing the whole thing because I was so hungry to be working. That way he'd get to see my work before having to commit to it. That suspicion, combined with my growing conviction that Sam hadn't the mentality to know how good a job I'd done if his *life* depended on it, and you can understand why I was beginning to feel a little bit locked out.

What I could do, to be sure, was not deliver the script until the contract had been signed and the proper moneys advanced. In any case, my old paranoia was coming out of the ground and looking for its shadow. I was having a tough time trying to coax it back into its hole.

Sam called that night. Late. About ten o'clock. He was still in his office and asked if I could drive down to see him. I didn't ask why because there was enough ur-

gency in his voice for me to know that it was important.
I decided not to bring my rewrite of "Hellbent for
Leather." Fuck him. If he wanted it he'd have to sign
the contract first—after the Writers Guild's approval of
it. If he balked at that, then I would have been working
all along for nothing. Still, he, too, would have nothing.
Nothing begets nothing better than nothing.

Sam and Randy Hampton were in Sam's office and
all I had to do was to step inside to know that things
were not good. Randy, ever-smiling, but not at me, simply got up and walked out, never acknowledging my
presence. Some kind of psychological warfare? I heard
him go to the elevator and I heard the elevator go
down. Still, I would have been more certain that he had
gone down had I heard his footsteps on the stairs and
not the elevator in the shaft.

I was alone with Sam Gaynor, not an especially good
position for any man to be in. Better to be in a cage
with a crazed lion. At least you can reason with a
crazed lion. "What's wrong with him?" I asked, referring to the dear-departed Randy Hampton.

"Sit down."

"No, thanks. I think I'll stay here, by the door. In
case of fire."

"Sit down, fucker. Ah'm gonna bring you up to
date."

"Okay." I sat, but never fully, always keeping enough
weight on the balls of my feet so that I could spring up
quickly if I had to—if it came to that.

He went around behind me, shutting the door and
locking it. Then he locked the door that led to Randy's
office. I had all the leeway of a rabbit on a spit. "How
you comin' with mah script, fucker?" There was no
lightness to his voice, no humor or gaiety. There was a
killer in the room and it wasn't me.

"I'll tell you when I see my contract." That was not smart of me. So what else was new?

"Don't piss on my buckskin shoes, boy. Ah asked you a question."

"Ah gave you an answer." How brave are those who know that cowardice will get them nothing. I looked around for a weapon, anything. I saw the brass radio microphone on Sam's desk. Properly wielded, Skip Gaynor's ten pound artifact could put a neat crimp into his son's strut. I calculated the distance between me and it. In a pinch—I could grab it.

"Your *contract*? Hey, boy—forget it. Ain't no contract, okay?"

"Okay." I decided to lay back and let him make his point. No sense in getting myself chopped up without first knowing why. Even in the worst films, the killer always tells the victim why. It was obligatory. It was my right.

He did not disappoint. "Those two scripts ah gave you—they ain't any good. They're lousy."

"You oughta know. You wrote 'em."

"No, ah didn't."

"Your name's on 'em."

"Ah·didn't write 'em. They've made the rounds. Turned down by everyone. They're dead scripts. Ah gave 'em to you 'cause ah figured you needed the exercise."

" 'Hellbent' can work."

"You can *make* it work, right?"

"Right."

"You can't make *anythin'* work, you shithead! You can't write a rat's fart worth!"

"Who made *you* a judge?"

He laughed, partly in admiration. "Sheeeet. Ah got

you locked in here with me—you want me to believe you ain't scared?"

"I don't care an elephant's burp what you believe."

He laughed. "Sheeet. Feisty little cocksucker."

"If you've got nothing else to tell me, I'm leaving."

"Want me to get to the point, is that it?"

"If you don't mind." I had the paperweight in my hand. And I let him see that I was holding it, hefting it.

"Oh, *please*, Daddy, don't *hit* me."

"Sam, you've got maybe ten seconds to unlock that door or I'm going to sing out the news right up your rectum."

"Well, ah am *not* gonna open that door—not yet. Not till you see this." He brought over a pile of scripts from a table and he plunked them down onto his desk in front of me. And he leaned on them as he spoke, cold venom in his voice. He was a hair's breadth away from blind rage. "See these scripts? 'Let There Be Love'—by Sam Gaynor. Ah mean, ah figured that, because *you* wrote it, ah figured it had to be good. Ah mean, you have a reputation—clever New York City writer, right? Ah mean, ah didn't even bother to read it. Still haven't. Just got myself a Form D and slapped a US copyright on it. Registered in the Library of Congress. "Let There Be Love,' by Samuel J. Gaynor. Only costs four bucks, fucker. You oughta try it."

"I sent in a prior copyright."

"Oh, the hell you did."

"I did." I didn't.

"Yeah, ah know. Those other scripts? The ones ah gave you? They're copyrighted in mah name, too. Both of 'em were originally written by some cowboy who didn't know his nose from the back end of a horse. Randy stuck a thou on him and the fucker went home like he discovered oil in his crapper."

"That won't work with me."

"Yeah? How you gonna prove you wrote it. And don't give me that copyright shit. Prior copyright, mah ass."

"People have read it."

"Who?"

"People at the Morris office."

"Oh, shit. Please don't fuck with me, Benny-Boy. Ah know all about frightened writers. Ah eat 'em up. Anyway, it don't matter. It don't matter and here's why." He flipped the scripts at me one at a time, as if flicking playing cards. "Warner Mothers—20th Century-Fucks—United Assholes—Universal Pussy—Columbia the gem of the shithouse—Metro-Goldwyn-Muffdive—Hey, Shakespeare, they all turned it down! Don't matter *what* name you put on it, it is *dead*! And *you're* dead! Wanna see letters of rejection?" He began floating the letters at me, his voice floating with them. "Here—'pedestrian,' 'banal,' 'hack,' 'saccharine'—man, they got you pegged every way to Sunday!"

I was slowly coming to a boil. "You submitted *my* script with *your* name on it?"

"Yeah! An' ah wish ah didn't! Now ah got a reputation as a lousy writer. Things are tough enough without gettin' hung with your fuckin' lousy failures!"

"You were doing it all along. Your two scripts—"

"Just a smokescreen, boy. Just to fake you out. Only, ah gotta tell you, ah just loved the idea that you were bustin' your balls on a cadaver. And one day—maybe when snow freezes in pussy-pie—if somebody ever wants to *buy* this piece of shit, *ah'll* still own the copyright. 'Let There Be Love,' by Samuel J. Gaynor." He paused, softened, and grinned. "Now then, let us turn our attention to a certain fucking television show in which a character name of Ron Garner caused me considerable embarrassment—"

That was my cue. As a dramatist, I knew a cue when it flew past me. I leaped up at him and slammed the bronze mike smack across his leering face. I heard his nose crack and watched him topple backwards. He sagged to the floor, his huge hands groping where his nose used to be. The blood flew as though someone had put an explosive charge inside a tomato. I stood over him and delivered the best dialogue I could find that might cover the moment. "I'm going to find out who that cowboy is, Sammy-boy. I'm going to find him and drag his ass back here and together, me and him, we're going to bend your cock around so that it goes up your ass and grows there. Then we're going to set fire to your one ball, and, while it's still glowing, we're going to stuff it into your mouth, rivet your mouth shut, and see if you can't whistle the Pepsi-Cola jingle. Your nose is broken, turd. It can be fixed—if you can find it."

I knew who I was when I left his office. I was Sam Spade, and I loved it. I was careful about making certain that Randy Hampton wasn't lurking around in some closet, then I beat it down the stairs, disdaining the elevator again. Elevators could get stuck—not feet. When I hit the street I saw Randy Hampton, sitting at the wheel of his snazzy car. He wasn't smiling. As a matter of fact, he looked pretty damned surprised at seeing me in one piece. I walked over to him and gave him a Bogart lisp. "Your partner's in his office. He just got hit by a truck and he don't look so good. As for you—you've got one hour to get out of town before the Fat Man comes around and finds that you've blown the caper. Using the name Joel Cairo just didn't work. As to the whereabouts of the bird." I slammed the hood of his car with the palm of my hand, as you'd hit a horse you wanted to send galloping off. "Shove off, matey. School's out."

Randy Hampton's eyes kind of jumped out of his oversized head, and he drove off and was never seen again. Then I got into my own car, lit a cigarette, and headed north for the Hills.

I tried to put it all together in my head as the windshield wiper smacked away at the sudden rain. It didn't take much doing. Sam Gaynor wouldn't lie around on his carpet all night. Also, he knew where I lived. The smart thing to have done would have been to call the cops, turn myself in, explain everything, and hire the best mouthpiece that Mary Astor's money could buy. But I wasn't very smart.

I found Jack Rush's address in my little book. Beverly Hills, naturally, and not too far. I gunned my Porsche and it responded. Inside of five minutes I was in front of Jack Rush's house. It was ten past midnight. He'd be asleep. Sorry about that.

I rang the bell and a dog barked. It was perfect Pavlov. An Oriental peered out a window at me. I sneered at him, "Open up, Moto—tell your boss it's important. Chop-chop."

The slant disappeared, displaced by Jack Rush in a paisley robe and ruby slippers. He opened the door and let me in. I walked passed him, flicking my cigarette into his rose bushes. "I wouldn't be here if it wasn't important, so let's not stand around in the rain."

He looked amazed, possibly because it was so late— also because it wasn't raining. I followed him into his study. Agents lived well, posh. I filled him in on everything that had happened. At first he was shocked. Then just surprised. Then—almost bored. "Everyone knows about Sam Gaynor," he said. "How the hell could you let yourself get sucked in like that?"

"Nobody loved me."

"What?"

"I took a chance."

"He's the local fraud. Put a red nose on him and he's a clown."

"I *did* put a red nose on him."

"Ben, it's difficult for me to follow you."

"Just tell me this—did he have a couple deals going at Columbia?"

"If you mean Colombia, South America, that's possible. Maybe he's got a banana plantation. But Columbia Pictures? Did he tell you that?"

"Yep. Looked me right in the eye and said it."

"Do you know what they say about him out here? They say that what Sam Gaynor lacks in talent, he more than makes up for with a lack of integrity. He wants to direct, too. He couldn't direct a Loony Tune."

"I'm beginning to see a pattern."

"And as for him copyrighting your script— you don't have to worry about it."

"I don't?"

"No. The reader at Paramount, Gail Rosen—do you know her?"

"Long hair, peek-a-boo bangs, about twenty-five, tewnty-six?"

"No."

"I know her."

"Anyway, she's a friend of mine. She read your script before sending it back to you because she liked the title."

"Good old Gail. I knew if I left a clue—Go on."

"She figured that 'Jackson Dowe' was a pseudonym because she'd never heard it before and the script was too professional to have been written by an amateur."

"Smart girl."

"She sent it back to you with the usual letter about not being able to read it because it wasn't submitted through—"

"Can we forget that and move on?"

"Yes. She noted that Jackson Dowe's return address was Ben Webber's address. She checked it out with the phone company."

"Smart phone company."

"Then she called *me* because she thought I was still your agent and she was curious as to why you were going around me. Ben? You all right? Want some coffee? You look funny. Why don't I have Wong make us some coffee?"

"Wong?"

"Yes."

"No, thanks."

"Anyway, Gail Rosen is your witness. I guess I am, too, because she told me the story of the script over the phone—all of that before Sam Gaynor could possibly have put a copyright on it. I'll swear to that."

"Did you like it?"

"Yes and no. I liked it because it was bright and rebellious. I didn't like it because it was a fantasy and fantasies just don't sell. Not anymore. That script will never sell, Ben, and it has nothing to do with the quality of the writing. No matter what they tell you, they can't tell you it's good because they're afraid to think that it's good."

"So you don't think I ought to worry about who has possession of the copyright?"

"Quite the opposite. You'll be doing the industry a favor by nailing Sam Gaynor."

"Oh. I certainly want to do the industry a favor."

"Get him on whatever the charge is. Piracy, plagiarism, bad breath—I'm no lawyer but I know you can

get him. As for those secretaries of his you mentioned—he keeps them around to con people into thinking he's got a flourishing little operation. Six nights a
week they work the bars along Santa Monica."

"What about his partner, Smiling Smedley?"

"Hampton? He's right out of the slime. I wouldn't be
surprised if he's served time. The rumor is that he has,
under a couple other names."

"A nest of vipers."

"The worst. How long ago did you leave them?"

"Half hour."

"They're probably on their way to your place right
now."

"Not Hampton. Unless I miss my guess, he's halfway
to Frisco by now."

"I'm talking about Gaynor."

"I took him once, I'll take him again."

"For God's sake, Ben, you're talking like a lunatic."

"In this business, it's required."

"Stay here tonight. Call the police from here. Tell
them what happened. Let *them* worry about it."

"No. No police."

"Ben? Did he hit you?"

"I never gave him the chance. I hit him across the
bridge of his nose with his father."

"Let me have Wong fix up the guest room for you."

"No. No Japs."

"He's Chinese."

"No guest rooms."

"Ben, maybe I ought to call a doctor."

"You don't feel good?"

"Ben, honestly. Where you going?"

"To my place."

"You can't mean that."

"I do. I left the phonograph running. It's my only Dooley Wilson record."

"Sam Gaynor is a potential killer. Your house is the first place he'll go.

"Everybody dies."

"I'll call the police, fill 'em in."

"You do what you like, Jack. It's every man for himself. Is there another way out of here?"

I drove home, my head still ringing from the blow on the head that Sam Gaynor almost gave me. It was maybe twelve thirty, twelve forty-five. The lights were on in my house, but I had left them on. If Sam Gaynor was waiting for me his nose would still be bleeding. Somehow I felt that he'd have the old schnozzola fixed up before dropping by for cocoa. That would give me the time I needed to prepare a little reception for him.

I pulled up to my garage and cut my engine. It was quiet. But that didn't mean that no one was there. He could have parked somewhere else and walked right in because I always left the house remarkably open.

I went around the back way, through the garage entrance, and slipped into the utility room, where the fuse box was. I opened the box and killed every light in the house. After about five minutes, I removed my shoes and socked into the bedroom, ever so mouselike. My eyes were used to the dark but I was still cautious. I listened intently, Indianlike. Every little sound had a meaning all its own—only there were no sounds. None at all. Nothing. No current running any appliances. No whir from the fridge. No hum from the old Victrola. No piano from Dooley Wilson.

Tweren't no one in the house but me. I went back to the fuse box and threw the current emphatically back on, like an executioner. And I returned to my living room where I sat down to think things out. There was no doubt but that Sam Gaynor would be coming after me. The only question was when. I had no weapons other than some salad forks. I'd use them if I had to.

Alone in my California funk, she occurred to me. Ginnie. Ginnie the Incredible. There I am, sitting and waiting for the wrath of Sam Gaynor, and my mind goes plying ghost mists in search of a faraway girl. And out of the swarmy myopia, her face comes through. One sweet face as if in answer to all the fool questions. One light in the attic. One carrot on a stick. One Rosebud. One Grail.

I loved her. God, how I loved her. From the apex to the brink, I loved her. I loved her once and I loved her still, and staying where I was, mired in inertia, was to accept the conclusion that, after paying every toll, catching every light, and hitting every drawbridge from Pittsburgh to LA, all I was going to end up with was a dead skunk on my bumper.

There had to be more. You don't start out life with a slap on the behind only to conclude it with a kick in the ass. I got back into my trusty car and pointed my life south, to the airport.

chapter twenty-six

ginnie

1953

After burning up New York City with countless weeks of shameless highlife, Johnny took me with him—first to San Francisco and then on to LA. San Francisco was indescribable. Glittering and expensive and fun. We spent weeks there and in the environs—Big Sur, Carmel, Monterey. Johnny would have to leave from time to time but I always found things to do as San Francisco was a fantastic place. And the drive down the Pacific Coast Highway, and San Simeon (Hearst's place), were beyond words.

But it was strange as hell being in LA because I knew Ben was there, somewhere—Hollywood or Beverly Hills or Bel Air, which was where we stayed—at the Bel Air Hotel in a suite they could have shot Ben Hur's chariot race in. Johnny spent a lot of time playing golf with bigwigs whom I never saw until dinner time. And, to keep me happy, he leased a little white Mercedes convertible—just for me. It was a dandy, like having a pony again.

The first day I had it I pranced it all the way out to Santa Monica, where I stopped to look at Southern California's view of the Pacific. There were some crazy surfers out there, trying to get killed, but nothing could kill them so I headed back for Bel Air.

Driving, I became aware of a sports car that was sure

as hell trailing me. It was the brightest red and, in my mirror, I could see the driver; but, because the sun was behind him, I couldn't make out his face. I figured he was some kind of death-defying kid, and because, a couple of times, he came so close to running into me I was determined to shake him off.

Making a hard right turn into a congested gas station, I watched the red idiot sail by. I waited awhile, apologized to the people I had almost killed, and drove back to the hotel.

Though I knew how to drive I was not quite the best driver because I had barely learned to drive before I was shipped off to those damned schools. Anyway, I got back to the hotel in one piece and got ready for dinner. We ate at Chasen's. Joan Crawford was there and it was all I could do not to run over to her and pester her for her autograph, or a lock of her hair, or a clove from her salad, or *anything*.

It was hard for me to keep track of the time. Everything was so meaningless, so frivolous. I took tennis lessons from some pro, only he wasn't really watching my stroke, he was watching my ass. And even though I was a beginner, I knew there was no such thing as an "ass" fault. I had to put the kibosh on that right away because I wasn't learning how to play tennis, and *he* was about ready to put a topspin on both of my boobs. So ended my tennis lessons—with a whimper and not a bang.

I swam a lot and sunned a lot and collected a crowd at the pool a lot, even though I didn't try, so I usually ended up driving out to the beach a lot. And I mean why out. Past Malibu. All the way to a little spot in some rocks where people left me alone. I dubbed it Point Vista, only don't ask me why. It was not pointed and had no vista at all. It just sounded like something

I'd heard in a movie somewhere. Very glamorous and lots of sand flies.

I would drive up to Point Vista, sometimes with a book, and just let my mind wander every which way. I was sneaking up on twenty-one years of age and I was beginning to feel that, once that happened, I would be over the hill and could no longer occupy myself with daydreams. Until that time, though, I'd still be a kid. Some kid. A millionaire's mistress, in a bikini, on a blanket, on a beach, a billion miles past childhood, a 180-degree turn away from virginity.

Johnny simply did not travel in any kind of Hollywood set. His friends wore blue blazers and white flannel trousers and were so WASP that they thought pastrami played second base for the Chicago White Sox. So there was no chance I'd ever run into Ben at any of their homes. Still, the thought of Ben's being so near often kept me awake at night, as well as beating the crap out of my days. I missed him. Not as a lover, I don't think, because that time was too long dead to exhume, but as a friend and as a part of my life when I was terribly young and frighteningly vulnerable and, I fear, alarmingly stupid.

The memories were not harsh. A year and a half had smoothed away the sharp edges. If I were to meet Ben again it would not be the classic meeting of the spheres. It would not be Siegfried crashing into Brunhilde at the Mardi Gras in New Orleans. It would be more like Donald O'Connor bumping into Debbie Reynolds at the roller rink in Yonkers. We'd say, "Hi, there," and go arm-in-arm, two turns around the rink, while the organ played "Abba-Dabba Honeymoon" and the pair of us ate our way out of cotton candy.

Ben Webber had been my first lover. I had given him

my so-called innocence. In him arms I had lost my virginity. What an archaic term—"lost my virginity"—as if it had been in a brown paper bag that I'd left on the Fifty-seventh Street crosstown bus. I had only known two men since Ben and none before—not a particularly high count for a racy woman of the world. Richie Pickering had been an affair without passion, a port in a storm and a misguided port at that. He had used me badly and I left him. Johnny Farrar, I had to admit, was an affair on the rise, a relationship based more on potential than on day-to-day fulfillment. I was allowing it to happen. I was giving it room and air. I was not lost in it, off the deep end in it, throwing caution to the wind in it. I was playing it as I had seen deep sea fishermen play a marlin. I was giving it all the line it wanted, and if I hooked it—great. I'd pose beside it for *Sports Illustrated*. But if it got away, hey, I'd just go chumming for another.

What I didn't like about my existence was that constant feeling of lukewarm. You can cook with lukewarm but you can never boil with it. And by the time something gets hot in it, you can already be bored with it. Lukewarm was steady-as-she-goes, when what I thrived on was hard-rudder-right, girl overboard.

Three weeks in LA and the outskirts (Palm Springs and Santa Barbara) and the ants were in my pants. Johnny was fine, delightful and attentive. But he was also a little possessive, which led to his taking me for granted, something I never could stand since my days as a kid sister. The only time I had gotten a rise out of him was when he walked in on my "dinner for five" that night in the Delmonico. I didn't know it then, but I liked that he was annoyed. I mean, he really looked at me when he looked at me. His voice had more charge when he spoke, his fists clenched, and his jaw twitched.

I knew I was alive is what I'm getting at. I knew it because I was afraid he was going to hit me.

Christmas in Palm Springs, New Year's in Acapulco. January telescoped in to February and April was goosing March. More restaurants, more parties, more idle wealth than I'd ever imagined. And more tedium than I'd ever been designed to tolerate. Johnny went away a couple times, to Denver, never staying for more than three days but leaving me alone at the Bel Air just the same. I handled the few mashers without incident, never breaking stride and never getting cornered. But what I could not handle was the pointlessness of it all, the waste of it. And the waste of me.

Had I come all those years to merely dress up a pool? Was that the measure of my worth, the depth of my contribution to the year 1954? Was I really in love with Johnny Farrar or did I just want to be? And should I wait around and then leave whenever I felt like it, as he had invited me to do, or should I cling around, and sweat it out, and hope to so fascinate him that he would beg me to marry him? And in that Atomic Age we then lived in—were those the questions that the history books would list as the most pressing of the time?

I felt like drinking but knew not to, at least not alone. I felt like screaming, and that I did—alone on Point Vista, where I had been spending most of my daylight hours. I had, of course, developed an incredible tan but at great expense as my skin began to feel like dried-out leather; and I wondered what to use on it—moisturizer or saddle soap.

When Johnny came marching home I was so gorgeous that even *I* couldn't take my eyes off me. And instinct told me that that was the time for me to make my move—my play, so to speak. For I would never be more beautiful. From that point on it would all be downhill. Wrinkles and flab, crow's-feet and triple chins. Stretch marks, liver spots, and facelifts so often that my feet would be off the ground.

So I got myself all made up like some kind of sacrifice to the Gods. White dress—snug, deeply cleaved, and slashed down one side. Flowers in my hair—courtesy of Ophelia. And barefoot. I was goddamned barefoot in the lobby of the Bel Air Hotel, and for no other reason than that the idea of it knocked me out. And when I saw Johnny coming in, I moved at him as if out of a dream, and I put my arms around him and surrounded him with my perfume. And as I tongued his ear, I whispered, "Welcome home, my Johnny. I have only one thing in mind." To which he replied, "Get dressed. We're having dinner with the Barringers. And, for Christ's sake, wear *shoes!*"

So much for bare feet and good intentions. As to dinner with the Barringers, it had been coming for some time. It was not merely a flash bulletin on the six o'clock news. I had, up till then, given a great deal of thought to how I might worm out of that appointment should it finally land on me. Johnny had mentioned it to me in New York, and because Johnny never concerned himself with anything but reality, I knew that the confrontation would one day take place. To get out of it I had considered and rejected: hepatitis, mononucleosis, turned ankles, false pregnancy, inexplicable vomiting, swoons, desertion, and suicide. There was no way to get out of it without turning invisible. I tried turning invisible. A tall, suntanned blonde cannot turn invisible so don't try it.

"I want you to look incredible," said Johnny, jumping into the shower. "You have to go all out if you're going to look good next to Maggie."

"Oh? Is she that special?"

"I don't know. Was Cleopatra special?"

"Cleopatra was sixteen. How old is Maggie Barringer?"

"Oh, maybe thirty."

"*That* old?" Fat chance, Johnny. Still, if anyone could have done it, it would have been Maggie. Except that it would have meant that she had me at nine years of age and Mary Ann at five. Very precocious—or a fucking miracle.

Oh, I knew it was going to be a trauma. Not for *her*—she'd probably find the reunion enchanting—but for *me*, because I would no doubt stammer and piss in my panties. The only advantage I had over Maggie was that I knew, ahead of time, that we'd be meeting at dinner. Unless—"Johnny?"

"Yeah?"

"Does Mrs. Barringer know anything about me?"

"No. Nothing."

"Not even my *name*?"

"I told her nothing. I want her to be surprised."

I didn't comment. Yes, Maggie would sure as hell be surprised—but not shocked. Nothing could shock Maggie, of that I was certain. Unless—unless when we met, Johnny was naked and I was standing behind him, pumping his cock while saying, "There'll always be an England." *That* might do it.

I was scared. I saw no reason to lie to myself about that. Whoever Kevin Barringer was, he was also my stepfather. I had a rich stepfather, goddamnit, which right away put me one up on Snow White. When had Maggie remarried? It would have had to have been almost two years prior, before the St. Regis fiasco because she was already using the name Barringer at the time. Also, to have remarried, she would have to have known about Daddy's death. She wasn't at Daddy's funeral so how soon after it had she learned of it? And had she made any claim on Daddy's estate—because, if she had, and was successful, then more than likely I was wiped out. My share of the estate, as well as Mary Ann's, disappearing into Maggie's treasure chest. Was Kevin Barringer really up to his ass in oil, or was he living off of what was formerly my inheritance? And me only weeks away from the age at which I had planned on claiming it. Things were askew in paradise as I dressed to the teeth for my meeting with Mama. Some skeletons were rattling around in the closet and wanting out. It promised to be a fun night.

Johnny—God, he looked beautiful. He was a beautiful man. Should have been a movie star. Could have been had he studied with Helga Nathan, as I had, and been able to withstand her flashing tit. He was wearing velvet—a midnight blue velvet tuxedo with silver piping about the lapels, and trousers to match. Me? I was so gorgeous, so breathtakingly beautiful that I could have been coronated and England would have bought it—a pale, powder blue satin evening gown so clinging that, had it been a flesh tone, I'd have been arrested for nudity. Low-cut back, down to my sweet ass, and low-cut front, down to my lowest rib, all of it held up by two cute boobs and a strong knot behind my neck. Diamond necklace and diamond earrings. Diamond ring, too, but because I had bitten off two of my best nails I chose to wear gloves to my elbows. So no one saw my ring.

We went by limousine but I don't know to where. It was dark and my mind wasn't so much on where we were going as on how the hell I'd act when we got there.

We were somewhere in Beverly Hills. Truesdale Estates or something. Imagine, a private section of already private Beverly Hills. It would be a private home, of

course, not a restaurant. And a frightening twinge electrified the nape of my neck as I asked myself the amus-
ing question, "Would Johnny and I be the only other
couple?" The answer: a rousing yes—because we were
the only other car in the driveway and were already a
fashionable one hour late.

The house was unacceptably unbelievable. Spanish.
White and wrought-iron things squiggling all about.
Gates and fences, big and black. And floodlights bouncing off the walls as if we were arriving for the world
premiere of *Gone With The Wind*. As to the swimming
pool, it was more of a lagoon. No, make that a lake.
Not just *any* lake, but Lake Michigan, done over with
underwater lights that gave everything an aquamarine
sheen. Obviously it was a house that MGM had built as
a memorial to Esther Williams, though she must have
been underwater at the time because she never would
have allowed it—it had no orchids, no Van Johnson, no
Lauritz Melchior.

Johnny was reading my mind. "Don't worry. It's
rented."

"From who? The Aga Khan?"

"Fellow named Tyler. Diamonds."

"And we're the only dinner guests?"

"Appears that way."

"Seems a shame to fill the lake just for us."

"What?"

"Shouldn't we have brought bathing suits?"

"I'm sure they'll have some for us."

"Yeah, but can platinum float?"

"Honey, I think, tonight, Maggie Barringer is going
to meet her match."

"You mean Greta Garbo's coming?"

The liveried chauffeur eased our battleship under a

marble portico and a man in a white jacket leaped to open the door. "Hurry!" I said to him, "the pains are coming every thirty seconds!"

Johnny gave me a little elbow-nudge in the boob to express his displeasure with my gamesmanship.

Our limousine disappeared as the white-jacketed footman (I guessed that he was the footman as he certainly wasn't a greengrocer) led us up the stairs to where another white-coated man (the pharmacist?) held the fortress door open for us. All I could see was hallway—a hundred miles of hallway, spotted every ten yards with black candelabra that had real candles going. I was either about to be initiated into some sorority or I had stumbled upon a witches' convention.

My heart did a timestep as our hostess came sweeping at us from the opposite end of the hall. Damn, but she moved well. Damn, but she had style in that black dress that billowed as if pushed along by a fan in a wind tunnel. And as she drew closer I could see that—damn—she was still beautiful. Wrong—she was more beautiful than ever, another of those slender, regal women whose age is never guessed at because it's never of any consequence. And I had a sudden rush of immense pride—my mommy was so pretty.

She saw me but if she recognized me she didn't let on, and Johnny made the introductions. "Maggie Barringer, may I introduce Ginnie Maitland."

Maggie extended her hand to me. "Ginnie, I'm so glad that you could come."

To which I said, "Vive la France." And Johnny figured I'd gone bonkers.

Maggie smiled but did not bat an eye. I had fired my Big Bertha at her, my Doomsday Weapon, and it had sailed right past her, out the window, over the pool, and on to Malaya where the dawn came up like thunder. It was the only line I had rehearsed. After that I was on my own. *The Stan Arlen Show* was never like that.

Maggie hooked an arm through one of mine, and the other through one of Johnny's and walked us into the bar. All of us were in step like we were opening the *Jackie Gleason Show*.

Kevin Barringer was white-maned and tall and looked the billion dollars he was reputed to be. There was a bartender and a waitress, plus the four of us, in a room as big as the Gay Nineties. Huge globed lights like the front of New York's Plaza Hotel. And everything was done in that dark stained mahogany that I always found so opulent. There was a Persian carpet on the floor that had to run the forty yards in record time, and set into the walls were floor-to-ceiling panels of stained glass that were lit from behind. And a bar—thirty feet long if an inch, polished with a slippery lustre and armed with a brass rail. Before it stood a dozen leather-topped chairs, each of them as tall as I was.

The small talk was decidedly small—minuscule, infinitesimal—most of it supplied and indulged in by Johnny and Kevin. I had trouble believing that Johnny was so fluent in that archaic tongue but he was. Polo and regattas and all the stuff that mattas.

Maggie and I were cutely sparring, getting ready for what we each felt the other might instigate. Maggie got off the best one by saying aloud, when the bartender popped the champagne "Vive la France!" The menfolk didn't know what it meant but I did and laughed. And it crossed my mind that, under different circumstances, Maggie and I might just have been sensational friends.

The men went off into the billiard room or the war room or the trophy room, and for the first time, Maggie and I were alone—in the center ring, fully lit. She smiled, that glorious smile on that incredible face, and asked, "Any questions?"

"Yeah. Lots."

"Fire away."

"Is Kevin my stepfather?"

"No. He's your mother's fella."

"You use his name."

"And his credit cards."

"You're not married."

"No more than you and Johnny."

"You know that Daddy's dead."

"Yes."

"You didn't come to the funeral."

"I didn't know there *was* one. I didn't find out until much later when I called your sister to wish her and Walter a merry Christmas and all that fa-la-la. And that was long after you found me and Ben. Want to talk about *that*?"

"I don't know. Do you?"

"Only because I'm curious as to what happened afterwards."

"What happened afterwards was that I left him."

"Did you ever give him a chance to explain?"

"Nope. Could he have explained?"

"He was a lovely, intelligent boy. And he didn't have the slightest idea that he was in both of our lives at the same time. Whatever became of him?"

"He's out here, writing movies."

"Do you see him?"

"Do you?"

"No, but I might like to."

"I'll get you his phone number."

"Please do. It would be nice to keep him in the family."

"How do you stand with Daddy's estate?"

"Exactly where I want. Out."

"You made no claim?"

"Did I have a right to?"

"You hurt him very much. You hurt me, too."

"Yes. I thought I might. But I couldn't go on with that hypocrisy. I was a lousy mother and would have hurt you even more if I continued to try to play that role. I was right. You're good. You're on your own. You're tough. And you're still young."

"I don't think I'm all that young anymore."

"You'll be twenty-one in a couple weeks. That ain't old."

"I'm surprised you remember."

"Don't be. Don't assume that I never look back—and wonder. And regret. I don't mind that you think me a hedonist and a whore. You have every right to think that. But don't think me a total nonperson. Because you'd be wrong."

"Okay."

"You'll be coming into a great deal of money."

"If Mary Ann hasn't already gone through it."

"She hasn't. It's in the State National Bank, in Stamford. All waiting for you."

"You keep tabs on it?"

"As much as I can in my crowded schedule."

"Do you like the life you lead?"

"Yes. Do you?"

"How would they take the news that we were mother and daughter?"

"With a grain of salt, I imagine."

"Wouldn't it—take the gloss off your image?"

"Decidedly. Planning on telling them?"

"I'm thinking about it."

"You've been thinking about it all evening. Do as you like. I'm sure you have no secrets from Johnny."

"Johnny and I are going to be married."

"Does he know it?"

"I think so."

"In that case, congratulations."

"How long can you go on as you're doing?"

"Probably until Kevin gets tired of me."

"He may never get tired of you. You're quite beautiful."

"You ain't bad yourself."

"Does Kevin give you money?"

"Oh my, yes."

"Do you save any of it?"

"Oh my, no."

"You might someday wish you had."

"No, my dear. Keeping the money makes a woman a whore. Spending it makes her—dangerous."

"I'll try to remember."

"Will we be friends, Ginnie?"

"I don't see how."

"Neither do I. Come. Let's go to dinner. Do you like squab?"

"Yes. Especially his Fourth Symphony."

"Funny."

"You've fucked-up my life, Maggie."

"By scaring off your Ben?"

"That's part of it."

"A secret. I'll tell you a secret, all right?"

"Please."

"If he loved you he would have come after you. He'd never have let you slip away without raising a ruckus."

"He tried."

"Not hard enough though—apparently."

"Well—"

"Come, dear. We mustn't let the squab get cold. Beats the shit out of the woodwinds."

Dinner was served in a diningroom that was czarist Russian. Heavy brass and clunky crystal. And draperies that had to have been smuggled out of Nicholas's palace before Lenin busted in to say, "Show's over, folks."

Eating squab is like dining on hollowed-out grapefruit. Most of it is air, the rest of it is skin. And the sight of that little dead bird served up in its entirety made me feel ikky because I identified with the poor thing. There, but for the grace of some hunter's arrow, was I, pretty on the outside, nothing on the inside, legs up and on my back ready to be taken because that's what I was best at. Forks up, gentlemen. Show's over, Ginnie.

Wine and wine and wine. Different bottles for different courses. Different jockeys for different horses. Different cups for different saucers. This rhyme is Spenser's—or is it Chaucer's?

"Ginnie? Are you all right?" That was Maggie, looking at me from over the lip of a brandy snifter. Brandy from Peru. Pasco Pisco. Whatever it was, it wasn't Nabisco. "Ginnie?"

"I'm fine. I love squab."

"That was two courses ago."

"My love is everlasting."

The men laughed. I wanted to Pisco in their Pasco. "Ginnie?" Maggie was standing, affecting a delicate tipsy. "I think I've had a little too much wine. I'd like to get some air. Will you come with me? These blokes are talking too much shop anyway. Would you gentlemen please excuse us?"

Johnny and Kevin jumped up like toy soldiers—rounded faces, squared-off shoulders. And Maggie, mercifully, steered me out of the room.

"Don't you just hate them?" I asked her.

"A little. Yes. I think it's required."

"They're so full of squab."

"The whole world's full of squab."

"Where we going?"

"Out by the pool. It's cooler."

"You're gonna throw me in, yes?"

"No. You'd swim away and I'd never see you again. Here, sit down."

"How'd you feel if I threw up in your pool?"

"Not too good, but you'd feel better. Put your feet up. For God's sake, relax! Christ, are you that afraid of me?"

"Yes."

"Good. Because I'm a little afraid, too."

"Ha-ha-ha."

"I am."

"Ho-ho-ho. Why are you afraid?"

"I'm not sure."

"You're afraid I'll tell 'em you're my mother."

"I told you, that's your privilege. Your weapon. If it's loaded, fire it."

"I'm loaded."

"I know. Sometimes you think more clearly when you're loaded. It strips away the artificials. And the truth jumps out and says 'Here 'tis!' And it's irresistible."

"*You're* loaded."

"Maybe. A little."

"I hate you, Mommy."

"Good. Feel better now?"

"You left me and never came back."

"I was running for my life. That's not an excuse, it's an explanation."

"I still hate you."

"As long as you do maybe I ought to give you a little more to hate me for."

"You ran away and never came back. Answer the question."

"What question?"

"How come you do me like you do, do, do?"

"That's not the question. You asked me why I was afraid."

"You said you weren't sure. That's no answer."

"I think—now I'm sure. Want to hear?"

"I ain't goin' anywhere."

"I know."

"Huh?"

"That's why I'm afraid. Not for me, but for you. When I ran away it was from a life I couldn't deal with, a marriage that was strangling me, kids that were sucking me dry. I had something to run away *from*. You're running away and you're not running away from anything. I was cowardly. You're just—nuts."

"Fuck you, Ma."

"Want me to stop?"

"No. That means continue. Whenever I say, 'Fuck you, Ma,' that's your signal to continue. Fuck you, Ma."

"Ginnie, I was fifteen years older than you are now when I took off. I knew what I was doing. You don't. Do you know what you're doing? I mean living with Johnny Farrar?"

"Yeah. I know what I'm doing."

"Then tell me, because I don't."

"I'm living with a man who makes me happy. He gives me everything I want—takes me places. I've lived in basements, Maggie."

"People get out of basements. They don't always get out of gilded cages."

"I can get out of living with Johnny anytime I want."

"Who sez?"

"He says. He *told* me. Anytime I want to go I'm free to go."

"He's too smart for you."

"Fuck you, Ma."

"You don't need him. In a very short time you'll have money of your own. It'll be close to half a million dollars. Christ, twenty-one years of age, an heiress, a body like Venus, a face like the Mona Lisa—why the hell are you locking yourself in with a phony like Johnny Farrar?"

"Johnny's not a phony. He's a very successful man. He's in electronics. Travels the world. Meets with consuls. Does business in *Russia*! Where the hell you getting your information from? You never met Johnny until a couple months ago!"

"Ginnie, I travel in a certain set. Three, four hundred people who know more about each other than they know about themselves. You're not in yet. When you are, you'll know everything that I know. What I'm doing now is trying to see to it that you're never in."

"What do know about Johnny? Jesus Christ, have you slept with *him*, too?"

"No. Not yet."

"Boy! You're something! How come you didn't meet him at the door and give him the old 'Vive la France'?"

"Ginnie, why aren't you and Johnny married?"

"Because he's not divorced yet!"

"Do you know why he's not divorced?"

"Because he's still married!"

"The reason he's not divorced is that he's *never* been married. Now, do you want to take a minute to let that sink in?"

"Fuck you, Ma."

"Johnny Farrar has a girl in Amsterdam, younger

than you. She's waiting for his divorce, too. And, there's a girl in Denver. A ski instructress."

"Denver?"

"Yes. We were there with them, Kevin and I. We just got back. Not the most beautiful girl but evidently great on the slopes. Ginnie, there's a sort of a code in our crummy set. We don't tell on one another. If we did we'd have no set. And we *need* a set, otherwise we wouldn't have each other—just ourselves, which would be pretty unbearable. As much as I love Kevin, the thought of being in his company one hundred percent of the time would have me running back to Stamford. I'm telling on Johnny because he's messing with my daughter. So—fuck the code. When Johnny Farrar goes to Moscow, he goes not to sell computers or electronics. That's all done automatically by a board of directors. He goes to plug in on Olga, or Natasha, or Catherine the Great—or whoever it is he calls comrade and beds down with in the Kremlin. Johnny Farrar is just playing and laying. That's all he does. When he gets to Kevin's age, perhaps he'll cut down and concentrate on just one. But he's got twenty years to go and I give you—maybe—two of those." She tossed her cigarette into the big pool and smiled at me. "Love is a crapshoot, Ginnie. You think you have gossamer—and it turns out to be orlon. Tell you what, here comes your Johnnykins now. I'll start the ball rolling and you can take it from there."

Johnny was walking toward us, carrying a drink and looking like the cat who just ate the squab. "What're you two girls gabbing about? You've been out here forever."

Maggie smiled at Johnny and gave it to him straight. "Ginnie is my daughter and we had much to talk about." Then she turned and walked back into the house, heading off Kevin who had been coming out to join us. She just turned him around in his tracks and took him back inside, leaving Johnny and me alone.

"What the hell was that all about?" He asked.

"The lady thinks she's my mother."

"Is she?"

"First I heard about it. I think your Mrs. Barringer's a little bit bombed."

"I guess so. She just didn't seem to be doing all that much drinking."

"I think she started before we got here. I think she started at reveille this morning."

"Hmmmmmm."

"Johnny. I don't want to end up like that."

"Come on. Let's go back in."

"She let it slip. She's not married to Kevin. He can walk out on her anytime he wants."

"Maybe so. But it works the other way around, too. She can walk out on him."

"At her age? Where does she go from there? Or maybe it isn't Kevin's concern."

"I don't know. I don't really know them all that well."

"I guess not. She didn't seem to know you were married."

"Well, I don't go around discussing my private life with everybody. Come on. Dessert's on the table. They set fire to Alaska just for us."

"Let it burn for a little while, okay? Johnny? If you were divorced, would you marry me? On the spot?"

"In a minute."

"Where does your wife live? Chicago? Maybe I can go see her, have a little talk with her."

"Since when did you become Bette Davis?"

"Since I decided to stop being June Allyson."

"Let me see if I understand this correctly. You want to see my wife, to talk to her, to ask her to—let me go, right?"

"Yes. Something like that."

"What you're really saying is that you don't think I have a wife."

"The thought has occurred to me."

"You think I've been lying."

"Well, there's only one way to find out, isn't there. And, if I'm wrong, I'll apologize."

"That's too easy. How am I supposed to feel at the fact that you distrust me?"

"Well, you might try being flattered. It shows interest."

"Ginnie, I am so disappointed in you—"

"I know. But where do I reach her? Give me a phone number, Johnny. Any number. Make one up. Hey—how about color of hair? Eyes? Any distinguishing features? Does she have any hobbies?"

"Nothing doing, Ginnie."

"Which, translated, means there is no such person. Well—there's a howdy-do."

"Where you going?"

"I don't know. Denver, Amsterdam, Moscow. Wherever the fair wind blows."

"Ginnie—"

"You told me I could leave anytime I wanted to. Well—I want to leave *now*."

"What did she tell you?"

"Not as much as *you* just told me by telling me nothing."

"Ginnie—"

"Love is a crapshoot, Johnny. You think you have gossamer and it turns out to be shit—something like that."

I walked around the edge of the pool and never, never looked back. The moon was in the pool and I wondered how come I was so high up that I could look down on it—but it didn't stop me from leaving. Bette Davis was leaving. I knew I'd compromised Maggie a little with those direct allusions to Denver and Amsterdam, but I figured she'd be able to work her way out of it. I also figured I was doing what she wanted me to. If Johnny wanted me, if he really, truly loved me, he'd come after me. I just didn't think he would. Ben hadn't. Johnny wouldn't. Maggie had said it and Maggie was right. Because when you get right down to it, mothers know best. I had learned something else. I had learned that a woman never leaves a man who tells her she can leave anytime she wants to. She only leaves the man who begs her to stay forever. Philosophy for a summer's night, while walking out on a rich boyfriend. Put that in your tampon and stuff it.

I found our limousine and driver out by the garage, behind the house. He snapped to as soon as he saw me, and he ran around to open the door for me. "Home, Miss?"

I got in. "I have no home."

He ran around to the other side, got in behind the wheel, and started up the boat while looking at me in the rear-view-mirror, puzzled as shit. "The hotel, Miss?"

"The airport."

"The airport?"

"Please."

He guided the car down the long driveway. "Would you want to stop back at the hotel and pick up some things, Miss?"

"No."

"Somebody sick, Miss?"

"Yes. Me. Of the whole fucking thing."

"Yes, Miss."

We drove to the airport where I selected American Airlines because I liked their advertising. And in my clinging blue gown and my elbow length gloves, I flew first class to New York, having first borrowed twenty bucks from my driver. It was all he had but it was twenty dollars more than I had. I would need it for pocket money, cabs and stuff for when I got to New York. Johnny would pay the man back. My plane ticket I charged to American Express, and to Johnny, and to experience.

Some of the passengers leered at me suspiciously, but the stewardesses seemed to know that it was an affair of the heart. Bless all stewardesses, in and out of love as frequently as they flew in and out of time zones. In my next life I would come back as a flat-chested stewardess in a trim business suit. And I would live in a big apartment with hospitable boys and make love against the bannisters.

But it was okay. Maggie had paid me back. We were even. If we were never to see each other again, she had made up for my losing Ben by bailing me out of Johnny. And I was no longer an orphan—and no longer had to cry. Vive la Mama!

New York felt cold. Especially for people who traveled in sheer evening gowns and open-toed sandals. I got a cab at the airport terminal building. I could have gotten a dozen of them, the way I was dressed—all those frothing cabbies practically driving over one another to get a shot at picking up "the Blue Slink."

The drive into Manhattan and I was elated, on fire. I was an Easterner, a New Yorker. And as much as I ever had a home it was in the East. In New York. I was cyclical and deciduous. I shed leaves and took on new colors almost in sync with the seasons. And I knew that, if I ever researched it, I'd discover that each time I'd shed old love for new, the exchange had taken place on the day of an equinox.

I pulled up to the Delmonico, where the doorman smiled because he knew me. It didn't bother him that I showed up in an evening gown sans luggage, for he had seen me show up in jeans with a cabful of wardrobe. He was used to Ginnie the Kook. I gave the cabbie the twenty dollars, not out of generosity but because I wanted very much to hit the suite without a sou to my name. Some kind of symbolism there, whatever.

Not that it proved anything. If I wanted money all I had to do was reach into my closet and whatever I came out with would be worth no less than a fifty. I poured myself such a shot of bourbon that my ears stood out. I did it twice. Maybe a third time—I don't remember. I woozied around the suite, feeling like a burglar. For it was no longer mine. You walk out on your landlord, kiddo, you walk out on your flat. That there's the Law.

I was drunk and knew I shouldn't be driving so I pulled over to the bed and lay down, reaching over to slide open my closet. I looked at all my clothing, hanging like ready-to-go showgirls. They were no longer mine either. Whoever came next would inherit them, though if she had any backbone, she'd burn the lot and make Johnny trot her out new.

All I wanted were my leotards, sneakers and jeans. That's what I had arrived in, and, if fair was fair, that's what I would leave in. And even as I thought that noble thought, I realized I was being the schmuckeroo of schmucks because another way to look at it—a better way—was that I had earned everything he'd given me, that by living with Johnny and being his mistress, all those goodies were rightfully and immorally mine. It was not as though we'd been engaged and that, because I changed my mind, I had to return his ring. I had been lied to and taken advantage of, stalled and balled with nothing to show for it but a bad reputation and a scolding from my mother.

So, finding my old luggage and loading up with a little of thissa and a little of thatta, I stood in my doorway, weaving about in my darling blue gown and asking myself that most pertinent question, "Where the fuck are you going?"

The telephone interrupted the questioning and, putting my bags down, I went over to answer. I got it on the fifth ring because the damned thing kept avoiding my every move at it. It was the hotel operator advising me that Mr. Farrar had called a number of times and that, if and when I came in, I was to call him back in Los Angeles. I told her that, if and when I came in, I would indeed call Mr. Farrar in Los Angeles—but—if and when I did not come in, would she please tell Mr. Farrar that I had jumped out the window and could not be reached. She told me to tell him myself as he was once again on the line.

"Ginnie?"

"No. It's Betsy Ross. How dare you call me after what happened at Concord?"

"Ginnie—I can't believe you took off the way you did. When Hawkins told me he took you to the airport—"

"Fuck Hawkins. What I want to know is how many stars do you want on this fucking flag, George? I mean, is Massachusetts in or out? They've got to make up their minds. If it was up to me, I'd say out because thirteen's an unlucky number anyway."

"I love you. I want you to come back."

"And what do you want me to do about this Christmas Eve deal? The boys are freezing their nuts off at Trenton, and *you're* going across the Barringer's pool in a fucking lounge chair!"

"I want you to listen closely, okay? I want you to close your clever mouth for just a little while and let me talk. Can you do that?"

"You always talk. You and that loudmouth, Patrick Henry. This would still be Merry Old England if it wasn't for you two—and I wouldn't be knitting this fucking flag! How do you spell 'Don't Tread On Me'?"

"Ginnie, let's do it this way. I'll be in New York on Wednesday. That's four days. We'll talk about getting married."

"Beautiful. And what are you going to tell Martha?"

"Who?"

"Your wife. Martha, from all the ice cream."

"You're drunk. Are you drunk, Ginnie?"

"You do have a wife, don't you, dollink?"

"No. But I'm going to."

"Anyone I know, dollink?"

"Kid name of Betsy Ross."

"Never heard of her. What shows has she been in, dollink?"

"Ginnie, I'll be there Wednesday. Can you find something to do till Wednesday?"

"Yes. I've been thinking of invading Mexico. Mexico or Canada. Either one. They're both in the way, you know."

"Stay where you are. Reinforcements are on the way. I love you. Bye."

"Bye, George."

We hung up. He was coming after me. "He's coming after me, Maggie. Did you hear that? He'll be here in four days. How's that for action? Is that fast enough? Well, what'd you *expect* him to do—get on the next plane? Really, Maggie, you're being quite unreasonable. I do *not* think he's stopping over at Denver! What? Yes. Yes, damn it. I suppose you're right, dollink. It is another con. Of course, it is. He's smooth-talking me. Figures he can put me on the back burner till I cool off. Well, I tell you, Mama, I ain't gonna hang around four days till Johnny comes marching home. I am leaving this place because everybody here is drunk!"

There was a letter for me. On the Louis XIV table. From Candy. Two weeks old. I opened it. Crazy. She and Don had gone on to New Haven, where Don would be directing Arnie Felsen's play. I wished them all Godspeed and then cried for myself as in days of yore—for I had no place to go and no friends to speak of and no phone number to hang up on just to prove he was there.

Ben. Sneaking through. The sonofabitch. I'd been able to keep the lid clamped on him pretty good, pretty good. But with my past ganging up on my present, and my future about as well-planned as a star-burst, the lid had come off. And out popped the boy who had me cry.

So much of him was me. So much of me was him that we never really knew where the separation began, where the zipper was or whether or not the seams showed. We were like the hands of a clock, neither of us knowing the right time if the other wasn't around. And how many times did the words come out of his mouth just as they were lining up in mine?

When we made love, when we did it right, it was so total that we climaxed into one person, slotting together so perfectly that we could have slid ourselves under a door. Oh, how we did flabbergast the mathematicians by continually proving that one plus one equaled one.

And, when we parted, how the suction rang like a Chinese gong. Still, I never really did let go; I only pretended to, doing the "good-bye" number, yes, but only as a grandstand play against being made to appear the fool.

As though with pins on a military map, I had been able to trace, at least for a while, all of his deployments. "Ben is here, having moved from there." "Now he's thither, on his way to yon." No exchanging of Christmas cards, no birthday presents arriving unerringly. None of that because the breech had grown too wide. But it didn't matter. We were together, like separated identical twins. Like the Corsican Brothers. Hurt him, I'd feel it. Hurt me, I'll bet he knew.

It was such a nice story we had going for us—two kids in the big city and all that. But somebody slipped some bad pages into the script, and all that love went a-squandering.

There should have been quatrains and cellos instead of silence and discords. There should have been pennants on tall towers and people granting boons. There should have been castles, I do believe.

I left the hotel wearing leotards, sneakers and jeans and leaving all else. Ashes to ashes and baubles to shit—it was the way I'd arrived and the way I'd depart.

chapter twenty-seven

ben

1954

Flying back to New York I had the unfulfilling feeling that I had blown LA, that my decorum in that city could hardly have been applauded as exemplary. I had heard that Faulkner and Fitzgerald had behaved with a similar peevishness, but they were Faulkner and Fitzgerald. I wasn't even Hammacher and Schlemmer.

I tried to suppress the woe, drowning it in drink, but there was a halo of "last chance" all about me and it discomfited me. It had boarded the plane with me and fought me for my window seat. And though I had elbowed it out of the way, it all the same set up camp in the aisle seat beside me. (There were so many empty seats that it could have sat anywhere, even in first class, or up front with the pilots, so why me?)

The "why me" was simple enough. I had invited it to do so. Right from the day I had arrived in California, right from the moment Steiner the Cougher picked me up and rumbled me to the Hollywood Roosevelt, I had comported myself with such a lofty arrogance that "last chance" could not fail to pick up my scent and shadow my missteps with the deadly certainty of a leopard tracking, attacking, and alacking a bunny.

I had been a fool in my dealings with the studios, and a bumpkin in my reliance on Sam Gaynor. I had alienated friends, irked agents, and debased women. I had minimized the human animal at every turn and, in so doing, had developed an early proclivity for self-destruction into a fine art worthy of a generation of lemmings.

The plane squatted down at Idlewild at about noon. As I had no luggage it was easy for me to be the first passenger to get a cab. I told the driver "Manhattan," and in Manhattan I told him, "East Eighty-third." And on East Eighty-third I said, "Here." And when I got out I was standing in front of ye olde building.

Five flights up. I figured Candy would be there. Or Don, or both. It was neither and the place was locked. And how long ago it suddenly seemed. I had played that scene before, returning from a different despair to find the castle similarly locked.

I sat down on the top stair that I had once sanctified with love and blew cigar smoke through the bannister curls. I had done that once before, too, and the image of her flew at me from all that time ago.

Laughing ponytail, cohabitant of the most perfect time of my youth, frozen in my memory by the wrenching suddenness of our parting. For almost two years she had lodged there despite all my efforts at casting her out. She had stayed on, an intransigent tenant, unchanged and unscarred by the event that had blown her away. Ginnie in my head, steadfastly defying eviction and erosion.

I was tired. Sleep, seconds away—blanketing in, lecturing me that the perfection of any given moment could sustain for only as long as the next moment could be held back, that pictures in sequence are destructive in that they each undermine the impact of the first.

Girl on the stairs, floating up as in a cubist painting, image over image. The face, like a photograph in the developer, slowly transforming from vague blankness to specific contour. Each step toward me endowing the subject with more contrast, greater clarity, sharper definition.

Girl. Blonde. Pretty. Ginnie.

chapter twenty-eight

ginnie

1954

Walking aimlessly up Park Avenue from the Delmon- ico, veering East on Seventy-second Street—it wasn't much further to East Eighty-third, so there I went, like some kind of fuzzy-thinking homing pigeon.

Four flights up, a turn at the fourth floor landing, and I saw him, sitting there, on *our* step, wearing cigar smoke, pushing it out at me.

Three steps up that last flight I took. Four. Slowly. Five, six—like a child caught with her hand in the cookie jar, too guilty to protest her innocence, but slow- ing nevertheless to at least acknowledge her capture. Seven, eight—God, can it be? "Ben?"

"Ginnie?"

Courage, girl. Poise. Sophistication. "Jesus Christ."

He stood. "We've done this before."

"I guess." Another step up. Wanting to run, to grab, to devour. But slowly, girl. Cool. Composed. "You out of the Army?"

"Ginnie, I've been bad."

"Me, too."

"I've blown it all. The whole thing. Soup to nuts. Memphis to Mobile."

"Natchez to St. Joe."

"I've got nothing. No clothes. No toothbrush."

"Me neither."

"No typewriter."

"So what? You can't type."

"A man may come looking for me, to kill me."

"Me, too. To marry me." Another step up. How to keep from flying.

"You look wonderful."

"My hair is different."

"The place is locked. Do you have a key?"

"Don't I always?"

"Yes."

Another step up. How tired he looks, how lost. "Guess what? In two weeks I'll be an heiress."

"In two weeks I'll be a plumber."

Standing beside him. Can he feel the heat of me? Fumbling for the key I always kept, no matter what bag, what purse. "I was the one who kept calling and hanging up."

"I know."

"It was childish." Key, get in the lock, *please.*

He takes the key. "Should we talk about it?"

"About what?"

Opening the door. "About Maggie."

"Okay. But a hundred years from now, who'll care?"

"We will."

The door is open and I'm walking in. Oh, sweet Jesus.

"I love you, Ginnie."

"Okay."

"Always have. And I honestly believe that—if two people, two intelligent people—"

"Ben?"

"Yes?"

"How about a little fuck?"

The door closes. Life begins. Was there ever such a ucky girl?

Dell Bestsellers

- [ ] **SECOND GENERATION** by Howard Fast $2.75 (17892-4)
- [ ] **SHARKY'S MACHINE** by William Diehl $2.50 (18292-1)
- [ ] **EVERGREEN** by Belva Plain $2.75 (13294-0)
- [ ] **WHISTLE** by James Jones $2.75 (19262-5)
- [ ] **A STRANGER IS WATCHING**
  by Mary Higgins Clark $2.50 (18125-9)
- [ ] **THE THIRTEENTH HOUR** by John Lee $2.50 (18751-6)
- [ ] **THE NAZI CONNECTION** by F.W. Winterbotham . $2.50 (16197-5)
- [ ] **TARA KANE** by George Markstein $2.50 (18511-4)
- [ ] **SUMMER'S END** by Danielle Steel $2.50 (18418-5)
- [ ] **MORTAL FRIENDS** by James Carroll $2.75 (15789-7)
- [ ] **BAD BLOOD** by Barbara Petty $2.25 (10438-6)
- [ ] **THE SEDUCTION OF JOE TYNAN**
  by Richard Cohen $2.25 (17610-7)
- [ ] **GREEN ICE** by Gerald A. Browne $2.50 (13224-X)
- [ ] **THE TRITON ULTIMATUM** by Laurence Delaney .. $2.25 (18744-3)
- [ ] **AIR FORCE ONE** by Edwin Corley $2.50 (10063-1)
- [ ] **BEYOND THE POSEIDON ADVENTURE**
  by Paul Gallico $2.50 (10497-1)
- [ ] **THE TAMING** by Aleen Malcolm $2.50 (18510-6)
- [ ] **AFTER THE WIND** by Eileen Lottman $2.50 (18138-0)
- [ ] **THE ROUNDTREE WOMEN: BOOK I**
  by Margaret Lewerth $2.50 (17594-1)
- [ ] **TRIPLE PLATINUM** by Stephen Holden $2.50 (18650-1)
- [ ] **THE MEMORY OF EVA RYKER**
  by Donald A. Stanwood $2.50 (15550-9)
- [ ] **BLIZZARD** by George Stone $2.25 (11080-7)

At your local bookstore or use this handy coupon for ordering:

Dell **DELL BOOKS**
P.O. BOX 1000, PINEBROOK, N.J. 07058

Please send me the books I have checked above. I am enclosing $_____
(please add 75¢ per copy to cover postage and handling). Send check or money
order—no cash or C.O.D.'s. Please allow up to 8 weeks for shipment.

Mr/Mrs/Miss _____

Address _____

City _____ State/Zip _____